The Eye of Icarus

Michael D'Ambrosio

The Eye of Icarus

Helm Publishing

For information address:
Helm Publishing
3923 Seward Ave.
Rockford, IL 61108
815-398-4660
www.publishersdrive.com

ISBN 978-0-9801780-2-9

Printed in the United States of America

I.   The Assignment

A long, white hovercraft, armed with twin cannons mounted on top, lurked in the trees near the Space Fleet Academy.

Inside the dark hovercraft, two alien creatures patiently monitored the guests entering and leaving the Space Fleet's graduation ball.

A ballroom parquet floor was filled with dancing couples. The perimeter was carpeted on three sides in plush teal fabric with dinner tables set fancifully for the celebration.

A young cadet with dark hair and cat-like eyes approached the marble bar and sat down in one of the burgundy, velvet chairs, from which vantage point he could eye his peers.

Long-sleeve, tan shirts and black pants portrayed their rank as Service Spec 1 cadets. This was the Fleet Academy's first graduating class trained to understand languages and cultures of alien races in addition to the regular fleet training skills required for crewmen on fighter craft.

A short, slender woman with long, wavy, brown hair stepped into the cadet's view. He eagerly acknowledged her.

"Hello, Zira."

"Mr. Saris. Why are you sitting here all alone on a special night like this? You should be celebrating."

"I'm waiting for someone."

"I was going to ask you to dance, but since you're not interested, I won't bother you."

"I'm sorry, Zira. It's real important."

"I only ask once and you were my first choice."

Will bit his lip as Zira sauntered away from him. He watched painfully as she approached another cadet and invited him to the dance floor.

Will mumbled, "This had better be worth it."

A burly bartender leaned across the counter and asked, "What can I get for you, sir?"

"Water is fine."

"A fine looking woman, she is. A friend of yours?"

"Kind of. She's more like a missed opportunity."

The bartender kidded, "It's never too late."

"For me it is."

The bartender handed Will a glass of water with ice.

Will sipped from the glass and stared. Zira snuggled closer to her partner during a slow dance. "That should have been me," Will complained to no one in particular.

His thoughts were suddenly interrupted by a familiar voice, "Will Saris. Look at you in your service uniform. I can't believe it." A tall, blond-haired woman with dark, brown eyes stood before him.

Will's attitude improved dramatically. He stood and exclaimed, "Maya! It's good to see you again."

Will stared at her shapely figure in a blue flight officer's uniform. Maya was twenty-four in Earth years, about seven years older than he was. The two embraced in a friendly hug.

Maya took a seat next to Will and gazed at him. She remarked, "My, how you've grown."

"So have you, Maya. You're not a little schoolgirl anymore."

Maya blushed and looked briefly at the dance floor.

"How did the Academy treat you?"

"Okay, I guess. I'm not sure why, but they taught me to speak one hundred and four alien languages. I thought that's what the translators were for. No one else had to learn so many."

"Your courses were selected based on certain abilities that you have as well as the assignment we have. That's the reason I'm here."

"I don't get it."

"You have certain traits that you inherited from your mother which make you quite different and of great value to the Fleet."

"For instance?"

"You can change into an alter-shape. You are a shape-shifter."

Will responded with a surprised look on his face, "A what?"

"A shape-shifter."

"How did that happen?"

"We're descendents from a Firenghian race of shape-shifters. We're the only ones in the Fleet."

Will rubbed his chin and pondered Maya's revelation.

"So what is my alter-shape?"

"That remains to be seen. Everyone is different based on their character."

"And you're a shape-shifter, too?"

Maya glanced about suspiciously and whispered, "Yes, I am."

Will looked around them to see who might be listening. No one was near enough to hear them.

He was curious about her secrecy and asked quietly, "What's your alter-shape, Maya?"

Maya replied defensively, "That's personal."

"When does this change happen to me?"

"Now that you're aware of it, it can happen anytime you suffer extreme emotional trauma or fright. It's like a defense mechanism. That's why I'm telling you about this now. You weren't ready before."

"Did my father have this ability?"

3

"Yes he did. He received this and other traits from your mother. Because he was human, he developed several unusual traits that set him apart from most other Firenghians. You might even have traits that I wasn't aware of which would make you different from your father."

Will grinned coyly. "Interesting," he mused.

"You do know about your keen senses, don't you?"

"Yeah, I figured that part out."

Maya continued, "And you have the ability to communicate with other individuals using telepathy. You can also discretely read the minds of anyone having telepathic ability as well. One thing special about your skill is that you can cloak your thoughts from others. This is a mutated trait."

"How did you learn all this about me?"

"I tested your skills against mine when we were young. You shut me out on many occasions."

"I don't see why it's such a big deal."

"It's a big deal because it makes you a secret weapon against the alien forces. If you can read their thoughts and cloak your own, then you have a distinct advantage over them. They can't detect you."

"Do many races have this telepathic ability?"

"It's quite common in many species. Another thing you might not have known. You'll heal much faster than humans can."

"Why didn't you mention this before?"

"If other cadets knew about this, you would have been subjected to many distractions in school and they would have treated you more like a circus animal than a gifted student."

Will complained, "The shape of my eyes didn't prevent any distractions. They did set me apart from the others."

Maya peered into his feline eyes and replied, "It seems to me that you've adapted quite well."

Will studied her eyes briefly. "Your eyes look less feline than mine."

"We're from different bloodlines."

"Does that make a difference in you and me?"

"It certainly does. Your mother was royalty among our people. Your eyes are a sign of your blood-line and proof of your royalty."

Will pondered, "So, what you're telling me is that I'm considered royalty in a race that is no more."

Maya surmised, "Perhaps someday, our race will be resurrected."

Will took another sip of water, and then he asked, "So was this the business that we so urgently needed to discuss?"

"No, there's more."

The bartender leaned across the bar and interrupted, "I see things are looking up for you, sir."

Will smiled and nodded.

The bartender directed his attention to Maya and asked, "Can I get you something to drink, ma'am?"

"I haven't had an Earth drink in a while. How about an Iced Tea?"

The bartender answered, "I'll be back in a moment."

"You like Earth drinks, huh?"

Maya answered cheerfully, "I like a lot of Earth things. The Earthers seem to have a zest for life. After spending some time with your dad and step-mom several years back on Earth, I found life on the other human worlds to be quite a bore. Earth is different."

Will inquired somberly, "Have you heard any news on my father's disappearance?"

"No. The Fleet Commander told me that several vessels were dispatched to Aramis-5 where his ship crashed. It's an oxygen-rich environment so, if he and Tera survived the crash, they could be alive."

"I heard that the ship was a wreck."

"It was, but your father has a knack for surviving situations like that. Your step-mom is a very unique person as well. She's pretty tough in her own respect. I wouldn't want to do battle with her."

Will recalled, "Aunt Rena and Aunt Penny told me some of the stories about Tera. I only met her once, though."

"What did you think of her?"

"At first I thought she was scary. She wore spikes and leather, kind of like a dominatrix. But after talking to her for a while, I found her to be really nice."

Maya saw a tear form in the corner of Will's eye. She recollected, "I liked her a lot, too. She was good for your father. After your mom died, things were really hectic. They were fighting the Andorans, the Boromeans and just about everyone else while trying to survive."

Will sighed. "I wish I knew my mother."

"You would have been proud of her."

The bartender set a tall, dark glass on the counter in front of Maya and warned, "It might be a little on the strong side so I suggest you sip it slowly."

"Thank you. I like it that way."

Will pushed the conversation, "So, back to business."

"Patience, Will."

Maya sipped the drink heartily.

Will pointed to Zira and her partner on the dance floor. "I turned down a dance with that young lady over there for our business, so I can't help but feel a little anxious."

"At your age, Will, you'll have plenty of girlfriends. Besides you'll be seeing her again soon, I'm sure."

"What do you mean by that?" he asked.

"She's been assigned to the *Ruined Stone*, the surveillance ship that's accompanying us on our mission."

Will looked surprised.

Maya drank the Iced Tea until only a few cubes of ice were left in the glass.

Will teased, "A little thirsty, are you?"

Maya giggled at him. "Every now and then, I get the urge to loosen up a little."

"I'll remember you said that."

"Smart ass."

Maya stood up and straightened her uniform. "Come on, Will. We have to go."

"Go where?"

6

"We have business to tend to. We'll discuss it on the way."

Will looked once more at Zira on the dance floor. He sighed and replied, "If you say so."

Maya and Will left the hall together and crossed the parking lot. Maya walked ahead of Will. He eyed her seductive strut and wondered what it would be like to spend a romantic evening with her.

Maya read his thoughts and stopped abruptly. She faced Will and said, "Remember, I can read your thoughts when they aren't cloaked."

After a brief pause, she continued apologetically, "There couldn't be any romance between us, Will. We're like family. It would be awkward."

Will blushed and remarked, "You knew what I was thinking?"

"Of course I did."

"How come you don't have a boyfriend?"

"Who says I don't?"

Will felt awkward and stuttered, "I just thought ..."

"You just thought that I'm all work, no play. I get that a lot."

Will noticed that she evaded his question.

They approached a white hovercraft with two large turbo-fans mounted on the rear. Will was impressed. "Is this yours, Maya?"

"No. It's a rental."

Maya unlocked the hatch to the hovercraft and climbed in. Will entered and took a seat beside her.

She toggled three switches and the craft sprang to life. The whirring of the fans was barely audible. The floor vibrated gently as air raced through the ducts underneath them. Maya gently eased the hovercraft forward onto the highway and accelerated until they were racing at maximum speed.

Will commented, "Boy, this baby is smooth."

"The Fleet is generous on rentals."

To Maya's dismay, Will giggled.

She inquired, "What's so funny?"

"Oh, I always heard that the Fleet was run by a cheap bunch of misers."

7

"They've always treated me just fine."

The road was dark but the headlights cut long traces ahead of them.

Maya handled the craft skillfully as she negotiated curves leading onto another highway. She remarked, "So I heard you were quite a prankster in school."

"Who told you that?"

"Some friends of mine. I kept tabs on you, don't worry."

After a brief period of silence, Maya asked, "Will, can I count on you to follow my orders?"

"Of course. Do you doubt me?"

"I have to be sure."

"I wouldn't let you down no matter what."

"Your father had his own way of thinking in the heat of battle. I hope I won't get that from you. I have a lot of responsibility and I don't need to draw the attention of the Fleet, especially now."

Will avoided making a response and changed the topic.

"I've heard my dad used to rile Aunt Penny up pretty good."

"Yes, he did. He and your Aunt Penny had many arguments."

Will admired Maya as she drove. "What is our special assignment?" he asked.

"We're going into the fourteenth quadrant to the planet Attrades."

Will thought back to his lessons on the fourteenth quadrant. Then he recalled with surprise, "Isn't that the heart of the alien empire?"

"Uh-huh."

"And we're going in there?"

Maya swerved to avoid an oncoming hovercraft and yelled, "Crazy driver!"

Will looked back and noticed that the hovercraft spun around. The lights were drawing nearer.

Will asked, "Are we expecting company?"

Maya looked in the rear-view mirror. "No. My presence here is a secret. No one knows that the *Luna C* is here either or that you're involved."

"The *Luna C*! That was my dad's ship."

Maya added proudly, "Now she's new and improved. She's been refitted for deep covert surveillance."

Will looked back at the approaching headlights and became uneasy. He warned, "I think you ticked them off. They're getting awfully close."

A bright flash lit up the air, followed by a small explosion. The roof of the hovercraft shattered and the pieces quickly dispersed into the wind.

Will was startled.

Maya warned, "You'd better get down. This is gonna get ugly."

Will slid down in his seat.

Maya steered the craft left and then right. Flashes of light followed by small, fiery explosions besieged the hovercraft.

She yelled into a silver transmitter fastened to her wrist, "Celine, I need an extraction for two, fast! We've got hot pursuit."

Fifteen seconds later, the shadow of a large object loomed over them in the night sky.

Will felt a strange, floating sensation as he was pulled from their craft. He glanced back and saw the hovercraft explode into a fiery mass.

Whisked up to the *Luna C*, Will landed on a platform in the center of a large room. He surveyed the area around him in astonishment. There were several control panels with colorful arrays of lights and monitors. Maya landed next him on the platform.

Maya urged, "Come on, Will. We have work to do."

Will followed Maya off the platform onto a polished steel floor. She hurried up two flights of stairs to the pilots' cabin. Knocking twice, the door slid open. She poked her head in and announced, "It's me, Celine."

Maya waited for Will to join her.

Will stopped on the second level and took note of the strange instrumentation mounted on the walls. He continued to the top of the stairs where Maya was waiting impatiently.

"You know, these craft were portrayed quite differently in class."

Maya explained, "The *Luna C* and the *Ruined Stone* are two of a kind. They are enhanced with very special technology."

Maya pulled Will by the arm into the cabin.

A dark-skinned woman with a wild hairdo tied back in a ponytail chastised her. "Well, Maya. It seems you still know how to make friends wherever you go."

Maya was befuddled and flustered, "I don't understand how they knew we were here."

Celine remarked, "You're lucky to be back in one piece."

"Who were they, Celine? Did you scan them?"

"Of course. They were Weevil, in human form, no less. I did take it upon myself to dispose of them, right after you were extracted."

"Nice work."

"It's ironic that they always seem to know where we are. I can't believe their spy network is that good," Celine commented.

Will suggested, "Maybe someone in the Fleet tipped them off."

Maya scolded him, "Bite your tongue. No one would ever do that?

Will rebutted, "Celine just said that the Weevil could take human form."

Celine explained, "It's not that easy but I guess an imposter could infiltrate the ranks of the Fleet."

Maya asked, "Where are Neelon and Saphoro?"

"Resting. They have the next shift in about an hour."

"Who are they?" Will inquired.

Maya answered, "They are our intelligence analysts. We find information, they decipher it. They also relieve Celine at the controls every other shift." Then she ordered Celine, "Contact the *Ruined Stone* and inform them that our cover's blown. We'll meet them at destination B."

Celine warned her, "We'll need to get supplies soon, Maya. You cut into our shopping time."

"Understood. We'll stock up on Aries-II. No one will expect us there."

Celine reached back for Will's arm and pulled him forward. She eyed him up and down.

"So, this is the young man."

Will was annoyed with the blatant disrespect and spoke defiantly, "Excuse me?"

Celine kidded, "Does he know anything, Maya?"

"Not much. We'll have to brief him."

Will snapped, "What do you mean 'not much'?"

Maya said calmly, "Let's go downstairs and talk."

Will glared at Celine warily before leaving the cabin.

Celine cackled loudly and yelled, "Fresh meat!"

Will and Maya returned to the lower bay. They sat in front of a large console with three monitors on it.

Sarcastically, Will asked, "What's her problem?"

"Relax Will. You're the rookie on board."

"Just what I need, a hazing."

"I'll ask Celine to back off. She puts up a tough front but she's a softie."

"I'd appreciate it, at least until I get to know everyone."

Maya explained, "My primary responsibility is to make sure your skills and traits are up to par for the mission. Then I need to deliver you to your destination."

"And that's why I was chosen for this assignment, my traits!"

"No, I requested you for this mission."

"So, what happens when we reach Attrades?"

"Officially, our mission is to find out what the alien forces are up to. Some strange things have been happening around Attrades regarding the positioning of their battle craft. Unofficially, there's another issue I need your help with."

"And what might that be?"

"A good friend of mine is being held prisoner on Attrades. He went down on the planet's surface to scout the Attradean stronghold. He gathered some important information but he was captured before we could make sense of it."

11

"So you are asking …" Will paused, waiting for Maya to finish his statement.

"Will, he means a lot to me. The Fleet would never sanction what we're about to do. You have the ability to find out where he's at and determine if we can rescue him."

"He means that much to you?"

"Yes, he does."

Will was somewhat surprised by Maya's request. "And we're going to walk right into an Attradean stronghold and locate him?"

"Not we. I'm asking you to find out where he is and if he's okay. We'll figure out how to rescue him later."

"What will you do in the mean time?"

"Monitor communications and make sure we extract you as soon as possible in case of an emergency."

"Why wouldn't you ask the Fleet for help?"

"The Fleet cannot know anything about this. I would lose my commission."

Will teased, "What if I refuse?"

Maya's face saddened. "Then I'll go myself and find him." Tears welled in Maya's eyes.

Will put his arm around her and hugged her. "I'll do it. I just want to make sure he's worth it."

Enthusiastically Maya answered, "He is."

"What's next?"

Maya turned a knob on the control panel in front of her and entered a six digit code through the keyboard. The screen glowed bright blue. Maya pressed four more digits and a palace appeared on the screen.

Maya explained, "This is the Attradian Palace." She turned the knob and the palace shrunk, exposing the surrounding area. Pointing, she said, "This is where the king's family resides."

"These guys actually have a king?"

"Oh, yes. He's quite a barbarian, too." She pointed to another area, "This three story cement building is where the guards are quartered. The white structure to the left is where the king does his official business. In the lower level of the adjacent building, we believe he is keeping political prisoners."

"Who are these prisoners?"

"All we know is that Baron's last message mentioned blackmail and forced allies. He also mentioned something strange about an eye for the future. We lost contact and haven't heard from him since."

"What do you know about the king's family?"

Scrolling down, a report appeared beneath the pictures. "It looks like he's got a spouse and one daughter," she read.

"I'll make sure I stop in and say hello."

Maya warned, "Don't do anything crazy. There's a lot at stake, here. Can you imagine what the Fleet would do to us if they found out what we're up to?"

Will cracked a smile and said, "I guess we'd all be out of a job."

Maya chided, "And why would we want that?"

"Just kidding."

"Remember, Will, you're a rookie. We've been together as a team for quite a while. Try not to get us into trouble."

"I'll do my best."

The intercom beeped and Celine's voice came across. "The *Ruined Stone* is enroute. We'll rendezvous at the depot."

Maya replied, "Thanks, Celine. I'll be up shortly."

Will asked, "What's this business about an eye for the future?"

"I don't know. I wonder if it was an analogy or a coded message."

Will rubbed his chin and said, "You mentioned that the Weevil spies always seem to be ahead of you, is that right?"

"Yes. What are you getting at?"

"What if they're working with the Attradeans and they developed a way to see into the future?"

Maya laughed at Will and said, "That's ludicrous!"

"It's just a thought, but if that were the case, you'd have to plan your defenses accordingly."

"What do you mean?"

"I think you'd have to keep yourself in a defensible position at all times. But it also means that you can predict what they're going to do as well."

"I can't see that happening."

"Maya, anything is possible."

Maya stood up and walked despondently to the stairs.

"What's wrong, Maya?"

"I'm afraid for you. This is my mess and I don't like risking the lives of those I care about."

"Look, Maya, I was born for adventure, not for classrooms or cadet duty. So as long as we're out here, I want to have some fun. If I don't want to do something, believe me, you'll know it."

"You're just like your father."

Will appreciated the compliment.

Maya instructed him, "Your quarters are in the last room down the hall on the left. I'm two up from you if you need me."

"Does everyone berth on this level?"

"No. The upper level houses the comm/nav equipment and three berths. Celine, Neelon and Saphoro use that level because of its proximity to the pilots' cabin."

Will examined several of the instrument panels. "What happened to the power bank for the cannon system?"

Maya replied, "It's been removed. A smaller one was installed but the firing system no longer has automated firing control or computer generated coordinates."

"So if we need it, we're firing manually."

"We're fitted for surveillance, not combat."

"I hope we don't get into a dogfight out here."

Maya said proudly, "That's what stealth is for. I have to meet with Celine. You can join me if you like."

"Maybe later."

"We'll be arriving at the depot in a little while."

Will answered, "Let me know if you need me for anything. I want to check out the turrets and cannons."

"Sure thing. Welcome aboard, Will."

"Thanks, Maya."

As she elegantly mounted the stairs, Will gazed in admiration and thought, "What a lady!"

Maya's voice carried back down. "Thank you, Will, but please try cloaking your thoughts next time."

Will ascended the ladder into one of the turrets and sat for several minutes, reminiscing about the short periods of time he spent with his dad and stepmother. He recalled the stories of the contests that his dad had with his step-mom, Tera, shooting down alien fighters while racing through the galaxies.

"Why couldn't things be different? I wish I knew my mother. Maybe Tera and dad are gone too."

Maya hesitated at the top of the stairs. She could still read Will's thoughts. She felt his loneliness and wondered how to ease his grief as she entered the pilots' cabin. She took the seat next to Celine.

Celine notified Maya, "I'm running a scan on Aries-II. So far, it appears deserted. No sign of life."

Maya grew concerned. "How about the depot itself? Any sign of activity, thermal trails or debris?"

"Not yet."

Celine continued to monitor the scanners, while Maya programmed the landing coordinates.

Neelon entered the compartment and sighed. "I guess we're going to hear Jack Fleming run his mouth about the bargains of the universe."

"Not this time. It looks like something happened down there."

Neelon was a short albino figure of a man with stubby hands and feet. He stood by a monitor located over Maya's head and pressed several buttons. The screen was full of information. He pressed another button and the information scrolled to the end of the report.

"So we had another encounter with the Weevil, huh, Celine?"

"Yeah. I don't get it. They're always two steps ahead of us, no matter where we go."

Maya interjected disbelievingly, "Will suggested that they might have some sort of device which allows them to see into the future."

Neelon laughed, "That's crazy! Your friend's been reading too many science fiction stories."

"That's what I think."

Celine asked, "What if they do have something that allows them to see, even a little bit of the future?"

Neelon scoffed at the idea. "If there was a way to develop a device with such a capability, I'm sure my people would have done so by now."

Maya replied cautiously, "Perhaps we should be open-minded to the possibility that they can predict what we're doing."

Neelon scoffed, "I wouldn't waste my time on such rubbish."

Celine inquired, "How did you make out with Will? Is he half what we've heard?"

"Yes, he is. He's very special. He just doesn't know it yet."

Celine remarked, "He is kind of cute."

Neelon inquired, "Is this the shape-shifter boy whose father solved the Andoran crisis?"

Maya answered, "Yes, he is. His dad was Bill Brock and his mother was Queen Seneca."

Neelon complained, "My father was on the original Council and he felt that Brock was a cancer. In fact, Brock coerced its members to disband the Council after the Andoran alliance was signed. Besides all that, I think this Firenghian mythology is a lot of hocus-pocus. Every tribal leader makes up stories to build up their characters."

Celine moaned, "Oh, boy! Here it comes."

Maya stood nose to nose with Neelon and informed him, "It's not mythology or hocus-pocus."

Neelon angrily declared, "Says who?"

"I say because I was there. I am a Firenghi. I watched Queen Seneca die at the hands of the Boromeans in her alter-shape. Shall I go further?"

Neelon grew red with embarrassment. "I'm sorry. I didn't realize …"

Celine chided, "Nice one, Neelon."

Neelon asked, "But how did you make it through the Academy. I thought … Never mind."

Maya responded, "You thought what?"

"Nothing."

Maya opened the door to leave, but Will blocked her path.

"Will! You startled me."

"I couldn't help overhearing the conversation."

"It's no big deal, Will."

"Obviously, Neelon thinks it is." Will's face reddened. "Don't ever talk about my mother like that again."

Neelon was not intimidated by Will and barked, "Or what? What will you do, little boy?"

Maya begged them, "Please stop. You don't want to do this."

Will replied, "I know what I'm doing, but it appears that someone else here doesn't."

Will suddenly looked ill and fell to one knee. He placed his hands across his stomach.

Celine asked nervously, "What's he doing, Maya?"

Maya ignored her. She cradled Will and whispered softly into his ear. "Not now. You have to control it. Hold it back."

Will trembled for several seconds, before he relaxed.

Neelon teased, "What a crock! A grown boy behaving like this."

Will stood up and glared at Neelon. His eyes opened wide and glowed red. Neelon's head ached terribly. Inside his brain was a terrible throbbing sensation. He desperately clutched at his ears and screamed, "Please stop! I'm sorry."

Will stared intensely at Neelon, forcing him to the floor. He blinked and his eyes returned to normal. He asked, "Is there anything else you'd like to discuss, Neelon?"

"No, no. I'm through."

A young oriental lady entered the cabin and asked, "What is going on? I can hear you people half way across the universe."

Saphoro was pale-skinned and brunette with long flowing locks. She had big, brown oriental eyes, which made her appearance a bit imposing.

Will forgot about Neelon and greeted her, "You must be Saphoro."

"Hi. Yes I am. I heard we were picking up a friend of Maya's."

She glanced down at Neelon and asked in a gentle voice, "Why are you on the floor, Neelon?"

"It's a long story."

Neelon got up and fixed his tunic.

"Now that we're all here, how about a formal introduction?" Will suggested

Maya took the hint and introduced Will first. "This is Will Saris. He's here to help us locate Baron on Attrades."

Celine extended a hand in friendship to Will. "I'm Celine, the co-pilot on the *Luna C.* I hope you didn't take the ribbing personally."

Will shook Celine's hand and asked, "Where did you get your hair done?"

Celine answered proudly, "It's part of my image. They think I'm a nutcase."

"Then we'll get along just fine."

Saphoro gave Will a hug and said, "Welcome aboard. I understand your father was from Earth."

"Yes he was."

"Earthers fight well. My mother was an Earther."

"Then we have some history between us."

"I imagine we do."

Saphoro smiled at Maya, indicating her approval of Will.

Will extended a hand to Neelon and said, "We can start over as friends if you like."

Neelon shook his hand and nodded. "I'd like that. I'm sorry for my ignorance. I didn't think there was any truth to the stories and Maya never told me that she was a Firenghi."

Maya responded, "I'm sure you understand why."

"Yes I do. My apologies, none the less."

Maya was relieved. She put her hand on Will's back and rubbed it. "Thanks for understanding and thanks for controlling your anger."

"No problem."

Maya suggested, "Let's go downstairs. It's getting crowded in here."

"Sure."

As they descended the stairs, Celine informed them, "We'll be on the ground in five tocks."

Will paused on the steps and asked, "What's a tock?"

Maya answered, "That's an astral second which is about one quarter of an Earth hour."

"I see."

When they reached the lower level, Maya pointed to the chair and said, "Sit, please."

Will sat in the chair and slid away from the panel.

Maya leaned against a table and stared at the wall. She looked very tired.

Will asked Maya, "Are you okay?"

"I am now. What happened up there?"

"Which part?"

"Were you shifting?"

"I could have, but I chose not to."

Maya paced back and forth nervously.

She replied doubtfully, "Okay."

Will sensed her uneasiness, "My eyes frightened you, didn't they?"

"What did you do to Neelon?"

"I went into his mind and created an illusion of pain."

"Please don't scare me like that again. These are my friends. We've been through the Academy together and accomplished many missions as a team."

"They didn't know you could change, did they?"

"No. Only Celine did."

"I thought so."

"I couldn't tell what you were thinking."

19

"Of course, not. I cloaked my thoughts."

"You mean you already knew how?"

"I'm not the naïve little boy you grew up with. I just enjoyed the attention."

Maya was surprised. "I'm sorry. I guess I always think of you like a baby brother."

Maya knelt down and hugged Will.

Will said confidently, "Don't worry. We'll get your friend, Baron, back."

"Thank you. I feel better knowing you can handle your abilities."

Will smiled and leaned back in the chair. Maya sat in the chair next to him.

"You wanted me to read your mind earlier, didn't you?"

Will was amused. "Yup."

Maya continued, "And hear all that romance stuff."

"Yup."

"Will Saris, you are so fresh."

Will chuckled and said, "Yup."

Saphoro descended the stairs and took a seat near Will and Maya.

"Homework time, people."

She depressed two switches on the console and entered a five digit code. The image of the palace and its surrounding grounds appeared.

Saphoro pointed to a large domed building on the left. She informed Will, "This is where Baron's last transmission came from. He mentioned that there were some key prisoners being held on the palace grounds. He also mentioned something about the future. We're not sure what he meant but it must have been important for him to risk contacting us from so close to the palace."

"That's what I hear."

Maya drew Will's attention to the area in the back corner of the palace grounds. "This is where we dropped Baron off last time. He seemed to have easy access from this area. Is that okay with you?"

Will surveyed the grounds. "No. I want to be dropped outside the wall."

Maya was surprised. "Outside the wall?"

"Yes. I have a hunch they're expecting me inside."

Maya explained, "I only want you to find out if we can rescue Baron and see if there's anything unusual going on. Nothing more."

"Why do you think something's going on?"

Saphoro explained, "There are only three ships on Attrades. The rest of the fleet left in a hurry a short while ago."

"What do you suspect they're up to?"

Saphoro answered, "I don't know. It's very strange to leave the kingdom with so little protection."

"I'll see what I can do."

Neelon descended the stairs and interrupted the conversation. "Celine has found one life form at the depot. It's probably Fleming. She also found thermal trails indicating that three Attradean vessels had been there about four pogs ago."

Will frowned and asked, "What's a pog?"

Maya explained, "It's about two and a half Earth days."

"Why can't everyone use the same time standard?"

Neelon bragged, "That will happen soon. My people are working on the conversion."

Maya asked anxiously, "Has she established contact with Jack yet?"

"Yes she has. We'll be docking shortly."

Celine's voice echoed from the intercom. "Maya, your presence is requested by Mr. Fleming."

Maya sighed. She stood up and asked Will, "Do you have any other questions?"

"No. I'm satisfied."

"Good. I'll be back soon."

Maya left them and ascended the stairs.

Saphoro asked Will, "You don't seem too concerned about this mission."

"No, not yet."

"How do you think you'll get around without attracting attention?"

"I might have to get their attention first. Maybe I'll pick up some collateral along the way."

Saphoro looked confused. "How would you do that?"

"I don't know yet. Can you do some research for me?"

"Sure. What do you need?"

"I can't believe all these alien races just fell in line with the Attradeans. Check out each race that's joined the Attradean alliance. See if there are any significant events that occurred prior to their enlistment."

"I'll start on it immediately."

"Thanks, Saphoro."

****

Maya entered the pilots' cabin and sat next to Celine. Jack Fleming's face appeared on the monitor in front of them.

Jack greeted Maya cheerfully, "Well, hello, Maya. It's been a long time. You don't even call to say hello, anymore."

"Sorry, Jack. Duty calls."

"Some of your friends paid me a visit and took all of my hired help."

"Why not you?"

"I was indisposed at the time."

"I see."

Jack asked, "So are you coming in the back door?"

"Don't we always?"

"You remember the key, Maya?"

"Of course."

"Good. I'll be waiting for you. How many guests?"

"Two."

"Only two of you?"

"No, two vessels."

Jack sounded disappointed. "Must be a big mission."

22

"Not really. If you're good, we'll try to get your hired help back."

"That would be nice. Good help is hard to come by."

Maya replied, "See you shortly."

"Aye, aye, Captain."

Celine turned the monitor off and complained, "What a jackass!"

"Some things never change."

"What's this 'back door' and 'key' business?"

Maya explained, "If we don't want our presence recorded on the computerized tracking system for the depot's database, we use the 'back door'. To get in, we need a 'key', which is usually about four hundred credits."

"So you have to buy our secrecy?"

"Yeah. One thing is guaranteed – Jack will keep his word and cover our tracks."

Celine eyed Maya intently, "Did you and Jack know each other aside from the depot?"

Maya chuckled.

"I can't get anything past you, can I, Celine?"

"You didn't answer the question. Was that on purpose?"

"Okay. We dated a few times but we had a conflict of interest when it came to our careers."

"No kidding."

"Yeah. He's not always the loud-mouthed jackass that you see. That's just his front."

"And that's the end of it?"

Maya explained, "We just knew that we had to go separate ways. It would never work out."

"And he charges you for protection?"

"Yeah. He says it makes him feel important, like I need him."

"What a crock!"

"I know, but there is some truth to it. We do need him."

Celine bellowed in disgust, "I'd rather die on an asteroid!"

"Now, Celine, you were nearly suicidal when we cancelled your shopping trip."

Celine kidded, "Well, maybe I'd just think about dying on an asteroid."

"That's better."

Celine and Maya watched the huge depot outer doors open on the monitor.

The *Luna C* and *Ruined Stone* glided into the outer bay. The outer doors closed and the inner doors opened. The doors squealed mightily as they reached the end of their tracks. The bay was an isolated over-sized garage with stained walls from years of neglect.

The ships eased toward the berths. Celine guided the *Luna C* smoothly into the first berth. She pressed a button on the video display system and the *Ruined Stone* came into view in the berth next to them.

Celine kidded, "Like a symphony in motion." She shut down the engines and turned on the auxiliary systems. "We're all set, Maya. Let's go shopping."

"Jack will want the code first for his 'key'."

Celine teased, "Oh, of course. What man doesn't want money before his woman?"

Maya snapped, "I'm not his woman."

"You know what I mean."

****

Neelon descended the stairs and approached Will.

Will and Saphoro watched the lower level video display system near the stairwell. The docking bay came into view.

"Looks like we're here."

Neelon asked, "Can I ask you a quick question, Will?"

"Sure."

"If you and Maya are Firenghian, does that mean that she can change into an alter-shape as well?"

Will chose his words carefully. "I don't know what her lineage is. It's possible but it seems to me that each Firenghian I learned about had different traits and abilities. If no one's ever seen her change or fight off a change, then maybe she can't."

"That's interesting."

Saphoro pressed several keys. The monitor scrolled several paragraphs of information.

Saphoro turned her attention from the screen and asked, "So it's true that you really can change shape?"

Will answered earnestly, "I haven't done it yet, so I don't know. I've heard that a shape-shifter only assumes one alter-shape and that is determined by his or her traits."

"I always wondered if it was really possible. Can you make others into shape-shifters?"

"I have no idea. I only know that shape-shifting is possible under certain circumstances and I don't have any idea what they are."

"That's really neat."

"You don't think it's freaky or anything?"

Saphoro grabbed his arm and squeezed it affectionately. "Everyone is different as is every planet. You are just like the rest of us in that respect. It's what's in the heart that counts."

"That's good to hear. When people see or hear about the other things I can do, they're frightened of me."

"Well, we're all one team here. I'm glad to have you with us."

"Thanks again."

Saphoro turned her attention back to the screen. She quickly scanned the data and said, "This is interesting, Will. It seems that the last eleven races to join the Attradeans did so after a key member of each was abducted."

Will asked, "Does it say by whom?"

"No."

"I wonder if these races are being blackmailed into joining the Attradean alliance?"

"It sure looks like a possibility."

"If I can rescue the prisoners, we might be able to shake up their alliance."

Saphoro warned, "I'd be careful if I were you. Tenemon is very dangerous.

Neelon interrupted, "Let's get ready for a walk. The bay should be pressurized by now."

Maya and Celine descended the steps and joined them.

Maya instructed, "Celine and Neelon, take care of the food and medicines. Saphoro, Will and I will get the maintenance supplies and parts. Remember, everyone, we have a budget. This stop is costing me a bunch."

Jack Fleming's voice blared from the speaker, "Welcome to Jack's Discount Depot. Of course I have to ask, Maya, do you have the 'key'?"

Maya spoke into the speaker, "Of course, Jack. Are you ready?"

"You wouldn't believe."

Maya covered the mike and whispered, "Always a smartass."

She retrieved her comm/link and typed in several numbers. She pressed 'enter' and transmitted them. Ten seconds later, Jack replied, "You're as good as gold."

Maya answered indignantly, "Flattery will get you nowhere and it obviously won't get me a discount."

"Always business, aren't you, Maya?"

"I thought you preferred business."

Jack answered coldly, "You haven't changed. The bay is pressurized and the oxygen level is sat. Come on in."

As Maya led her crew to the rear hatch, Will kidded her, "Do I detect a little more to the conversation than it appears?"

"You can read my thoughts. Why are you asking?"

"Because I won't read your thoughts. I won't invade your privacy. If I do, I'll make sure you know first."

Maya was pleasantly surprised. "You would do that for me?"

"Of course."

"Thank you."

"You're welcome."

Maya proceeded through the hatch, first.

Celine nudged Will and said, "Boy, you really know how to make an impression."

Will just smiled at her.

II.   **The Depot**

Maya was the first to step off the *Luna C* onto the stainless steel dock.

Jack Fleming waited anxiously to greet her. Jack was a few years older than Maya. He was tall, medium build, with shoulder length, dirty-blond hair. He wore high, black leather boots, with tight, brown pants, and a white, loose-fitting shirt. It was tucked into the pants at the waist and tied with a black sash.

"Welcome to my humble abode, your highness."

Maya blushed but replied firmly, "Save it, Jack. How are you?"

Jack held his arm in front of Maya, welcoming her through the main hatch.

"I'm fine when the Attradeans aren't trying to put me out of business."

Maya asked curiously, "How is it that you managed to escape them?"

"I've been asking myself that same question. I hope they don't know you were coming. I'd hate to see what they'd do to my business next."

"Don't worry. No one knows our itinerary but us."

"I hope you're right. If not, it would put us all in a vulnerable position."

Will stepped forward and introduced himself. "Hi, Jack. I'm Will Saris."

Jack shook Will's hand.

"Nice to meet you, kid."

Maya interjected, "He's family."

Will asked, "Have you searched the depot since the Attradeans left?"

"Only the operational areas. I still have the cargo holds to check out."

Will suggested, "Perhaps we should take a look. They might have left a calling card."

Jack stared at Will, making him uneasy. "You know something about this, kid?"

"No, but I have suspicions."

Maya ordered, "Leave him be, Jack. He's new out here."

Jack ignored her and inquired, "And what would they be?"

"We should evacuate this place, including you."

Jack was genuinely interested in what Will had to say. "Enlighten me, boy."

"There's an alien presence here. I can sense it. I wonder, though, since the Weevil always seem to be ahead of us, why would the Attradeans come here, coincidently ahead of us?"

Jack added, "If they knew you were coming, did they leave without searching for me on purpose? Is it possible they wanted you to come inside the station?"

Maya barked, "That's nonsense! You two are being paranoid."

Jack paced the deck and replied, "The kid's right. There is something peculiar about this. It has all the makings of a trap."

Maya grew irritable and complained, "This is ridiculous."

Jack ordered, "Follow me."

Maya reprimanded Will, "Don't start scaring people with your 'seeing the future' stuff."

"I told you before that we can't discount the Attradeans' foresight. We're putting ourselves at risk."

Two women from the *Ruined Stone* disembarked from the ship.

Will spotted Zira, his lady friend from the dance.

Zira yelled across the bay. "Will! Will Saris! What a small galaxy it is. Imagine meeting you here."

Will ignored her and asked Maya. "What about them?"

"What about them, Will?"

"Maybe they should stay on the *Ruined Stone* until we check the place out."

Maya was embarrassed and demanded, "Stop it, Will! Stop it right now."

Jack heard Will's suggestion and replied, "That might be a good idea. The Attradeans are too sneaky to go away without leaving some kind of surprise."

Maya complained, "Don't think the two of you are going to order me around like this."

Will and Jack stared at Maya in disbelief.

Maya whined, "Fine. I'll tell them."

Maya met with Talia, the *Ruined Stone's* commander.

Talia sensed Maya's apprehension. "What's wrong?"

"The men seem to think this is a trap set by the Attradeans."

"That sounds unlikely, but I guess it can't hurt to take precautions."

"I'll go with Jack and search the cargo bays. Stay inside the ship until we've finished."

Maya left Talia and followed Jack down a long corridor.

Talia returned to the *Ruined Stone.*

Zira anxiously cornered Will near the hatch. She grabbed Will by the arm and asked, "Are you avoiding me, Will?"

"No, Zira. Why would I?"

"You told Maya to send us away. I thought you'd be glad to see me."

"I am glad to see you but something is wrong here. I'm not sure what but I think we're in danger."

"Well, I hope you're right. Maya doesn't seem too happy with you."

Will complained, "It seems that women never are."

Zira looked hurt. She replied, "That wasn't nice."

"I'm sorry. That's not what I meant. I sense an alien presence around here."

"Do you think we're being set up?"

"I sure do. How many ships with surveillance capabilities like ours are there in the fleet?"

"Just these two."

"And they're both inside this depot right now. That makes a trap more than likely."

"I see your point. I'll talk to Talia. Maybe we're better off moving the *Ruined Stone* outside the depot."

"It wouldn't hurt."

"You and I should talk later. I'll see you in a while."

"Thanks, Zira."

Will watched her strut away in her seductive manner. That was part of her evil spell she used on every man she fancied. Part of him was attracted to Zira but he also knew that she was a free spirit. She could never belong to one man for long and he didn't care to be her play toy, especially now.

Saphoro startled him and asked, "Are you coming, Will?"

"Sure. I was just thinking about something."

"I see."

Will blushed at her comment as they proceeded to the elevator.

Maya and Jack were already inside, holding the doors open.

Will followed Saphoro inside and stood in the corner. The door squeaked as it slid shut with a bump.

No one spoke as the elevator ascended several floors. Jack finally broke the silence and asked, "Hey, kid. Do you have any idea what kind of trap the Attradeans might set?"

"Your computer system…was anything tampered with?"

Jack responded, "They accessed my records to see who's been here over a lengthy period of time."

"Where did you hide during the intrusion?"

"The air conditioning duct on level C."

Maya interrupted, "We did a scan of the depot. The only life form was you, Jack."

Will countered, "What life forms are the sensors calibrated for?"

Maya retorted, "How should he know?"

"I'm serious! It's important."

Jack replied, "I'm not sure. Anything that walks or crawls should be traceable. Plant life forms probably wouldn't. Anything in between, I don't know."

"Did you hear anything unusual from the duct?"

"They messed with the grating in the mechanical bay but it didn't sound like they had much luck getting it off."

Will asked, "Where are we going now?"

"To the control room. I'll do a quick scan of the bays before we go down there."

Maya complained, "We have a tight timetable, Jack, so I'd like to get in and out as quickly as possible."

"It seems that I've heard that before. You're always in a hurry, Maya."

"Jack, we ..."

"Look, Maya. I'm past that. It doesn't matter anymore."

Saphoro rolled her eyes in annoyance.

Will stared at the floor, wondering what happened between Maya and Jack in the past.

The door squealed open in time to break the mounting tension.

Jack entered the control room first and took a seat in front of four monitors. He pressed a series of keys and watched intently as images appeared from four different bays.

Saphoro and Will looked over Jack's shoulder and examined the monitors.

Maya waited impatiently behind them.

Jack focused on the ceiling of the first bay and zoomed in with the camera.

"It looks like I've got a bit of a mold problem in the instrument bay."

Will asked, "Do you have sensors in your ducts?"

"Yes, oxygen sensors located at several junctions."

"Can you run a check on the closest sensors to that bay?"

"Sure. What are you thinking?"

"We'll see in a minute."

Jack entered a series of digits and a chart appeared on one of the monitors, "This sensor, OX245-5, must be malfunctioning. It shows only 3.5% oxygen in that duct."

Will warned, "I don't think it's malfunctioning."

Jack complained, "It's only mold. What's the big deal?"

"I'll bet if you check the mechanical bay, you'll find the same oxygen level."

Jack entered another code and the screen showed a new report. The bay sensor showed 3.5 % oxygen.

He remarked, "Well, I'll be a son of a …!"

Jacked pressed three more buttons. The camera inside the mechanical bay zoomed closer to the ceiling.

Jack howled, "They've infected my depot with mold! Those bastards!"

Will advised, "I don't think it's just mold. Do you have oxygen packs around here?"

Jack became very concerned and replied nervously, "Yeah, in the cabinet by the door."

Will alerted Maya, "We'd better seal the *Luna C* shut until we're ready to leave."

Maya snapped, "We don't even know what this stuff is and your panicking, Will."

Jack interrupted, "Maya, the kid's right. If this stuff has airborne spores, we don't know how far or how fast it will spread."

Maya was agitated and yelled, "Fine! We'll seal the *Luna C*."

She contacted Neelon and Celine on the radio and ordered, "Return to the ship and seal the hatch until we return."

Saphoro asked Jack, "Can I use your computer? I'd like to analyze your database."

"Sure, but for what?"

"They might have implanted a monitoring device to track any incoming signals."

"Have at it. We're going down to the mechanical bay. I want to see this stuff for myself."

Will opened the cabinet and pulled out four respirators, one for each of them, and distributed them.

Jack instructed Will and Maya, "Each mask has a radio transmitter and receiver built in so we can communicate clearly."

He unlocked another cabinet and took out two RG-23 pulse blasters and a TT-5 flame-thrower.

Maya asked, "What are you going to do with those?"

Jack handed the flame-thrower to Will and one of the RG-23s to Maya.

"We're going to get your parts and sterilize my station."

After donning the masks and setting the air flow rate, they entered the elevator.

Jack asked, "Everyone ready?"

Will and Maya nodded.

The elevator descended to the bottom level.

Jack did a radio check, "Saphoro, can you read me?"

Saphoro's voice echoed to each of them, "Loud and clear. Hey, Jack, you have a mite in your system."

"What's a mite?"

"If you transmit an SOS, it will shut your system down permanently."

Jack mumbled, "Somebody wants me dead."

"I also found a critter."

"Come on, Saphoro, I don't know what that computer lingo is."

"The Attradeans know we're here. They're monitoring your communications. They heard our entire conversation with you."

Maya fretted, "Their damn spies are everywhere."

Will contradicted her, "I don't think it's the work of a spy network. There are too many coincidences."

Maya chided, "We'll see how your conspiracy theory plays out. And when we find that you're wrong, I don't want to here any more about it."

Jack chastised Maya, "You don't know half what you think you do. Give the kid a break."

Maya replied sharply, "Let's not make this personal, Jack."

Jack glared at Maya through his mask.

Will heard Jack breathing heavily over the speaker. He wondered what happened between Jack and Maya to generate so much emotion and tension between the two of them.

The elevator door squealed as it slid open.

Jack stepped off and proceeded to the exterior hatch. He pressed four digits on an electronic lock. The outer hatch door opened, leading to an inner chamber. Jack motioned for Will and Maya to enter first.

The outer hatch closed behind them, leaving them inside the quiet chamber.

The chamber reminded Will of a tomb. He waited nervously for the interior hatch to open."

Maya asked, "Why all the security?"

Jack replied, "It's not security. It's for containment in case of an emergency or a breech to the outside. Gotta' do something to keep oxygen inside this tub."

Maya pondered aloud, "I wonder how the Attradeans got in so easily."

"The computer has all of this information in a secure data base. They obviously knew how to access all of my classified codes."

The inner hatch opened slowly. They peered past the large steel door, eager to see what waited for them on the other side.

Jack asked Maya, "What parts do you need?"

"A twelve-tooth compressor gear, six feet of V9 piping and a three way double-action valve actuator."

"I have them in aisle three. Cover me."

When the hatch fully opened, Jack stepped out first. The bay had a gloomy atmosphere and the mold formed a thick layer across the high ceiling of the bay. Several of the lights were covered, as were two of the cameras.

"Hey, Jack," Will asked, "You said that the hatch was for containment, right?"

"Yeah. Why?"

"How does the process of containment work with the ducts?"

"Dampers isolate the bay from the remainder of the ship."

"What about the sensor which read low oxygen? Was that in the isolation zone?"

"No."

Jack yelled, "Damn, I see your point. The mold is already spreading into other parts of the station. The Attradeans must have jammed open the dampers to spread the mold."

Jack thought for a moment and ordered, "Will, stay here and guard the hatch. Maya follow me."

Will scanned the ceiling and inspected the mold.

Maya and Jack disappeared up aisle three. Jack switched his radio to 'local'. He reached over and switched Maya's to 'local' as well.

Maya asked, "What are you doing?"

"Time for a private conversation."

Jack pulled a six-foot section of V9 piping from a shelf and handed it to Maya.

"Why do you do this to me, Maya?"

"Do what?

"You break my heart and you keep coming back to rub salt in the wound."

"If I didn't care, do you think I would come back at all?"

"Then what's the problem?"

Maya's head drooped and she sniffled.

Jack could tell she was crying. "Come on, Maya. Throw me a bone here. What's the big deal?"

Maya looked up and glared at him. She screamed, "You really want to know why? Will is part of the reason. My background is the other."

Jack became confused. "The kid? You had an affair with the kid?"

"No, stupid! He has unusual abilities. He got them from his parents."

"Well I certainly hope he did."

"No, you don't understand. I'm Firenghian. I have these traits, too. If we had a relationship, they would be passed on to you."

"What's so bad about that?"

"It would ruin everything. I don't want to pass traits to anyone."

Jack was confused. "How do you avoid that?"

"By avoiding you, Jack! This is so damn hard on me. I can't have a lover without this responsibility hanging over my head."

"Is it so bad to have a family like that?"

"What if it doesn't work out? What if you left me and you had these abilities?"

Jack hollered, "And what if I didn't leave you? What if we lived happily ever after?"

"I can't take that chance."

Jack became angry.

"So this whole business about careers first was just a lie to keep me away from you?"

"Yes it was."

"I can't believe you think I'm that shallow. Look in the mirror, sister. It's you that's shallow."

****

Will noticed several tentacles emerging from the mold on the ceiling. The tentacles slowly descended over one of the aisles. He spoke urgently into the transmitter, "Jack! Maya! Get out of there, fast!"

Will received no response. He tried to connect with Maya mentally but something in the bay blocked him out. He grew concerned and screamed into the transmitter several times, "Maya! Jack! Answer me."

Saphoro became alarmed and asked, "What's going on down there, Will?"

"I can't reach them. Something's down here."

Saphoro asked, "What is it?"

"I don't know. I'm going after them."

"Be careful, Will."

Will left the hatch and hurried to aisle three. He saw Jack and Maya facing each other. He could tell by their motions that they were arguing. The tentacles hung about fifteen feet above their heads.

Will fired the flame-thrower but he was just out of range of the tentacles.

Jack and Maya saw the bright light from the flame and looked up. Jack quickly pushed Maya toward Will.

The tentacles became excited by their quick movements. They whipped at Jack and Maya, thrashing about.

Will fired again, igniting one of the tentacles.

A loud squeal came from the mold above them. Another tentacle lashed out and struck Maya on the side of her head. She tumbled across the floor into the side of a large steel box and fell to the ground. Two more tentacles stretched hungrily toward Maya's prone body.

Will fired frequently but the tentacles danced about so fast that they were difficult to hit. Just as the tentacles reached Maya, Jack dove onto them and attempted to wrestle them away from her.

Will fired again but the flame-thrower failed to fire. A red light indicated the fuel was spent. He angrily threw the weapon down on the floor and raced to Maya's aid.

The tentacles eagerly curled around Jack.

Will grabbed Maya's arms and dragged her to the safety of the hatch. He returned to aisle three and retrieved Maya's pulse blaster.

Jack was hoisted halfway to the ceiling fighting desperately to free himself.

The mold pulsed with hunger as Jack was drawn closer to a large opening where the tentacles emerged from.

Will climbed up the shelves and fired the RG-23, hoping to stop the tentacles from pulling Jack into the huge bio-sac. The blast slowed the tentacles briefly.

Will climbed higher until he reached the top of the shelves and was ten feet from the quivering mass. He fired again but one of the tentacles lashed at him, knocking him backward onto a crate.

The tentacle swung down at him. Will rolled off just as the tentacle smashed the crate, sending pieces of wood, packing and metal raining down on the floor below.

He got up and fired again. The mold parted like a biological gate. Inside was a horrible gargoyle-like creature. It reached its long jagged claws eagerly toward Jack.

Will seized the opportunity to fire again at the creature. He struck the inner lip of the opening, which caused the mass to reverberate. The creature lost its balance and fell from the opening. It hung by one of the tentacles and struggled to pull itself up.

Jack flailed desperately as the creature swiped at him twice, nearly catching him with its sharp, clawed hands.

Will got a close look at the creature and was horrified. It had a huge head with a large gaping mouth and double ridges of sharp teeth.

Will fired at the creature and then at the tentacles around Jack. The creature lost its hold and tumbled to the floor. Will fired again and struck the creature's head. It collapsed on the floor and lay motionless.

****

Saphoro called frantically over the radio for her friends several times. There was no response. She switched on the station radio.

"Come in *Ruined Stone*. This is *Luna C*. Do you read me?"

Talia answered, "Go ahead, Saphoro. What's your status?"

"We're in trouble. Be ready to evacuate the depot. I repeat, be ready to evacuate from the depot."

Talia asked, "What's going on there?"

"Something is taking over the depot. I lost contact with Jack, Will and Maya. I'm going down to the bay to look for them."

"Saphoro, get out of there. We'll pick you up."

"No, I'm staying."

Saphoro went to the elevator and pressed the button. While waiting, she tried repeatedly to raise her friends on the radio but there was still no answer. Finally the elevator arrived. She entered and pressed the button for the bottom level.

When the elevator finally stopped, the door slid open noisily. She hurried to the hatch and pressed the 'Open' button. Nothing happened. She studied the digital keypad. She pressed "1, 2, 3, 4" then 'enter'. The keypad displayed, "Activating...."

Saphoro thought, "Leave it to a man to use the first four numbers for a lock."

****

The creature stirred and stood up in the main aisle. It shrieked, as it looked up at the other creatures in the huge sack on the ceiling. It waddled down the aisle until it saw the light from the hatch. As it approached, it saw Maya's prone body lying inside on the floor.

It shrieked again, delighted to find such an easy prey. It stepped into the hatch and hovered over Maya. Suddenly the inner hatch door began to close. The creature stepped toward it and watched curiously. A hissing sound filled the chamber as the air was purged and oxygen was vented in. The creature began to wobble as it turned its attention back to Maya. It staggered and fell lifeless to the ground.

After a minute, the outer hatch opened. Saphoro entered and saw the creature lying on the floor beside Maya. She trembled at the sight of such a horrible creature. Even worse, she saw Maya's hair was streaked with blood from a laceration on the side of her head.

Saphoro realized the creature was dead and pulled Maya out of the chamber. She quickly pressed the 'Close' button and watched the hatch seal. She checked Maya's pulse and was relieved that she was alive.

"Come on, Maya. Wake up."

Maya didn't move.

Saphoro sat Maya up and pulled the mask off of her face. "Come on Maya. I can't move you by myself."

Finally, Maya stirred.

Saphoro pulled her to a standing position. "Come on. We've got to get out of here."

Maya's head listed sideways. "I can't. I … can't."

"Come on. If not, we'll be eaten like Will and Jack."

Maya had a vague look in her eyes but she lifted her head and spoke weakly, "Where are they?"

"I think they're dead."

Maya moaned weakly, "They can't be dead?"

"It sure looks that way and so are we if we don't get out of here."

Maya sobbed, "No it can't be. I have to go back."

"You can't go back in there with those creatures?"

"What creatures?"

"You didn't see the creature in the hatch with you?"

"No. There were tentacles in the bay. Giant tentacles."

"Well you're one lucky woman."

Maya struggled to walk with Saphoro's help. They slowly made their way onto the elevator. Maya sat down again on the floor.

"I'm so tired Saphoro, but we have to help them. We have to …" Maya passed out again on the floor. When the elevator door opened, Saphoro dragged her to a chair and sat her up. She took a seat in front of the microphone.

"Come in, *Ruined Stone*. It's *Luna C*."

"Go ahead, Saphoro. It's Talia."

"I've got Maya here but she's injured."

"What happened down there?"

"I'm not sure. I found her inside the containment hatch with a dead creature. Oh, it was horrible."

Talia warned, "We're coming in."

"No. Neelon and Celine can help me. They're onboard the *Luna C.*"

Talia advised her, "They didn't answer our calls on the radio. You get Maya out of there and I'll try to raise them again."

"Thanks, Talia."

Zira's voice came across the intercom. "Where's Will? Is he okay?"

"Negative. No sign of him or Jack."

Zira muttered, "Shit."

****

Will slung the pulse blaster around his shoulder and lunged onto one of the tentacles. He climbed toward the opening in the bio-sac as Jack was pulled inside. When he got close to the top, he was horrified to see more of the creatures inside, waiting anxiously for their prey to arrive.

The tentacle stopped trying to shake Will and retracted into the mold. He unharnessed his weapon while clinging tightly to it.

Suddenly, the tentacle whipped and tossed him through the opening. He landed against something solid under the mass that hurt his back.

Jack lay on his back next to Will.

"Are you okay, Jack?"

"Yeah, just rattled. How the hell do we get out of this mess?"

Jack scrambled to his feet.

"What's this thing behind us?"

"It's a crane hook. Why?"

"Does it have power?"

"Of course."

Jack stared at it for a few seconds and looked at Will. "Are you thinking what I'm thinking?"

One of the creatures crept up behind Jack.

Will answered, "You bet. If we can lower the hook ... Watch out!"

Will raised his pulse blaster and splattered one of the creatures daring enough to approach them. The other creatures quickly dragged the carcass away and devoured it.

Will blasted another creature to keep them occupied. Will and Jack kept their eyes on the creatures, alert for any movement.

"How many of them do you think are back there, Will?"

"I see about fifteen."

"You see in the dark?"

"Yeah."

"This has to do with those Firenghian traits, I'll bet."

"Uh-huh. Sore topic with you and Maya?"

"Yeah, you could say that."

Will looked around the living chamber that imprisoned them. He suddenly realized what was happening.

"This is a biosphere! This thing creates its own atmosphere. I'll bet the creatures can't survive in an oxygen rich environment. That's why the sensors read so low."

Jack replied, "So we had better get out of here before our oxygen runs out."

"You got that right. This thing is filling the chamber up with gas as we speak. I can see it seeping out of its walls."

"Great. Give me the gun."

"For what?"

"I have to get above the pulleys to actuate the hook."

Jack took the gun from Will and blasted the mass above the hook until he could see the platform. He handed the gun back to Will.

"Keep those things off my back. This won't take long."

Jack climbed through the hole and pulled himself onto the platform. He unlatched the clips on the electrical panel and swung the door open.

"Hmm, contactors. Now, which one?"

Jack pushed one of the contactors in and a loud bell filled the air. The whole mass shifted briefly when the trolley budged.

"Oops. Wrong one."

Jack pushed another contactor in and the reel began to rotate slowly. He could feel the mass vibrate as the weight of the hook dropping began to tear at it.

Will yelled from below the platform, "It's working, Jack! It's tearing away at the belly."

"How far are we from the top shelf?"

"About ten feet."

"I'm going to shift the trolley. Let me know when we're over the shelf. Hold on in case this mess breaks loose."

Will leaned back against the wall and replied, "I'm ready."

Jack pushed the first contactor in and the bell rang again. He griped, "Damn, I hate that sound."

Will yelled, "Six feet, Jack."

The mass tore away from the ceiling in sections.

"Three feet, Jack. We can jump."

"Another couple of seconds, Will."

Will pleaded, "Hurry! This thing's breaking loose!"

Will watched anxiously as the crane eased over the top of the shelves.

"That's it, Jack! Come on."

Jack slid through the hole and landed next to Will. "What are you waiting for, kid? Let's get out of here."

Will jumped out of the mass and tumbled onto the shelf. Jack jumped and landed beside him. Will saw one of the creatures about to leap from the mass onto Jack's back. He instinctively grabbed a basketball-sized gear and swung it at the creature's head as it leaped.

The gear caught the creature in the face. It tumbled from the shelf and fell thirty feet to the floor.

"Nice shot, Will. By the way, that's the 12-tooth compressor gear Maya wanted. Hang on to it."

Will warned, "Let's get out of here, fast."

The huge mass rippled violently as it sagged and tore away from the ceiling. The vibration alarmed the creatures enough to keep them away from the gaping hole.

As Will tossed the gear down to the floor, Jack grabbed his arm and said, "Thanks. You saved my life."

"And you risked your life to save Maya's. Why?"

"Later. Last one down buy's a round at the bar."

The two men scurried down the huge racks. Jack was surprisingly agile and reached the bottom first.

He kidded, "Looks like you're buying."

"I'd be happy to."

Will picked up the compressor gear and headed for the hatch.

Jack looked down the aisle and saw the V9 pipe.

"Ah, what the hell."

He picked up the pipe and headed for the hatch.

They kept an eye on the creatures overhead in case any were bold enough to make the jump.

Jack pressed the 'open' button. The hatch door slowly opened and they entered anxiously.

Will was the first to acknowledge the dead creature's presence. "Geez, look at that thing."

Jack replied, "Our theory was right. When the hatch closes, the chamber purges and fresh oxygen is vented in. It looks like the oxygen did kill the creature."

****

Saphoro struggled to lift Maya from the chair. She tried to get Maya to the dock where Neelon and Celine could help. She heard voices on her radio, faint at first, but growing louder."

"Will! Jack! Is that you?"

"It sure is," Will hollered. "Did Maya make it back?"

"I have her here. She's unconscious."

"Where are you?"

"The control room."

"We'll be right up."

Jack pulled off his mask and said, "I don't think spores are the problem here. It was the gas."

Will pulled his mask off and breathed deep. "Ah, fresh air."

44

The two men sat on the floor inside the elevator and waited. Will stared at Jack until he responded, "What's the matter?"

"You risked your life to save Maya's."

"Yeah. So?"

"Why? I know there's more between the two of you than she lets on."

"Let me ask you a question first."

"Sure."

"You and Maya are both Firenghian, right?"

"Yeah."

"What's the big deal that she won't even kiss me?"

"My father was human and my mother was Firenghian. Just by kissing, several of her traits were transmitted into his body. He is the only human to receive traits from a Firenghian. His traits were slightly mutated, or different for lack of a better word. He was actually better than the Firenghians when the traits finished affecting his body."

"I've heard that you guys can, you know…"

"Change shapes?"

"Yeah."

"Yes we can."

"Why didn't you change in there?"

"Should I have?"

"I've heard that fear and high emotions cause Firenghians to change to their alter-shapes."

"My genes mutated. I can control when I change."

"What do you change into?"

"I don't know. I haven't done it yet. All I know is that I felt it but repressed it."

"What about Maya? Can she change too?"

"I don't see why not. I don't know if she ever has. She seems intent on keeping it a secret from her crew, though."

"And me as well."

"You really care for her, don't you?"

"Yes I do. I thought she was jerking me around like a fool all this time."

"And now?"

"Now I can understand the situation. It makes it easier to accept."

"Well, I think you'll have plenty of time to work on it. I don't think you'll be staying here."

"You've got a point."

The elevator stopped and the door slid open. They found Saphoro sitting on the ground with Maya in her arms.

Jack uttered, "Jesus. She's a mess."

Will took the pipe from Jack.

Jack pulled her mask off and picked her up.

"We're getting out of here, now."

Saphoro threw her mask down and followed. She was relieved to see her friends alive again.

When they reached the dock, Neelon and Celine were packing cases of food and drink onto the *Luna C*.

Will asked angrily, "What the hell are you two doing?"

Celine replied, "We needed supplies, so we stocked up."

Will scolded Celine, "You were supposed to seal the *Luna C*."

Saphoro complained, "We've been trying to reach you on the radio."

Celine saw Maya lying unconscious in Jack's arms and fretted, "Is she okay?"

"We don't know. Get on board, quickly."

Will looked at Neelon and then at the crates. He conceded, "Alright. I'll help, but we have to hurry up."

Will tossed the pipe and gear inside the ship.

Neelon hurriedly passed the crates of supplies to Will. Will stacked them inside the hatch.

When they finished, Neelon closed the hatch and called Celine on the intercom,

"We're ready for take off."

Celine responded indignantly, "Well it's about time."

****

Jack carried Maya in his arms. Saphoro led him to Maya's quarters. He set Maya down on the bed and pulled off her boots.

Saphoro felt bad for Jack. She saw how much he cared for Maya. Reluctantly she interrupted, "Come on, Jack. Celine needs you to open the bay doors."

Jack hesitated for a second, then leaned down and kissed Maya's forehead.

Saphoro smiled at him.

Red-faced, he remarked, "Don't ask."

Saphoro giggled and led him up to the pilot's cabin.

When they entered, Celine hollered at Jack, "Well it's about time! You men are making a habit of dragging ass around here."

"Lady, you don't know the half of it."

"So what do we do to get out of here?"

"Lend me your headset."

Celine removed her headset and passed it to Jack. He dialed a frequency into the computer and said, "Jack Fleming – 7-5-3-1."

The bay doors began to open. Jack handed the headset back to Celine.

She looked at him curiously and asked, "That's it?"

"Sure is."

"I could have done that."

"Not without duplicating my voice."

Saphoro teased, "Like the Attradeans did?"

"Yeah, like they did. How did that happen?"

Celine replied, "Who knows? They're doing all sorts of unusual things these days."

Jack said, "I've got to check on Maya."

"See ya', Jack. Nice to have you aboard."

"Smart ass."

Celine laughed loudly as Jack left the cabin.

****

When Jack reached Maya's quarters, Will was sitting on the edge of the bed with a wet towel on Maya's head.

47

Jack asked, "How is she?"

"She'll be okay."

"I guess she'll need stitches."

"No. Too late. She'll have a nasty scar on her scalp though."

"What do you mean 'too late'?"

Will made a face at him.

Jack nodded, "I get it. Another one of those Firenghian things."

"Yeah, but keep it between us."

"Sure, Will."

"You called me 'Will' instead of 'kid'."

"Is that all right?"

"Yeah, it feels good to be acknowledged like that."

"Well, we made a heck of a team back there."

"We sure did. Did you ever see creatures like that before?"

Jack answered, "No, but I've heard about them. I didn't think they really existed."

"Who told you about them?"

"There was a freighter, several years ago, that came into the station. The captain was known to indulge in piracy among the alien colonies. He told me about a species of creatures that existed on Eremus, not too far from Attrades. Eremus is a small planet surrounded by an ammonia atmosphere."

Will sniffed at his shirt, "Can you smell it?"

"What?"

"Our clothes are tainted with ammonia."

"I guess we know where those things came from. But why on my station?"

"I think we'll find the answer on Attrades."

"Attrades? We're going there?"

"Uh-huh."

"Whose crazy idea is that?"

Maya sat up and muttered groggily, "Mine. If you don't like it, we'll take you back to the station."

Jack was relieved to see her awake and coherent.

"No, no. I'm happy to be here."

"I'll bet you are."

Jack quipped, "I guess it's a good thing I didn't type in the codes for your space credits. We'd both be a lot poorer."

Maya asked, "Why didn't you?"

"Because I wanted to know the truth about us."

"And what do you think now?"

Jack asked, "Now?"

"Yes, now that you know about the traits."

Maya cast a long glance at Will as she waited for Jack to answer.

Jack was embarrassed. He stammered, "Oh. You know that I know?"

"Yes, I do."

"I feel …"

Will stood up and excused himself.

Jack sighed and breathed deeply. He regained his composure and said, "I feel better now that I know why you behaved like you did. I may not like the idea of not being in a physical relationship with you but I can live with that. I still want to be with you."

Maya smiled and said, "Jack Fleming, you are a strange man."

"Yeah, I know."

"Thank you for saving my life."

"Will had a lot to do with it. He saved both of us."

Maya smiled at Jack and pushed the hair out of his eyes.

Jack covered Maya with a blanket and suggested, "You should get some rest. That's quite a whack you got."

"Haven't you learned? I heal quickly."

"Good. I want you in one piece. I'll be back to check on you."

Maya closed her eyes and drifted off into a deep sleep.

III.   Attrades

Jack entered the pilot's cabin, where Will and Celine were conversing. Celine smiled deviously at Jack and asked, "How is Maya?"

"She'll be okay. She needs to rest for a while."

Celine couldn't resist teasing the men. "So the dynamic duo saved the day and now the fairy princess is happy."

Jack glanced at Will with a confused look. Will shrugged his shoulders, acknowledging mutual bewilderment.

Celine uttered, "Let's try this again. Have you and Maya finally come to terms, Jack?"

Jack asked innocently, "What are you talking about?"

Celine lectured him, "Come on. Everyone knows she has a thing for you."

"Yeah. Everyone but me."

"Did the three of you clear things up?"

Will was baffled by his inclusion and asked, "What do you mean the three of us?"

Celine rolled her eyes and exclaimed, "You guys are killing me! Will, did you explain to Jack about Maya's habits?"

"You mean traits?"

"Habits, traits, whatever you call them."

"Oh, yeah. We discussed them."

"Good. Now we're getting somewhere."

She paused for a moment to enter the coordinates for their new course. After pressing several digits on a small keypad, Celine continued, "So, did you discuss the said traits with Maya?"

Jack answered, "Not really. She's aware that I know about them now and that's it."

"So are the two of you on or off?"

Jack became frustrated and asked, "Celine, can't you speak in a way that I can understand?"

Celine cackled. "Man, you've been cooped up on that farmer's market of yours for way too long. Have you and Maya connected yet?"

Jack looked at Will for help but Will just rolled his eyes.

Jack answered, "I don't know. We might have but she didn't say."

Celine pleaded, "Well, tell me. What did she say?"

"She said 'I'm a strange man'."

Celine became annoyed and bellowed, "That's it? I could have told you that!"

Jack replied dejectedly, "Well, that's all there was."

Saphoro entered the cabin and took a seat. She asked, "Am I missing anything good?"

Celine answered, "No. There's more excitement at a funeral than with these guys."

Saphoro giggled, drawing Will's attention.

He asked defensively, "What's so funny?"

"Oh, I was just thinking about something to do with you."

Will mused aloud, "What in the world could that be?"

She took a deep breath and tried to be serious. "Okay. If you insist."

Celine glanced at Saphoro and asked, "Am I going to enjoy this?"

"Maybe."

"Then by all means continue. I'm bored to death."

"When I was in Jack's control room, I radioed the *Ruined Stone* and told them that I lost contact with you guys. When I brought Maya back there, I told them that I thought you were dead."

Will asked impatiently, "So what's the punch line?"

"Well, Zira, the new girl on board the *Ruined Stone*, was asking about you."

Will's eyes lit up as he thought for a moment that Zira might have actually cared about him.

Saphoro continued, "She seemed more disappointed than upset. Will, I don't think she's …"

Will cut her off and said, "I know. You don't have to tell me. I'm just a convenience."

Will was embarrassed and left the cabin. He descended the steps to the lower level and entered his quarters. He pulled his shirt off and angrily threw it at the wall. He thought about Zira for a moment and lay down on the bed."

Jack asked Saphoro, "Did you have to shatter his dreams like that?"

"It's not all that bad. Maya told me that Will is already aware of Zira's shallowness."

Then Jack asked Celine, "Have you told Zira that Will is alive?"

Saphoro waited anxiously for Celine's response.

Celine said coyly, "Well, I mentioned that we rescued Maya and escaped. I don't think I said that you guys made it back safely."

Jack exclaimed, "Well, damn, woman! Get on the horn and tell her. I want to hear her reaction."

Celine cackled and said, "Good idea, Jack."

She turned on her Display Monitoring System (DMS) and selected the *Ruined Stone's* frequency.

"Come in, *Ruined Stone*. This is *Luna C.*"

Talia's face appeared on the monitor from the *Ruined Stone*, "Go ahead, *Luna C.*"

"Hi, Talia."

"Hi. How's Maya doing?"

"She'll be okay. It's a good thing Jack and Will were able to rescue her."

Talia asked in a surprised tone, "They're both alive?"

"Sure are. They put Maya in the containment hatch and fought off the creatures."

Talia replied happily, "No kidding! Hey, someone wants to speak with you."

Zira's face appeared on the monitor. She spoke excitedly, "Hi, Celine. I'm Zira. Did I hear you say that Will is alive?"

"Yes you did. He's lying down right now but he's okay."

Zira replied icily, "Lucky for him. Good men are hard to find out here."

Celine tilted her head back and poked a finger in her mouth. She pretended to be enthusiastic toward Zira, "I'm glad to hear that you were concerned about him."

Talia resumed the conversation, "Celine, this is Talia, again. Give my regards to Maya. We're glad everyone is safe, even Jack Fleming."

Jack sneered quietly from the corner of the cabin, "That bitch."

Celine and Saphoro laughed heartily. Celine said, "We'll talk to you later."

Talia replied, "Adios, girls."

Celine turned the DMS off and teased Jack. "She's got your number!"

Jack responded defensively, "Why me? I'm just an honest businessman."

Celine suggested, "Maybe your prices were too high."

Jack quipped cynically, "Just what we need around here - a comedian."

****

Hours later, the *Luna C* and the *Ruined Stone* passed through the last portal en route to Attrades.

Will wandered down the stairs to the lower level and intercepted Maya leaving her quarters.

Will asked, "How are you feeling, Maya?"

"Much better. I still have a splitting headache."

"You were lucky you didn't get killed."

"I was lucky that you and Jack were there to save me."

"Speaking of which," Will mentioned, "I have a question for you."

Maya cringed and said, "I knew this was coming."

"You have a thing for Jack, don't you?"

"You have to ask? I thought you'd figured that out by now."

Will continued, "I'm risking my life to find Baron. You did tell me that Baron is special to you, right?"

Maya replied calmly, "Yes, I did."

Will asked, "I don't get it. Which of these guys is the one you really like or are you playing them both?"

Maya answered defensively, "Will, I wouldn't play anybody. When you meet Baron, you'll understand."

Will sighed and conceded, "I guess I'll have to trust you."

Maya questioned him, "You don't want to go to Attrades, do you?"

"It's not that. I just don't like the way things are going in general."

Maya was confused and asked, "In regard to what?"

Will answered boldly, "The way this war is being fought. The Fleet has no idea what they're doing."

"Do you know a better way to run the war?"

"I think so. Do you remember studying Earth History at the Academy?"

Maya answered, "Vaguely."

"Do you remember how the Americans fought the British in the Colonial period?"

"Refresh me."

Will explained, "Instead of confronting the enemy head on, which was the British army's strength, they resorted to tactical hits on the officers only and waged guerilla warfare."

"So how does that apply to us?"

"What if we were to make tactical hits on the leaders of different alien outposts, and maybe pillage them in the process?"

Maya asked skeptically, "What good would that do?"

"It would confuse them. They aren't organized for that kind of warfare."

Maya chastised him, "Will, you fantasize too much."

"Call it what you want, it would work."

Maya warned him, "This mission is my responsibility. I owe you and Jack my life, but we will stick to the plan."

"I understand, but if the Attradeans know we're coming and we aren't prepared, it could be disastrous."

Maya became agitated and rebuked him, "Will, they can't see into the future! Forget that notion."

"How do you know?"

Maya declared assuredly, "You'll see when we get there. They won't have a clue that we're coming."

Celine's voice sounded from the intercom. "Attention, everyone. We're nearing our destination. We'll be in position shortly."

A few seconds later, Celine requested, "Maya, if you're available, I'd like to see you in the pilots' cabin."

Maya pleaded, "Please, Will, be patient and trust me."

"I'm trying."

Maya ascended the stairs to the upper level.

Will wondered what was going on in her head. He was tempted to read her mind but she would know. After all, he did promise to respect her privacy.

Will sat down in front of the imaging console. He pressed the 'recall' button and studied pictures of the Attradean compound.

Jack entered the main quarters and approached Will.

"Mind if I join you?"

Will looked back, surprised to see someone else in the room. "No, not at all."

"What's happening on Attrades?"

"I'm not entirely sure. I'm supposed to locate a prisoner and gather some information."

"It must be someone very important to risk two ships and their crews. Isn't Attrades the headquarters for the alien forces?"

"It sure is."

"Mind if I go with you?"

"Why would you want to do that?"

"Oh, I don't know. Maybe it's the sense of adventure."

"Jack, what made you want to run a depot? Isn't that boring?"

"I used to be in the Fleet a while back. I didn't follow orders too well, so we parted ways. I needed a job so I started a depot."

Will was surprised. "You? In the Fleet?"

"Yeah, I was."

"What did you want to do with the rest of your life?"

"I dreamed of becoming a space pirate."

Will laughed. "A space pirate! That's cool."

"Yeah, but it's just a dream."

"I'd like to be something like that. It's a lot more exciting than following stupid routines. I loved hearing the stories about marauders' adventures."

Maya descended the steps and pulled up a seat between the two men.

Jack greeted her, "Hello, Star Princess."

Maya blushed but said sternly, "Don't embarrass me, Jack."

Will asked, "So what now?"

Maya replied stoically, "It's time."

Will stood up and proclaimed, "I guess I'm as ready as I'll ever be."

Maya added, "Neelon is getting you some equipment and a weapon."

Jack informed Maya, "I'm going, too."

"No, Jack. You can't."

"Why not?"

"They can read your thoughts. Will can cloak his and you can't."

Will patted Jack on the back and said, "Thanks for trying. I'll be all right."

Jack warned, "If you get into trouble, I'm coming down."

Maya glared at Jack, much to his chagrin.

"What's the matter, Maya?" Jack asked.

Maya stated defiantly, "I'm in charge and I'll tell you if you need to go down there or not."

Jack looked at Will for support. Will shrugged his shoulders and replied, "It's her show."

Neelon entered the room with an equipment vest, an RG-23 pulse blaster and a backpack. Will examined the equipment and asked Maya, "How long do you think I'll be down there?"

"Two days at the most. Remember, if you contact me, they'll know. Save it for the extraction. We can track you and monitor your speech but that's all we can do."

"I can live with that."

Maya explained, "The *Ruined Stone* is in position at a distance for monitoring the Attradeans. They'll be tracking you in case you get into trouble. We'll be standing by quietly to react in the event of a situation. Any questions?"

"No, but I'm sure they already know I'm coming."

Maya snapped, "Will you stop it already!"

Will fired back, "Forget I said anything!"

Maya pointed to the transport platform. Will promptly obeyed. He stepped onto the platform and waited.

Jack hollered, "Good luck!"

Will waved and disappeared in a flash of light.

Jack asked Maya, "Are you sure this is a good idea?"

"No, but I don't know any other way to do this. Maybe you have a better plan."

"No. I'm the new guy on the block. Can we really monitor him while he's down there?"

"We can't but the *Ruined Stone* can. We would risk being detected at this close range. Talia will let us know if he's in trouble, though."

Jack complained, "I've got a bad feeling about this."

Maya pressed the intercom switch and inquired, "Celine, do you have the *Ruined Stone* yet?"

"Yes I do. Talia's keeping the link open. They have Will on their scanners."

"Good. Keep me posted."

****

Will surveyed the area outside the palace walls. He searched the area for an entrance to the palace but saw none.

The woods were thick and the foliage was dense in most places. Eerie noises emanated from the trees when the wind blew.

Will crept along a narrow path until he reached a small clearing. The sound of snapping twigs and branches brushing against something caught his attention. He retreated into the bushes and hid.

A young Attradean female passed him and entered the circular clearing. She sat on a rock at the rear.

Will cloaked his thoughts and studied the female. This was the first real alien he had ever seen.

Her face was dappled yellow and green. Although she possessed a number of human-like qualities, she had several distinct Attradean features. She possessed onyx eyes, webbed hands and fanned-out ears. Her lips were pursed and her pointed teeth reminded Will of an underwater creature.

Will interpreted her thoughts and learned that she was very sad. She was distraught with her father. He noticed that she had tears in her eyes.

Deciding to try something daring, Will stopped cloaking his thoughts and used his telepathy to communicate with her.

"Why are you crying?"

The Attradean female looked nervously around the clearing. "Who are you? Show yourself."

Will spoke aloud, "I don't want to frighten you. Can we just talk?"

She asked, "Why would you want to talk to me?"

Will explained, "I feel your sadness. Maybe I can help."

"No one can help me."

Will asked, "Why not? Give me a chance."

"Well, alright."

She paused for a moment to gather her courage.

"My father is King Tenemon and he's a horrible tyrant."

Will couldn't believe his luck. To find the king's daughter outside the palace walls alone was more than he could have hoped for.

Will inquired vocally, "Has he hurt you?"

"No, not directly. My boyfriend is from a small village in the mountains. Father forbade him to see me anymore. The guards caught my beau and imprisoned him."

Will was shocked.

"He did that just because he was seeing you?"

"That's the kind of person he is."

Will suggested, "Maybe I can free your beau."

"That's impossible. He's too well guarded."

"What's your name?"

"Laneia. What's yours?"

"Will Saris."

****

Talia's voice rang frantically from the DMS, "Celine, he's communicating with an Attradean!"

"Are you sure?"

"Of course, I am. I'm listening to him as we speak. Get Maya now!"

Celine barked into the page, "Maya, get up here fast! We have a problem."

A few moments later, Maya and Jack burst into the cabin.

Maya asked, "What's wrong, Celine?"

"I think you'd better talk to Talia."

Maya sat down in the seat and looked at the monitor.

"What's going on, Talia?"

"Your boy! He's talking to an Attradean woman."

"What? You've got to be kidding!"

"No. We're picking up faint pieces of conversation between him and the Attradean."

Maya fretted, "I hope he knows what he's doing."

Jack pressured Maya, "Send me down. I'll find out what's going on."

Maya responded, "No. It's too risky. We'll give him a chance."

Maya, Jack and Celine waited anxiously for Talia to report back with additional information.

****

Laneia asked, "Can I see you, Will Saris?"

"Only if you promise not to be frightened."

Laneia became curious. She asked, "Why would I be?"

Will stepped out of the bushes and stood before Laneia. Her eyes widened with surprise.

Will pleaded, "Please don't be afraid. I won't hurt you."

Laneia collected her composure and replied, "I'm not afraid. I just wasn't expecting to see a human. In fact, I've never seen a live human before."

"I'm not all human. I'm part Firenghian, which is a little different."

"Forgive my ignorance, but I know very little about other races. My father believes all races are inferior to the Attradeans."

"That's not true. All races are different, not inferior."

Laneia asked anxiously, "Do you still think you can help me?"

"I think so. I'll need your help, though."

"What can I do?"

"I'm looking for someone named Baron. I believe he was captured and imprisoned inside the palace."

Laneia waved her hands excitedly. "I know Baron. He used to talk to me when I sat out here. He's been imprisoned and placed in a special cell."

"Why a special cell?"

"Because of his size, silly."

Will was bewildered. "His size? What about his size?"

"He is so small and cuddly."

"Maybe I'm missing something here. What is Baron?"

"I'm not sure. I've never seen a creature like him before."

Will paced back and forth, trying to understand Maya's connection with Baron. He asked, "Can you tell me where to find him?"

"Sure. He's in the white building, three floors down. That's where my father keeps all the prisoners."

"What about your beau?"

"His name is Breel. He is there as well."

"Do you know how many guards are inside?"

"Six."

Will was surprised that there would be so little security in the prison. He exclaimed, "Only six!"

"That's right."

"Where are the rest of them?"

"Most of them are assigned either to the Seers or inside of the palace."

"The Seers? Who are they?"

"Five priestesses who take care of the Eye. The Eye shows them things before they happen."

Will's eyes widened with keen interest. "Have you ever seen the Seers or the Eye?"

"No, but I heard the guards talking about them."

"Do you know where they are?"

Laneia answered, "They are kept in the bottom level of the prison house. My father never lets them out of their area."

"That's interesting. As soon as darkness falls, I'm going inside the palace grounds. If Breel is in there, I'll find him."

"Will, there's something else you should know."

"What's that?"

"They're expecting you or someone like you."

"I would have been disappointed if they weren't."

"You're a strange one, Will."

Will asked, "Where will you go after I free him? You can't stay here, can you?"

"No, I can't. I guess we'll hide out in the mountains."

"I can bring you both back with me if you'd like a new start."

Laneia replied, "So long as Breel and I can be together."

"We'll meet in the morning and I'll have my ship extract us."

"Thank you, Will."

"You're welcome."

****

Talia reported to Maya, "Your boy just made arrangements to bring two Attradeans back with him at daybreak."

Maya exclaimed, "He did what?"

Talia replied, "You heard me. It appears that the Attradean is the king's daughter."

Maya's jaw dropped. She panicked and snapped, "He'll have the whole Attradean fleet hunting us!"

Talia added, "They also discussed seers and an eye."

"Don't tell me. They can see the future?"

"Well, she did call them Seers."

Maya conceded, "He must have some kind of plan. I guess we'll wait and see what happens."

After a pause, Talia asked, "Are you sure we can trust Will?"

"I certainly hope so. I just wish I knew what he's up to."

****

Will asked, "Do you know any discreet entrances into the palace where the guards aren't likely to be watching?"

Laneia answered, "Nothing big enough for someone your size to pass through."

"Let me worry about that."

Laneia looked puzzled. She instructed him, "Down at the stream is a big, old tree. I mean it's really old. If you climb up a ways, you'll find a large hole in it. The inside of the tree is hollow. If you were smaller, you could fit into the hole like Baron did and follow it down through the ground. The hole leads into the lower level of the prison. That's where the Seers are. You need to get one level up from there to find Baron and Breel."

Contemplating the situation for a moment, Will asked, "Where is Breel in relation to Baron?"

They are three cells apart. Breel is in the first cell."

"That doesn't sound too bad."

"But even if you get in, how would you get out?"

Will took Laneia's webbed hands in his. He said confidently, "As I said before, let me worry about that?"

Will sniffed the air around them. He searched the perimeter of the clearing, then slid into the trees and disappeared from sight. A few moments later, he returned.

Laneia asked, "What in the world are you doing?"

"I found them! Dusselberries."

Laneia asked, "What are Dusselberries?"

"Dusselberry juice will make you sleep. It's very potent."

"Are you sure you know what you're doing?"

"Of course."

Will laid out a small pile of the tiny, blue berries. Laneia watched curiously.

Will wrapped the berries in a wide green frond. He placed them in the outer pocket of his knapsack. "Where do your father's ships dock?" he asked.

Laneia pointed to a large docking facility on top of a nearby hill.

"There are only two or three ships up there. Most of the ships usually berth a short distance from here in the main facility. I've never been inside either of them, though."

Will studied the building from a distance.

"What are you thinking, Will?"

"They'll expect us to escape in my ship. What if we do something different?"

Laneia asked, "Like what, take one of my father's ships?"

"Exactly. I'll need to find someone to pilot it, though."

"I think I know someone who'll help us."

Will asked cautiously, "Can we trust him?"

"Without a doubt."

"Good. Meet me at dawn near the side of the hangar."

Laneia promised, "I'll be there with a pilot."

"How long before your father realizes you're missing?"

"It will take a few days. He doesn't pay me any attention. Be careful, Will."

Will advised, "When you go inside the palace, walk around and let as many people see you as possible. That reduces the likelihood of them noticing your absence right away."

Laneia hugged Will. "If you can do this, I will be indebted to you for life."

"Don't worry about it. I'll see you in the morning."

"Thanks, Will. Good luck."

Will waved to her and disappeared into the forest.

****

Back inside the ship, Maya chewed on a fingernail.

Celine slapped her hand away.

"Stop that!"

Maya complained, "I can't help it. I'm worried."

Talia's voice sounded from the intercom, "He's going away from the palace! I don't get it."

Maya asked, "Did you hear anything else?"

Talia answered, "Something about berries and ships. It's very difficult to comprehend from this distance."

Maya asked, "What should we do, Celine?"

"Don't look at me. You picked him because of all these immaculate qualities he has."

Maya covered her face with her hands and sighed.

Celine added, "He's not stupid. Maybe he knows something we don't."

"God, I hope so."

Celine suggested, "Maybe it runs in the family. The stories about his father were pretty extraordinary."

Maya replied, "But they were all high risk actions. We can't afford that."

Celine explained, "The higher the expectation is, the higher the risk will be. Did you think this would be easy?"

"No, but I expected him to follow orders."

"Whose orders? Yours?"

"Of course. How else could we do this?"

"Maya, you are obsessed with controlling every situation. You have to relax and trust people."

"I can't. I'm afraid things will go wrong."

"Like with you and Jack?"

Maya snapped, "That's low, Celine!"

"Think about it. You're a difficult person to deal with. You're high maintenance for any man to deal with."

Maya griped, "I have responsibilities."

"Like what? Getting your stupid promotion. You already lost Baron. Now you're risking Will's life. You've lost touch with your human side."

Maya asked pathetically, "I'm not that bad, am I?"

"Ask Jack."

Tears rolled down Maya's cheek. She blurted, "I never meant it to be like this."

Talia called, "Are you still there, Maya? What do we do?"

Maya wiped her tears away and answered Talia, "Nothing right now. I think Will knows what he's doing. Keep me updated."

"It's your call."

Maya responded, "Thanks, Talia."

Maya stood up and approached the door. She paused and said, "Thanks, Celine. I needed that."

"What are friends for?"

****

Will hiked through the thick foliage in the forest. Daylight faded, but he found the stream. He easily located the old tree as it stood out among the others like the grandfather of all trees. Its branches and bark looked brittle, reflective of its age.

Setting his backpack behind a clump of bushes, Will removed his RG-23 pulse blaster from the holster on his belt. It would do him no good when he shifted to his alter-shape. He also removed the tracking devices on thin silver chains from around his neck and carefully stowed them inside the backpack. He undressed and stashed his clothes nearby. He took the wrap of Dusselberries from the front pocket of the backpack and set them on the ground, nearby.

Nervously mumbling to himself, he stated, "This had better work."

He knelt down and focused until a strange sensation overtook his body and he began to transform. He felt his insides cramp up and his bones ached. His muscles stretched and pulled in different directions.

Will thought about Maya from his younger days to forget the pain. He remembered how she changed, as she grew up. She was so attractive to him, but he was so young. He thought about Zira as well. Would she ever change? Sometimes events can change people. Sometimes things just weren't meant to be.

The pain passed. Will looked about him in awe. Everything was much bigger than before. He crawled to the stream for a drink. He was amazed and proud to see his reflection as a young wolverine. He recalled that his father's alter-shape was a wolverine.

Will took the leaf wrap in his mouth and scaled the tree. He reached the second large branch and found the hole, just as Laneia said.

Will entered the opening and scurried down the middle of the hollow trunk of the tree. When he reached the bottom, he entered a small dirt tunnel, which wound under the roots. The tunnel seemed to spiral downward infinitely. Sometimes it was just barely wide enough for Will to squeeze through. He saw a dim light ahead and was relieved. Unfortunately, the tunnel grew narrow and he became stuck. He was so close, yet so far. There was no way to turn back. He began to panic, thinking to himself, "What can I do?"

Will tried to relax and control his breathing. He focused on the light ahead and tried to psych himself, "Come on, Will. You're a shape-shifter. You can get out of this."

He backed up a few strides and stretched. He inched forward only to be squeezed again. He struggled backwards to a wider section.

"Okay. What next? Think."

Will began to claw at the sides of the tunnel. He realized that he could push the dirt under him with his front legs and push it behind him with his rear legs.

"Hey! I think I'm learning to act like a wolverine."

After a few minutes of digging, he was able to squeeze through the narrow section of tunnel onto a damp stone floor in a dark corner. He promptly searched the area for any sign of trouble but no one was near.

Will set the leaf wrap on the ground and rested for a few moments. The sound of women's voices in the distance caught his attention. He crept toward the source of the sounds.

Will turned the corner and entered a large chamber. Torches high above him cast eerie flickering shadows across the floor. He noticed gray mist near the center of the gigantic stone chamber. The mist covered a wide channel, which surrounded a granite island. The island had a narrow catwalk, which led to a small room lit by a torch in the rear.

At the edge of the channel atop five stone steps, Will stopped. Something bothered him about the mist in the channel. He inched closer and grew nauseated from a familiar smell. Will backed away and thought for a moment, "Where have I smelled that odor before?"

Suddenly he recognized the smell. "Ammonia! Why is there ammonia down here?"

Will looked closer and saw five women on top of the island wearing red cloaks. They were huddled around an oval crystal on top of a golden pedestal. It looked like a large diamond with many smooth faces on it.

Will was quite interested.

"I wonder what they're doing. Do I risk opening my thoughts to read theirs?"

Suddenly one of the women stood up and approached the edge of the platform near the ammonia cloud. Will sensed that she could see him. He opened his thoughts to her.

"Who are you?"

The woman responded, "Shanna of Yord. What do you want?"

"What is that thing you congregate around?"

"Why does a creature like yourself care? Why is a creature like yourself able to care?"

"What do you think I am?"

"I think you could be someone else in that creature's body."

"Maybe I am. If you are from Yord, why do you hide here in the dungeon of an Attradean tyrant?"

"I'm not hiding."

"Then why are you here?"

"My sisters and I were taken prisoner by the Attradeans and brought here from our world."

"Why would they keep you like this? Wouldn't it be easier for them to kill you?"

"You ask a lot of questions, silly creature. Who are you?"

"My name is Will. Will Saris."

"Why have you come here?"

"I have come to rescue some friends from this wretched place."

Shanna asked kiddingly, "Have you come to rescue me?"

"Do you need to be rescued?"

"Yes, but I doubt you can help me."

"Why are you here?"

"We are Seers. We must read the Eye of Icarus everyday for Tenemon or he will feed us to his creatures."

"What creatures does he keep?"

"They hide in the mist. They can only survive in the mist."

Will remembered the ammonia odor.

"The creatures at the depot!"

Shanna saw the images from the depot in his mind and responded, "So you are human!"

"Not entirely. If I were, I wouldn't be here."

"Can you save us?"

"Perhaps. What do you see in this Eye?"

"We can see certain events in the future. Sometimes they are vague and other times they are quite clear."

"Did you see me coming?"

"We saw a man coming, a man who would humble King Tenemon. That man would take his daughter from him and free his enemies."

"It certainly sounds like me."

"If it's you, then you'd best beware. King Tenemon's wrath will lead him to hunt you for the rest of your life."

"So you think I'll live long enough for him to chase me?"

"I can't say."

"Why?"

"There are reasons."

"Do I rescue you?"

"The Eye will not show a sister of Yord her fate."

"Then we'll have to be creative."

"Be advised, the king will send a ship after your friends in the morning. They must flee or be destroyed. He knows of their presence but he isn't aware of yours yet."

"Good. His surprise will be so much better."

"Can you help me to escape?"

"I think so. I know a little about these creatures' habits so I'll create a diversion for you. When I tell you, take a deep breath and cross the channel."

Shanna fretted, "But the creatures, they'll kill me.

"If you want to get out of here, follow my directions exactly. When I tell you, hurry across the channel."

"I will obey. Please don't let the creatures get me."

"I promise, they won't harm you."

Will took a deep breath and scurried down the steps into the mist. He slipped into the lair and spied seven of the creatures lying still, with their eyes open.

Will stayed close to the wall away from their line of vision. He crept up to the first creature and lunged at its shoulder. He buried his teeth into its rubbery flesh. The creature shrieked in pain.

Will then bit into the creature's neck. The creature flopped about spasmodically. Will released his hold and leapt toward the steps. The other creatures saw their wounded peer and immediately attacked it.

Will ordered Shanna, "Quickly! Cross the channel."

Shanna looked back at her friends. They took notice of her.

The elder of the group yelled, "Shanna, what are you doing?"

Will urgently ordered her again, "Go, now!"

Shanna took a deep breath and rushed down the steps. She held her breath as she crossed the twenty-foot wide trench. When she reached the other side, she coughed and choked as she tried to climb the steps.

Will dashed to the steps and saw Shanna gasp for air. She fell three steps from the top into semi-consciousness.

Will panicked. "Oh no! Not now, Shanna."

He reached the steps and began to transform into his human shape. He stumbled several times during the transformation. He grew as he grabbed Shanna by the arms and pulled her to the top of the steps.

The creatures finished devouring their prey. They sensed an intruder in their midst and scanned their area. They saw Will climbing the steps with Shanna in his arms and rushed after him.

Fully transformed and naked, Will staggered to the top of the steps with Shanna. He carried her clear of the steps.

Two creatures lunged at Will, barely missing his leg. One of the creatures leapt from the mist and tackled Will. It clawed at his back, opening several gashes.

Will screamed as he struggled to free himself from the creature's grasp.

Shanna coughed and breathed hard. She saw the creature on Will's back. She struggled to her feet and removed her cloak. She threw it around the creature's head and held it tightly.

The creature flailed wildly while trying to reach her. It gasped horribly and threw her off. She fell hard onto the ground and slammed her head. Feebly, the creature crawled back toward the channel.

Shanna grabbed the clawed foot and held it tightly. The creature pulled desperately at the top of the steps but died before it could reach the safety of the ammonia mist.

Will was semi-conscious on the ground in a doubled-over position. His head spun from the quick transformation. Blood seeped from the wounds on his back.

Shanna wept as she crawled near the creature and recovered her cloak. She covered Will's naked body with it.

Will looked up at her face. A stream of blood trickled down her nose from a cut on her forehead. He wiped the blood from her nose.

Shanna blurted, "You did it! You've freed me. Thank you so much."

"I told you I would."

She hugged him and kissed his forehead. The other Seers were stunned at Shanna's escape.

Will was still light-headed when he got to his feet. He thought about rescuing the other Seers but decided that the creatures wouldn't be fooled twice. He kicked the dead creature down the steps.

The remaining creatures swarmed on it, devouring its carcass hungrily.

71

The elder woman yelled to Shanna, "What do I say to Tenemon?"

Shanna replied triumphantly, "Tell him the creatures got me."

Will remarked, "He'll get over it."

Shanna asked, "What can we do for them?"

Will assured them, "We'll be back for you."

The women grew giddy and held each other's hands in hope that they might escape their exile soon.

Will took Shanna's hand, "You saved my life. Thanks."

"You saved mine first."

"But you could have kept going without me."

"And you could have left me there, too, but now you're stuck with me."

"I'd do it again."

Shanna kissed Will's cheek and he blushed.

Will explained, "I have to get something I left in the corner."

Shanna watched him curiously. He disappeared around the corner for a moment. When he returned, he had the leaf with the berries wrapped inside.

"These should help with our escape."

Shanna was confused. "A leaf! How will that help us?"

"Not just a leaf. Inside the leaf are Dusselberries."

"What good will those do?"

"The berries have a concentrated chemical in their juices. We squeeze the juice from the berries onto a rag and add some water. We can use it to put the guards to sleep."

Shanna looked unconvinced. "If you say so."

****

Maya chewed incessantly on her fingernails. Celine slapped her hand away from her mouth. "Will you stop it already? Go for a walk or something."

Maya asked, "How long has it been?"

"Eight hours. Why don't you get some sleep?"

Maya complained, "We haven't heard anything from Talia in a while."

"If I call her, will you get some rest?"

"I promise."

Celine pressed a switch and the Display Monitoring System (DMS) initiated.

"*Ruined Stone*, are you there?"

Talia's face appeared on the monitor.

"Yes, I'm still here."

Celine sensed fatigue in Talia's tone. "What's wrong, Talia? What have you heard?"

"Nothing."

"What do you mean nothing?"

Talia explained, "I'm not picking up anything at all."

Maya pleaded, "Talia, talk to me."

"I can't track what I can't see and I'm not picking up any conversation."

"How long has this been going on?"

Talia replied, "Oh, for quite some time."

Maya informed her, "I put the tracking device on him. Maybe it failed."

Talia explained, "It would be possible except that I can't pick up any conversation either. It's as if he removed the devices."

Maya added, "…or his clothes."

"You think he shifted, Maya?"

"It could be. That would explain it."

****

Will took Shanna by the hand and led her up the granite steps. They peered around the corner down a long, ebon stone hallway. On either side of the hallway were several cells.

Shanna asked, "Who are you looking for?"

"I'm not really sure. One is an Attradean boy. Another, well, I don't know."

Two guards stood by the entrance to the hall. Four guards were playing cards inside an office nearby.

Will took a ewer of water from a small table near the doorway into the stairwell. He squeezed the leaf wrap until the juices streamed into the ewer.

Will whispered, "This should quiet them down for a while."

They could smell a faint trace of the berries in the air.

Will shook his head a few times. "Whew! Don't breath in too much of this stuff."

Shanna stepped back a few steps and took a deep breath. She blurted, "Wow. I feel a little light-headed."

Will warned, "This stuff is really strong."

He tore the leaf in half and soaked it in the ewer.

"Are you ready, Shanna?"

"I guess so."

"You take the guard on the left. I'll take the guard on the right."

Will reached into the ewer and took out the pieces of the leaf. He handed one to Shanna.

The two of them crept past the doorway. They quickly slapped the leaves over each guard's face. Both were quickly immobilized.

Will pulled one of the sleeping guards into the stairwell. He removed the body armor and clothing from the guard.

Shanna grinned slyly as Will started to remove her cloak from around his body.

Will asked politely, "Shanna, would you mind turning around?"

Shanna responded playfully, "Why?"

"So I can change my clothes."

Shanna teased, "Do I have to?"

"I'd feel better about it."

Shanna reluctantly obeyed.

Will donned the guard's uniform.

Shanna eyed him up and down before nodding in approval. She complimented him, "You make a handsome guard, Will."

"Thanks, but I hope not to make a habit of it. Wait here. I'll be right back."

Shanna watched Will closely. She was already attracted to him. His self-confidence, unusual characteristics and kindness created a passion in her.

Will strolled into the office. The guards paused and stared at him.

One of the guards bellowed, "What is it? Can't you see we're busy?"

"I have something you should see."

Will approached the table and held out the leaf in his hands. All four guards leaned forward to see what Will had. Instantly, they fell to the ground in a deep slumber. Will set the leaf on the table and propped the guards up in their shabby wooden chairs.

He returned to the stairwell and informed Shanna, "So far, so good."

Shanna offered, "I can take care of the rest. You go find your friends."

"What? You!"

"You'll be surprised when you see what I can do."

"Come get me if you change your mind."

Will proceeded to the third cell. The outer lock was a simple latch.

He thought gleefully, "This couldn't be easier."

He unfastened the latch and cautiously opened the door. He peered inside, expecting to see Breel, but there was another door with a hand reader.

Will griped disappointedly, "What in the world...?"

He analyzed the reader and hurried into the hall. He grabbed one of the sleeping guards by the arms and dragged him into the cell. He took the guard's right hand and held it on the scanner.

Shanna entered the cell. "Will! What are you doing?"

Will answered, "What do you think I'm doing? I'm trying to open the door."

Shanna realized why and shrank with embarrassment. "I'm sorry."

Will waited but the lock didn't activate.

Shanna suggested, "Try the other hand."

Frustrated, Will replied sarcastically, "That won't make any difference." He placed the guard's left hand on the scanner anyway. The door hummed and slid open.

Will muttered, "Yeah, I know. You were right."

Shanna smiled proudly.

He cautiously entered the inner cell. He wondered who or what Breel would be.

"Hello. Is anyone in here?"

Will took three steps in and announced, "Laneia sent me. Are you in here?"

The walls of the cell emitted a dim glow from a luminous coating. Will looked around the room but saw no one. Suddenly, someone dropped on him from above. He fell to the ground with the attacker on top of him.

He screamed, "Get off me!"

Shanna heard Will's cry and rushed in. She jumped on the attacker from behind just in time to prevent him from punching Will in the back of the head.

She yelled, "Stop it! Stop it! He's here to rescue you, stupid."

The assailant pushed Shanna off. He barked, "Who are you? I don't know you."

Will breathed heavily with the Attradean on his back. He explained hoarsely, "Laneia asked me to rescue you. Now, would you please get off of me?"

The attacker hesitated and asked, "Laneia really sent you?"

Will answered raspily, "That's what I said. You do know her, don't you?"

"Yes I do. I'm Breel."

Will replied impatiently, "If you don't mind getting off of me, I have others to rescue. Time is wasting."

Breel stood up and extended his hand to Will. Will took it and allowed Breel to help him up.

Will finished the introduction, "I'm Will Saris and this is Shanna. We've got to move quickly."

Will and Shanna left the cell, followed by Breel.

Breel asked anxiously, "Where is Laneia?"

"We're meeting her in the morning."

Breel's eyes grew wide with excitement. "Are you serious?"

"Yes, I am."

Will opened the door to the fourth cell. "Damn! We need the guard's hand again."

Breel offered, "I'll get him."

Will asked Breel, "Would you mind putting all of the guards in one cell. It would make a nice present for Tenemon."

Breel replied enthusiastically, "My pleasure." He rushed out of the cell and down the hall.

Shanna asked, "How did Tenemon's daughter get involved in this?"

"She was distraught outside the palace." Will explained. "I spoke with her briefly and she gave me some valuable information like how to get inside here."

"And she asked you to rescue her boyfriend?"

"Sure."

"Of course you graciously agreed."

Will asked innocently, "Why wouldn't I?"

Shanna replied, "Oh, I'm just curious."

There was an awkward moment of silence until Will spoke up. "Shanna, thanks for helping me out with Breel. I don't know what I would have done if you weren't there."

"Oh, it's okay. I think we make a good team."

"I think so, too."

The two chuckled until Breel entered the cell, dragging one of the guards.

Breel held out the guard's left arm. "Here's your key, Will."

"Thanks, Breel."

Breel dropped the guard on the floor and exited the cell.

Will placed the guard's hand on the scanner. The door opened like the previous one. He breathed easier. "That's better."

He entered the room with Shanna. They found a small box, about three feet square, on a stone table.

Will inspected it for a moment and asked, "What do you think, Shanna? Any ideas?"

"Maybe it works off of body heat. I don't know how else it could function."

Will suggested, "Let's give it a whirl."

He placed his hands on the box, then changed position to the other side. Nothing happened.

Shanna offered, "Let me help."

She placed her hands on two sides and Will placed his hands on two sides.

The box shivered for a few seconds and grew warm. Suddenly, the sides and the top ejected. One side smacked Will in the chest, startling him. Another whizzed by Shanna's head.

Will remarked, "Wow! That was crazy."

A small furry creature was bound to a miniature seat. It appeared to be undernourished.

Will exclaimed with surprise, "So, this is Baron!"

Shanna ran her hand down Baron's arm. She spoke to him.

"Hey little guy. Are you alright?"

Baron's eyes stirred and his head bobbed.

Will untied Baron. He carefully moved his arms and legs to make sure nothing was broken.

"He seems to be in one piece."

Shanna picked him up and cradled him like a baby.

"I'll take care of him for you."

"Thanks, Shanna."

Baron spoke weakly to Will, "I knew Maya wouldn't forget me. You must be Will."

"Yes, I am."

"Maya spoke highly of you."

"And you, as well. Save your strength."

Shanna asked, "Where are we going next?"

"To free the other prisoners. I have reason to believe that they are political prisoners, not criminals."

IV.   Escape from Attrades

Breel explained, "The left side is maximum security. That's why there are two doors. The right side is all single doors."

"Thanks, Breel. Help me release the prisoners."

The two of them hurried down the hall, opening all the doors.

Three humans and nine aliens gathered in the hallway. One of the humans asked, "Who are you? What's going on?"

Will explained, "We're getting out of here. I'll answer your questions later."

Will, Shanna and Breel led the prisoners up three flights of granite steps. When they reached the top, they searched for an exit.

Breel pointed to a door down the hall. "That's the only way out. There is a guard stationed around the corner from the door."

Will asked, "Any idea how to get rid of him?"

Baron suggested, "I'll lure him away from his station. When he comes around the corner, you guys take care of him."

Will, Breel and Baron crept to the end of the hall.

Shanna was waiting at the rear of the group when one of the human councilors asked her, "Who is this man who rescued us?"

Shanna answered, "Will Saris. He rescued me as well."

"I am Arasthmus, Councilor of Lott."

"I've heard of you, Councilor Lott."

Another human councilor named Regent interrupted them.

"You're one of the Seers, aren't you?"

"Yes I am. Why?"

The councilor inquired, "What happened to the others?"

"They are still captive. Will plans to go back for them later."

"He couldn't rescue all of you at once?"

"No. There wasn't enough time to get the others past Tenemon's creatures."

Regent asked, "Are they in good health?"

"Tenemon took care of us in that regard."

The councilor was very concerned and promised, "I'll get him whatever resources he requires. Whatever he needs, he'll have."

"You'll have to discuss that with him, Councilor. I have no idea how he plans to execute a rescue."

"Thank you, Shanna."

"Anytime, Councilor."

Regent rejoined the other councilors.

****

Will asked Baron, "Are you strong enough to do this?"

Baron replied in a soft, gentle voice, "Yes I am."

Will set Baron on the ground.

Baron staggered into the aisle muttering strange noises.

The guard at the counter bellowed, "You, there! What are you doing?" He stormed out from behind the counter and headed angrily toward Baron. Baron coughed and fell to the ground. He lay motionless. The guard knelt down to examine Baron.

Breel whispered to Will, "I got this one."

"Go get 'em, tiger."

Breel stepped around the corner and smashed the guard's head into the floor. He picked the guard up and tossed him over the counter, smashing a chair in the process.

Will was impressed with Breel's strength. Breel had the same average build as Will, but was much stronger.

Will opened the door slowly and stepped cautiously into the courtyard.

Shanna hurriedly scooped up Baron.

Baron nuzzled against Shanna's neck as she comforted him.

She promised, "We'll get you something to eat soon. Hang in there, little fella'."

Breel followed closely and warned, "There's one guard in each of those two towers. Two guards scout the grounds just outside the king's hall."

Will asked, "Do you know how Laneia gets outside the palace?"

"Yes, I do. Behind the servants' quarters is a broken oxcart. It covers a hole in the wall. We can exit through there."

Will instructed, "Stay close to the wall. Hopefully the darkness will hide us from their view."

"There's just one problem," Breel informed Will.

"What's that?"

"Attradeans can see in the dark."

Will sighed. "Well, so much for that plan."

"That's okay. I have an idea."

"I'm listening."

Breel explained, "We can cross over the top of the wall. I doubt the guards would expect anyone up there. When we reach the servants' quarters, we can climb down using the roof and a trellis on the side of the quarters."

"You lead them. I'll keep an eye on the rear to make sure we don't lose anyone."

Will motioned for everyone else to exit the building and follow Breel.

Breel asked, "In case anything happens, where are we supposed to meet Laneia?"

"She'll be outside Tenemon's docking facility on the hill and she'll have a pilot with her."

Breel was surprised. "We're taking one of Tenemon's ships?"

"Yes we are."

Breel answered happily, "Oh, I'm loving this, more and more."

Will warned, "Don't get too cocky. We're not out of here yet."

"See you outside."

Breel motioned for the prisoners to follow him up the steps to the top of the wall.

Will watched anxiously as each one passed. Shanna came up last, carrying Baron. She informed Will, "I'm staying close to you. You're my good luck charm."

"I'm beginning to think that you're my good luck charm, too."

Will placed his arm around Shanna's shoulders and escorted her up the steps.

When Breel reached the servants' quarters, he instructed the men where to go once they reached the ground. He sent the first pair onto the roof.

They crept to the eave, where they jumped onto a pile of hay. When they were out of sight under the oxcart, Breel sent the next two.

When Will and Shanna reached the servants' quarters, Breel was grinning. He said giddily, "Looking good so far."

"Don't jinx us, Breel."

"I can't help it. I'm so excited."

Will asked, "Would you go next and carry Baron? I don't think that either of us can climb down while carrying him."

"Sure thing."

Breel extended his hands and gently took Baron into his arms.

Will informed Baron, "Maya and Talia are waiting for a signal to pick you up. If something goes wrong, you know how to contact them."

"I sure do."

Baron blinked his beady eyes at Will and continued, "I can communicate with her now that I'm outside the prison walls. Thank you very much, Will."

"You're welcome, Baron."

Breel easily descended the roof and leaped onto the ground. Two guards stepped out of the shadows with their weapons drawn. They crept up on Breel.

Will whispered to Shanna, "We've got to do something. Follow me."

Will and Shanna crept to the edge of the roof.

One of the guards asked, "What have you got there, Breel?"

Breel hid Baron behind his back.

The other guard teased. "Tenemon isn't going to be happy with you."

Breel glanced up at Will and moved away from the building so the guards wouldn't see them.

Breel said coyly, "Can we talk about this, guys? This is all a misunderstanding about Tenemon's daughter. You understand, don't you?"

The guard ordered, "Stop babbling. What are you hiding?"

Will leaped off of the roof and punched the nearest guard in the back of the neck as he landed on the ground. The guard crumpled easily.

Before the other guard could react, Shanna landed on him. The two fell onto the ground.

Will quickly came to Shanna's aid and grabbed the guard's neck from behind. In one fluid motion, he snapped the guard's neck.

Breel gave Will and Shanna a thankful salute and said excitedly, "Hurry! Let's go find Laneia."

They crawled under the oxcart and passed through a gap in the wall. Two of the human councilors helped them through a cluster of bushes onto a worn path.

Will explained, "There is something I have to do first."

Breel asked, "What is it?"

"There's a stream not far from here. I left some things near an old tree."

Breel answered, "I know exactly where it is."

"We won't be long. Keep everyone together."

83

"I will."

Will and Shanna left the group and headed to the old tree.

"Shanna, I need a few minutes to gather my things."

"What can I do to help?"

"Behind that rock is a small bag. Would you get it for me?"

Will untied the armored plate on his chest.

Shanna poked around the bushes near the rock and found Will's backpack. She brought it to him.

"Thanks. Can you wait behind the tree?"

"Sure. Any particular reason?"

"Yeah, I have to get changed."

Shanna kidded, "You don't really want me to leave, do you?"

"Well, it's a little embarrassing…

Shanna giggled at him. "That's okay. I'm a big girl."

Shanna sat on a stump and watched Will.

Will blushed. "This is a little unnerving."

Shanna teased, "We don't have a lot of time, so I suggest you do something quickly."

Will was confused by her reply. He opened the backpack and removed his clothing. He set his RG-23 pulse blaster on the rock. "I don't think this is a good time, Shanna, if you're expecting something to happen between us."

Shanna approached him and rubbed his shoulders. "Relax, Will." She unbuckled the Attradean armor from around Will's chest. She slid the pants down from his waist and feasted her eyes on Will's half naked body.

Will quickly grabbed his pants and covered himself. Shanna laughed and said playfully, "I'm not going to hurt you."

Will replied, "It's just that … oh, never mind."

Shanna placed her arms around his neck.

Will sighed. "I guess there's no way out of this."

Shanna looked hurt. She said defensively, "Would it be that bad making love to me?"

Will was embarrassed by his awkward choice of words.

"No, that's not what I meant. I'm just not ready to romance you right now."

"I understand."

Shanna turned away from Will and walked toward the stream.

Will called to Shanna, "Wait!"

She paused and responded seductively, "What is it, Will?"

Will ordered her, "Come here."

Shanna came to Will and stood in front of him.

"You wanted something."

"Yes I do."

Will placed his arms around Shanna's waist and kissed her, softly at first, then passionately.

A few minutes later, Shanna asked, "What are you telling me, Will?"

"Have you ever had a boyfriend before?"

"No. You're the first."

"You're kidding?"

"Not at all. I was sent to Yord when I was very young. The Council sent all women who were different or defective to Yord so they wouldn't breed."

"Are you serious?"

"I swear to you."

Will exclaimed, "That's horrible!"

"So, of course I'm happy to be rescued by a handsome young man like you."

Will was stunned by the idea of banishing women to an empty colony.

"Right now is a bad time for me to start a relationship. I have a lot of things on my mind and some very important decisions to make."

Shanna asked, "Do you want to talk about it?"

"Not now. And you aren't ready for a serious relationship either."

Shanna became angry and replied sarcastically, "I see. And you're an expert in this area."

Will explained, "No, but I'm afraid the first time you see other men, you'll leave me."

Shanna smiled. "I know what's in your heart already and I hoped you would know what's in mine."

Will explained, "I want you by my side. I like being with you, but I'm afraid if we go too fast, things won't work out."

"Then I should give you something to think about." Shanna disrobed and cuddled up to Will. She placed her arms around him and pressed her body against his. She kissed him softly and seductively. Will felt his knees grow weak. Shanna stopped and dressed.

Will asked dizzily, "Where are you going?"

"I only wanted you to have something to think about. I'll leave you now."

Will fell awkwardly against a tree. He was stunned by Shanna's beauty but wondered if he was disposable to her the way he was to Zira.

Shanna mentioned, "That's what's waiting for you when you're ready. Don't wait too long, though."

Will was dazed. He watched her as she walked to the stream and knelt down. He breathed deeply and said, "Wow!"

Will watched eagerly as Shanna sipped from the stream. She glanced back and smiled. He could feel his blood boiling and thought to himself, "Maybe I'm making a mistake – a big mistake."

Shanna suggested to Will, "We should get moving."

He reached down for the backpack. "Uh, yeah. Let's get moving," Will replied nervously, removing two metal objects on chains from the side pockets and placed them around his neck. He strapped the pulse blaster and holster to his waist.

Shanna asked seductively, "Are you ready?"

Will gazed into her lovely blue eyes and asked guiltily, "For what?"

She giggled at his nervousness and said coyly, "To get out of here."

Will was once again embarrassed. He replied meekly, "Oh, yeah. Of course."

****

Celine and Maya were asleep in the pilots' cabin at the controls. Jack slept soundly on the floor behind Maya's seat. His hand rested on Maya's leg.

Zira's voice from the DMS startled them. "Maya! Celine! We've found him."

Maya awakened, rubbing her eyes.

"Talk to me, Zira."

"He's with or around several people."

Celine caught part of Zira's message as did Jack. Celine whispered, "Who else could be down there with him?"

Maya replied quietly, "Beats me."

They looked at Jack. He just shrugged his shoulders.

Zira continued, "I heard names which sounded like Breel and Shanna."

Maya ordered, "Keep listening, Zira. We're going to prepare for an extraction."

Maya stood up, still groggy from inadequate sleep.

Celine asked, "Are you alright?"

Maya suddenly looked ill.

Celine stood up and grabbed Maya's arms.

"What is it, Maya?"

Maya mumbled, "Shanna. Shanna. Do you know who Shanna is?"

"No. Should I?"

"Shanna was the name of one of the Seers supposedly imprisoned by Tenemon. He accused them of having special powers that threatened him."

Maya retrieved the comm-link from her pocket and dialed three digits.

Saphoro answered, "What is it, Maya?"

"How good are you on Attradean history - recent Attradean history?"

"Pretty good. Why?"

"What do the names Shanna and Breel mean to you?"

87

Saphoro explained, "Shanna was one of five Seers captured by Tenemon a while ago. Shanna was believed to be the youngest of the Seers. Rumor has it that Tenemon also captured an object which belonged to the Seers. They used this object to foretell the future on their world. No one knows if it's real or mythical."

Maya asked, "Where were they held captive at?"

"On Attrades. Supposedly they are guarded by Eremites, carnivorous predators that live in a toxic atmosphere."

"What would happen if one of the Seers, perhaps Shanna, escaped?"

Saphoro continued, "If the myth is true, that would greatly reduce the ability of the others to foretell the future. There are supposed to be five Seers to effectively use this object."

"Any idea what this object is or how it works?"

"I read in Yordic history where they once had a crystal sphere called the Eye of Icarus. This was a very ancient sphere that was seen by very few, thus casting its existence in doubt. It's named after the son of Daedelus in ancient mythology. Icarus flew too close to the sun with wax wings. The wings melted and he fell into the sea. Of course, he drowned. The point is he could see everything from above."

"What about Breel? Any idea who that is?"

"I seem to remember from previous intelligence reports that Tenemon had a daughter named Laneia. She had a lover named Breel. Tenemon didn't want Breel seeing his daughter and imprisoned or killed Breel. There is no definitive history available on it."

"Thanks, Saphoro."

"Why do you ask?"

Maya replied, "Zira heard something over the tracking system."

Saphoro's voice squeaked in a high pitch, "Oh, no."

Maya asked, "What?"

"Think about it. Why would Will be involved with both of those people at once?"

Maya shouted. "No! It can't be! Laneia, Breel, Shanna. He's bringing them all back!"

Saphoro warned, "We'd best prepare to haul butt out of here. Tenemon is not the type of person you want hunting you."

"Thanks, Saphoro."

Maya turned off the comm-link. She stared blankly.

Celine pleaded, "Well, tell me what you think is going on!"

"Contact the *Ruined Stone* and put them on alert status. Whatever Will is doing, it's going to happen fast."

Celine complained, "Damn, that boy's having all the fun. I'm going with him next time."

Jack complained, "I knew I should have gone with him, too."

Maya glared at both of them, before leaving the cabin.

Celine declared, "He sure is a piece of work."

Jack quipped, "Reminds me of myself in younger days."

Maya's voice echoed back from the stairwell, "That's enough, both of you!"

Celine whispered, "Can't you do something with her?"

Jack replied quietly, "I'm trying."

****

Shanna carried Baron like a mother would her newborn.

Will beckoned Shanna to walk with him.

Will asked Baron, "How well do you know Maya?"

"She rescued me from a Boromean patrol. They killed most of my species. I was a lucky that her ship landed nearby."

Will inquired, "So how is it that you wound up on Attrades?"

"I asked Maya to help me return to Attrades. Tenemon took many of my species captive. I had to find out if there were any survivors. Of course, there weren't."

"I'm sorry, Baron. I didn't know."

"Maya asked me to do her a small favor and gather some information. I thought I could manage without getting caught."

"How long were you captive down there?"

"Oh about four cycles. The king thought I might be someone else. He wasn't taking any chances and locked me up in that little box. It's designed to prevent me from communicating with anyone."

Will pondered what Maya's logic might have been for letting Baron return to Attrades. He remarked, "I'm surprised that Maya would agree to that."

Baron replied, "I promised to get her valuable information on the Attradean stronghold."

Will asked, "What kind of information was Maya looking for?"

Baron thought for a moment and replied, "She wanted to know how the Attradeans were gaining allies. Too many races were falling in line with them. I found out that the king was using an eye of some sort to see into the future. He could coerce kingdoms to join his alliance against their will."

Will informed him, "There is an object called the Eye and Shanna was one of the Seers who used it to foretell the future to King Tenemon."

Baron was surprised and said, "So it is true."

Baron looked at Shanna reverently and said, "You are a most holy individual. It's an honor to be here with you."

Shanna blushed. "I'm not a holy person. I have some powers, but I'm just an ordinary person."

Baron remarked, "Neither of you are ordinary. To rescue us like that, you must be destined to be together. You have great powers that you have yet to discover. I can sense them."

Shanna suggested, "Maybe you should take a hint, Will."

Will replied playfully, "I don't know about all that, but I am enjoying my new friends."

Regent and Arasthmus followed Will closely. Regent called out, "Will, can we have a few words with you?"

Will thought, "Just in time."

He answered the councilors, "What can I do for you?"

Regent explained, "We want you to know that we appreciate what you've done for us."

"I understand and I appreciate your gratitude."

Arasthmus, the second human councilor pointed out, "We also want to reward you for your kindness. What can we do for you when we return to our worlds?"

"You don't have to do anything. I didn't do this for hire. Perhaps some day, if I need a favor, you'll find it in your hearts to assist me."

Regent replied, "Whatever you need, just ask."

"Thank you both."

Regent asked, "Do you foresee making a rescue attempt for the other Seers in the near future?"

Will was curious that Regent would ask so direct a question.

"Most definitely. The timing is critical, though. If we move too soon, we could put the Seers in great jeopardy."

Regent responded thoughtfully, "I understand. I am willing to help in any capacity."

"Is there a personal reason for your interest?"

Regent answered uncomfortably, "I guess you could say so. I'd really like to partake in the rescue operation."

Will patted Regent's shoulder and said, "I'll make sure that you're with me when the time comes."

"I won't let you down, Will."

"Thanks, Regent."

The two councilors dropped back with the others.

Will, Shanna and Breel led the group through the forest, toward the docking facility.

Breel commented, "I think you missed a golden opportunity, Will."

"No, not really. I don't want their wealth, but someday I may need their support."

Shanna remarked, "That's an interesting approach."

Breel asked, "What are you going to do when we get off of this planet?"

Shanna added, "Yes, Will. I'm curious, too."

Breel pointed out, "Laneia and I have no place to go."

Shanna mentioned, "My real home is Yord."

"I don't know. Now that we've almost pulled this off, I guess I have to make some decisions."

Breel asked, "Did you ever dream about being something you're not?"

Will replied, "Everyone does."

Breel asked Shanna, "How about you?"

"I dream of being free. I dream of sharing exciting adventures with someone special."

Breel related, "I dream that I could be royalty and wed Laneia."

Shanna asked, "Is Laneia your love?"

"Yes, she is. I haven't seen her in so long."

Will informed him, "She's anxious to see you."

Breel asked, "How did you meet her?"

"When I first arrived here, I found her crying in the forest. She cried for you."

"And you offered to rescue me for her."

Will teased, "Since I was in the neighborhood, I thought I might as well."

Shanna asked calmly, "And I guess the same goes for me?"

"No. Something else happened there."

"Please tell me about it, Will."

"I can't explain it. It's just one of those things."

"Please, Will."

"Well, I felt sort of an attraction to you, as if it were fate. Then, inside the prison, we worked so well together, as if we were meant to be. Then, oh never mind. It gets foolish."

Will blushed.

Breel inquired, "What do you dream of becoming, Will?"

"You'll laugh at me if I tell you."

Shanna pleaded, "Come on, Will. You haven't told me anything about yourself. I won't laugh, I promise."

Will took a deep breath.

Breel noticed his apprehension and kidded, "This should be real interesting."

Shanna added impatiently, "Come on, Will. We're waiting."

"Okay, here it is."

Will took a deep breath and said, "I want to be a space pirate."

Breel and Shanna were amused.

Breel quipped, "A space pirate?"

Shanna exclaimed, "That would be exciting!"

Breel countered, "But you're a member of the Fleet. How would they react if you left to become a pirate?"

"It would be a big problem. I'd be better off dead."

Shanna replied, "Not if they didn't know."

Laneia rushed out of the trees.

"Breel! It's really you."

Breel caught Laneia in his arms. He spun her around and kissed her repeatedly.

Will looked sad as he watched them.

Shanna asked, "Are you okay?"

Will said glumly, "Look at them how happy they are."

"You caused all of this. You should be happy for them."

"I know. I don't understand it."

Shanna suggested, "Perhaps it was fate. Perhaps you're looking for that same happiness."

****

Jack rubbed Maya's shoulders. "Try to relax. Everything will be fine."

Maya snapped, "That's easy for you to say."

Jack sat next to Maya and stared at her. He said stoically, "I think we're at a crossroad, you and me."

Maya quieted her tone. "What are you talking about, Jack?"

"You've changed. Everything is about you, isn't it?"

Maya chastised Jack, "This is my ship and if you don't like it, you can leave."

Jack stood up and looked at her with pity.

"I'm going to take you up on that. I'm going to miss you but I'd rather remember what you were than what you've become."

Jack exited the pilots' cabin. He passed Celine outside the door.

Celine sensed the discord and entered the cabin cautiously.

She informed Maya, "Neelon and Saphoro offered to take watch for you if you need a rest."

Maya looked up and tears filled her eyes. "I'm fine."

Celine bellowed at her, "You're not fine. Look at you. I've known you a long time and you were never this messed up."

Maya blurted out, "Someone's got to take charge."

Celine snapped back, "Take charge of what? This tin can in the middle of nowhere."

"Our job's very important!"

"Bullshit, Maya. If we disappeared today, they'd never miss us."

Maya asked between sniffles, "Then why are we out here?"

Celine glared at her. "Do you think it's because you're the Fleet's prized commander? They'll never promote you because of what you are! I'm sure they know you're Firenghi. That's why you're out here, with a low probability for survival."

Celine stormed out of the cabin.

Maya cried for several minutes, until Zira's voice sounded from the intercom.

"Maya, it's Zira. Are you there?"

She wiped away her tears and pressed the DMS 'receive' switch. Zira's face appeared on the monitor.

"Go ahead, Zira."

"The tracking device is working again!"

Maya asked anxiously, "Where is he?"

"He's still outside the palace. He's actually moving away from the palace toward a building on top of a nearby hill."

"Hold on a minute."

She took out her comm-link and dialed Saphoro's number.

Saphoro answered, "What's up, Maya."

"How did you know it was me?"

"Just a guess."

"I'm sure Celine had something to do with it. I need you up here, pronto."

"I'm on the way."

Maya put away the comm-link.

She informed Zira, "I asked Saphoro to join us."

Zira explained, "My computer has identified nine voices with other unknowns."

"Nine! Who are they?"

"It sounds like the voices belong to Breel and Laneia, Shanna the Seer, Baron, Will and three of the captive councilors."

Maya moaned, "Just great. The Fleet wasn't supposed to know about this expedition and Will's bringing back half of the planet."

Zira sounded confused. "But this is good news, isn't it?"

Maya muttered, "No. Not really."

"I guess Will screwed up."

"Yeah, big time."

Zira suggested, "Don't be so hard on him. He seems like an overachiever."

Maya replied, "That's the problem. He's just like his father."

Saphoro entered the cabin. "What's going on, Maya?"

Zira greeted Saphoro from the DMS, "Hi, Saphy. How are you doing?"

"I'll let you know after I hear the news."

Maya explained, "It appears that Will has quite a few people with him. They're heading to a building on top of the nearby hill."

Saphoro replied, "That's strange. That particular building is used for docking extra ships. Why would he ...?"

Maya screamed, "I'll kill him! If he steals one of Tenemon's ships, I'll kill him before Tenemon does."

Saphoro suggested, "We should get out of here in a hurry."

Neelon rushed in. "Sorry to break up the party but there are ten Attradean battle cruisers leaving the Strontarion galaxy. They appear to be headed this way."

Maya asked, "How much time do we have?"

"They're still pretty far out. I'll monitor their speed and let you know if anything changes."

Maya instructed, "Tell me when they get close."

"Understood." Neelon paused and asked, "How is Will doing?"

Maya yelled, "Don't ask!"

Saphoro interjected, "It seems he's doing pretty well under the circumstances, Neelon. We're waiting to see how he wants to leave Attrades."

"You mean there's more than one way out?"

Maya replied sarcastically, "For Will, there's always more than one way out."

Neelon rolled his eyes at Maya and left the cabin.

****

Breel put Laneia down on the ground. She hugged Will so hard she almost knocked him over. "I can't believe you did it! How can I ever repay you?"

"Just tell me you found a pilot to fly us out of here."

Laneia yelled, "Bastille! Come on out."

A rough-looking, bearded, dark-skinned human approached them. He shook hands with Will and introduced himself, "I am Bastille."

"It's good to meet you, Bastille."

Laneia explained, "Bastille was tortured by Tenemon's troops a while ago and left for dead in the forest. I found him and nursed him in a cave until he recovered."

Bastille spoke sarcastically, "I hate Tenemon and I'd do anything to get even with him."

Will suggested, "If you can get us out of here, it would be a good start."

Bastille boldly demanded, "Show me the ship."

"Follow me."

Will, Breel and Bastille approached a locked door on the outside of the building. Will mulled over how to deactivate the door lock.

Breel noticed and picked up a rock. He struck the locking mechanism solidly, smashing it to pieces. The door swung open freely.

Will remarked cynically, "Nice touch, Breel."

"Sorry. I get a little excited."

Will drew his pulse blaster and entered the building. Inside was a huge hangar with three docks constructed at even intervals. Two ships were berthed at the last two docks.

Will ordered, "Stay here until I give the okay."

Breel complained, "I want to go with you."

Will stated firmly, "No, Breel, we can't risk the both of us getting killed. If something happens to me, you're taking charge."

"Who, me?"

"Yes, Breel. You'll make sure everyone makes it on board that ship and gets out of here safely."

Breel was surprised that Will had such confidence in him.

Will said calmly, "Don't let me down if anything happens to me."

"I won't, Will."

Bastille offered, "I'll cover you from here."

"Thanks. I'll make this quick."

Will raced across the hangar to the first dock. He searched the area thoroughly but saw no one. He thought to himself, "This is too easy."

He climbed the steel stairs to the dock and proceeded to the ship.

Everyone gathered anxiously just outside the door to the hangar.

Shanna fretted aloud, "He needs someone to watch his back. I'm going in there."

Laneia yelled, "No, Shanna!"

Shanna rushed across the hangar floor toward the steps before anyone could stop her.

Two Attradean guards crossed the dock and took aim at Will.

Shanna screamed, "Will, look out!"

Will fell to the ground and fired, striking one guard, which killed him instantly.

The other guard fired at Shanna. She stumbled and fell to the ground.

Will cried out, "Shanna! No!"

He fired at the second guard and killed him.

Breel rushed to Shanna's aid. Her shoulder was a bloody mess.

He picked her up and carried her toward the dock. Shanna asked weakly, "Is Will okay?"

Breel replied, "Yes he is. You saved his life."

Shanna forced a smile.

Breel climbed the stairs to the dock. "Will, she needs medical attention."

Will hugged Shanna. "Why did you do this, Shanna? Why?"

Shanna answered faintly, "Someone's got to look after you."

Breel suggested, "Let's get her onboard the ship, then we can try to help her."

"I'll lead. Follow me."

Will angrily crept forward toward the ship's hatch. A guard stepped out from the second ship and aimed at Will. Will fired first and struck the guard in the throat area, killing him instantly.

When Will reached the hatch, two guards rushed at him. He fired and hit the first one. The second guard fired and struck Will's thigh. Will fired again and hit the guard in the head. The guard fell limply to the ground.

Will staggered through the hatch and searched the main quarters. No more guards were present.

Breel entered and lay Shanna down on a table. He pulled a seat cushion from a chair and placed it under her head.

Breel exited ship and called the others to come aboard.

Will knelt down next to Shanna and held her hand tightly. He pleaded, "Please be okay, Shanna."

Shanna said tearfully, "It hurts, Will."

"I know it does. I promise, if you pull through this, I'll make it up to you."

"Don't pity me, Will."

"I mean it, Shanna."

"You'd better."

Will leaned forward and hugged her tightly. He peeled back her blood-soaked robe and cloak. Fortunately, the wound was closer to her arm than her chest.

Bastille, Baron and the councilors boarded the ship.

Arasthmus promptly attended to Shanna and examined her. He felt the inside of the wound with his fingers.

Arasthmus ordered Breel, "Find me a medical kit, quickly. There should be a room with medical supplies, somewhere near the pilots' cabin."

Breel called Laneia, "Help me find a medical kit."

Laneia followed Breel up the stairs.

Bastille entered last and closed the hatch. "This is everyone, I assume."

Will answered, "Yes it is, Bastille. Get us in the air, fast."

"Consider it done."

Bastille hurried up to the pilots' cabin.

Regent joined Arasthmus and Will.

"What can I do to help?"

Arasthmus asked, "Do you know what a Molidium laser is?"

"Yes, I do."

"See if you can find one in the maintenance cabin."

Regent hurried down the hallway.

Will looked down at his lap. It was covered with blood.

He uttered, "Look at all the blood. Shanna's bleeding badly."

Arasthmus glanced up at Will and complained, "That's you bleeding all over the place, foolish boy."

Will looked down again at his lacerated thigh. His face became pale and he felt nauseous.

Arasthmus consoled him, "Don't worry. We'll fix you up, too."

Breel and Laneia returned with the kit. Breel set it on the table and opened it. He looked at Will's leg and said, "Come on, buddy. You need a seat."

Breel and Laneia helped Will to a nearby table and hoisted him on top of it.

Regent returned with a Molidium laser. He connected the cable to a power source and handed the laser to Arasthmus.

Regent asked, "Will she be alright?"

"I think so."

"Can I do anything else?"

"Yes. Cut off Will's pant leg and examine his wound. Let me know if the artery was hit."

Regent tended to Will and cut away his pant leg.

****

Breel entered the pilots' cabin. "How's it going, Bastille?"

"Take a look, my friend. We are leaving this wretched planet."

"This is great! I've dreamed for cycles about getting away from Tenemon and his creeps."

Bastille chuckled.

"You might want to find out where we're going."

"You got it."

Breel returned to the main quarters. He stopped at Shanna's table and asked Arasthmus, "How is she?"

"Why don't you ask her yourself?"

Breel looked surprised. Shanna's eyes were open and she was coherent. "I'll be okay, Breel."

"I'm glad, Shanna."

Breel moved to Will's table. "How's it look, Regent?"

"He should be fine. Fortunately, he didn't catch the full impact of the blast."

Will asked, "Hey, Breel. How's it feel to get away from Attrades?"

Breel replied, "I feel marvelous except for one thing."

Will asked, "What's that?"

"Do you know where we're going?"

Will thought for a moment. "Now that you mention it, no."

Shanna interrupted, "We can go to Yord. I'll give Bastille specific instructions as soon as Arasthmus finishes with me."

Will consented, "That works for me."

Arasthmus interjected, "Both of you need to chill out. You've lost a lot of blood."

Breel volunteered, "I'll see if Bastille knows the way to Yord."

Arasthmus remarked, "Good. The two of you stay put until I say so."

Breel returned to the pilots' cabin. "Bastille, can you find Yord?"

Bastille pressed several buttons. He put on a headset and spoke, "Computer, give me coordinates for Yord."

A series of numbers appeared on the monitor. Bastille instructed, "Computer, set 'autopilot'."

"Autopilot Set" appeared on the monitor.

Bastille informed Breel, "We're on the way." He exited the cabin with Breel to check on Will and Shanna.

Arasthmus finished using the laser to cauterize Shanna's wounds. As he placed Shanna's arm securely in a sling, she winced. Moving over to Will's table with the medical kit, he blotted his wound with antiseptic.

Bastille sat down next to Shanna's table. He said passively, "I presume you know how to get us into Yord."

"Yes, I do."

"Good. I've never been there, but I've heard stories."

Shanna explained to Bastille, "When we arrive at Yord, you'll need to locate a long, narrow canyon called Devil's Crossing. Take the ship to the bottom of the canyon. Look for a large cave, big enough for a ship. Take us in slowly. There is a huge rock wall. It opens through sensors mounted in the walls. It should let us in."

"I'll enter the search info into the computer."

"It won't acknowledge Devil's Canyon. It's an old, secret Fleet base so it doesn't exist in databases."

Bastille rubbed his beard, "Ah, I see. Why did they build a secret base on a planet like Yord?"

"I think that's why they sent misfit women there. It made a good front."

Bastille asked, "Why did they abandon it?"

Michael D'Ambrosio

Shanna explained, "They never got to use it. The war broke out and the Attradeans quickly took control of the area.

Laneia sat down with Shanna and talked. Will was glad to see the girls becoming friends.

When Arasthmus finished repairing Will's leg, he advised Will, "Stay off of it for a little while."

"Thanks, Arasthmus."

"Take it easy, Will. There's no rush to get up."

Will interrupted the girls. "Laneia, can you do me a favor?"

"Sure, Will. What is it?"

"Can you ask Bastille to contact Maya on the *Luna C* and Talia on the *Ruined Stone*? Have him explain where we're going and tell them I'll talk to them later."

Laneia obediently left the main quarters and entered the pilots' cabin. She relayed the information to Bastille.

102

V.   Journey to Yord

Maya sat alone in the pilots' cabin, wondering what happened to her life. Everything became so complicated, ever since Will came along. Even Jack was back in her life again.

Jack waited outside, wondering if he should try and talk to Maya. She needed someone to lean on and he wanted to be there for her.

Talia's voice startled her. "Maya, are you there?"

Maya pressed the DMS 'receive' button. Talia's face appeared on the monitor.

"Go ahead Talia."

"Ten Attradean vessels are headed this way in an odd formation."

"We know about them."

"Also, a cruiser just left a remote building on Attrades. The tracking devices indicate Will is onboard. What do you want to do?"

Maya freaked, "He should have contacted us. What the hell is he doing?"

Jack entered the Cabin.

Maya yelled angrily, "What do you want?"

Jack ordered her, "Sit down and shut up."

He sat in the co-pilot's seat and said, "Talia, it's Jack. Where is the cruiser headed?"

"Toward the Burness Galaxy at a high rate of speed."

"Follow it."

The monitor beeped three times. Maya became excited. "It's him! It's got to be him."

"Stay on their tail, Talia," Jack commanded. "We have an incoming signal. I'll get right back to you."

Maya pressed the 'receive' switch again. "This is the *Luna C.* Go ahead."

"*Luna C.* This is *Darien's Fang*, an Attradean cruiser. Is Will Saris a member of your party?"

Jack put his hand up for Maya to hush. "This is Jack Fleming, co-pilot. Why do you ask?"

"Jack Fleming! It's Bastille. How are you, you old dog?"

"Bastille! Bastille Brashore! I heard you were dead."

"So Tenemon thought. Is Will a member of your party?"

"Yes he is."

"He is here with us. He's recovering from an injury. He asked me to inform you that we're headed to Yord. We have some refugees as well. There is a place for us to hide on Yord until the Attradean forces pass us by. We strongly recommend you follow us. I'm sure that Tenemon is going crazy right about now."

Jack replied, "I'll bet he is. We'll see you on Yord."

"Roger."

Jack looked at Maya and asked, "Are you okay?"

Maya regained her composure. "I'm better now." She sniffled and wiped her eyes. "I really lost it. Thank you for helping me."

"You're welcome."

"I'd better get back to Talia."

"Good idea."

They looked into each other's eyes. Jack leaned forward to kiss Maya. She closed her eyes and waited. Jack withdrew.

"I'm sorry. I shouldn't have …"

Maya grabbed Jack by the collar and pulled him toward her. She kissed him hard for several seconds. Jack pulled away from her but kissed her again, slowly and passionately.

Maya pressed the DMS 'standby' switch.

Talia's voice interrupted them. "Maya... Jack. Are you there?"

Celine rushed into the cabin. "Talia's on the …"

She saw Maya in Jack's arms, kissing. She was shocked beyond belief.

"I'll… I'll come back later."

Celine anxiously left the cabin.

Maya and Jack giggled. Maya suggested to Jack, "How about I talk to Talia and you meet me in my quarters?"

Jack asked, "Are you sure about this?"

"As sure as I've ever been."

"I'll be waiting."

Maya pressed the DMS 'receive' switch. "Hello, Talia. It's Maya."

"Hey, girl! We heard Bastille's message. Looks like we're going to Yord."

"Yes, we are. Neelon picked up the ten Attradean ships on the long range sensors. Isn't that strange for so many of them to travel back to Attrades at one time?"

Talia added, "Yes it is. Also, they're in an oval formation. That's really unusual."

"This is interesting news."

"Zira will be at the controls for a while. I'm going to get some sleep."

"Good idea. I'm going to do the same. Celine will be here if Zira needs us."

"See you later, Maya."

"Bye."

Jack passed Celine in the hall.

Celine asked, "Hey, Jack. What's going on with Maya?"

"I think she's had a change of heart. Got to go."

Jack hummed as he strolled down the hallway.

Celine warily entered the cabin. She sat down in the co-pilot's seat and glared at Maya.

Maya informed Celine, "We have a place to hide until the Attradean forces pass."

Celine questioned Maya, "Are you sure you're okay? You sounded like you were losing it a little while ago."

"Oh, Jack has a way of bringing out the best in me. Sorry about that."

"So everything is alright?"

"Yes. I'm going to my quarters for a little while."

Maya rushed to her quarters to meet Jack.

Celine shook her head and complained, "And they tell me I'm the crazy one. Imagine that."

****

Will lifted the gauze from his leg and examined the wound. He expected to see some healing. He called Arasthmus over.

"Something's wrong, Arasthmus. My leg isn't healing."

Arasthmus studied the wound. He complained, "It's obviously not healing yet and infection is setting in. I don't know what else to do right now."

"Arasthmus, I'm a Firenghi. We're supposed to heal fairly quickly. I know something is wrong."

"Get some rest. Maybe you're worn down."

"I hope you're right."

Will closed his eyes and drifted off to sleep.

****

Laneia entered the main quarters. "Hi, Shanna. How are you feeling?"

"Much better, thanks."

Arasthmus instructed Shanna, "Leave the sling on until your shoulder is healed. That was a nasty wound."

"Thanks, Arasthmus. What about Will? Shouldn't he be getting better?"

"Yes, but he isn't. I don't understand it. If he's Firenghian, he should show some sign of healing by now."

Arasthmus paced the floor and pondered, "I wonder if something else could be causing the infection."

Shanna explained, "There are creatures that live in a poisonous mist surrounding the Eye. One of them jumped on Will when he rescued me. It clawed his back badly."

Arasthmus exclaimed, "Why didn't you tell me?"

"I didn't think it was relevant."

Arasthmus shook Will repeatedly. "Wake up, Will."

Will awoke miserably. "What's the matter? I just dozed off."

Arasthmus ordered, "Turn over. I want to inspect your back."

"What for?"

"Animal wounds."

Shanna remarked, "Remember the cuts on your back?"

Will grumbled, "So what?"

Arasthmus pointed out, "It's an alien creature from a foreign environment. That's the worst form of infection you could get."

Will removed his shirt. His back had seven deep gashes that swelled and oozed pus.

Arasthmus was appalled. I've never seen infection this bad. I want to lance the wounds open and examine them more closely. Perhaps we can scrape them and cauterize them."

Regent opened the medical kit and asked, "What do you need, Arasthmus?"

"Hand me a scalpel."

Arasthmus took the scalpel from Regent. He sliced open each of the wounds and scraped away the infected tissue.

Bastille entered the main quarters. "Excuse me, ladies and gentlemen. We have a problem."

Regent asked, "What is it, Bastille?"

"An Attradean cruiser is approaching from dead ahead."

Will said tiredly, "I've got to get up. This is important."

Arasthmus warned him, "I'll have Breel sit on you. You aren't going anywhere until we're done."

Shanna informed Bastille, "I have an idea. Come with me."

Shanna and Bastille entered the pilots' cabin and sat down. Shanna asked, "Who did you talk to on the other ships?"

Bastille replied, "Celine is on the *Luna C*. Talia is on the *Ruined Stone*."

"Ask them if their ships can become invisible."

Bastille laughed. "That's ridiculous."

"Ask them. If they were near Attrades the whole time Will was rescuing us, then they must have done something to keep from being seen."

Bastille selected the proper frequency and pressed the DMS 'call' switch.

Celine was dreaming about a beach on a tropical island. Men in grass skirts waited on her, bringing her drinks and food. Her dream was interrupted by three beeps.

Saphoro pressed the DMS 'receive' switch. "I got it, Celine. Go back to sleep."

Celine answered groggily, "That's okay. I'm awake, now."

Bastille's face appeared on the screen. "Sorry to bother you, ladies. This might sound dumb but do your ships have some sort of cloaking device?"

Celine answered, "Yes they do, but only when the engines are shut down. It's a power issue. Why do you ask?"

"There is an Attradean cruiser heading directly toward us."

Celine glanced at her screen. "I don't see it yet."

"You will. I suggest that both of your ships take position ahead of us and do your disappearing act. We'll play crippled and let them come into firing range. They'll never expect two invisible ships waiting for them like a gauntlet. When they enter your firing range, you should be able to take care of them with little difficulty."

Celine replied, "I see it, now. Your ship has better range than ours."

Bastille replied, "We'll try to take advantage of it."

Celine asked, "Zira, did you get that?"

"I sure did."

Bastille informed them, "We're shutting down to drift."

"Understood. Good luck."

"Thanks, ma'am. You, too."

Celine commented to Saphoro, "A true gentleman. That's a rarity in space."

Bastille heard her and chuckled.

Saphoro asked Celine, "Should I get Maya?"

"No, not yet. Please, not yet."

"Why?"

"She's in therapy."

Saphoro asked with a wide grin, "With Jack?"

"Yup."

"Oh, thank goodness."

The girls laughed heartily and high-fived each other.

****

Arasthmus finished cauterizing the wounds on Will's back.

"This should help improve things."

Shanna returned from the pilots' cabin and sat next to Will's table. "How is he?"

Arasthmus replied, "We'll know soon. I removed the infected tissue and cauterized the wound so it doesn't return. The key is how fast the rest of his body reacts."

Shanna picked up a clean towel from the drawer below the table and wiped the sweat from Will's forehead.

She exclaimed, "You're burning up, Will."

Will answered, "I don't feel well. What's going on with the Attradean vessel?"

Shanna informed him, "Your friends will take care of it for us. We're going to lay low for a little while."

Arasthmus placed his hands on his hips and admired his handy work. "Looks like I'm finished with you, Will."

"Thank you Arasthmus."

"You're welcome. I'll be back in a while to check on you."
Arasthmus left the room.

****

Bastille congratulated Shanna. "That was a great idea. They'll never suspect an ambush from us."

Shanna remarked, "It doesn't make sense to confront them head on."

"Not yet, anyway."

Bastille shut down systems one by one. The monitor beeped three times. Bastille muttered impatiently, "Now what?"

He pressed the DMS 'receive' switch and Zira's face appeared on the screen.

"Bastille, I'm Zira from the *Ruined Stone*."

"Hello, Zira. What can I do for you?"

"How is Will doing? I haven't heard anything in a while."

"Not so well. Shanna's with him at the moment. I hear he's battling a bit of an infection from an Eremite wound."

"Who's Shanna?"

"She's a friend of his."

Zira grew agitated, "What kind of friend?"

Bastille sensed her jealousy. "I don't know. She's been looking after him."

"What's Will think of her?"

Bastille snapped impatiently, "Zira, I don't know."

"When he's able, I want to speak with him."

"Sure. I'll pass that along to him when he feels better. I've got to go."

"Don't forget."

"I won't, Zira. Goodbye."

Bastille placed his hands on the back of his head and stretched. "Oh, what a pain in the tail!"

Breel entered and sat next to Bastille. "Who's a pain in the tail?"

"Some girl from the *Ruined Stone*. She wants to know all about Will and Shanna."

Breel mused, "Perhaps Will already has a paramour."

"No. This one is too catty. I'm sure Will has better judgment than that."

They chuckled over the issue.

Laneia entered and sat on Breel's lap. "And what might the two of you be laughing about?"

Bastille replied, "Oh, nothing. Just guy talk."

Laneia looked at them suspiciously. "That usually means females are involved in the conversation."

Breel looked guilty.

Laneia asked, "Is this something I should know about?"

Shanna was about to enter the cabin but stopped to listen.

Bastille explained, "It's not a big deal. Some girl from the *Ruined Stone* was asking a lot of questions about Will and Shanna."

Laneia asked, "Do you think she's Will's real girlfriend?"

Bastille looked confused. "What's a 'real' girlfriend versus a girlfriend?"

Laneia grew uncomfortable.

Breel quipped, "Remember, you started this discussion."

Laneia explained, "A real girlfriend is the one that counts. The other girlfriend is a situational girlfriend. When the situation changes, so does she."

Shanna entered and said curiously, "This sounds like an interesting conversation."

Bastille and Breel shook their heads sideways indicating no.

Laneia blurted out, "A female from the *Ruined Stone* is asking questions about you and Will."

Breel said nervously, "I have to do something important."

He quickly left the cabin.

Bastille added, "I think I need to use the lavatory. Laneia keep an eye on things."

Laneia looked disgusted. "Typical males."

Shanna asked sadly, "So what do you think? Does Will have a girlfriend already?"

Laneia asked, "What has he told you so far? Has he made a play for you?"

"Actually no. He's been quite gentlemanly. I thought he was shy, but maybe he already has someone else."

"I doubt it. You're too special to him."

Shanna blushed, "Thanks, Laneia. That means a lot."

****

Bastille and Breel hid near the back of the ship, away from the women.

Bastille complained, "Can't never have a descent conversation with women around."

Breel replied, "I can't believe she told Shanna about the other woman. Shanna's going to feel real bad."

Bastille explained, "Women are cold-hearted, my friend. It's the nature of the species. They relish the idea of another woman's pain."

"So what can you do about it?"

Bastille grinned and replied, "Nothing."

"Well that's no help."

"It's been going on for eons, my friend, in every species, all over the universe. Get used to it."

"So I have to take the bad with the good."

"Exactly. Now I'd better get back to the controls before they take over my ship."

Bastille walked up the long aisle and entered the main quarters.

Will slid off of the table. He saw Bastille and asked, "Bastille, what are you up to?"

"Uh, lavatory run."

"Where's Shanna?"

"I think she's up front with Laneia."

"I'll walk with you."

Bastille asked nervously, "Are you feeling well enough to walk?"

"Yes, I'm much better. My leg is healing, finally."

Bastille explained, "Arasthmus is a good person to have around. He used to practice medicine on his world before he entered politics."

Will commented, "He's a good man in many regards."

"What do you think of Shanna? I mean like is she special to you?"

"Oh, yes. She's special."

"That's good to hear. Maybe you should tell her that. It would mean a lot to her."

Will responded, "I think she knows where she stands with me."

The lights shut down and the room darkened.

Will asked, "What's going on?

Bastille explained, "The non-vital systems are shutting down. The Attradean cruiser is getting close."

"Whose idea was it to ambush the cruiser like this?"

"Shanna's."

"No kidding. She surprises me more and more for a Seer."

Will and Bastille entered the dimly lit pilots' cabin. Laneia and Shanna looked surprised to see Will. Shanna asked, "What are you doing here? You should be lying down."

"I'm feeling better. How far off is the Attradean cruiser?"

"We're almost in its range."

Bastille took his seat at the controls. The DMS beeped three times.

Bastille moaned, "Not again. That thing is annoying."

Laneia mentioned, "Zira called from the *Ruined Stone*. She was asking a lot of questions about you and Shanna."

Will replied curtly, "So?"

Shanna said, "Leave it alone, Laneia. It's not a problem."

Laneia persisted, "She acted like she was your girlfriend or something – real possessive. I was curious if she was."

Breel tried to keep the peace. "We think Laneia is reading too much into it."

The monitor beeped three times again.

Bastille suggested, "We should respond. It could be important."

Will replied irately, "So now I have to account for everyone that I know?"

Bastille pressed the DMS 'receive' switch.

An angry, bearded, Attradean face appeared on the screen.

"So, I finally meet the thief who has stolen from me."

Sarcastically, Will asked, "What do you want?"

Bastille whispered to Will, "That's Tenemon."

Will suddenly took interest in the conversation.

Tenemon remarked arrogantly, "We have a problem."

Will laughed. "We have lots of problems, Tenemon. Pick one and wait in line."

"You won't be so cocky when I get my revenge."

"And how do you plan to do that?"

"You're about to find out."

"Look, I have a busy schedule. How soon is that?"

Tenemon screamed, "Don't disrespect me like this, you impudent rodent. You take my prisoners and kill one of my Seers. You embarrass my guards and steal one of my cruisers. I'll teach you respect."

"Maybe you need better guards."

Tenemon screamed, "You've crossed the line now!"

Breel pushed Shanna off to the side away from Tenemon's line of sight.

Shanna glared at him.

Breel whispered to her, "He thinks you're dead."

Shanna replied softly, "Oh, yeah."

Will asked defiantly, "So what should I do, Tenemon?"

"Beg for mercy."

Will rationalized, "Look. You've got to understand that this is a business. Nothing is personal."

"What do you mean 'business'?"

Will winked at Bastille. "My employer paid me handsomely to kill your prisoners. The Seer was an accident. I was also paid to kill your daughter and her friend. As a courtesy, I asked your daughter if she had any last words for you."

Tenemon waited impatiently. "Well."

"She said that you suck."

"I never cared for that little vamp anyway. She was an accident."

Will grinned at him. "I hope you die with as much dignity as she did."

Tenemon yelled angrily, "I hope there's a good reason for this debauchery. Why would you dare…?"

Will interrupted Tenemon, "Ah, yes. The age old question 'why'? My employer doesn't like the way you take on new allies. Double-crossing your constituents isn't a good thing among planetary rulers."

Irritated, Tenemon asked "Is this going somewhere?"

Will elaborated on the consequences. "If word gets out that you killed the prisoners, then you've lost your leverage with your allies. They will desert you."

Tenemon screamed, "Who are you?"

Calmly, he answered, "Will Saris, your friendly, neighborhood businessman."

A small, fiery explosion appeared in the distance. Bastille checked the tracking screen. He whispered to Will, "The cruiser's been destroyed."

"Gee, Tenemon, did you just lose another cruiser? That's a sloppy way to run a military operation."

Tenemon glared at Will from the monitor. "You will pay tenfold for everything you have done to me."

Will stood up and looked fiercely at the screen. He said firmly, "If you want to play games and keep score with me, I'll run the score right up your fat ass. I will kill you for free."

Tenemon was incensed. "You don't know who you're dealing with, Saris."

Will became aggravated and swore, "One day, when you least expect it, I will be standing behind you and you will pay again and again and again."

Tenemon retorted, "It'll be a long time before that happens."

"Good. That gives me plenty of time to make your life a living hell."

Tenemon yelled, "I want my ship back, too!"

Will chuckled. "I'll see what I can do. Maybe next time we can do lunch."

"Screw you, Saris!"

"No, screw you, Tenemon. Good day."

Will changed the DMS frequency to that of the *Luna C* and the *Ruined Stone*.

Will reached for Shanna but she kept her distance.

"Shanna, come here."

"Perhaps later."

Will remarked, "So Zira is making a nuisance of herself."

Shanna ignored his comment and asked, "Is Zira your woman?"

Will laughed. "Heavens no. I wouldn't wish her on anyone."

Shanna cheered up. "Really?"

"Really. Would you care to experience a conversation with dear, lovable Zira?"

Bastille added, "What a charmer she is?"

Shanna replied, "No, I'll take your word for it."

"I have to check in with them anyway. You can stay if you like."

"No, thanks."

Shanna giggled and went to the door. She stopped and glanced back at Will.

Will looked at her and kidded loudly, "What?"

Shanna explained happily, "I never imagined you getting so upset about anything. Were you mad at Laneia and me for asking about Zira?"

"No. I was just playing around."

Bastille laughed hysterically.

Breel and Laneia joined in the laughter as well.

Bastille told them, "I was shaking in my boots. I thought Will had gone mad."

Breel admitted, "That was a damn good act."

"Well, part of it was an act. I was a little upset that you would be concerned with anything Zira says. Tenemon just picked a bad time to bother me."

Shanna crooned, "All that over me?"

Will blushed. "Yeah, I guess it was."

The DMS beeped again.

Bastille complained, "Who can it be, now!"

Talia appeared on the DMS. "Hey, Maya, are you there?"

Celine answered, "No she's still indisposed."

"What about Bastille? Are you on?"

Bastille replied, "This is Bastille. Go ahead Talia?"

"Is Will available?"

"He's right here. Would you care to speak with him?"

"Yes I would."

"Hi, Talia."

"Will, how are you feeling?"

"Much better, thank you."

"What happened to you?"

"I had scratch fever from an Eremite."

"What's going on? I understand you've got quite a crowd there."

"Yes, I do. I have the councilors who were held captive. I have King Tenemon's daughter and a close confidant of hers here as well. I also have one of the Seers with me."

Talia asked, "How much do you know about Seers, Will?"

"Not much, but I'm learning fast."

Shanna became concerned and looked at Breel and Bastille. They shrugged their shoulders in ignorance of what Talia might say. Shanna left the pilots' cabin quickly.

Talia responded, "So I've heard."

Will asked, "What else did you hear?"

"About what?"

Will chuckled and said, "From Zira."

"Oh, that. It was nothing."

"Come on, Talia. I enjoy a little gossip."

"Well, since she's not here. Zira is under the impression that you and the Seer have a thing going on."

"And ..."

"Well, she thinks the Seer is out of your league. You know, being that they are witches and all that."

Will's face grew serious. "Where did you hear that?"

"It's a proven fact. That's why the Seers were disbanded to Yord."

"Are all of the women on Yord Seers?"

"No. Undesirables were sent there as well."

Will looked for Shanna but she was gone. Everyone's faces grew serious. Laneia followed after Shanna.

"That's interesting. Why are you telling me this?"

"I didn't know if you understood what the background of your friend was."

"I've got a pretty good idea."

Talia asked, "So what is up with you and the Seer?"

Will replied cynically, "Ask Zira. She seems to know more than I do."

"You're not saying, are you?"

"Perhaps when we land, I'll have more to say on the matter."

"That was a great plan you came up with to get rid of the cruiser."

Will remarked, "Shanna and Bastille thought of it. The timing of the explosion was perfect."

Talia asked, "Why?"

"Because Tenemon was trying to get a leg up on me on the DMS. It gave him something to think about."

"Don't tell me you made things personal with Tenemon?"

Will asked innocently, "Would I do that?"

Talia responded nervously, "Does he know who you are?"

"Oh, yes. I told him."

"He's gonna' kill you and probably the rest of us as well!"

"No he won't. I have a plan for him. Besides, he's looking over his shoulder for whoever paid me to kill all of his prisoners who happen to be with me."

"You told him that!"

"Yeah. He doesn't know who to go after."

"Will, I hope you know what you're doing. This is a dangerous game."

"I'm aware of that."

"Just remember. We're in this, too."

"You don't have to be. I'll explain later."

"Will, this had better be good."

"Believe me, it's very good. I'll see you on Yord."

Will stood up slowly. He winced in pain.

Breel attempted to help him.

"It's okay, Breel. I can do it."

Will looked for Shanna.

"Where did Shanna go?"

Breel said, "She left abruptly when Talia spoke about the Seers."

"Oh, boy. I'll be back."

Will exited the cabin and hobbled through the main quarters. He approached one of the alien councilors. "Councilor Triton, have you seen Shanna?"

"She went upstairs a little while ago."

Will was about to ascend the stairs but had second thoughts. He selected a berth on the main level and decided to rest for a while.

****

Bastille guided the cruiser across the barren Yordic terrain. He searched carefully for the Devil's Canyon. He pressed the DMS 'call' switch and inquired, "Hey girls, are you on?"

Talia replied, "I'm here, Bastille."

Celine also responded, "I'm here, too."

Bastille informed them, "We'll be dropping down into the canyon shortly. When we get there, slow down and space yourselves. We'll be looking for an opening in the lower side of the wall. I've never been here before so this is new to me."

Talia said, "We'll drop in behind the *Luna C.*"

119

Celine replied, "We're on your tail, Bastille."

Bastille saw the narrow canyon approaching on his left. He slowed the ship and eased into the deep crevice. The cruiser gracefully glided along the canyon bottom. Bastille spotted a large opening under an outcrop of rock.

"Well, ladies, I think I see it."

Celine responded, "We'll hold back until you give us the word."

"Good girl."

Bastille steered the cruiser into the opening and hovered in front of a rock wall. He turned on the outside sensors and listened for telltale sounds. He was about to back up, but heard rocks grating. He watched carefully as the wall opened up like a huge garage door.

Bastille chanted, "Looks like pay dirt, ladies. Come on down."

Bastille piloted the cruiser into the cave. The cave led to a large cavern, which housed a complete facility, including docks for the ships. Bastille spun the cruiser around and eased it into the first berth.

He shut down the engines and turned off the main power. On the monitor, he watched the *Luna C* and the *Ruined Stone* gliding past him.

VI.   Will's Pirates

Will slid out of bed and exited the cabin.

Breel sat in the main quarters alone when Will entered.

"What's going on, Breel?"

"We just landed on Yord."

Shanna stepped off of the stairs with Baron in her arms and exclaimed, "I can't believe it! I'm home."

Will asked, "Why did you leave so fast? I wanted to talk to you."

Shanna replied humbly, "I didn't want to hear what your friends had to say about me. There are things I wanted to tell you about me when the time was right."

Will laughed, angering Shanna.

She asked defensively, "What's so funny, Will?"

"Who cares what they say about you? I sure don't, and there was nothing said that you should be ashamed of."

Shanna looked surprised and answered sheepishly, "Oh. I just assumed ... Well, never mind."

Will patted Baron on the head. "How are you doing, Baron?"

"Very well, thank you. It felt good to eat, sleep and drink like a civilized being."

"Thanks for your help earlier."

"Thank you. I am extremely grateful to you for rescuing me."

The hatch of the *Darien's Fang* was open and the councilors had already exited the ship. Bastille waited for Will and Shanna.

Laneia descended the stairs and hooked her arm in Breel's.

Will's commanding voice rang out, "Shall we go?"

Bastille exited first, followed by Breel and Laneia.

Will offered his arm to Shanna and asked, "Would you accompany me to the dock?"

Shanna graciously accepted. She asked, "Are you sure they didn't say anything we should be concerned about?"

Will escorted Shanna and Baron off of the ship. As they walked, he asked her, "Like what?"

"Anything."

"What are you so paranoid about?"

They walked away from the ship.

Shanna snapped, "Forget I said anything."

Will whispered in Shanna'a ear, "Don't worry. Everything is fine."

Shanna sensed that Will learned something about her background but she couldn't be sure. Whatever he knew, it didn't seem to bother him.

Will looked across the dock and saw a few surprises.

Bastille wasted no time in meeting Celine face to face.

Breel and Laneia had a few intimate moments behind a nearby stairwell.

Maya and Jack exited the *Luna C* holding hands.

Will and Shanna approached Maya and Jack. Maya saw Baron and rushed to him. Shanna gently handed Baron to her.

Maya cried, "Baron, it's so good to see you again! I told you we could count on Will to get you back."

Baron remarked, "Will did very well."

Will couldn't resist teasing Maya. "Well, well, well. What's with the hand holding, Maya?"

Maya exclaimed, "Wait a minute! I'm the one who should be asking you the questions."

Jack winked at Will, who quipped, "I guess a picture is worth a thousand words."

Maya sniped back, "You have a lot of explaining to do. By the way, who is your friend?"

Will introduced everyone, "Shanna, this is Maya, my pseudo-sister and her companion, Jack Fleming. Jack and I met during a hair-raising adventure. Since then, we've become good buds."

Will pulled Shanna in front of him and placed his arms around her. "This is Shanna, a very good friend of mine."

Maya exclaimed, "You're Shanna, the Seer!"

Shanna replied timidly, "Yes, I am. I hope that's okay."

"I'm amazed. I never expected to meet a real Seer."

Shanna explained, "I'm a real person just like you and Will."

Maya gave Shanna a funny look and said, "I don't think so. Will and I aren't quite human."

Shanna replied, "That's okay. Neither am I."

"I can see you and I have a lot to talk about if you're going to be with Will. I think we'll be very good friends."

Shanna replied happily, "That would be great!"

Jack asked excitedly, "Will, I have to know, what in the world happened on Attrades? You had everybody going crazy."

"It's a long story."

Maya added, "I was worried about you."

Will teased, "No way. You were too busy being mad at everyone."

Jack explained, "Maya's looking at things in a different light now. I think you'll appreciate her new outlook."

Jack kissed her cheek and she blushed.

Will kiddingly demanded, "I want the details over dinner. This is hard to believe."

Maya answered, "You're the one who'd better have details."

They chuckled together.

Will took Shanna to meet Talia and Zira.

When they gathered near the *Ruined Stone*, Talia joked, "Well if it isn't the walking dead."

Will replied, "You wouldn't believe what I've been through."

"Bastille told me all about it."

Zira spoke indignantly, "Will, I hope you haven't settled on her. She's way out of your league."

"Yes, Zira. We've already heard your opinion on things."

"If we're ever going to have a future, you and I need to straighten some things out."

Will rolled his eyes.

Talia giggled and looked away.

Zira snapped at them, "This isn't funny. I'm serious."

Will placed his arm around Shanna and explained, "Zira, we have no future. Don't you remember? We already agreed to that."

"We did. Well, maybe we need to discuss it some more."

"No. I have things to do."

Zira was stunned.

Talia pulled Zira with her. "Come on, girl. You have work to do."

Zira moaned, "But Talia ..."

Talia remarked, "By the way, Will, nice job on Attrades. I'm sorry I doubted you."

"Thanks, Talia."

Will explained to Shanna, "Maya is a little older than I am. When she was younger, she raised me while my mother was fighting the Boromeans. She really is like my big sister."

Two women approached them. One was a middle-aged woman with long auburn hair, dressed in a long red robe. The other was young, with long blond hair, much like Shanna's. She wore a white robe with gold trim.

The older woman approached Shanna and exclaimed, "This is a miracle. You've grown so much since we last saw you."

Shanna embraced her and asked, "How are you Mariel?"

"I'm well. How did you ever escape from Tenemon?"

"Will rescued me."

Shanna looked at the young girl and cried, "Brindy! Look at you."

The two girls embraced.

Shanna introduced them, "This is my aunt, Mariel, and my sister, Brindy."

Mariel nodded with a smile.

Shanna continued, "This is Will Saris. Will rescued me from Tenemon."

Will greeted her, "It's a pleasure to meet you."

Brindy waved and said, "Hi. It's nice to meet you, too."

Mariel surveyed Will's friends on the dock. She remarked, "What an interesting group of beings? You have Attradeans, a Chinubian, humans and you, a Firenghi."

Will asked, "How did you know I was Firenghi? Other species have eyes like mine."

Mariel replied with a smile, "I, too, am Firenghi."

Will was stunned by this revelation. "You, a Firenghi!"

"That's right, Will."

"But how?"

Mariel replied, "In time. What of the other Seers?"

"We couldn't get them this time."

"Assemble your friends and come with us. We're preparing a meal for you."

Will whistled loudly and motioned for everyone to join them. They gathered at the dock area and followed Mariel up a long stretch of granite steps to a beautiful, marble concourse. Across the concourse were two sets of double-doors made of oak. Mariel opened the doors and waited for everyone to catch up.

Will and Shanna stood with Mariel.

Shanna exclaimed, "I've never seen this place. It's amazing!"

Will questioned her, "You grew up here, didn't you?"

"I grew up on the surface. When Tenemon's forces came, they destroyed everything we had."

Will and Shanna entered the hall behind Mariel. There were four glass tables in parallel and one on an elevated floor at the front of the hall.

Mariel stood behind the higher table and welcomed everyone inside the hall. She extended a special invitation to Will and Shanna. "Please join me up here."

Will commented to Shanna, "Looks like we're the guests of honor."

Shanna whispered, "I wonder what she has in mind for us."

"It should be interesting.

Will's friends sat at the first four tables.

Women dressed in light green robes entered the hall with trays of food and ewers of wine.

Mariel announced, "Everyone, please enjoy your meal. My servants will accommodate your needs."

Will said politely, 'Thank you, Mariel, for your hospitality."

Mariel remarked to Will, "It's so good to see Shanna again. She was one of my brightest students."

"Shanna is a very smart girl."

Mariel sat down and looked seriously at Will.

"Tell me about the other Seers."

Will was surprised by her directness. "What is it that you want to know?"

"Can you rescue them?"

"I think so. It's going to take a little time, but I'm working on a plan."

Mariel seemed pleased. "It's hard to believe you got Shanna out of there. No one has been able to get into the palace, let alone escape from it."

Will explained, "It took a trick or two. Once I rescued Shanna, she helped me free the others."

Mariel asked, "How close are you and Shanna?"

Will pondered if she had an underlying reason for asking these questions. He answered carefully, "We're very good friends. She and I seem to be a good match."

"I would love to see your relationship come to fruition."

Will became suspicious and said, "Mariel, don't be offended, but I sense that you're fishing for something here."

"You're very perceptive."

Shanna slid her chair between them. "Hey, I'm here, too. What are you two talking about?"

Mariel commanded her, "Hush, child. This concerns you, too." She sipped from her glass of wine and began, "The Eye of Icarus brought us much fortune when our Priestesses possessed it. We knew the weather, the outcome of critical events and what enemies to protect ourselves from. If we had the Eye back and the Seers who tended to it, we could once again rise to become a resourceful world."

Will inquired, "I don't understand. How could you be prosperous when your population consists of misfit women?"

"We had a near perfect situation. No one paid us any mind until we emerged as an economic galactic power. That's why Tenemon ravaged our world and took the Eye."

Will mused, "That's interesting."

"Yes, it is. Seers are reclusive in nature. If the Eye were returned to us, we would become reclusive again. Unfortunately, the other women would need someone to rule for them on the surface."

"I see. And who would that be?"

"You and Shanna would be perfect."

Will became more intrigued and asked, "How do you know?"

Mariel explained, "There are many things that our race can become. The two of you would rule wisely. People would come to our world again and we would rise in prominence."

Will asked, "But is all this really about wealth and prosperity?"

Mariel asked in surprise, "You don't want wealth?"

"I'm not exactly concerned about it right now. I'm enjoying my life so far."

"Then how about galactic peace? What if you could end the great war?"

Will quipped, "If only it were that easy."

"It will never be easy but it could be within your grasp."

Will explained, "I think that certain goals of mine coincide with your hopes, but, I don't want anyone to dictate how I accomplish them."

Mariel softened her stance and replied, "I didn't mean to imply that I wanted anything from you, only that there are opportunities."

"I think we've discussed Yord's future enough. Now, I'm curious to know some things about you."

"Like what?"

"You mentioned that you are also Firenghi. How is it that you wound up here?"

"Are you sure you want to know?"

"Yes, I am."

"I joined the Fleet as a young girl. Things went well until I was injured in an accident. When the masters at the academy saw how fast I healed, they became suspicious of me. Soon after, I was discharged and placed on a freighter with a number of other 'suspicious' women."

Will was shocked. "The Fleet really did that to you?"

"I'm sure you find it hard to believe, especially since you're one of theirs."

"No. It's just hard to believe that you were punished for being Firenghi."

Mariel looked into Will's eyes and asked, "Who are your parents?"

"Queen Seneca was my mother and Bill Brock was my father."

Mariel shrank back from Will. Her eyes were wide with surprise. "Queen Seneca?"

"Yes."

"So you are Firenghi royalty."

"There isn't much left of Firenghia to be royalty of."

"There were many stories of your mother's courage. Your father was human, if I'm not mistaken."

"Yes he was."

"You say 'was'. They are deceased?"

"My mother was killed by the Boromeans when I was very young. Maya was older than me. She helped raise me. My father is missing and perhaps dead. The Fleet is searching for him."

"I sensed a familial closeness in the two of you. So what are your plans? Will you be leaving us?"

"I don't know yet. I have some things to discuss with my friends before I set a course."

"You are welcome to stay here, as are your friends."

"As the ruler of Yord?"

"No. In any capacity you choose. Your destiny will find you in time."

"That I can live with. I'll consider your offer."

Mariel was satisfied with the results of their discussion. She explained, "I must tend to other issues."

"Thank you, Mariel."

Mariel nodded and left them.

Shanna remarked, "You sure made an impression on her."

"How could you tell?"

"Every test she baited you with, you passed."

"I can't believe Mariel was once in the Fleet. That's ridiculous what they did to her."

Shanna pointed out, "That could have happened to Maya, as well."

"Now I understand why Maya was worried about the Fleet knowing her background."

Will finished eating his meal. "Come on, Shanna. Let's talk with Maya and Jack."

"Is it a good idea to bring this issue up to Maya?"

"I'm afraid she'll find out anyway."

Will and Shanna visited the table where Maya and Jack sat.

Maya teased, "It's nice of you to join us."

Will replied, "Sorry. We had formalities to discuss."

Maya asked, "How is Mariel?"

Will replied stoically, "She used to be in the Fleet."

Maya was stunned.

"What happened? How did she get here?"

"They found out she was Firenghi. She was injured and healed too quickly."

Maya suddenly lost her appetite.

Jack took her hand and asked, "Are you okay?"

She just stared at the table.

Jack asked Will, "Are you certain of this?"

"She knew about my mother. She also knew that my father was human. I do believe her."

Jack became silent.

Breel and Laneia looked from the end of the table and sensed that something was wrong.

Breel called to Will, "Is everything okay?"

"Yes. Just some surprising news."

Jack changed the topic. "What do you plan to do next, Will?"

"I think I'm going to stay here. I like the idea of being a pirate, as you suggested."

Jack asked giddily, "You're not serious, are you?"

"Were you serious when you first mentioned it?"

Jack's face grew somber. "I would do it in a heartbeat."

Will proclaimed, "I hijacked my first ship. I'm already a wanted man. It's a good start."

Maya chided, "You two are talking nonsense."

Will explained, "This is the perfect base. I'm sure we can round up a crew."

Jack indicated, "Bastille is a good pilot. He'll stick with us."

Maya complained, "This is ridiculous."

Will replied, "I like being a renegade and making my own decisions."

Jack was excited. "Me, too. We'd be a great team."

Maya glared at him.

Jack asked, "What's wrong, Maya?"

"You have to ask?"

Jack realized that he omitted Maya from their plans.

"Would you leave the Fleet to join us?"

Maya replied coldly, "No, I couldn't do that."

Will asked sternly, "Even after what they did to Mariel?"

"I can't just walk away from something I've done for so long."

Breel and Laneia joined them. "What are you conspiring, Will?"

Will announced proudly, "Piracy. We're discussing the possibility of becoming pirates."

"Laneia and I will follow you anywhere."

Maya asked skeptically, "You're not really going to do this?"

Will answered, "Yes I am. I'll tell the others, later."

Maya was irate. She got up from the table and stormed away

Shanna said excitedly, "I'm in, too!"

Will warned her, "It's gonna' be dangerous, Shanna."

"We've already been through quite a bit of danger."

"But you could get hurt."

Jack teased Will, "It sounds like somebody's falling in love."

"Stop it, Jack. We're just friends."

Shanna's eyes widened with surprise and disappointment.

Talia approached the table and sat down next to Will.

"Maya told us what you're planning."

Will rolled his eyes and replied, "I know. You're against it as well."

Talia responded, "Not quite. I have some suggestions though."

"Go ahead. I'm listening."

"Our mission is to monitor the Attradeans. The Fleet expects us to stay out here and continue that mission."

"True."

"Maya will take the councilors to Alpha-17. They can get transportation home from there."

"That makes sense, but then what? I know there's a punch line here, somewhere."

"We'll continue to use the *Luna C* and the *Ruined Stone* to eavesdrop on Tenemon and his friends. We feed you the information and you do what you have to do."

"Why would you do this for me?"

Talia replied, "Because we were hung out to dry by the Fleet. Because Celine wants to stay with Bastille. Because Jack's staying and Maya wants to keep seeing him."

Will laughed.

"No kidding! And what about you?"

Talia reluctantly answered, "I need a little excitement in my life. I'm getting older and I'm bored."

"And you're comfortable with this?"

131

"I think so. If not, I can always leave."

Will exclaimed, "That's great!"

Talia asked, "So what do you foresee as our first adventure?"

"Since Maya's taking the councilors back to Alpha-17 on the *Luna C*, that leaves just the *Ruined Stone* for surveillance. How many ships were coming from the Strontarian galaxy?"

"Ten. Why?"

"What if they weren't coming for us? There's no way Tenemon could have summoned a task force that big to come after us on such short notice."

Talia thought for a moment. "You've got a point. What do you think they're up to?"

Will said, "That's what I want you to find out. I also want to know what kind of ships they are."

"We believe they're battle cruisers. I'll take the *Ruined Stone* out tomorrow. As soon as we get more information, I'll contact you."

"I want to rescue the remaining Seers and recover the Eye."

Talia asked curiously, "What's the big deal with this Eye?"

Will informed her, "That's how Tenemon knew what we were up to. He sent the Weevil ahead of us to do his dirty work."

Talia was surprised. "You mean that 'Eye' story is real?"

"It sure is."

"But won't Tenemon expect you to come back for the priestesses?"

"I don't think so. Just the same, I want to be prepared."

"I don't blame you."

Will promised, "Talia, I won't let you down."

Talia replied, "I know you won't. I have a few things to take care of so I'll talk to you later."

"Talia."

"Yes, Will."

"Thanks."

Talia put her hand on Will's shoulder.

"You're welcome."

Talia rejoined her group at the other table.

Jack blurted, "I feel like a kid. This is something that I always dreamed about doing."

Will explained, "I had a hard time making this decision but I feel much better about it now that I've made it."

Jack explained on a serious note, "I've heard from some of my trader friends that the Attradeans have been impounding ships from anyone deemed a threat. I also heard that the Attradeans are building a new class of ship – a destroyer."

"No kidding."

"Do you think that the task force could be an escort for this new ship?"

Will pondered, "That would make sense, but where are they escorting it too?"

Jack commented, "I know you're thinking of something devious."

"I have to work out the logistics, but I think it would break Tenemon's heart to lose his new ship after losing two cruisers already. Perhaps that could also be the perfect distraction for rescuing the Seers."

Shanna remarked, "That's a pretty bold plan, isn't it?"

"Yes, it is. We're going to need some help to make this happen."

Jack suggested, "I know a few men who might fit the role."

"Good. Where can we find them?"

"There's a rest stop about forty jimmies from here. It's called 'Eve's Garden of Paradise'."

"I think we'll take a trip there tomorrow and check it out."

Shanna asked, "Can I go, too?"

Will looked at his friends and announced, "I think we'll all go."

Jack exclaimed, "That's great! I know a lot of the people who hang out there."

Will asked, "How's parking? I mean we are traveling in an Attradean cruiser."

"Fine. Nobody asks questions in a place like that."

"Then we've got a date."

"I'll inform the others."

"Thanks, Jack. I'll be on board the ship if you need me."

Will spoke loudly, "Good night everyone."

Will's friends replied in unison, "Good night."

Will left the table and departed the hall.

Shanna looked down at the table in disappointment. It seemed that Will forgot about her. She walked away without being noticed.

Jack asked, "Anybody know how to paint?"

Laneia answered, "I can. Why?"

"We need a good paint job on the ship. We can't travel with the Attradean colors. That would be embarrassing."

Laneia asked, "What should we put on it?"

Jack suggested, "Skull and crossbones. Maybe some eerie décor along the sides."

Breel asked, "What about 'Phantom' for a name?"

Jack replied, "That will work. Let's ask Mariel's servants if they can get us some paint."

They left the hall and cornered the first servant they met.

Jack made arrangements with the servant for the paint to be brought onto the dock.

****

Will took the last berth at the end of the hall. He entered and sat comfortably on his bed. He was keenly aware of the quiet hall through the open door. As soon as he leaned back against the wall, he closed his eyes.

A short while later, Shanna entered the room. "Are you still awake, Will?"

Will opened his eyes and replied, "Sure. Come on in."

"I thought you forgot about me. What's wrong?"

"I'm worried that it might be too dangerous for you."

Shanna was irked. "I can take care of myself."

"But, Shanna. These places are dangerous."

Will got up and paced about the room. He lectured, "I care about you. If something happens and we're outnumbered, I can't help you. I'd never forgive myself."

Shanna explained, "Yord is full of women. How well do you think they got along? Everyday, I had at least one fight."

"But, Shanna. This isn't about fistfights. This is knives and guns."

Will leaned against the doorjamb with his hand and placed the other on his hip. "Please, do this for me. Stay here."

Shanna opened a drawer. Inside the drawer was a fork, a knife and a glass plate. She took the knife and held it up.

"How well do you value you're thumb and forefinger?"

Will was amused and asked curiously, "Why?"

Shanna fired the knife at Will's hand. The knife stuck in the right doorframe between Will's thumb and forefinger. Will turned ashen.

"What was that for?"

Shanna explained proudly, "I throw a knife very well."

Will grew uncomfortable. He foolishly placed his other hand against the left doorjamb.

"Tell me the truth. That was a lucky throw, right?"

Shanna took the plate and broke it over the edge of the table. She fired a piece of the plate at Will's other hand. The plate buried itself in the left doorjamb.

Will yelled, "Hey, you almost cut my hand!"

Shanna glared at him, "Look again. I never miss."

Will removed his hand from the left doorjamb. Blood trickled down the jamb where his hand had been.

Will asked arrogantly, "How many other surprises do you have for me?"

Shanna retorted angrily, "Quite a few."

She stood face-to-face with Will and stared into his eyes. "I had hoped to save a few of them for you but I'm changing my mind."

Will asked coolly, "What are you talking about?"

135

Shanna spun him away from the door and pushed him onto the bed. She took his shirt off.

Will asked, "What are you doing?"

Shanna replied defiantly, "I want you now."

Shanna closed the door.

"But, Shanna, we talked about this."

"I changed my mind. Besides, I want you tonight for me, not for you."

Will complained sarcastically, "Well that sounds real romantic."

Shanna removed Will's shoes and pants. She stood over him and removed her white robe. She taunted him, "Still want to wait?"

Will was speechless. Shanna's beauty astounded him. Shanna took control and made love to Will in every way she desired.

When Shanna was finished with Will, she got up and dressed. She went to the door and pressed the digital lock. The door slid open.

Will asked, "Where are you going?"

Shanna turned seductively toward him and said, "I'm going out. I'm finished."

Will complained, "Just like that? You're done."

"Yeah."

"I thought there would be a little love and romance in it, not just a tussle in the sheets."

"Sorry, Will. You'll have to wait for love and romance. I won't. I just wanted a friendly frolic."

Shanna brazenly exited the berth.

Will was confused and worried. Something went terribly wrong. He tried to sleep but tossed and turned most of the night, trying to sort things out.

The next morning, Will showered and dressed. He took a walk up to the hall where his friends were eating breakfast. He entered the hall and looked for Shanna.

Mariel intercepted him in the doorway.

"Good morning, Mariel."

"Good morning, Will. I trust your night was well spent."

"Why do you ask?"

"A young man like you is a hot commodity around here. Good news travels fast."

"And your point is?"

"I see Shanna marked her territory."

Mariel examined a series of marks on Will's neck. Will blushed and covered his neck with his hand.

Mariel commented, "It wasn't what you expected was it."

Will glared at her. "What do you mean by that?"

Mariel explained, "You must not underestimate the females on this planet. They are more dangerous than any male, human or otherwise."

Will asked, "What are you getting at, Mariel?"

"Since you weren't anxious to consummate your relationship with Shanna, she had to take the initiative or risk losing you."

Will was surprised. "To whom?"

Mariel said, "Don't be coy. Look around the concourse. You'll see."

Will saw that he had the attention of many of the females from servants to priestesses.

Mariel turned and walked away.

Will called out, "Wait, Mariel."

Mariel stopped and turned around. "You wanted something?"

"What happens if someone wants me more than Shanna?"

"That's the interesting part. She'll have to fight to keep you."

"What kind of fight?"

"Oh, any fight will do. The only way to win is by killing your opponent."

Mariel left him feeling devastated. Shanna was doing all of this for him.

Will spotted Shanna sitting with Maya, Talia, Zira and Laneia. At the adjacent table sat Jack and Breel.

Will was embarrassed by the events from the night before. How could he face Shanna?

Maya waved to Will. She motioned for him to come over.

Will cringed. He approached the table and sat down.

Maya said, "I'm leaving in a little while for Alpha-17. I'll be back in a half cycle."

Will inquired, "Are you okay with the councilors?"

"I'm glad you asked. It seems that Arasthmus and Regent want to join your merry little band."

Will was taken aback by his friends' decision. He asked, "Is that a problem?"

"Only that I have to explain where they are."

Will replied smartly, "They joined a resistance group on the surface of Attrades."

Maya said cynically, "I see you have the answer again."

Will used his telepathy to speak with Maya.

"What was that for?"

Maya responded telepathically as well.

"I heard what happened. How does it feel to not have control of a simple situation?"

"That's cold, Maya."

"I wish you well. I hope you know what you're doing."

"Thanks. You, too."

Laneia asked, "Is something wrong?"

Will answered, "No, why?"

"You two seemed to be staring each other down."

"Just a private family matter."

Shanna commented, "You're good, Will. You can cloak your thoughts very well."

Will replied, "You shouldn't pry into someone else's business without being invited."

Shanna giggled, "My, aren't we fresh today."

Talia cut in, "We're leaving as well. I'll be in touch as soon as we hear something on the Attradean armada."

Will replied, "Thanks, Talia. Be careful."

Talia added, "Don't mind Maya. She and Jack have some things to work out, similar to yours."

Talia left the table and exited the room.

Zira stood up and smiled. "Good luck, Will. See you when we get back."

Zira followed Talia out of the hall.

Will asked, "Can we talk, Shanna?"

"About what?"

"About last night."

"There's nothing to talk about."

Will used his telepathy to make their conversation private. "I'm sorry."

Shanna was curious. "Why are you sorry?"

"I put you in an awkward position last night."

"It wasn't awkward and it wasn't about love."

Will grew more confused. "What was it about?"

"It's about you treating me as an equal. I am as capable as anyone else here in defending myself and my friends."

"Mariel told me ..."

Shanna interrupted, "I would have been content to let you find out the hard way about the women here because, as you said, we discussed it and didn't want to rush into anything."

Will responded, "I'm really sorry if I hurt you. I realize how much you mean to me and now I've lost you."

Shanna corrected Will, "You never had me."

"I don't understand, Shanna."

She ignored his comment and smiled, "Some day you will. See you on board."

Shanna and Laneia left the table and exited the hall.

Will moved to the next table and joined the men.

Will asked, "Where's Bastille?"

Jack replied, "He's coming. He and Celine have developed a bit of a friendship."

Will frowned.

Breel asked him, "What's wrong?"

Will grumbled, "Women. Who needs them?"

Jack said, "By the look of your neck, you had a good night."

Will muttered, "No, not really."

"Don't ever take women too seriously."

"Gee, thanks, Jack."

Jack exclaimed, "Hey, we've got something to show you."

"What is it?"

"We have to go out to the ship."

Jack and Breel stood up and left the table.

Jack beckoned Will to follow them.

The three of them approached the ship. They turned to Will and pointed at it.

Will looked up at the ship in amazement. It was painted black with a skull and crossed swords on the tail and nose. There were sheer flowing robes painted on the wings and keel. The broad sides sported a laughing skull. 'Phantom' was written underneath the skull in fancy letters.

Jack asked proudly, "What do you think?"

Will was amazed. "Who did this?"

Jack answered, "All of us. Laneia did the finer things like outlining the skull and painting the robes on the wings. We did the easier painting."

"It's fantastic!"

Breel declared, "Now we're ready to go out and act like pirates."

Will ordered, "Get on board, mates. It's time to set sail."

The three of them eagerly boarded the ship. Arasthmus and Regent were waiting at the hatch.

Arasthmus greeted Will. "I figured that you needed a doctor on board."

"Always. Glad to have you with me, Arasthmus."

Regent shook Will's hand. "If there's any chance of rescuing the Seers, I know you'll be the one to do it."

Will asked Regent, "Why are you so interested in the Seers?"

"One of them is my childhood sweetheart, Keira. She was taken from me by the Fleet and shipped out here to Yord. When Tenemon's troops invaded, they found her in the sacred shrine with the other Seers. They took the Seers away and I haven't seen her since."

"We'll get her back. Just be patient," Will promised.

Will searched the main quarters for the women, but didn't see them.

Arasthmus noticed and said, "They're in Shanna's quarters, upstairs."

"Scheming, no doubt."

Will wondered what they were up to. He thanked Arasthmus and proceeded toward the pilots' cabin. He sat in the co-pilot's seat and wondered what might lie ahead. His thoughts were suddenly interrupted.

Bastille and Celine entered the cabin. Bastille said politely, "I beg your pardon, Will. You'll have to vacate the co-pilot's seat for the co-pilot."

Will looked back and saw Celine. "What are you doing here?"

Celine pushed Will out of the way and answered, "Somebody has to keep an eye on this big lug."

Will backed out of the way. "Welcome aboard, Celine. What made you join us?"

Celine cackled and gazed at Bastille.

She replied, "It's the paint job! I love it."

Will asked, "The paint job?"

"Hell, yeah! I've been trying to get one for the *Luna C* for a long time. The Fleet says it's too expensive and wouldn't be appropriate."

"Well, keep Bastille straight. He needs all the help he can get."

Bastille chuckled, similar to Celine. He asked, "Are we ready to leave?"

"Yes we are. Anytime you're ready, we can depart."

Will left the pilots' cabin and headed to his berth. Jack was waiting for him in the main quarters. "Are you alright, Will?"

"I'm still stinging from Shanna's behavior."

"Don't tell me she broke your heart?"

"I don't know what happened. I crashed and burned."

"You'd best get over it fast. We've got work to do."

"I'll be alright. If you need me, I'll be in my quarters at the end of the hall." Will walked away dejectedly.

Jack shook his head sideways and mumbled, "Women."

VII.   Eve's Garden of Paradise

The *Phantom* was bigger than most of the ships at Eve's, so it was limited to a wide berth at the end of the huge bay. A tube-shaped gangway swung out toward the hatch and sealed in place against the *Phantom's* side.

Jack rapped on Will's door.

"Come in."

Jack announced, "It's party time." He opened the door and entered Will's room.

Will lay in bed with the pillow over his head.

Jack scolded him, "What is wrong with you, boy?"

"I can't help it. I'm depressed."

"Well, I know exactly what you need to fix that. Come on."

Will followed Jack into the main quarters.

Arasthmus and Regent were engaged in a chess match.

Breel, Laneia and Shanna waited anxiously near the hatch.

Bastille and Celine entered from the pilots' cabin.

Will remarked, "I guess everyone's going."

Jack answered, "They sure are."

Will frowned and asked, "Are you sure it's safe for the women to go?"

Jack replied, "It's dangerous wherever they go, so let's have fun."

"If you say so."

Jack teased them, "We're only here for one night, so don't make any long term commitments.

Everyone laughed.

Bastille opened the hatch. He and Celine entered the gangway tube, followed by Shanna, Laneia and Breel.

Jack urged Will, "Let's go, partner."

They followed the tube into a long, dimly lit corridor. At the end of the corridor was a huge lobby with fancy blue, neon lighting. A bright red sign read, "Welcome to Eve's Garden of Paradise".

Another sign nearby flashed "All weapons prohibited".

Music blared from inside the lounge area. Various species of humans and aliens wandered in and out of the lounge. Will's crew entered the lounge and dispersed.

Will followed Jack to the long L-shaped bar. They sat on the velvet-cushioned seats.

An alien bartender caught Will's attention. It had a frog's head and six arms. It wore an interpreting device on its huge neck and a voicemitter across its wide mouth.

Jack noticed Will's surprise and explained, "He's from Gyrath-407; part amphibian and part human."

Will responded, "Interesting. I've never seen an alien like that."

Jack pointed out, "They're very friendly people. They are also very good listeners. They hear quite a bit of what's said in this place."

The bartender stopped in front of them and greeted them, "Welcome to Eve's. I'm Cookie. What can I get for you?"

Jack answered, "I'll have a whiskey sour."

Will thought for a few seconds and replied, "I'll have an Ice Tea."

Cookie asked, "With hair on it?"

Will looked at Jack for a translation. Jack said, "Yes. Make that a double hair."

Cookie left them.

Jack explained, "He wanted to know if you prefer the Ice Tea with alcohol in it."

Will was slightly embarrassed and said, "I guess you can tell I don't get out much."

The bartender returned with six drinks. He set two down in front of them and moved on to four other patrons at the end of the bar.

Jack held his glass up for a toast. Will raised his glass as well.

Jack exclaimed, "To friendship and prosperity."

Will replied, "I'll second that."

They tapped their glasses and drank.

Will noticed Shanna across the dance floor, socializing with three male strangers. Breel and Laneia were with her so he relaxed.

Jack said, "I'll be right back. Don't go anywhere."

Will remarked dryly, "Where would I go?"

He stared at his glass and gulped its contents down.

Cookie stopped on the way by and asked, "Another for you, sir?"

"Sure."

Cookie returned a moment later with another drink. Will thanked him and watched Shanna.

One of the men placed his arm around her waist. Will became envious.

Jack returned and sat down.

"I saw a couple of old friends I had to speak with."

Two women approached Jack and Will. One of them had long dark hair, pale complexion, and a dark satin dress. The other had auburn hair, slightly tanned and wore a gold tunic.

The brunette spoke first, "Good evening. I'm Mynx and my friend is Neva. We're from Alpha-17."

Jack replied, "I'm Jack Fleming and this is Will Saris."

Mynx asked politely, "Mind if we join you?"

"Not at all."

Mynx sat next to Will and Neva sat next to Jack. Will couldn't help but notice that Shanna was watching him now. He felt good that the shoe was on the other foot.

Will asked, "What brings you all the way out here from Alpha-17?"

Mynx explained, "We work for Galactic Security Services. We're on an assignment."

"I never heard of your company before."

"That's by design. Very few people have."

Jack interrupted, "Neva and I are going to dance for a bit. Are you okay, Will?"

"Sure. Have fun."

Mynx asked, "What brings you out this way?"

"Just a night out with some friends."

Mynx warned, "Be careful. There are shadows in here."

Will wondered what she meant.

Mynx saw the perplexed look on his face. "There are some creatures in here that impersonate humans and they're up to no good."

"I'm sorry. I understand now. What kind of imposters are we talking about?"

"It's not good to talk in a place like this."

Will whispered, "Do these imposters happen to be Weevil?"

Mynx looked sharply at Will. "What do you know of the Weevil?"

"Enough to know who they work for and what they do."

"Perhaps later we could talk in private."

Will replied coolly, "That could be arranged."

Mynx mentioned, "When you arrived, you came in an Attradean ship. Nice paint job but it doesn't quite change the design."

Will became suspicious and said, "So?"

"There's a hefty bounty on your head from Tenemon, the Attradean ruler."

"Let me guess. You're looking to collect on the reward."

Mynx slapped him across the face.

"That was uncalled for."

Jack noticed from the dance floor and laughed.

Will was at a loss for words.

Mynx pointed out, "You're a bit naïve, aren't you?"

"Maybe."

"We're looking for something much bigger than any bounty. I can't discuss it here."

"So what do you want to do?"

Mynx grinned slyly. "I thought you'd never ask. Let's dance."

She took Will by the hand and led him to the dance floor. They danced for several consecutive songs.

****

Shanna tapped Laneia on the arm.

Laneia asked, "What's wrong?"

"Look at Will. What's he think he's doing?"

Breel pointed out, "You're socializing with these men. He doesn't seem too concerned."

Shanna stared angrily at Will and Mynx.

Laneia suggested, "Can you read his mind?"

"Yes, but he'd know."

"Maybe you should go over and join them."

Shanna explained, "If I go over, it will look like I'm keeping tabs on him."

Breel asked, "Well, aren't you?"

Laneia advised Shanna, "Sometimes it's not what it seems. Relax."

Shanna bristled as she watched.

****

Will and Mynx finally sat down at the bar. Jack and Neva already ordered another round of drinks for them.

Will saw the fresh glasses on the bar and commented, "Easy Jack. I've got to get up in the morning."

Jack teased, "Sometimes you have to let your hair down a little bit."

Will picked up his drink and joined Jack in another toast. "Why not?"

Jack said proudly, "To free enterprise in the universe."

Will sipped his drink. He thought about what Jack just said. He busted out laughing and spit on the floor.

Jack asked, "What's the matter?"

Will replied, "That's classy. I like it."

Mynx asked, "What else would you call it? Piracy?"

Will's grin disappeared quickly. "Why would you say that?"

"Piracy is a form of free enterprise."

Jack added, "In a number of ways to be exact."

Another couple joined them.

Mynx introduced the strangers. "This is Kalin and his friend, Sandal."

Will and Jack shook hands with them. Will offered, "Would you care to join us?"

Kalin replied, "Sure. Thanks."

Kalin had a thick black mustache and beard. His hair was shoulder length. He wore blue jeans, a flannel shirt and snakeskin boots.

Sandal was tall and muscular for a female. She wore black jeans, a low-cut white blouse, and black leather boots.

Will asked, "What brings you to this neck of the woods?"

Kalin replied, "I'm unemployed right now. My ship was confiscated by Tenemon's goons and some of my crew was taken prisoner."

Jack asked, "What line of business were you in?"

"I guess you could say I'm an independent merchant."

Mynx remarked to Will, "You guys might have something in common."

Jack asked Sandal, "Do you work with Kalin?"

"No. My husband did. He was taken prisoner by the Attradeans."

"No kidding. I see Tenemon's been busy, lately."

Kalin explained, "I put together a group of mercenaries to go after my ship but there are spies everywhere. My men were captured at the dock."

Will inquired, "Do you have funding to try again?"

"Yes I do. I just don't have the people and no one wants to risk their ship being confiscated."

Will asked Jack, "Are you thinking what I'm thinking?"

"It's got potential."

Mynx asked, "Is there someplace private where we can talk? This is becoming a very sensitive conversation."

Will suggested, "Perhaps we should go back to the ship. I agree that this conversation has taken a serious turn."

Kalin suggested, "I should leave first. Sandal works here. Her shift starts shortly so she'll stay here."

Will asked Sandal, "Can you keep an ear for information that might pertain to us?"

"Gladly."

Will added, "Perhaps, with a little luck, your husband will be coming home soon."

She replied, "That would be nice."

Will instructed Kalin, "Meet us at berth seventeen in a little while."

"Thank you for taking the time to consider this matter."

Will responded, "In the spirit of free enterprise, us merchants need to stick together."

Kalin left his seat while chuckling and walked to the door. He paused in front of three men.

One of the men stared at Kalin.

Kalin stared back and said something.

The man drew a knife from under the table and attacked Kalin.

After a brief scramble, Kalin got off the floor. The other combatant didn't.

Kalin quickly exited the lounge.

The two remaining companions carried their dead comrade out an alternate entrance.

Will asked Cookie, "Could I have one more round for the four of us?"

"Certainly. I'll be right back."

Will watched Shanna carefully to make sure she was safe.

He pondered aloud, "I wonder what that was all about."

Mynx explained, "I think that was the Weevil that ratted Kalin out to the Attradeans."

Jack commented, "Well, I'm glad he handled that well."

Cookie placed four drinks on the bar. He asked, "Will there be anything else?"

"No. Could I pay the tab now?"

"Sure, sir."

Cookie brought over a digital device and pressed in two numbers. "That will be forty credits, sir."

Cookie handed Will the device. Will entered his account code and the amount. Will looked up at Cookie and asked, "What is your transfer number?"

"Why would you need that, sir?"

Will replied sincerely, "I'd like to send you a tip for your friendly service."

Cookie was elated. He exclaimed, "Why thank you, sir!"

Will held the device out and Cookie punched in the codes for an account transfer.

Will entered an amount to transfer into Cookie's account. Cookie thanked him and moved on to other customers.

Will noticed that Shanna glared at him continuously. He pretended not to notice. He proposed a toast. "To new friendships and prosperity."

The four of them raised their glasses and saluted. They finished their drinks and left the lounge together.

****

Shanna was appalled. She poked Laneia and said, "Look at that. Will and Jack are leaving with those two tramps."

Breel remarked, "Maybe you played the game too long. Perhaps Will gave up."

Laneia slapped Breel's arm.

"You shush up. Will shouldn't even be talking to another woman."

Breel asked Shanna, "Are you jealous?"

Laneia reminded Breel, "You shouldn't interfere with women's business. Keep your comments to yourself."

Breel rolled his eyes.

"Perhaps I'll get one more drink from the bar."

He walked away from the table and sat at the bar.

Cookie approached him and asked, "Can I help you, sir?"

"Yes, I'd like a double strong Mindbender."

"Coming right up."

The two men returned from disposing of their friend. They sat next to Breel.

Breel asked, "Can I help you, gentlemen?"

The first man replied, "Just a couple of questions. Who is the girl with you?"

Breel became suspicious and answered, "I really don't know. She doesn't say a whole lot."

The second man asked, "Did she ever do anything strange or mention anything unusual?"

Breel answered, "That's a vague question. Anything females talk about is strange."

The first man explained, "We're looking for a Seer. There's a huge reward and we're willing to share it with you if you have information."

Breel asked, "What if we lied and said she was a Seer? Could we still collect the reward?"

The first man grew impatient and snapped, "This is serious!"

The second man asked, "What ship did you come in on?"

Cookie set down a drink in front of Breel. He overheard part of the conversation.

The first man barked, "We know you're with the two guys who sat here earlier."

Breel grew nervous and said, "It's none of your business who I came in here with."

The second man warned, "We're about to make it our business."

He held his arm straight and a twelve-inch blade slid out from under his sleeve. The first man grabbed Breel's arms and held them back. He was amazingly strong for a human or Weevil.

Cookie's arms stretched across the bar and grabbed both men. He slammed their heads repeatedly into the bar until they were dead.

Breel was shaking. "Thank you so much. Why did you help me?"

Cookie explained, "Your friends sat here earlier. They were very nice to me. These men are Weevil. I hate Weevil."

"I'd better get going. Thank you again."

Breel hurried back to the table with his drink.

Laneia glared at him.

"What did you do to start with those men?"

Breel became upset and replied sharply, "They were Weevil. They wanted to know about a Seer and the ship we came in on."

Shanna grew worried. "I'm sorry, Breel. I never meant to drag you into this mess. You could have been killed."

"Tenemon knows you're alive. Next time we should stick together."

Laneia was embarrassed. She said nothing more.

Breel ordered, "We're leaving now. Come on."

Shanna and Laneia obediently followed.

****

Will, Jack, Mynx and Neva walked down the long corridor.

Kalin waited anxiously in a small alcove. He stepped out of the shadows and teased, "I was afraid you forgot about me."

Will responded, "No, just being careful. Sorry for the wait."

151

They proceeded to the gangway and boarded the *Phantom*.

Kalin was amazed and asked, "How did you get your hands on an Attradean cruiser?"

Will replied, "Would you believe I walked in and took it, with a little help from my friends, of course."

Kalin complimented them, "You guys are good."

They entered the *Phantom* and passed through the main quarters where Arasthmus and Regent were playing chess. Both councilors were surprised to see strangers with Will and Jack.

Will greeted them, "Good evening, gentlemen. We have business to tend to so if you could, make sure no one disturbs us.

Regent answered, "Yes, sir."

The five of them entered Will's quarters. Will and Mynx sat on the bed. Jack leaned against the door. Neva sat at the desk and Kalin sat on the edge of a table.

Will suggested, "Since Mynx and Neva are the honored guests from Galactic Security, why don't you begin?"

Neva explained, "The Attradeans are building large destroyers at an undisclosed location. These ships are equipped with some very high tech weaponry and surveillance systems."

Will asked, "Why isn't the Fleet handling this matter?"

Neva continued, "Because someone is selling the Fleet's new technology to the Attradeans. It's the same technology being used on our new surveillance ships."

Will queried, "You wouldn't be referring to the *Luna C* and the *Ruined Stone,* would you?"

"As a matter of fact, I am. You know of them?"

"Intimately."

The girls waited anxiously for further explanation.

Will disappointed them. "Sorry, that's sensitive information right now."

Mynx whispered in Will's ear, "I can seduce it from you."

Will teased, "You could try but I don't think it would work."

Mynx elaborated, "We're looking for someone to disable the plant and help us find the traitor."

Will casually remarked, "You do know that one of the ships has already departed for Attradea, don't you?"

Mynx looked rattled. "How do you know that?"

Will explained, "It left the Strontarian galaxy with a large escort about four cycles ago."

Neva exclaimed, "I've got to get this information to the Agency and to the Fleet!"

Will suggested, "Why don't we wait until we evaluate the situation further."

Neva inquired, "Why would we do that?"

"A better opportunity might arise if we leave Fleet and GSS out of it."

Neva looked to Mynx for a response.

Mynx nodded her approval of the idea.

Will asked, "What are they offering for the job?"

Mynx answered, "Five million credits."

Jack's eyes lit up and it was his turn to stare at Will for a reaction.

Will kept a straight poker face and said, "No dice. We're going to risk at least one ship and all of our lives to destroy an entire shipbuilding plant, which is likely protected by a military base. Then we're going to snag your snitch and get out of there in one piece."

Mynx said, "Well, Mr. Saris, name your price."

"Twenty million credits into non-Alliance accounts to be designated by us, half up front. A five percent commission for the two of you in the account of your choice, half up front."

Mynx remarked slyly, "I like your style. Consider it done."

Neva complained to Mynx, "They won't pay that kind of money."

"There are some things you can't put a price on."

Neva asked, "How do we explain this?"

Will interjected, "One ship has already left the plant. If they want that ship captured or destroyed, they'll pay it."

Neva asked, "What if they only pay half and default on the rest?"

Will explained, "I fully expect them to default. We will have a destroyer in our possession that's worth a lot more than twenty million credits to the highest bidder. Then, they'll wish they did pay on time."

Mynx asked, "You wouldn't sell to another bidder would you?"

Will teased, "You wouldn't tip our hand to the Fleet or your agency, would you?"

"I see your point. We can make this work."

Neva spoke, "You know what we want. Now it's your turn."

****

Shanna, Laneia and Breel entered the ship.

Regent and Arasthmus were still engaged in their chess match in the main quarters.

Regent asked Breel, "If you are in for the night, would you please close the hatch?"

"Sure. Are Will and Jack back?"

Regent nodded affirmatively. He moved his rook three spaces forward.

Shanna inquired, "Is Will alone?"

Arasthmus declared, "He has company and I wouldn't disturb him if I were you."

Arasthmus focused on a chess move. He slid his bishop diagonally and took Regent's rook.

Regent bellowed, "Ah, you bastard!"

Arasthmus snickered.

Shanna asked, "How about Jack?"

"He's busy as well. They might be a while."

Shanna became angry and charged toward Will's quarters.

Regent hollered, "Shanna, he specifically requested not to be disturbed."

Shanna yelled back from the hallway, "I'll disturb him anytime I want!"

She barged into Will's quarters in a fit of rage. She looked around the room and realized that they had an important discussion going on. Shanna became red-faced with embarrassment.

Will asked, "Is there something important that you wanted? We're discussing business."

Shanna whimpered sheepishly, "No. I'm sorry. I, uh, never mind."

Shanna retreated from Will's berth and returned to the main quarters.

Laneia asked, "What happened?"

Shanna burst into tears and said, "I made a fool of myself."

Laneia suggested, "Let's go back to Eve's and get another drink."

Breel advised, "Don't you think we should call it a night?"

Laneia defended Shanna, "It was an innocent mistake. Right now, Shanna needs us."

Breel rolled his eyes and muttered, "Just great."

Regent asked, "Shall I inform Will of your whereabouts when he comes out?"

Breel answered, "I think that would be a good idea."

Breel, Laneia and Shanna departed the ship and returned to Eve's.

****

Will asked Kalin, "What exactly do you want out of this?"

"I want my ship back. The Attradeans impounded it and my crew was imprisoned. I can only offer twenty five thousand credits."

Will countered, "If we recover your ship and crew, will you assist us in two other ventures?"

Kalin asked curiously, "What kind of ventures?"

"We're going to recover the Eye of Icarus and rescue the Seers of the Eye from Attrades."

Everyone looked at Will in surprise.

"You mean the Eye really exists?"

"Yes it does."

Jack asked nervously, "Are you sure you know what you're doing?"

"Yes I do. Eventually we're going to disrupt Tenemon's recruiting ploys as well."

Kalin responded, "So you want my help in addition to the twenty-five thousand credits?"

Will laughed. "No, no, no. Just your help. I think we can make more than enough in the long run by working together."

"I'd be a fool to turn this kind of offer down."

Mynx pressed Will, "You haven't answered our question yet, Will. What do you want out of this?"

"Just a little fun."

Mynx replied in sinister fashion, "I like fun."

Jack asked, "Will you girls be spending the night on board?"

Neva answered, "No, I'll return to the lounge and arrange for a transport. I'll go back and relay the offer to the agency."

Will asked Jack, "Why don't you show Kalin to his berth? Then, we'll escort Neva back to the lounge."

Mynx announced, "I have a few things I'd like to discuss with Will alone. We'll be out in a little while."

Jack kidded, "Some business, huh?"

Mynx countered, "Wouldn't you like to know?"

Jack led Neva and Kalin from Will's berth and closed the door.

Mynx wasted no time in seducing Will. She undressed him while she kissed him. When she had Will unclothed, she slid out of her dress and pressed Will down on the bed. They kissed passionately and reveled in each other's arms.

Mynx asked, "Will you tell me about the other ships?"

Will replied, "Do you want to end this little escapade now?"

She looked into his eyes lustily.

"Forget I asked."

****

An hour later, Will emerged from his berth. He crossed the hall to the lavatory area alone. After a quick shower, he dressed and returned to the main quarters.

Will was surprised to see Regent and Arasthmus still involved in their chess match. "You guys are still at it."

Regent confessed, "Arasthmus is a worthy opponent."

Will sat down next to Regent and watched a few moves.

Arasthmus mentioned, "Your friends went back to Eve's."

Will asked, "Did Jack and Neva go, too?"

"No. They're up front with Bastille and Celine. I believe they're waiting for you."

"Thanks, guys."

Will entered the cockpit. Neva was briefing Bastille on the suspected location of the Attradean factory and base.

Jack acknowledged Will, "I see you've concluded business."

"Yes and productive it was."

"I think you handled things quite well."

Will beamed.

Neva said, "I'm going back to the lounge. I'll keep you posted on any new information I receive."

Will replied, "Jack and I will escort you. I hear it's dangerous around there, particularly if you're alone."

Neva graciously accepted the offer.

Jack and Will escorted Neva back to "Eve's". They entered the lounge portion of the establishment and proceeded to the bar.

Sandal approached them and warned, "Your friends are in trouble. Look in the corner."

Will looked down the bar toward the corner. Two men stood behind Shanna and two stood next to Breel and Laneia. Will noticed that Breel and Laneia were held at knifepoint.

Sandal added, "They know that the girl is a Seer."

Shanna refused to answer questions and one of the men slapped her.

Will instinctively rushed across the bar and tackled him. He punched the man twice in the face. Another man jumped on his

157

back and rode him to the floor. The other men were distracted from Breel and Laneia by Will's attack.

Jack joined the fray and tackled one of them. Breel turned on the other and knocked him to the ground.

Neva pulled out her comm-link and dialed three digits. She ordered, "Nester, I need a hit team at the pickup point now. We have trouble here, class 5."

After a short pause, Neva screamed, "What do you mean 'negative'? Get a team down here now!"

Neva shoved the comm-link back in her pocket and quickly studied the other clientel. She recognized three more Weevil in human form.

Neva went to the bar and yelled to Sandal, "There are more Weevil over there. We're outnumbered. Can you help us?"

Sandal opened a drawer and took out a knife. She looked at Cookie for approval. Cookie reminded her, "You know the rules. If you use a weapon in here, you're fired and banned from the premises."

Sandal replied, "Yeah. I'm sorry."

Cookie encouraged her, "Do what you gotta' do, girl."

Sandal jumped over the bar and went to Will's aid.

One man grabbed Will by the shoulder from behind. Shanna watched in horror as blood appeared on Will's shoulder from the man's grip.

Shanna grabbed two glasses and slammed them upside down into the table. The rims broke and shattered glass onto the floor. Shanna took the two stems and slammed them into the man's temples.

The man fell to the floor and shook violently. The flesh began to fall off of his body, revealing a horrible insect-like creature.

Sandal dove on another assailant and planted the knife in its head. She pulled Will off of the man but saw that the claws from the man's hand were buried in the front of Will's shoulder. Will seemed to be in a daze.

Shanna grabbed the arm and began to pull the claw from Will's shoulder.

Sandal screamed, "Wait! Don't do that!"

Shanna was confused and asked, "What's wrong?"

Sandal severed the arm from the man at the elbow. She explained, "If you pull it out, you'll kill him. Let's get him out of here."

Shanna and Sandal got Will to his feet and escorted him out of the lounge. Laneia caught up with them and helped move Will.

Jack rolled across the floor in a battle with one of the men.

Neva broke a chair and took the spindle from the seat. She stabbed one of the men in the back of the neck. He fell to the floor motionless.

Breel slammed the remaining attacker into the concrete wall, shattering his head. Breel snapped the neck of another and went to Jack's aid. He threw the assailant off of Jack.

Neva stabbed another man in the ear with the spindle. He shivered violently and fell to the floor. The flesh fell from his body revealing another of the horrible creatures.

There were no more attackers. Jack, Neva and Breel rushed out of the lounge and down the corridor to the gangway.

VIII.   Flirting with Death

Regent checkmated Arasthmus.

Arasthmus complained, "I should have put you away when I had the chance."

Shanna hollered from outside the hatch. "Arasthmus! Will needs help."

The girls dragged Will through the hatch.

Will was delirious and feverish.

Arasthmus and Regent cleared the table off. Regent retrieved a plastic cover from a nearby cabinet and blanketed the table. He and Arasthmus took Will by the arms and helped him onto the table. The Weevil's arm still dangled from Will's shoulder.

Arasthmus was shocked and inquired, "What's going on here?"

Breel answered, "We were attacked by Weevil in human form."

Arasthmus lifted the arm and examined the claws. "Wow. The claws have extended into his shoulder. I've never seen anything like this."

Mynx entered the main quarters. She hurried to Will's side.

"Are you sure they were Weevil, Neva?"

"Yes, I'm sure. We were ambushed at the lounge. I called in a hit team but Nester denied my request."

Mynx became enraged and snapped, "That rat! Who gave him the authority to deny a request for support?"

Jack asked Mynx, "Is there anyone you can trust at the agency?"

"Yes. I do have a close friend I can count on."

"See what he can tell you about this Nester character. He sounds suspicious."

Will groggily asked Jack, "Can you set up non-alliance accounts for everyone on board."

Jack replied, "Sure. What about the girls' commissions?"

"Forget that."

Neva and Mynx looked surprised at Will.

Will coughed but managed a smile.

He instructed Jack, "Make them equal partners. I think they're going to be active players in this game whether they like it or not."

Mynx looked at the Weevil's arm and instructed Arasthmus, "Cut across the back of the hand until you see the tendons."

Arasthmus was uncertain about the procedure but obeyed. After peeling back the skin, he asked, "What now?"

Mynx took a small bottle from her pocket and sprayed the tendons. The cold spray caused the tendons to contract and withdraw the claws from Will's shoulder. The arm fell lifelessly to the floor.

Mynx examined the wound and informed them, "He's been injected with poison."

Shanna added, "He was injured on the other side of his shoulder as well.

Arasthmus pulled Will's shirt down further and looked at the backside of his shoulder.

He asked Mynx, "What do you think? You seem to be the expert on Weevil."

Mynx lowered her head and explained sadly, "That much poison is lethal. He probably has half a cycle to live."

Will sobbed, "That sucks."

Arasthmus yelled, "There must be something we can do! We can't just let him die."

Mynx muttered sadly, "If there was, I'd know."

Will coughed up a small amount of blood.

Jack left the quarters, teary-eyed.

Tears rolled down Shanna's cheeks. "Can we give him some privacy? I'd like to spend some time alone with him."

Regent and Arasthmus picked Will up and carried him into his cabin.

Regent said solemnly, "I'm gonna' miss you, friend."

Arasthmus added, "Who else can I take care of? I'll miss you, too."

Will smiled weakly and waved with his fingers. His eyes filled with tears.

Shanna quietly asked Breel and Laneia, "Can you keep everyone out for a while?"

Breel asked, "Why?"

"I'm gonna' try something."

Shanna closed the door and knelt next to Will.

Will squeezed her hand and said, "I love you Shanna. If only I had the chance to show you."

She sobbed as he lost consciousness.

Shanna threw herself on Will's chest. She begged like a little child, "Will, please don't leave me."

Shanna searched the drawers and found a shaving kit equipped with a box of razor blades and three towels. She took out a razor and cut Will's shirt off. She uttered several prayers in the Yordic language. She then cut into Will's chest, making several deep lines until a Yordic symbol was formed. The blood flowed slowly from the wounds.

Shanna sopped up the blood with the towel. She cut the same lines in each of Will's wrists. She placed a towel under each wrist to catch the blood.

Shanna ran her hand along Will's face. She sobbed and said, "I love you, Will."

Shanna removed her robe and cut the same lines on her chest, over her heart. She then cut the same lines on her wrists. After uttering more incantations, she climbed on top of Will. She leaned over him, placing her hands on his. The blood flowed from her wrists onto his and from her chest onto his. She gazed sadly at his face, praying constantly.

Shanna could feel the poison from his blood mingling with hers.

She began to feel faint. She climbed off of Will and knelt in front of him. She prayed, "My life for his. My life for his. My life for his."

****

A crowd had formed outside the room.

Laneia sat with her back against the door. She could hear Shanna's words faintly and feared that she might take her life.

Mynx pressured Laneia and Breel, "We should go inside. What's she doing in there?"

Breel chastised them, "Grant Shanna some privacy with Will."

Mynx pressed the issue, "Why the secrecy?"

"She's a Seer. Maybe she can do something for him."

Laneia promised, "We'll let you know if anything changes."

Everyone finally dispersed.

****

Shanna felt her life slipping away from her until she lost consciousness.

Laneia heard the thud as Shanna hit the floor.

She hollered, "Shanna, are you alright? Shanna?"

Laneia looked at Breel for direction.

Breel suggested, "I think it's time to go in."

They burst into the room and were horrified at the bloody mess.

Laneia moaned, "What has she done?"

"Those wounds are symbols. It's some kind of ritual."

Shanna lay on her back, her bare chest covered with streaks of blood, as were her wrists and hands. Small pools of blood collected on the floor.

Will's body was bloody in the same manner.

Laneia asked, "What do we do, Breel?"

"Do you trust her?"

"What do you mean?"

"Do you believe that she could help him?"

"Of course I do, but I don't see how that helps."

"Let's clean everything up. There's no need to frighten everyone."

"Is she alive?"

Breel checked her pulse. "Yes she is. Wash both of them up and we'll put them in another room."

Laneia sobbed as she washed the blood from the wounds on Shanna and Will's bodies. Tears streamed down her cheeks.

"Breel, the wounds aren't bleeding anymore!"

"Keep believing. Maybe they'll be okay."

Breel wiped the blood from the floor. As soon as Will and Shanna were clean, Breel carried them into another berth. He placed them side by side on a bed and closed the door.

Laneia finished removing the covers from the bed and tossed them into a bag. She suggested to Breel, "We should get some clothes for them."

"Shanna has a cloak in her room. Will doesn't need a shirt."

"But what about the marks on his chest? What will everyone say?"

"You're right. I'll find something."

Laneia entered the pilots' cabin and asked Bastille, "How long before we reach Yord?"

"Not much longer. Is something wrong?"

"Yes."

Bastille pointed to a yellow planet ahead of them. "There she is."

Bastille looked at Laneia's teary eyes and red face.

"What is it, Laneia?"

Laneia shook her head sideways. She couldn't answer.

"Laneia, we're friends here. Talk to me. Has Will passed away?"

She explained what transpired in the room and was visibly shaken.

Bastille spoke softly to her, "You've never seen a Seer work, have you?"

"No."

"I have."

"Then you knew she was a witch?"

"Not a witch, a Seer. Witches delve in the unholy. Seers beseech the Almighty. No one understands them and I sure don't try. I do know that they can summon powerful forces."

Bastille checked several screens on the tracking monitor.

"Laneia, you and Breel did right by concealing Shanna's work. There are many who fear Seers because of their power."

"What should we do now?"

"Leave them be. There's nothing any of us can do for them."

"Thanks, Bastille."

"You're welcome."

Laneia exited the pilots' cabin. She leaned against the wall, shaken from the vision of what Will and Shanna looked like in the room.

Breel entered the main quarters and saw Laneia. He sat next to her and hugged her. She nestled her head against him and closed her eyes. In a few minutes, they were both asleep.

****

Will's eye twitched. He opened his eyes and rubbed the side of his head. He strained to sit up but he felt weak. When he turned his head, he saw Shanna. Suddenly he remembered the poison.

Will wondered what was going on. He felt better but in an odd sort of way. He turned onto his side and gazed at Shanna's face. Something wasn't right. Shanna looked very pale. Will whispered into her ear, "Shanna, it's me."

Shanna didn't budge. Will propped himself up and stared at her face from a different angle. She was breathing but faintly. Will shook her but she didn't move. He slid the cloak back and saw the scars over her heart.

Will thought, "That's strange. She healed like the Firenghi do."

Will leaned forward and kissed her. He spoke softly, "Wake up, Shanna. Are you okay?"

Will grew nervous. He shook her and pleaded, "Please, Shanna, wake up."

Suddenly, Shanna trembled. Her eyes grew wide with horror and she gasped for air.

Will hugged her tightly. "It's okay, Shanna. It's okay."

She coughed and gasped. Finally she said, "Will, is it really you?"

"Yes, it is."

"Oh, thank goodness!"

"I don't understand what you did but it worked."

Shanna was elated. "I can't believe it!"

Will remarked, "So you really do have magical powers."

"Yes, although this one was a surprise." Shanna looked down at the floor shamefully. She asked humbly, "Do you still want me after all this?"

Will was taken aback by her question.

"Of course. Why wouldn't I?"

Shanna became worried. "I've got to tell you what happened."

"About what?"

"About how I healed you."

"Take it easy. You're getting all worked up."

Shanna said persistently, "Look on your chest and your wrists."

Will looked at the scars and noticed that Shanna had the same scars. He asked curiously, "What did you do?"

166

Shanna fidgeted. "It's an ancient rite that I learned from the elder Seer."

Will commented, "It looks like it was pretty dangerous."

"It was. In essence, I offered my life for yours. By virtue of love, I think I was granted my life back."

Will asked in a teasing manner, "How do you know I love you?"

"Because you kissed me, after all that we've been through."

"Oh, come on. That wasn't a kiss. This is."

Will leaned over Shanna and kissed her passionately. Will felt invigorated and strong. He caressed Shanna's golden blond locks.

He asked teasingly, "Could you handle being a pirate's woman?"

"I certainly could. Could you handle being a lady pirate's man?"

Will teased, "I'd have to think about it. Well, okay."

He stood up and reached for Shanna's hand. He helped her up. She adjusted her cloak and stood up.

Will thought, "She is so beautiful. I'd love to squeeze her tightly and kiss her."

Shanna pulled Will close to her. She stared into his eyes and said, "Why don't you squeeze me tightly and kiss me."

Will was surprised. "What did you say?"

Shanna replied, "You heard me."

Will answered back, "But I always cloak my thoughts."

Shanna giggled. "Isn't that funny? I guess I can read through your 'cloak'."

Shanna looked at her wrists and was amazed at how fast the cuts on her skin healed.

She said, "I don't understand how I healed so quickly. How did this happen?"

Will explained, "If the rite that you performed resulted in our blood mingling, you probably have some of the healing qualities that I had in my blood. I didn't think males could pass these traits, though."

Shanna asked, "How do you feel now?"

167

"I feel different."

"Perhaps you're a Seer, too. Maybe you'll have some of my powers."

Will queried, "What other powers do you have?"

"You and I need to spend some time with Mariel. She'll need to educate both of us on these things."

Will was silent for a moment as he took in everything that happened. He thought about how badly he felt when Shanna shut him out.

Shanna apologized, "I'm so sorry. I didn't know that you really felt this way. I thought you just wanted to use me as a convenience."

Will explained, "I really do care for you. I want to know everything about you."

"I would really like that."

Will felt a union develop between Shanna and him. He was elated about it and couldn't wait to consummate this union.

Shanna blushed and suggested, "You'd better get out there and check on your crew before we get into something serious."

Will kissed Shanna and walked out the door.

Shanna exited behind him and went to her berth.

Breel and Laneia stared at Will in amazement.

Breel asked excitedly, "Will, is it really you?"

Will put his arms around the two of them. "Of course it's me. It's great to be back."

Will entered the pilots' cabin.

Bastille, Celine and Mynx discussed coordinates and locations. They looked up and were surprised to see him.

Mynx stood up and checked him out from head to toe. She exclaimed, "Will, you're alive! I've never seen anyone survive one poisoning let alone two."

Will responded, "I have someone special looking out for me."

"Well, I'm glad to see you're back."

Will patted Bastille on the shoulder. "How are things going?"

"We'll be landing on Yord shortly."

Mynx informed him, "The money is in the bank. I talked to my contact and gave him the information as you requested."

Will remarked, "This should be interesting."

"It already is. My contact got back to me already. Nester left no record of Neva's request or his denial of support. Another interesting point: he left to meet with a contact immediately after he was notified that our ship was going to the Strontarian Galaxy."

"Good. Can we track him with the long range sensors?"

Celine replied, "If the *Phantom's* sensors are anything like ours, I think we can."

"Good. That makes looking for the planet where they're building the destroyers a whole lot easier."

Will looked at the monitor and saw the planet Yord.

He asked, "Any word from the *Ruined Stone*?"

Celine answered, "Yes. They have information for us. They're returning soon. The *Luna C* will also be back soon. Talia says that Maya has important news for you."

Will paced the cabin. "Good. Where's Jack?"

Mynx responded, "He's with Kalin and Neva. Probably in Kalin's quarters."

Will left the cabin and walked through the main quarters.

Arasthmus was ecstatic. He commented, "You look pretty well for a dead man."

Will kidded, "I don't have time to die."

Regent replied happily, "I'm so glad to see you looking well."

Will continued down the corridor to Kalin's berth. He rapped on the door.

"What is it?" yelled Kalin.

Will entered the berth and held his arms out. He exclaimed, "Well!"

Jack jumped up and screamed, "Will! You're alive!"

Will hugged him and said, "I certainly hope so."

Neva hugged him and exclaimed, "What a surprise? It's especially good to see you up and about."

Kalin was relieved. He shook Will's hand and said, "I was worried that we wouldn't be able to execute the plan without you."

"Why's that?

"Because you seem to have all the answers."

Will replied humbly, "It's all about opportunity."

Jack quipped, "At the very least, we're a wealthy bunch of people."

Will explained, "When we land on Yord, we'll take a little time to unwind. Talia and Maya will be back soon and they have important information for us."

Will looked around the room. He asked, "Where's Sandal?"

Kalin replied, "Oh, she's enjoying a good long sleep before she returns to Eve's. It's been a while since she had a bed to sleep in."

"How come?"

"The Attradeans destroyed her home when they took her husband."

"That's terrible."

"Now you see why she's committed to our cause."

"So we have a cause?"

"Yes we do and you're the leader."

Will was proud of his friends. "I'll see you all on Yord. I have some things to tend to."

Will exited Kalin's berth and walked to the stairs. He thought about Shanna and used his telepathy.

"Hi, Shanna. Want me to come up?"

To his delight she responded. "Sure. I'm waiting for you."

"I'm on my way."

A few minutes later, Will entered Shanna's room. Three candles were lit and placed around her quarters. She lay across the bed on her side, wearing a sheer negligee.

Will lay next to her. He gazed into her eyes and thought about how much he missed her.

Shanna pleaded, "Please don't ever leave me, Will.

"I promise I won't. You're stuck with me."

Will placed his arm around her and kissed her tenderly. She rolled on top of him and placed her hands on both sides of his cheeks. She kissed him passionately. They made love and consummated their union.

IX.   A New Home

Shanna kissed Will on the cheek. He opened his eyes and smiled at her.

"I'll see you later on, Will. I want to spend some time with my sister."

"Okay. I'll see you at dinner."

Shanna warned, "Don't be late."

Will kidded, "I'm never late."

Will got out of his bed and looked into the mirror. He couldn't believe how fast his life changed over the last several days. He dressed himself and exited the berth.

He arrived in the large, empty hall and sat at the head table. A servant brought in a ewer of wine and poured some in a glass for him.

The servant asked, "Do you really think you can free the other Seers and bring them home?"

Will sipped from the glass and said, "I think so."

"That would be great. We'll all pray for you on your mission."

"Thanks. I'm sure we can use it."

The servant thanked Will and left the hall.

Mariel entered a short time later and saw Will sitting alone. He acknowledged her with a friendly wave.

"Come on up, Mariel."

Mariel walked regally to the table and stood before Will.

"I see you have much on your mind."

"If you only knew. Would you sit with me for a little bit?"

Mariel walked around the table and took a seat next to Will.

Will opened his shirt and revealed the scars on his chest. He then held out his wrists revealing scars of the same symbols.

Mariel was stunned.

"What happened, Will? Who did this to you?"

Will pointed to the scars on his shoulder from the Weevil claw.

"Shanna saved my life."

Mariel couldn't believe her ears.

"Shanna performed this rite on you?"

"Yes she did. I understand there are complications as a result of this."

Mariel was at a loss for words. "I don't know what to say. She shouldn't be alive."

"How about telling me what this means to us? We have a big mission ahead of us and before we risk our lives to save the Seers, I want to know what's happening to us."

Mariel smiled. "I think destiny has caught up with you."

"You'll have to explain a little better than that."

"You and Shanna are united as one. Her powers are your powers. Your powers are now her powers."

"We pretty much figured that part out. What powers are we talking about?"

"You will be one with the Seers and the Eye. What they see, you will know, as will Shanna. The range of your telepathic abilities has increased tenfold. You will have the power to heal others in certain situations. There will be certain powers that are specific to you that you must discover for yourself."

"What about Shanna?"

"Shanna will be like you. She will be able to shift. Her senses have become keener. She will, for all practical purposes, be just like a Firenghi."

Will asked curiously, "Are there other Firenghi on Yord?"

"Yes, there are."

"Were they banished here by the Fleet as well?"

"Yes, but for different reasons. When the Great War started, the Firenghi moved to another planet. The planet was a frozen, desolate wasteland on the surface, but underneath was a perfect paradise. The Fleet later decided that it was a strategic location for a base, so they displaced the Firenghi females to this planet. The males were conscripted into the Fleet and given the most dangerous tasks. As a result, most were killed. Ironically, the Fleet also decided that Yord was an ideal location for a secret base. The base was built but, when the Attradeans took over the quadrant, it became too dangerous to operate it. As a result, the Fleet abandoned it."

Will wondered aloud, "Why is it that I despise the Fleet more and more each day?"

Mariel asked, "Do you see now why you and Shanna could rule Yord? These are your people. Those who aren't Firenghi are Shanna's people."

"That does put a different spin on things."

"Why wouldn't you want to rule Yord?"

"I've never been a ruler nor did I ever plan to be. My dream has always been to roam the galaxies without obligation to anyone. I want to harass our enemies. I want to plunder their spoils and cause discontent among their forces. I don't know how being a ruler fits in to all of this."

"Does Shanna feel this way, too?"

"It seems so. Let me think about this. Perhaps there is a better way to handle this problem."

"Wise move, Will."

"Thanks, Mariel."

Mariel excused herself from the table and left the hall.

Will sipped from the glass and pondered the possibilities. He thought, "Seers are reclusive in nature and rulers are bound to their kingdoms. Perhaps that would allow me to be a renegade part of the time and rule Yord the remainder of the time. I could have the best of both worlds."

Will's friends entered the room.

Will left the high table and joined them on the main floor.

When he saw the servant waiting dutifully by the door, he requested, "Can you bring glasses for my friends and more wine?"

The servant nodded and left the hall.

Will sat down next to Jack and asked, "What do you think so far?"

Jack exclaimed, "I'm still in shock over this deal with Mynx and Neva. We're wealthy individuals because of it. How did you think of all those details in a few minutes?"

"Ask Regent and Arasthmus. They can explain it much better in terms of chess."

Shanna entered the hall and walked elegantly toward the table. Will sensed instinctively that she arrived. He was stunned by her beauty.

Shanna wore a long, flowing light blue robe. It was wrapped snugly around her body, highlighting her slim figure. Her long gold locks were wrapped in a bun with two curly strands running down each side of her head.

The table was quiet as she approached.

Mynx broke the silence. "Wow! Will, you dog!"

Will whispered innocently, "Why am I a dog?"

Mynx teased, "She even looks good to me."

They chuckled.

Will stood up and offered Shanna his seat. He retrieved a seat from another table for himself. He used his telepathy and said, "You are by far, the most beautiful woman I have ever seen."

She answered telepathically, "You made me a woman last night. You made me your woman."

Shanna addressed everyone, "Good morning. I hope you all slept well last night."

Laneia remarked pleasantly, "It sure looks like you had a good night."

Shanna smiled gracefully.

Will announced, "I'm sure everyone has met Kalin, Mynx and Neva by now. They are new and important members of our group."

Will noticed that Mariel and three other women stood in the doorway.

Mariel spoke telepathically to Will and Shanna, "Do you mind if we monitor your meeting? We'd like to know if we could help in some way."

Will and Shanna both assented.

Will paced the floor around the table and explained, "We're going to the Strontarian galaxy." Then he asked Bastille, "Have you or Celine had any luck in tracking the ship we talked about?"

Bastille replied, "Yes we have. The sensors are locked on and the computer is logging information about the ship, its origin and its course. Soon we'll have a projected destination."

"Excellent. When we reach our destination, I'll be counting on the *Luna C* and the *Ruined Stone* to provide cover on key buildings and defenses."

Mynx interrupted, "You didn't tell me that the *Luna C* and the *Ruined Stone* were involved in this operation."

Will kidded, "You didn't say 'please'. Is that a problem?"

"No, that's great!"

"Our primary mission is to take out the facility which is building destroyers. The reason this is so important is that the destroyers have been equipped with vital surveillance equipment compliments of a traitor in either the Fleet, Galactic Security Services or possibly both. If those ships can cloak, the war is pretty much over. Their firepower would be phenomenal and they'd be untouchable."

Will took a sip of wine and continued, "Mynx and Neva will deal with Nester. That's an agency problem. We have to keep a protocol if we are to interact with these groups."

Neva sniped, "I want that little weasel."

"Then you girls understand your role. Take care of the mole."

Will walked behind Bastille and Celine. He placed his hands on each one's shoulder. "I want you to find the database and download any information about the installation of the surveillance equipment."

Celine suggested, "That might be a job for Saphoro. Neither of us can do that."

"We'll see if she cares to join us. You'll remain on the ship then. When you receive this information, I want you to learn all that you can about the equipment; how to remove it and how to install it on the *Phantom*."

Jack said giddily, "I know where you're going with this."

Will nodded with a smile.

Jack added, "Tenemon's going to have a stroke when this is over."

Will quipped, "Saves me from having to kill him."

Everyone laughed. They waited anxiously for more details.

Will stood near the end of the table and sipped coolly from his glass.

"We're looking to land where the Attradeans have been impounding ships. Kalin, you'll take Breel and Laneia with you. Search for your ship. When you find it, get on board and contact Bastille or Celine. I want you out of there quickly with your ship for other reasons."

Will walked behind Shanna and placed an arm on her shoulder. "Shanna and I will find and rescue Kalin's crew. When we do, we'll have the *Luna C* or the *Ruined Stone* extract us."

Will walked over to Jack.

"Jack, you'll take Regent and Arasthmus with you. You'll protect Saphoro and cause as much mayhem as possible. Take whatever weapons you need from the *Phantom*."

Kalin asked, "What about their defenses? I'm sure the facility is well guarded."

"I'm glad you asked. We're going to tow the *Luna C* and the *Ruined Stone* into firing positions nearby. This allows for them to be cloaked. On sensors, the *Phantom* looks like just another Attradean cruiser. The *Luna C* and the *Ruined Stone* will provide firepower when we encounter resistance. If you're stuck, you'll contact them by comm-link and they'll handle it from there."

Mynx asked, "Why do you want to know about their surveillance equipment?"

"Do you remember when I said that the destroyer would be worth a lot more to the highest bidder and that GSS would wish that they had paid that balance?"

Mynx answered skeptically, "Yes, but..."

Will continued, "We're going to remove that equipment from the destroyer and install it on the *Phantom*. We'll initiate a bidding war for the destroyer and sell it. I'm sure Tenemon will give his first born to retain that ship."

Laneia kidded back, "Hey, that's not funny. I'm already gone."

Will teased, "Then he has no collateral except lots and lots of credits."

Mynx added, "But so do GSS and the Fleet."

Will pondered aloud, "What a tough choice that would be? Now how do we keep everyone happy? We provide Tenemon the opportunity to get his destroyer back, but with a few of us onboard. When they depart from the pickup point and the balance of credits has been transferred, I'm sure they'll want to cloak and destroy us. When they realize they've been had, we'll take over the ship and do whatever is necessary to escape with it."

Neva asked, "Where would you hide a ship that big?"

"On Yord. We'll park it in the bay and forget about it. The Fleet is happy because Tenemon doesn't have it. They have no idea who the pirates were that took it. They know the cloaking device and surveillance equipment wasn't on board. As far as Mynx and Neva are concerned, this destroyer didn't have the equipment installed. The others were destroyed so the problem is solved. As far as GSS is concerned, the mole issue is also resolved thanks to Mynx and Neva."

Regent asked, "When do we rescue the Seers?"

Will sat down next to Shanna and held her hand. "While all of this is happening, Tenemon's kingdom will be in chaos. We'll return to Yord and regroup. Shortly after, we'll strike Tenemon's palace and rescue the Seers. I have a personal appointment with Tenemon."

Laneia asked, "You're not going to kill him, are you?"

"No. I just want to cause him lots of misery. Besides, he's still your father."

Laneia seemed relieved. "Thank you, Will. I despise him but it would kill my mother if she knew I participated in his murder."

Will patted her on the back and said, "I thoroughly understand."

He paused at the head of the table and asked, "Any questions?"

Everyone clapped and cheered.

Will added, "It will be a few days before we are ready to leave, so I suggest you have a good time between now and then."

Will took Shanna's hand and said to her, "We have some things to discuss with Mariel. I think you'll be pleased."

Will's friends vacated the hall.

Shanna smiled and accompanied him to the hall entrance. Mariel applauded graciously. "That's quite an ambitious plan you have. Do you really think it'll work?"

"I think it's destined to be. Isn't that what you told me?"

Mariel complimented Shanna, "You have become quite a woman."

"Thank you, Mariel."

"I guess you won't be resuming your duties as a Seer anymore."

Shanna nestled against Will and replied, "I guess not."

Will inquired, "Can we sit down and discuss our situation? I'd like to make a proposal."

Mariel answered, "Of course."

They proceeded to the head table. Will and Shanna sat together in the middle. Mariel sat next to Will and her three aides sat next to Shanna.

Mariel sensed what was coming and had difficulty containing her excitement. She turned her chair toward Will and Shanna.

She remarked, "I trust this will be quite interesting, this proposal of yours."

"Yes and I don't think it's quite the proposal everyone is expecting."

Shanna wondered what Will was up to. She didn't want to enter his mind and ruin his announcement so she waited anxiously.

Will explained, "I've considered many of the options available to me and how they affect everyone involved in my life. I want to address a most important issue in my life first. I'd like to ask Shanna if she'd consent to be my wife."

Will gazed at Shanna and waited expectantly for her response.

Shanna covered her face. Her jaw was agape and her face reddened. She was awestruck.

"I don't know what to say?"

Shanna looked excitedly at Mariel and her aides, then back to Will.

"Of course, I'll be your wife."

Shanna jumped up and down, screaming. She hugged Will and kissed him.

Will stopped her and said, "There's more to this which requires the presence of Mariel, since she is in charge of most things that go on around Yord."

The women waited anxiously for Will to give further details. Shanna was still awestruck and sat with her hands clenched together tightly.

Will explained, "Since I left the academy, I've learned a lot about the Fleet, my heritage and historical events that I never suspected could occur. I've considered Mariel's proposal to rule Yord and I would like to make it known that if Shanna chooses to rule Yord, then I will rule by her side."

Shanna was even more stunned by this revelation than the marriage proposal.

"But, Will! What about your crew and your ship? What about traveling around the galaxies? That was your dream."

"Yes it was and it still is."

"But why would you give that up?"

"We're not giving it up. Mariel told me that Seers are reclusive. That is the perfect cover for us to continue our

179

escapades. We'll build Yord back into the economic power that it once was. We'll establish allies by breaking Tenemon's hold on many of the alien races. We'll become the center of a new alliance that will someday restore peace to the universe."

Shanna's eyes filled with tears. "Oh, Will. I am so happy."

Mariel asked Shanna, "Would you accept the responsibility to rule Yord?"

Shanna asked, "But how can I rule Yord. I'm not royalty."

Mariel explained, "Your mother was the first ruler of Yord. She foresaw the Attradeans attacking Yord and decided that the only way for you to survive was to develop your skills as a Seer and take on the role of Priestess of the Eye. The other four Seers were selected specifically to tutor you."

Mariel sipped from her glass. "I already know about Will's lineage. The Firenghi that live among us will be proud to see Will as your male counterpart."

Shanna was so surprised. She stood up giddily and almost fell. Will put his arm around her waist and sat her on his lap.

Mariel decided, "We'll arrange for the wedding to be in twelve cycles. That will give you time to resolve your current issues and for you to learn etiquette. Your positions will give you immunity from persecution for any events that occur in your other life outside of Yord."

Shanna asked, "Can I tell everyone?"

Mariel replied, "Of course. Go and spread your good news."

Shanna pulled Will by the hand. Will thanked Mariel and followed Shanna out of the hall. They raced around the facility like little kids, telling everyone they could find about their good news.

****

The next morning, Will awoke in his quarters. He groggily climbed out of the bed. He thought about everything he decided yesterday. It felt good to have all those weights lifted off of his back.

Will crossed the hall to the lavatory and showered. He wondered how it would feel to be the ruler of a kingdom. Then he remembered Tenemon.

"Boy, he'll be angry with me! He can't do a thing about it as his empire crumbles to the ground."

Will considered if it wouldn't be better to keep his role on Yord a secret. He didn't want to endanger the people of Yord.

Will returned to his quarters and opened the cabinet drawers. Someone took the liberty of supplying him with clothes. He examined the selection and was pleased.

After dressing, he entered the main quarters.

Regent and Arasthmus were debating some insane issue when they noticed him.

Arasthmus greeted him first, "Good morning, Will. You're looking well, today."

"Thanks, Arasthmus."

"Congratulations on your new appointment."

"Thank you."

"I've been thinking about some of the responsibilities I'll have on Yord. I'll have to appoint individuals to various positions. Perhaps the two of you will be able to help fill them.

Arasthmus was elated. "I would be honored to serve under you."

Regent smiled but didn't respond.

Will asked, "What's wrong, Regent?"

"I think I would be satisfied just to see Keira safe again."

"I understand your feelings. Perhaps when things are behind us, we'll discuss it further."

Regent explained, "I would be honored to stay on as an advisor in some capacity but I think I've had enough politics for one lifetime."

Will complimented him, "Well spoken. I'll consider that."

Arasthmus added, "The *Ruined Stone* returned a little while ago. Talia and her crew are in the hall."

"I'd better get over there and see what's going on."

Will exited the *Phantom* and hurried to the hall.

181

As he approached, he heard his name surface numerous times. Will bit his lip and entered the hall. He immediately became the center of attention. He took a deep breath and approached the tables. He noticed Talia and Zira sitting at the table together with his crew.

He greeted them, "Good morning, everyone. Welcome back, Talia and Zira."

Talia declared, "It sounds like congratulations are in order."

She hugged him. "Will. I wish you all the luck in the universe. You've earned it."

"Thanks, Talia."

Zira waited behind Talia and said, "Congratulations. I should have been more patient at the dance. Perhaps I could have been in Shanna's shoes."

Will hugged her. "Don't worry. There's a certain person out there just for you."

Zira asked, "Did you ever think that we had a future together?"

Will whispered in her ear, "No, I didn't, but I wished quite often that there could have been."

Zira smiled at him and said, "Good luck."

Will sat down at the table across from Talia. "So what news do you have for me, Talia?"

"Well, it appears that the armada heading to Attrades is definitely in an oval formation. That is highly unusual. Further analysis showed a dense shape in the middle of that oval with an abnormal power application inside."

"That would be the new destroyer."

Talia was worried. "You mean it has the ability to cloak and probably sensors too like the *Luna C* and the *Ruined Stone*? Do you realize how much that could impact the war?"

"Precisely. That's why I have a plan."

"Don't you ever run out of plans?"

"Perhaps one day."

"It's a multi-stage plan which begins with an assault on a manufacturing plant."

"Why do I suspect we are going to the Strontarian galaxy?"

182

"Because that's where the Attradeans are building their destroyers and equipping them with the technology stolen from the Fleet."

Talia was shocked. "How could that happen?"

Mynx responded, "We're going to find out."

Will introduced Mynx and Neva. He explained, "They are here to handle the traitors. Oh, by the way, if you check your list of accounts, there's a new one which.includes your cut for this whole operation."

"What?"

Will explained, "We've been paid for half of the job. When it's over, we'll get a lot more."

Zira asked, "The other half?"

Will laughed and explained, "No, I don't expect them to pay the other half, but there will be more."

Zira greedily took out her comm-link and dialed in several digits.

The others wait anxiously for further explanation.

Will continued, "The ransom for the destroyer which we are going to highjack."

Talia said, "You can't be serious."

"Why not? We hijacked one ship. Why not another?"

"I don't doubt that you'd hijack another ship, I'm confused about the ransom part."

"It's simple. We're going to remove the stolen technology from the destroyer and install it on the *Phantom*. When someone pays the ransom, they get the ship minus the cloaking and surveillance technology. While they're trying to figure out what happened to it, we'll hijack it again and park it for good. Thus, no destroyers for the bad guys."

Talia asked, "So what do you need us to do?"

"We're going to tow the cloaked *Ruined Stone* and *Luna C* into the Strontarian Galaxy and drop you in a firing position. You'll monitor the raid and provide cover as required."

"Why do you need to land at the site? Why not blast it from space? I'm sure the cruiser has enough firepower."

"Mynx and Neva are going to hunt down a traitor named Nester. We're tracking his ship into the Strontarian Galaxy as we speak. We're also going to recover Kalin's ship and crew from the Attradeans. We believe it's impounded near the plant."

Talia looked at Kalin and said, "I presume you're Kalin."

Kalin was enamored with Talia. He took her hand and kissed it. "It's a pleasure to meet you, Talia."

Talia blushed. "It's my pleasure, Kalin."

Kalin suggested, "We must talk later."

Talia replied seductively, "I'd like that."

Will rolled his eyes at Talia.

Talia said apologetically, "I'm sorry, Will. Go ahead."

"We'd like to use Saphoro to tap into the database at the plant."

Talia looked at Saphoro and asked, "Would you mind?"

"How dangerous will it be?"

Will shrugged his shoulders and replied, "Don't worry. We'll protect you while you operate."

"I'll do it."

Talia concluded, "Then it's set."

"Do you have any other information?"

"The Boromeans are mounting a force near Earth's solar system. The Fleet suspects they are preparing an attack."

"Sounds like we'll have to give them something to think about."

Talia was concerned by Will's comment but before she could question him, Shanna entered the hall and captured Will's attention.

Shanna joined them at their table and greeted Will.

"Good morning, Honey."

Will kissed her forehead and greeted her, "Hello, Sweetheart."

Talia remarked, "So you're going to be Will's wife? I have heard so much about you."

Everyone looked at Zira.

Zira was embarrassed and shouted, "What? I didn't do anything."

Talia continued, "Congratulations. We'll have to take you out one night before your wedding."

Will suggested, "That's probably not a good idea."

Talia glared at Will and said, "Where did you take her?"

Will was reluctant to say but Talia pressed him for an answer. He buckled and said humbly, "Okay, we went to Eve's Garden of Paradise."

Talia was shocked.

"You're kidding me, Will! People get killed in that place."

"No kidding. I almost did."

Talia said sarcastically, "Why do I think there's a story behind this?"

Jack grinned at the end of the table.

Talia spoke louder, "Why do I think Jack Fleming had something to do with this?"

Jack looked straight-faced and innocent.

Talia suggested, "I know a nice place where we girls can go."

Shanna replied, "That would be nice."

Bastille entered the hall and sat down next to Will.

"I'm sorry to interrupt but we've received a message from Maya."

"What is it, Bastille?"

"Your father and stepmother. They're dead."

Will turned pale.

"What happened?"

"They were killed by Boromeans. There was a funeral ceremony at the academy."

"You said there 'was' a ceremony."

"That's what Maya told me."

"How about that? I'm glad the Fleet saw fit to notify me about it."

"Maya has some of their belongings. She thought you'd want them."

"Thanks, Bastille."

"They'll be here in a day or so."

Will replied cynically, "It's nice to hear someone refer to time in days instead of cycles. I'll be in my quarters if anyone needs me."

Will exited the hall and returned to the ship.

Shanna excused herself and pursued Will.

Bastille apologized to everyone. "Sorry for ruining the mood."

Talia responded, "It was important for him to know."

Bastille felt badly and departed the hall.

Kalin suggested to Talia, "Why don't we go for a walk. This is a beautiful facility and I'd like to see more of it."

"That's a good idea."

Zira examined her accounts on the display of her comm-link.

"Talia! Look at all the credits I have in my account."

Talia looked at the display on Zira's comm-link and immediately checked hers. When the display came up, she was stunned.

"Where did all of these credits come from?"

Kalin explained, "We all received the same amount. Don't worry. It's a non-alliance account so it can't be traced."

Talia replied, "You'll have to tell me how Will pulled this one off."

"It's a complicated story. I'd have to explain from the beginning."

"Well, we've got plenty of time. Start talking."

The two of them left the hall.

$$**********$$

Shanna knocked on the door to Will's quarters.

Will answered, "Come in, Shanna."

Shanna opened the door and peered in.

"Are you alright, Will?"

"Yeah. I knew it was coming, I just don't know how to accept it."

Shanna sat on a chair across from Will. She looked at the doorjamb and noticed that the glass shard and the knife were still embedded in it.

"Are you saving those for souvenirs?"

"No. They reminded me of someone."

"Why don't you tell me about it?"

My stepmother, Tera, was pretty adept at things like that. She was tough and handled herself much like you. When I saw that side of you, it was an eerie reminder of Tera."

"Is that bad?"

"No, it was eerie in a good sense. I tried not to think about them because I knew they were dead. It's as if a part of me died with them."

Shanna moved onto the bed next to Will. He laid his head against her breast and was quiet for a while. Eventually, he fell asleep against her.

Shanna leaned back against the wall and held him close to her.

A few hours later, Will woke up. He lifted his head off of Shanna's chest. He kissed her forehead and she awoke.

Shanna asked, "Are you feeling any better?"

"I'm alright. Thanks for staying with me."

"I'm glad I could help. Can I ask you something?"

"Sure."

"Do you really want to rule Yord with me?"

"Only if you want to. I thought about it for a while and I hoped my decision would make you happy."

"You wouldn't believe how happy I am. But are you happy?"

"Yes, I am. I still get to live my alter-life as a pirate and I get to share your world with you."

"I was afraid you didn't really want to do this. If you didn't, I wouldn't hold you to it."

"Shanna, we're in this together. I think we've got plenty of adventures ahead of us."

Shanna kissed him on the cheek. "You've made me the happiest woman in the world."

She kissed him again and stood up. "I've got to speak with Mariel about some of the wedding arrangements. I also promised Brindy that we'd spend more time together."

"That's fine. I'll see you at dinner then."

"I'll be waiting."

Shanna departed from Will's quarters.

****

Will sat on the edge of the dock thinking about the upcoming mission.

Mynx approached him and asked, "Mind if I join you?"

"No. I could use a little company."

"Are you mad about our encounter?"

"No. Should I be?"

"I didn't realize you and Shanna were so close, otherwise I wouldn't have acted that way."

Will explained, "Things happened kind of fast between us. We were on, and then we were off. You and I had our business encounter, and then I almost died from the Weevil poison. Shanna saved my life. That one event fixed all the problems we were having, so don't feel guilty."

"I'm usually cold-hearted and bitchy but I'm glad for the two of you. Things have really worked out in your favor."

Will confided, "One thing bothers me, Mynx. What if one of us gets killed? I mean any one of us. This is my dream and everyone else is along for the ride. What if someone dies because of my quest?"

"Any one of us could die at any time. You were the perfect example. If it bothers you, perhaps you should give up the mission and take the safe way out. You'll still have Shanna and a new life here on Yord."

"I'd never forgive myself if I backed out now. Regent and Mariel are counting on me to rescue the Seers and the Eye. Kalin and Sandal are counting on me to recover their ship and crew. The

Fleet and GSS are counting on us to prevent the Attradeans or their allies from using our surveillance technology."

Mynx sympathized with him. "That's a lot of responsibility. I must admit, though, your plan has a lot of merit to it. If all goes well, there'll be much to celebrate in addition to your wedding."

"Thanks, Mynx."

Celine exited the *Phantom* and joined them. "Got room for one more?"

Will answered, "Sure. Three's a party."

Mynx said, "Sorry, I have to head back. I'm supposed to meet Neva and Kalin."

Celine suggested, "You may want to hear this, Mynx."

Mynx paused.

"The craft we were tracking landed on a planet called Ramses-3. Jack knew someone operating a smuggling operation in the area. He sent out an encrypted message to his acquaintance. He received some pretty detailed information back."

Will asked, "What kind of information?"

Celine continued, "We know that there is a military base near the factory. It has a large spaceport with a number of impounded ships parked there. He also said that the crews are imprisoned in the plant because there isn't enough room on the base."

Will surmised, "So we can't blow up the factory until we get Kalin's crew out."

"Correct. He also pointed out that one cruiser arrives at the same time every day and departs at the same time."

"We can be that cruiser!"

Mynx added, "I believe you're right. If we can delay or destroy the scheduled cruiser, we can arrive in its place."

"You're learning fast, Mynx."

"I've got to run. Good job, Celine."

"Thanks."

Mynx departed the dock area and ascended the granite steps.

Celine said, "Congratulations. You're getting married. You're going to rule a new kingdom. Man, you have a busy life."

"How are you doing, Celine?"

"Fine. Why?"

"Are you glad you stayed with us?"

"I miss being on the *Luna C* but I love being on the *Phantom*."

"So no regrets?"

"None. And I even got Bastille to boot."

"How are you two getting along?"

"Like birds of a feather. I'm really sorry about your dad and stepmom."

"Thanks. It's hard to believe."

"Maya's worried about you. She asked me to keep an eye on you."

"Did you tell her about me and Shanna?"

"No, it didn't seem like the appropriate time."

"I guess I'll be getting an earful when she finds out."

Celine kidded, "Hopefully Jack's therapy helps."

Will became curious and inquired, "What therapy?"

"Oh, let's just say she got what she so richly deserved."

Will laughed. "You're kidding?"

"No. She and Jack were together in her quarters for quite a while."

Will was pleasantly surprised.

"Well, how about that!"

"Perhaps you'll find Maya a little more understanding."

"I hope so."

Celine suggested, "I'm meeting Bastille in the hall for some of that fine Yord wine. Why don't you join us?"

"Sure, why not."

X.   Revenge

Will walked quietly alongside Celine as they ascended the granite steps.

Celine asked, "What's wrong, Will?"

"The Boromeans have been skating along in this war as long as I can remember. They killed my mother."

"Maya told me about it."

"They are grouping their forces near the Solar System. I hear they even placed a base in the vicinity."

Celine became uneasy. "What are you thinking?"

"Let's put a hit on the Boromeans now! Their sensors will see us as an Attradean cruiser. They'll have no reason to suspect anything."

"I don't know about this, Will. Let's see what Bastille thinks."

Bastille sneaked up behind them in the hallway. "Did I hear my name?"

Celine answered, "Yes. We need your opinion."

"Shoot. I'm listening."

"Will wants to put a hit on the Boromeans near the Solar System."

Bastille looked surprised. "What? You want to hit the Boromean base?"

Will answered confidently, "Yes, indeed. They'll think that Tenemon is blind-siding them. What a mess he'll have on his hands."

Celine asked, "What do you think, Bastille?"

"I hate Tenemon. You know I would do anything to make his life miserable."

Celine asked, "So this is a go?"

"Yes it is."

Bastille informed Will, "Consider this a wedding present from Celine and me."

"I accept your gift graciously."

Celine said, "I'll get the others."

Will stated adamantly, "No. This is just us. Bastille, do you know the weaponry on the *Phantom* yet?"

"Absolutely."

"Is there anything I can fire?"

Bastille explained, "You'll love the cannons on this baby. The firing system and targeting system is so much more advanced than that of the Fleet's ships."

"Good. I want to personally dish out some punishment."

"I'll teach you how to use it. When do you want to go?"

"How about now?"

"Let's go."

Celine was worried. "Shouldn't we tell somebody?"

Will asked, "How long a trip is it?"

Bastille thought for a moment. "We can use three Fleet portals to get there and back before morning if you know the portal codes?"

"I sure do."

"Then we have a job to do."

Will told Celine, "Don't bother the others. We'll be back before they know it."

Celine asked, "What about Shanna?"

Will answered, "She's busy with the wedding plans."

"You guys are treating this like a walk in the park."

Will quipped, "No. It's more like a run."

Celine remained edgy about the decision.

Together, they boarded the *Phantom.*

Regent and Arasthmus were playing chess again in the main quarters.

Arasthmus asked, "Another meeting, Will?"

"No. We're going on a little trip. Is anyone else on board?"

"Just us."

Regent asked, "What are you up to, Will? I know that look."

"We're leaving a calling card for Tenemon."

"Oh, that's fine. I thought maybe you had something crazy in mind."

"Who me? Never. Want to go for a ride with us?"

Regent answered, "Sure. Why not?"

Will winked at Bastille and Celine. Celine rolled her eyes at Will and whispered, "That's mean."

Will winked at her and grinned.

Bastille took Celine by the hand and led her up the stairs to the pilots' cabin.

Will sat down and contemplated their mission.

Bastille quickly piloted the *Phantom* through the tunnel into the cavern.

A short while later, Will entered the pilots' cabin. He knelt between Bastille and Celine.

Will kidded, "Come on, Celine. I thought you wanted a little adventure out here."

Celine replied, "This sounds like one of those stupid things that men like to do for kicks."

Will and Bastille laughed.

Bastille set the coordinates and placed the ship on 'autopilot'.

Bastille informed Celine, "I'm going to teach Will how to use the cannons. I'll be back shortly."

Celine frowned at him. She leaned back in her seat and activated the sensors, both long and short range.

****

Bastille showed Will how to activate the turret and operate the targeting system.

Will pretended to fire at several asteroids and other passing debris.

He remarked, "This isn't bad at all."

"I told you. It's easy."

"I'd like to sit back here for a while and think. Let me know when we get close."

"Sure."

Bastille climbed down from the turret.

Will called to him, "Bastille."

"Yes."

"Thanks. This means a lot to me."

"That's okay. I've been dying for some real action."

"Maybe this is therapy for both of us."

Bastille laughed as he walked away.

****

Celine turned on the DMS and dialed in the frequency for the *Ruined Stone*.

"Hello, *Ruined Stone*. Anyone there?"

Zira's face appeared on the screen. "Hi, Celine. You got duty tonight, too?"

"Kind of. You're not going to believe this, but we're on our way to put a hit on the Boromeans."

"What? Whose crazy idea was that?"

"Guess."

"Is Will out of his mind? Maybe he doesn't want to get married and this is an honorable way out."

"I don't know what he's thinking, but we're on our way. We should be back by morning."

"Do you want me to notify Talia?"

"Don't disturb her. Just let her know we're going after the Boromean base near the Solar System."

"That's a long way out unless you know the portal codes."

"Will knows them."

Zira fretted, "Can you imagine what'll happen when the Fleet's ships see an Attradean cruiser passing through their portals? They'll go bananas!"

"You and I both know this is a bad idea but Bastille and Will are determined to do this. We're coming up on the first portal. I'll contact you on the way back."

"Good luck, Celine."

"Thanks. I'll need it."

Bastille entered the pilots' cabin. "Everything okay, Celine?"

"I'm just peachy."

Bastille contacted Will on the intercom. "We're coming up on the first gate. What are the codes?"

Will answered back, "Alpha-seven-alpha-seven-six-delta-five."

Bastille entered the codes and repeated back to Will, "Alpha-seven-alpha-seven-six-delta-five."

"That's correct."

"We're passing door number one. I'll call you in a little while."

"Roger."

Celine asked, "Do you realize we're passing through Fleet portals in an Attradean cruiser?"

"They'll get over it."

"We have a pirate paint job, for heavens sake!"

Bastille calmly explained, "Tenemon had me tortured and left for dead. I've been dying for a chance to repay him for his kindness."

Celine then realized that this was personal for Bastille as well as Will.

"I'm sorry, Bastille. I thought that this was a game or something."

"Hell, no! I wouldn't have brought you along if it were a game."

A short while later, they reached the second portal. Bastille called Will on the intercom. "Are you awake back there?"

Will answered, "Sure am."

"We're ready for the second set of codes."

"Alpha-seven-alpha-five-three-foxtrot-five."

Bastille read the codes back, "Alpha-seven-alpha-five-three-foxtrot-five."

"That's correct."

"We'll call you in a while."

"Roger."

The tracking system beeped five times. Celine pressed two buttons and the screen showed four Fleet vessels approaching them.

Celine muttered, "We have company. They're coming fast from the port side."

Bastille increased their speed to maximum. They passed through the portal before the Fleet ships could get within firing range.

Celine complained, "You do know they'll be waiting for us when we return."

"Don't worry about it. I have a feeling they'll come in handy on the way back."

Celine monitored the screen, expecting the Fleet ships to follow.

Bastille remarked, "They didn't follow, did they?

"How did you know they wouldn't?"

Bastille explained, "Because they're responsible for that side of the portal. They can't leave their zone."

Celine asked, "What about this side of the portal?"

"I'm sure they're notifying their superiors right about now."

Will called Bastille on the intercom.

"Hey, partner. I could have lit up those Fleet boys."

Bastille was surprised, "You saw them?"

"Of course. This targeting system is awesome."

"Good, because we're probably going to see them again on the way home."

Will replied confidently, "Not if things go according to plan."

Celine cut in, "I hope you're right."

Bastille suggested, "Why don't you get some sleep? I can handle things."

Celine was tired. "Okay. Just promise me you'll wake me if anything comes up."

"I promise."

Things were boring until Bastille noticed the third portal coming up too soon.

He thought, "That's strange. I didn't expect this one for a while."

Bastille called Will on the intercom. "Something's not right, Will."

"What do you mean?"

"We're coming up on the third portal a bit early."

Will advised him, "Slow down. When you enter the codes, watch carefully for the portal to blink. If it doesn't blink, break away and we'll regroup."

Bastille shook Celine and said, "We're going through the third portal."

Celine rubbed her eyes. "I'll be back. I have to use the lavatory."

Celine left the cabin.

Bastille informed Will, "We're coming up at half speed."

Will called out the codes, "Three-five-delta-foxtrot."

Bastille replied, "That's it? Three-five-delta-foxtrot."

"That's it."

Bastille warned, "Be prepared in case we enter a hornets nest."

"I'm ready."

The portal blinked as expected and the *Phantom* passed through. As soon as they exited, Bastille saw the rear of a Boromean armada ahead of him.

He called urgently to Will, "Take a look. We're in no man's land!"

Will hollered back, "Fire away and get the hell out of here."

Bastille armed twelve torpedoes and fired at the armada. He waited anxiously for the next twelve to load and arm.

****

Will turned on the live fire switch and peppered away at the Boromean ships. He destroyed three of them quickly. Will covered his eyes from the torpedo flashes. Nine more ships exploded.

Bastille hollered, "I'm waiting for the torpedoes to reload. You have to cover us."

"I'm on it!"

Will quickly targeted ship after ship. He destroyed five more.

The Boromeans finally realized that the gunfire was coming from behind them and broke their pattern.

Suddenly the *Phantom* was swamped with flashes from enemy gunfire."

Will yelled to Bastille, "There's the base, straight ahead. Make one run and go for the portal."

****

Celine entered the cabin. She freaked at the number of Boromean ships ahead of them.

"Bastille! What the hell is going on?"

"Not now. How many torpedoes are left?"

"After this volley, about twelve more."

Bastille headed for the base. The Boromean ships trailed them but were forced to hold their fire or risk hitting their base.

Bastille saw ships exploding left and right.

"Keep it up, Will. You're looking good."

"Are you loaded, Bastille?"

"Right ... about ... now!"

The 'ready' lights flashed and Bastille fired twelve more torpedoes. He veered away from the base and headed for the portal. The torpedoes found their mark and turned the base into a fiery mass.

Will cheered loudly across the intercom.

"Nice shooting, Bastille."

Celine sat frozen in her seat.

"When we get back, I'm gonna' kill him."

Bastille tried to calm her. "We're doing fine."

Celine exploded on him, "What do you mean we're doing fine?"

Will called to Bastille, "We've got a lot of company behind us."

"What do you want to do?"

"Pedal to the metal. Don't go through the portal, though. Break right at the last possible second."

"That's a ballsy move, Will. What if they don't bite?"

The ship shuddered and the power flickered from gunfire.

Bastille concluded, "Never mind. We'll do it."

The *Phantom* went full speed at the portal and broke right. Many of the Boromean ships were so eager to follow them through the portal that they couldn't change course. They crashed into the closed portal, which became a glowing mass of burning metal.

Bastille yelled, "Yee-hah! It worked."

Celine noticed that the torpedoes had reloaded. She programmed them for 'target acquisition'.

"You've got 'readies' on the torpedoes, Bastille."

"That's my girl."

Bastille did a complete loop and headed for the portal again.

"Any special instructions, Will?"

"Five-five-zero. Let them follow. I'm sure the Fleet ships are waiting on the other side."

Bastille fired another compliment of torpedoes and steered for the portal. Twelve more Boromean ships exploded.

Will yelled, "Spectacular! There are only ten left."

Celine mocked him, "Only ten left."

Will advised him, "When we pass through, take a three-three-five heading. If the Fleet ships are waiting, we'll avoid them."

Bastille entered the codes and the portal opened. He quickly took the prescribed heading.

Six Fleet battle cruisers waited for them. The quick maneuver allowed the *Phantom* to skirt the ships. The Boromean ships passed through and immediately engaged the Fleet battle cruisers.

The Boromean and Fleet ships seemed to forget about the *Phantom* and battled each other.

Bastille stood up and howled. He picked Celine up and hugged her.

Will burst through the door and jumped on Bastille. He screamed, "We did it!"

Celine asked dryly, "Can we get back to Yord in one piece before we celebrate?"

Bastille teased her, "Come on, Celine. Wasn't that a rush?"

Will yelled, "We just destroyed a Boromean base and three quarters of their armada! How about that?"

Bastille bellowed, "I feel like a million credits."

Celine snapped, "Hey, boys. The next portal is coming up."

Will recited, "Three-three-seven-delta."

Bastille entered the codes and they shot through the portal.

Bastille crooned, "Just like clockwork."

Celine softened her attitude and suggested, "Why don't you two get some sleep. I'll take it from here."

Bastille suggested, "How about we share a bottle of champagne or two?"

Will replied heartily, "I couldn't agree more."

He then notified Celine, "The next portal is five-delta-delta-kilo."

She answered confidently, "I've got it. Go have some fun. You guys earned it."

Will and Bastille entered the main quarters.

Will asked, "Where are Regent and Arasthmus?"

Bastille looked around and saw no one.

The chess board was still on the table with pieces in place.

"Beats me."

The door to the first berth slid open slightly. Arasthmus peered out. "Is it safe to come out?"

Will and Bastille laughed at him.

Will ordered, "Get out here. We have some celebrating to do."

The door slid all the way open. Arasthmus and Regent nervously entered the main quarters.

Arasthmus said humbly, "If you don't mind me asking, what just happened?"

Bastille slapped him on the back and said, "We just put a big dent in the Boromean forces."

Will said jovially, "Can you imagine Tenemon trying to explain this to the Boromeans? One of his ships was hijacked and turned loose on them. They'll never buy it!"

Bastille hollered, "I'd love to see his face on the screen."

Will suggested, "Maybe we should call him when we get back."

"Absolutely."

Bastille unlocked a refrigerator and took out three bottles of chilled champagne.

"I got these from Eve's for such an occasion."

****

Celine passed through the last portal without any further interference. She pressed two buttons for the DMS and waited patiently. Finally Talia' face appeared.

Talia asked excitedly, "What in the world is going on, Celine?"

"You wouldn't believe it if I told you."

"Yes I would. We're positioned near Attrades and we're monitoring their transmissions. They're going nuts down there!"

"We made a major strike on a Boromean base in the Solar System. The base is destroyed and just about all of their ships in that sector as well."

"Well, the Boromeans have attacked several of Tenemon's outposts and there are four or five battles raging in different parts of the galaxy. Tenemon is trying desperately to convince them that it wasn't him."

"You can thank Will and Bastille for that. I think it was a foolish idea but it worked."

"What a maniac! Well, it's good to know that you're safe."

"Thanks Talia. We'll be back soon."

"We'll be coming in, too."

"See you then."

Celine glided the ship into the canyon and entered the cave. The large door opened on cue and she guided the ship into its berth.

Celine was relieved when she shut down the *Phantom's* engines. She leaned back in her seat and took a deep breath.

****

Will sat up and grimaced. His head was pounding and he was dehydrated. He shook Bastille and said, "We're home, buddy."

Bastille grumbled, "Let me sleep."

"Sure."

Will entered the lavatory and washed up. The hot shower invigorated him. He walked slowly across the main quarters to the hatch. He looked down at Regent and Arasthmus, lying on the floor. The two of them snored loudly. Will thought better of waking them. He opened the hatch and exited the ship.

He immediately saw Shanna sitting on the granite steps. Her eyes were red from crying and her face was tear-streaked. She didn't run to him, but only stared at him.

Will approached her and sat next to her.

"Are you okay, Shanna?"

She glared at him and said, "I should be asking you that. What was that all about?"

She looked at the *Phantom*. The side and top was seared from gunfire. The top left engine was smoking. "Look at your ship! Was it worth it?"

"Will explained, "Something went wrong. The third portal was in a different location. This should have been simple."

"Will, you think everything is simple. I was worried sick about you. I didn't know if you changed your mind about us and ran away or what."

"I'm sorry. I figured you were so busy that you'd never even notice we were gone."

Shanna said coldly, "I waited at dinner for you for hours and you never showed up."

"I'm really sorry, Shanna. I was so incensed about my parents that I forgot about dinner."

"It's a good thing Celine called in and told Zira what was happening. Suppose you were killed or the ship crashed someplace. How would we know where you were?"

"I see your point."

Shanna added, "Besides, maybe the rest of us wanted to come."

Will apologized and lowered his head to the ground.

"Where are Bastille, Celine and the councilors?"

"Inside the ship. They're asleep."

"They're asleep!"

"Well, maybe a little drunk and asleep."

Shanna said sarcastically, "I figured as much. I saw Bastille sneak three bottles onto the ship from Eve's. Thanks for inviting me to your party."

"I'm really sorry. I didn't use the best of judgment, did I?"

"No you didn't."

Will stood up and walked sadly away.

Shanna asked, "Where do you think you're going?"

"I caused enough trouble for one night. I'm going to my quarters."

Shanna replied, "Not without me, you aren't."

Shanna walked with him onto the ship. She saw Bastille and the councilors sleeping on the floor and snoring loudly.

"This is really classy! Just like a bunch of pirates."

Will was confused.

"I thought that's what we were."

"That's what I mean, smarty."

"Oh, I get it."

Shanna asked, "Your quarters or mine?"

"For what?"

"You owe me. I worried about you all night. Now it's your turn to make amends."

Will finally understood what she meant.

"Let's go to your quarters. I like the candles."

Shanna led him into her quarters and lit two candles.

Will asked, "Why only two?"

"Because I'm only in a two candle mood."

Shanna pushed him onto his back across the bed and climbed on top of him. She kissed him and stroked his hair. She nibbled at his neck.

Will kissed her and nibbled on her neck agressively.

Shanna whispered, "What are you doing?"

"Marking my territory."

"You're bad, Will."

****

Several hours later, Will heard banging in the distance. He opened his eyes and saw Shanna sleeping next to him.

Talia yelled, "Will! Are you in there?"

Will mumbled, "Oh, boy. Here it comes."

Shanna opened her eyes and pulled him back.

"Don't go. Stay here with me."

"I'd love to but I think it's time to get my punishment."

Shanna teased, "I can punish you if you like."

"No. You rest. I'll see you later."

Will kissed Shanna.

She pulled him to her and kissed him passionately.

"Damn, Shanna, you're making this difficult."

She giggled. "I know. That's the idea."

Will quickly dressed and exited the quarters.

Talia waited with her hands on her hips.

"You've got some nerve. How can you indulge like that after everything that just happened? Come on. You have explaining to do."

Will asked, "What's the big deal?"

"Maya's back."

Will's eyes widened with surprise. "Oh, no! I didn't expect to see her until much later today."

Will followed Talia into the hall.

Maya and Jack embraced each other and kissed in the doorway. Saphoro and Neelon were eating breakfast at the table.

Talia ordered Will, "Follow me."

She sat down next to Saphoro and Will sat next to Neelon.

Neelon teased, "Looks like you've been having one heck of a party out here."

"It seems like it. How are you guys doing?"

Talia added, "Not nearly as well as Tenemon this morning. He's up to his elbows in Boromeans."

Will suggested, "I should give him a call and see how he's doing."

Saphoro interjected, "I wouldn't do that now. Wait until we see what the end result is between him and the Boromeans."

Will noticed Maya and Jack embracing.

"Why don't they get a room?"

Saphoro chastised him, "Don't push it, Will. This has been great for us. You wouldn't believe how different she is."

"I can't believe she was so tough."

"I'm sorry about your dad and stepmother."

Neelon added, "We hoped that things would have worked out for the better."

"Thanks, I appreciate it."

Maya and Jack came over and sat with them.

Will teased, "Well, it's nice of you two to come up for air."

Maya replied, "Don't be jealous. Where is your fiancée?"

Talia kidded, "She's sleeping after a rough night."

"Drinking?"

"No, waiting for Will to come home."

"Ah, yes. That's right. Will went out to play last night."

Will asked, "Is this going to take long?"

"Are you in a hurry?"

"No."

"The Fleet commander is climbing the walls because an Attradean ship passed through three of their portals, twice."

Will asked coolly, "Can you imagine that?"

"Strangely enough, a Boromean base was taken out and all but ten of the Boromean ships were destroyed by this mystery vessel."

"No kidding!"

"But that's okay. The Fleet battle cruisers disposed of the remaining ten. It seems the only legible identification from a distance on this ship was a skull and crossed swords."

Will kidded, "That sounds spooky."

"Well, the commander wants to know why I don't know who it is."

"What did you say?"

"I'm looking into it. She doesn't know if they should offer a reward or a bounty."

"I think you should contact her and tell her you've set up an arrangement. Give her our transfer numbers and tell her for a nominal fee, we'll continue to harass the enemies of the Fleet. We have no interest in crossing them."

"Jack and I already discussed that. It's done."

Will was impressed. "Boy, Jack has got you back on top of your game."

Maya looked suspiciously at Will, "What do you mean by that?"

Will winked at Jack. "Oh, nothing in particular."

She glanced at Jack.

He smiled and said nothing.

Maya informed him, "You'll find that you, Bastille, Celine and the two councilors each have two hundred thousand credits deposited into your accounts, compliments of the Fleet."

"Wow. This is getting better and better."

"And now for the bad news. You heard about your dad and Tera?"

"Yeah. Thanks for passing that along."

"Well, it seems that they were ambushed by Boromeans on Kappa-5. They held out for three cycles before the Boromeans overtook them."

Will was shocked.

"That's not what the Fleet told us before!"

"I know."

"Why did they lie?"

Maya explained, "A good friend of mine told me that they didn't send a rescue team out there until after the Boromeans departed the sector."

Will roared, "Those sons of ..."

Maya cut him off sternly, "Shut up and sit down."

"We're all defecting from the Fleet unofficially. We're going to stay out here and work with you on Yord. If we officially defect with the two ships we have, they'll have everyone in the galaxy hunting us."

"So what's to stop that from happening now?"

"Because we have the use of their portals. They won't interfere with us so long as we work parallel to them. Besides that, they'll keep paying us while we're out here."

Will complimented Maya, "Not bad. You're becoming a businesswoman."

Jack corrected him, "She's my business woman."

Maya blushed and said, "Don't say it, Will. I know what you're thinking."

Will teased, "No you don't."

Maya mentioned, "I brought back two trunks of items that belonged to your dad and Tera."

Will said, "Thanks, but I don't know what I'd do with their personal items."

"I think you'll find these personal items worth looking at."

Will became curious and asked, "Like what?"

"Oh, there's a sword and scabbard; a box with a golden skull and some other goodies. Tera's trunk has some things that Shanna might like."

Will kidded, "I don't even want to know."

Jack asked, "Why?"

"You didn't know Tera. I could only imagine what's inside that trunk."

Talia prodded Will, "Don't you have some important news for Maya?"

Maya quipped, "Yes. I hear some dramatic things are happening in your life."

Will hesitated and looked up. He noticed Shanna entering the hall.

Shanna saw them and came to the table. She dressed in a gold robe with a black sash around the waste. She wore her hair down over her shoulders.

She greeted them, "Good morning everyone."

Will stood up and kissed Shanna's cheek.

"You're just in time. Maya wants to hear about our good news."

Maya repeated curiously, "Our good news?"

Will explained, "I've asked Shanna to be my wife and she's accepted."

Maya yelled, "That's great! I'm surprised it happened so fast, but that's great."

Maya hugged Shanna.

Will complained, "Gee, Maya. I see you're really glad to be rid of me."

Maya laughed at him. "No, not at all."

Saphoro whispered to Will, "I told you."

Will continued, "A few other things came into play here. Since my bloodline is Firenghian royalty, and Shanna's bloodline is Yord royalty, we were asked to become the rulers of Yord."

Maya was astonished. "You mean like king and queen?"

"Let's just say 'rulers'. It gets more interesting, though."

"What could be more interesting than all of this?"

"We had a brawl inside Eve's Garden of Paradise."

Maya was appalled.

"What were you doing in there? That place is dangerous."

Talia looked at Jack. He blushed and turned away.

Maya glared at him and remarked, "I should have known."

Will continued, "We had an encounter with several Weevil and I was poisoned."

"No way! You'd be dead."

"I nearly was."

"Not even a Firenghi can overcome a Weevil's poison."

"But a Seer can."

Maya looked at Shanna in astonishment. "You did that for him?"

Shanna nodded. She and Will held their wrists out.

Will opened his shirt and displayed the scars.

Maya spoke in disbelief, "But I've heard that only the Rite of the Dead can restore someone from certain death."

Will nodded in affirmation.

Maya told Shanna, "I can never thank you enough for saving him. But how did you survive? I always thought that one person had to die."

"I guess our love was stronger than the rite itself."

Maya sat down and said, "Wow! What else did I miss?"

Will teased, "What else? Isn't that enough?"

Jack reminded him, "Don't forget about the GSS girls, Will."

Maya looked sternly at Will. "What did you do to get GSS involved?"

Will replied, "It's a long story but they're working with us on a big assignment."

Maya rebuked him, "GSS doesn't just work with you. What happened?"

"Check your list of accounts. You'll see a new non-alliance account with a significant amount of credits in it."

Maya was worried. "Will, did you blackmail them?"

Will laughed. "No, of course not. There's a traitor in the Fleet who sold the cloaking and surveillance technology to the

Attradeans. We're being paid to dispose of their new destroyers with the Fleet's technology and nail the rat."

Maya exclaimed, "That's insane!"

Jack countered, "But he's got a great plan."

Maya bit her fingernail and paced.

Will advised her, "Your role is easy. Just follow the plan. We'll be in and out like clockwork."

"Will, you've turned the war upside down with that little escapade of yours last night. No one is sure who's fighting who."

"Better for us."

Maya asked Shanna, "When is the wedding?"

"About twelve cycles from our departure."

"What departure?"

Will answered, "Our departure to the Strontarian galaxy."

"That's a big place to look for ships."

"Okay, how about Ramses-3?"

"That's in a bad part of town."

"Yes it is. You and Talia will be watching our backs from the sky."

Maya asked Jack, "Can you get me a glass of wine, honey. I feel faint."

Jack obeyed and went to the kitchen.

Maya asked Talia, "What do you think?"

"I think we're getting wealthier every day. I like the plan."

Kalin entered the hall and joined them. He placed his arm around Talia's waist and kissed her cheek. "Good morning, Talia."

Talia blushed.

"Kalin, this is Maya. She's the commander of the *Luna C*."

Kalin nodded to her. "It's a pleasure to meet you, Maya."

Maya was stunned. "Talia!"

"Now, Maya. Don't be jealous."

"I'm not. I'm just surprised."

She teased, "We all need a little therapy from time to time."

Talia explained to Kalin, "Maya and I are like sisters, so if anything sounds strange, you'll understand why."

"I'm sure I'll be amused."

Jack returned with a ewer and a glass. He poured a glass of wine for Maya and handed it to her.

"Thanks Jack."

Maya drank the wine in one gulp.

"Another one, please."

Jack grinned deviously as he poured.

Will informed him, "Maya just found out about Talia and Kalin."

Jack encouraged Maya, "There's a whole ewer here, honey. Drink away."

Maya glared at him and sipped from the glass. She said humbly, "This is more excitement in one day than I've had in my whole life. I need time to absorb all of this."

Will advised her, "Take some time to relax. We're not leaving until tomorrow morning."

"Tomorrow morning?"

"Yes. We have an aggressive schedule and I have a wedding coming up."

Everyone but Maya laughed.

Maya drank the balance of the wine and handed the glass to Jack. He promptly filled it again and handed it to her.

Will suggested, "I think we should prepare the ships this afternoon and have a nice relaxing evening."

Everyone agreed.

Will asked, "Are you okay, Maya?"

"I will be. I'm stunned. So much is happening."

"We're only warming up. The best is yet to come."

Maya hugged Will. "Congratulations. Do you really love her that much?"

"You wouldn't believe how much."

"Maybe I would."

Maya put her arm around Jack's waist.

"I'm going to lay down for a bit. I'm feeling a little tipsy."

Jack offered, "I'll escort you to your quarters."

"You'd better."

Jack winked at Will.

****

Will entered the hall for breakfast. He wondered how it was that everyone always got there before him when it came to a meal. Shanna was the only one missing.

Will sat at the head table next to Mariel and greeted everyone. "Good morning, friends."

Everyone replied in unison, "Good morning."

Will quipped, "You guys are like a finely tuned bunch of students although you hardly look like them."

His friends laughed heartily.

Will continued with his speech, "Today marks the return to an era of prosperity and peace here on Yord. Although the rest of the universe doesn't know it, we're taking over. With the return of the Eye of Icarus and the Seers, we'll build a kingdom that surpasses all others. We'll dismantle Tenemon and the other alien races that choose to fight this senseless war. And most of all, we'll monitor the Fleet because of their unscrupulous activities of the past."

Everyone cheered for a moment.

Mariel and her aides stood and clapped as well.

"As you have heard, Shanna and I will be the new rulers of Yord. We plan to set up a democratic system, which can function efficiently while we continue our role as pirates for peace. I'm sure a few of you are thinking about wealth too."

He drew laughs from his friends.

"Even after we establish peace, we'll continue to roam the stars looking for new adventures for those of you who get bored easily."

Will stepped aside for Mariel.

She announced to the group, "I'm here on behalf of the surviving people of Yord. We wholeheartedly support Will and Shanna as the new rulers."

The room erupted in an exuberant roar.

Will wished them cheerfully, "Enjoy your meal. We leave afterward."

He used his telepathy to contact Shanna, "Hey, Sweetie. Where are you?"

She replied telepathically, "I'm almost through."

"What are you doing?"

"Maya gave me Tera's belongings to look through."

"Did you find anything good?"

"Well, she had some very interesting things."

"Will you be down soon?"

"I'm coming. Be patient."

"I can't. I miss you."

"I know you do."

Will finished his meal and stepped down to the floor.

Shanna entered the hall. She wore black leather slacks; studded straps on her arms, wrists and ankles; a leather headband; short curled knives strapped to each arm and thigh; black leather boots and her hair was tied up in a pony tail.

Will was stunned as he eyed her.

Everyone was awed by her appearance as well.

She swaggered up to Will and asked, "What do you think?"

Will replied unsteadily, "You.... You look dangerous."

"Thank you."

Jack kidded, "What are you supposed to be dressed up for, Shanna - Halloween?"

Shanna took one of the knives and threw it at Jack's hand. The knife stuck in the table between Jack's thumb and forefinger.

Jack snapped, "Hey, you almost cut me."

Shanna grinned as she approached the table.

"Take another look."

Jack looked at his hand and saw a small slit in the webbing between his fingers.

Shanna pulled the knife out of the table and stowed it in the armband.

Jack looked at his hand again and said, "Will, did you know she could do that?"

Will held his hand up, revealing a small scar in the webbing between his fingers.

"Yeah, I did."

Jack apologized to Shanna.

Mariel gleamed with pride.

Maya, Talia, Celine and Zira clapped for Shanna.

Maya said, "Well done, Shanna. Well done."

Jack asked, "Whose side are you on, Maya?"

Maya replied, "You have to learn to respect women for their abilities."

Jack rolled his eyes.

Shanna asked Will, "Have you looked through your dad's things yet?"

"No, I'm avoiding it."

"Come on. Let's see what he left. It could be fun."

"Well, alright. You talked me into it."

"We'll see you all on board in a little while."

Mariel hugged Shanna and Will.

"Good luck to you both. Come back safe."

Will replied, "Thanks. We'll see you soon."

Will and Shanna walked out of the hall, arm in arm.

****

Shanna sat on the bed and watched as Will slid the trunk away from the wall. He opened it slowly and removed a sword and scabbard. He held it up and examined it. "I like this."

The sword had a hilt made of silver, with a skull and red gems for eyes. There were roses around the skull.

Will took out a fancy box and opened it. Inside was a brown sack with a golden skull in it. The sack had a clip on it for hanging."

"Looks like dad was obsessed with skulls."

Shanna suggested, "Maybe the skull has some kind of magic power."

"I don't know anything about it."

Will put the sack back in the box and stowed it. He poked through some clothes and found a strange device. Attached to it was a note.

Will read it aloud, "Consult Xerxes before operating."

He asked Shanna, "Any idea who Xerxes is?"

Shanna looked befuddled and suggested, "Maybe Maya knows."

"Remind me to ask her about it later."

Will returned the device to the trunk. He closed the lid and pushed it back into the corner.

"I don't see anything else worth looking at."

"There's another package next to my trunk."

"Maybe later. I've seen enough."

Shanna strapped the sword and scabbard around Will's waist.

"You're getting there. I can make you some clothes to match your image."

Will asked, "How about a cloak like yours?"

"I can do that. You know, there's only one thing better than dressing you."

"What's that?"

"Undressing you."

Shanna unfastened the sword and scaffold. She set them neatly on the table.

Will remarked, "I can see where this is going."

Shanna smiled devilishly and removed his shirt.

XI.　　Assault on Ramses-3

One by one the ships exited the canyon and ascended into the sky. The *Phantom* took the lead with the *Luna C* and the *Ruined Stone* on the wings.

Bastille ordered Celine, "Activate the tractor beams and attach to the ships."

Celine operated a panel on her right. After pressing several switches, she slowly slid a short double-pole lever forward.

"I'm increasing the power of the beams, Bastille."

"That's it, Celine. Nice and easy."

Bastille set the DMS switch to 'call' and spoke, "*Ruined Stone. Luna C.* Are you there?"

Maya answered, "We're here, Bastille."

Talia echoed, "We are, too."

Bastille requested, "Let me know when you feel the pull of the tractor beams."

Celine reached seventy-five percent.

Maya answered, "We're sensing it."

Bastille ordered, "Cut back on your engines to fifty percent."
The sister ships reduced power and stayed with the *Phantom*.
Celine informed Bastille, "We're at eighty percent."
Bastille ordered, "Cut engine power on both ships."
Maya notified him, "We're shut down, Bastille."
Talia said, "We are, too. It's working. We're keeping pace."
Bastille replied, "Excellent. Now activate your cloaking system."
Celine looked out of her transparent shield. "The *Luna C* is invisible."
Bastille looked out his side and replied, "As is the *Ruined Stone*."
Maya announced, "We're cloaked, Bastille."
Bastille teased, "Now's the boring part. Relax and enjoy the ride."

****

Will practiced with his sword in the cargo bay. He repeated several strokes while stepping forward and backward. Shanna sat on a crate nearby and was amused by his intensity.
Will asked, "What's so funny?"
"I guess it's safe to say that yours is bigger than mine."
"If only I could handle mine as well as you handle yours."
Shanna giggled. "It took me a long time to learn how to throw like that?"
"What made you want to throw so accurately?"
"When I was a young girl, there were three women in particular who always came around and took whatever I had. I couldn't fight them so I drew a picture of them and threw stones at it. After a while, I graduated to pieces of glass. When I became bored with that, I borrowed knives from the kitchen."
"You worked in a kitchen?"
"No, I hung out with some friends there. That's why there was so much resentment when my mother sent me to the temple to spend time with the Seers."

Will thought aloud, "I wonder how well my father could handle a sword."

Shanna laughed.

"Isn't this ironic?"

"What?"

"Look at us. I'm wearing Tera's battle garments and you're using your dad's sword. Do you think they'd be proud of us?"

"Yes, I do. I wish they were still here."

Shanna embraced Will. "That's why you went after the Boromeans, wasn't it?"

"Yeah, I guess it was."

"Do you feel any better?"

"A little bit. At least they finally paid for their actions. They hadn't been touched so far as I know but they've done the most harm to my people."

"I always heard that they were elusive."

"Well they weren't so elusive when we ran up their butts."

"What? How did that happen?"

Will explained, "We were only going to fire a few torpedoes at their base and split. Well, the third portal wasn't where it used to be. When we came through, we were behind the whole armada and they were heading away from the base."

Shanna laughed and said, "That's either incredibly good luck or unbelievably bad luck."

"Fortunately, Bastille is one hell of a pilot."

"Well, I heard that you came up with one hell of a plan for Bastille to follow."

"Who told you that?"

"Bastille and Celine told me about the double loop at the portal."

Will noted, "It's funny how Celine tries to boss him around and he calmly overrules her."

"She really likes him."

"Isn't it strange how some people are attracted to others?"

"Look at us? I knew you were the one as soon as I met you."

Will laughed. "I was in my alter-shape. How could you know that?"

"You were so cute and cuddly."

Will pretended to be offended, "Wolverines aren't cute and cuddly."

"Okay, you were mean and scary."

"That's better."

"Can I ask you a serious question, Will?"

Will stopped doing the sword strokes and sat down next to Shanna.

"Of course."

"Do you think I could change shape like you did?"

"I don't know. It seems that our telepathy became considerably better after your ritual."

"What's it like to change?"

Will took a deep breath and answered, "It's hard to say. I was so caught up in the moment that I really can't remember much about it."

"Did it hurt?"

"I think it felt strange more than it hurt. I did have cramps but I don't recall anything else. Why do you ask?"

"I was just thinking about what it would be like."

Will begged her, "Please don't become obsessed with it. Maya told me that my dad's relationship with my Aunt Penny was ruined because she was so obsessed with her alter-shape."

"Don't worry. So long as I'm with you, I'm happy. It doesn't matter what shape we're in."

Will teased, 'That's good because I'd be really unhappy if you got fleas."

Shanna hollered, "That's mean."

She smacked his arm twice. He grabbed her arm and pulled her toward him. They kissed passionately and rolled back across the crate.

Shanna asked, "What if someone comes in?"

"I'm sure they won't stay."

They giggled and embraced each other.

Celine called the *Ruined Stone* and the *Luna C*, "We're approaching the drop off point."

Maya responded, "We'll let you know when to terminate the beam."

Zira replied, "Ditto, here."

Will entered the pilots' cabin and sat down in the pilot's seat. "Where's Bastille?"

Celine replied, "He'll be back shortly. He went to his quarters to rest."

"How are we looking?"

"The drop off point is coming up soon. How about you?"

"Everyone is waiting anxiously in the main quarters."

Celine said stoically, "There's a good chance we won't make it back."

"There's always a chance we won't make it back."

Will called the *Luna C*, "Good luck, Maya. We're counting on some sharp shooting from you and Talia."

"You make sure you take care of Saphoro down there. She's my best intelligence officer and a good friend."

"I'll do my best."

"Will, take care. I mean it."

Will swallowed hard and said, "I know you do."

"Keep an eye on Jack for me."

"I will, now get on those cannons."

Maya added, "Come back safe."

Will felt a tear form in his eye. He got up from the seat and left the cabin.

Celine knew he was concerned about the potential for failure and loss of life. She was amazed that he could keep such a cool head about it.

Maya exclaimed, "This is it, Celine! Drop us here."

"Roger."

Celine toggled off the switch for the first tractor beam.

"You're on your own, Maya."

Zira called, "We're coming up soon, Celine."

"I'm ready."

Bastille returned to the cabin. "How are you doing Celine?"

"One down, one to go."

Zira called again, "Now, Celine!"

Celine depressed the next switch and pulled the lever back to zero percent.

Celine announced, "The beam is shut down. You're on your own, Zira."

"Good luck, Celine."

Celine pleaded, "I'm counting on you, Zira. Keep them off of us."

"We've got you covered."

Celine turned the intercom off.

"Well, Bastille. It's show time."

"Yes it is."

Bastille leaned over and kissed Celine.

Celine looked at a monitor and pushed him away.

"Look, Bastille! We have company."

An Attradean battle cruiser appeared on the tracking screen.

Bastille muttered, "What timing!"

He flipped the intercom switch to 'on' and announced, "Will, come to the cabin, pronto."

Celine asked, "Should we attack it?"

"I don't know."

Will hurried into the pilots' cabin.

"What's the matter?"

Bastille pointed to the tracking screen.

Will laughed sadistically and said, "Lady Luck is smiling on us already."

Celine and Bastille were confused.

Will switched the DMS to 'external'. He called the *Ruined Stone* and the *Luna C*. "Hello, girls. It's Will. Are you out there?"

Maya asked, "What's up? I thought we were on radio silence."

"There's an Attradean battle cruiser coming. You're going to take it out and we're going to take its spot on the schedule."

Talia answered, "We've got it covered."

Will explained, "The fireworks should be started by then."

Maya replied, "Don't worry. We can handle it."

"Thanks, girls."

Will turned his attention back to Bastille and Celine.

"Don't worry. We're right on schedule."

Mynx entered the cabin.

"We've got images of the surface. You'd better take a look."

Will leaned over Celine's shoulder and turned on the secondary monitor.

Mynx informed him, "Channel C."

Will changed the selector to 'C'. The first image showed a long rectangular building.

Mynx pointed out, "That's your factory. We don't have enough firepower to destroy it."

"What powers it?"

"Two reactors located at the south end in the lower level."

"That should do the trick."

"Then we'd better be out of here when it blows."

"Shanna and I will take care of it. What else do we have?"

Mynx pressed 'enter' and an image of the base appeared on the screen.

"We estimate about one hundred and fifty troops are based here."

"Do you think we can keep the reinforcements at the base away from the plant?"

"Talia and Maya will be busy but there are only two entry points to the plant so we'll know where to stop them."

Mynx pressed 'enter' and another image appeared. Mynx explained, "This is the impound sector. I talked to Kalin and he believes that this ship here is his."

Mynx pointed to a mid-sized merchant ship docked between three freighters.

Will pointed out, "This could be a problem for Kalin. There's a lot of room for an ambush."

"What then?"

Will explained, "We have to free Kahlin's crew first. They'll help him recover his ship. Breel and Laneia will help protect Saphoro instead. I'm sure there are other crews imprisoned as well. They'll be happy to fight for their freedom."

"I'm glad you're so confident. I'm getting nervous."

Will asked, "Did you see Nester's ship?"

"Yeah. He's docked on the plant roof."

"Good. We'll use the other entrance. It keeps the element of surprise in our favor."

"If you say so."

"Pass the information along to the others. We'll be landing shortly."

Mynx promptly left the cabin.

Will asked, "Celine are you sure you're okay here?"

Celine replied, "I have the easy job. It's all of you that I'm worried about."

"We'll be fine."

Will departed the cabin and went to Shanna's quarters. He knocked and entered.

Shanna was praying on her knees. She finished and stood up.

Will informed her, "It's nearly time."

"I know."

Will hugged her tightly. "We can do this."

"I know we can."

Will kissed her gently. "Are you ready?"

"Yes. Let's show everyone that we're worthy to rule."

"That's my girl."

Will and Shanna descended the stairs side by side and entered the main quarters.

Will screamed, "Are we ready to rock?"

Everyone yelled in unison, "Yes!"

"Kalin, Jack, Mynx, you know what you have to do?"

Jack answered, "We're ready. Let's start the party."

Arasthmus handed out radio headsets to Kalin, Will and Jack.

He informed them, "You'll need these to coordinate your efforts. Celine can hear you as well on this frequency."

Will congratulated Arasthmus on his find.

"Nice work! Where were they?"

"I found them in a cabinet on the middle level. They're charged up."

"Excellent."

****

Maya and Neelon watched the tracking screen carefully as the cruiser drew closer. Maya spoke softly into the intercom, "Are you there, Talia?"

Talia answered back faintly, "I'm here."

"How does it look from your end?"

"The ship's almost in range."

"We'll coordinate our firing and target the area just behind the pilots' cabin. They'll never get a peep off."

Talia replied, "The ship is in range now."

Maya ordered, "We're almost in locking range. Three. Two. One. Fire!"

Cannon fire from both the *Luna C* and the *Ruined Stone* drilled the cruiser in the targeted area. It exploded instantaneously into a large fireball.

Maya changed frequency and called the *Phantom*. "This is Maya. The cruiser is destroyed. I repeat, the cruiser is destroyed."

****

Celine's voice came over the intercom.

"Will, the approaching ship has been destroyed."

Will beamed and said proudly, "Beautiful."

Celine continued, "We're landing now. There's a welcoming party of about thirty five soldiers waiting for us."

Will ordered, "As soon as we touch down, take them out."

"My pleasure."

The *Phantom* gracefully landed and the soldiers waited impatiently for Will and his friends to exit the ship.

Celine programmed two torpedoes for 'anti-personnel' and fired. Two large explosions wiped out most of the soldiers.

Celine hollered into the intercom, "We're on the ground. Go! Go!"

****

Will and Shanna exited the *Phantom* first. They took positions near the entrance to the plant.

Twelve soldiers fired from behind barricades on the roof.

Will instructed his friends, "Shanna and I will cover you. Get into the plant as fast as you can. We'll be right behind you so hurry."

Will asked Shanna, "Are you ready?"

"Ready as ever."

Shanna and Will stood up and laid a barrage of gunfire across the top of the roof. Jack led the remainder of the group across the grounds into the plant.

They were met by gunfire in the main hallway.

Jack led them down a secondary hallway. He fired and wounded one of the soldiers.

He ordered, "Grab him."

Mynx yelled, "Cover me!"

She crawled spryly down the side of the hallway toward the attackers. Jack and Neva fired at the two remaining soldiers.

Mynx aimed her pistol and picked off one of the soldiers. The other stepped out and fired at her. She rolled but the shot caught her left arm.

Jack hit the soldier twice and killed him. He and Neva rushed to Mynx' aid.

Jack ordered, "Kalin, get the wounded soldier and pull him into one of the rooms. We need directions fast."

Jack carried Mynx into one of the rooms.

"It's not too bad, Mynx. I think you'll live."

"Thanks for the sympathy, Jack."

Jack examined her arm. The flesh was burned to the bone. He tore his shirtsleeve off and wrapped her arm to stop the bleeding.

"Neva, get over here."

Neva entered the room. She was stunned by the blood on Mynx' clothes.

"Oh, Geez, Mynx. Your arm."

Jack ordered, "Neva, shut up. Can you get her back to the ship?"

"Yes, I can. What about Nester?"

"Get her back to the ship first. Then we'll worry about Nester."

****

Will and Shanna were pinned down from gunfire on the rooftop.

Will called to Celine, "We need some cover. We're caught."

Celine replied, "I'll relay the message."

"Tell them to keep it light. We don't want to bring down the plant on our heads."

"Understood."

Will and Shanna waited for a few minutes.

A quick pulse from the sky destroyed a portion of the rooftop and the soldiers on it.

Will and Shanna rushed inside only to be met by more gunfire. They lay on their stomachs as the soldiers fired at them.

Will called on the radio, "Jack, where are you?"

"Down the right hallway. We've got a live one."

"We'll be there shortly."

Will darted across the lobby to the right hallway. Shanna followed in a hail of gunfire.

Pieces of the wall and ceiling shattered all around them. One of the light fixtures fell from the ceiling and struck Shanna on the head. She stumbled and fell.

Will pulled her around the corner. "Are you okay?"

"Give me a minute. My head is spinning."

Will's gun beeped. The 'arm' light illuminated.

Will noticed and took Shanna's gun as well. Her gun beeped and the LED illuminated for 'arm'. The guns were recharged.

"I don't think we have a minute. Get down the hall. I'll cover you."

Will reached around the corner and fired several shots with both guns. He hit four of the approaching soldiers. He rolled across the floor of the hallway and fired again. He hit six more of the soldiers.

The remaining four retreated back to a barricade.

Will raced down the secondary hallway after Shanna.

She staggered awkwardly down the hall toward Jack's team.

Will caught up with her and yelled, "I thought you were okay?"

"I am!"

"You don't look like it."

Will helped her into the first room. He sat her down on the floor. He noticed a laceration on the back of her head. The blood dripped down onto the back of her leather vest.

Will ordered her, "Stay put."

Shanna placed her head in her hands and closed her eyes. She was dazed and in pain.

Kalin stood over the wounded soldier with one foot on the soldier's arm. He pointed his gun at the soldier's head.

Will asked, "What are you doing?"

"Helping him remember."

"Has he told you anything yet?"

Kalin replied, "A little bit. We know where the computer system is located. We also know where the prisoners are kept. I'm having a hard time helping him remember where the main power comes from."

Will knelt down by the soldier and stared into his eyes. Will focused intensely until his eyes glowed red.

The soldier cowered and tried to pull away.

Will grabbed the soldiers chin and said, "Think hard, my friend. Your's could be the next life taken."

The soldier began to shake and scream. "Alright! Stop already. I'll talk."

Kalin became frightened and stepped back fearfully from Will.

Will said calmly, "It's okay, Kalin. I'll explain it later."

Kalin cautiously came forward and stepped on the soldier's arm again.

Will asked, "Where is your main power generated from?"

The soldier trembled before him.

Will's eyes glowed again.

The soldier screamed, "On the bottom level! Take the elevator. In my pocket is a keycard. You'll need it to enter the area."

Will ordered Kalin, "Stand him up. He's going with me."

Will called Jack on the radio.

"Did Kalin give you directions?"

"Yes he did. We're in the upper hallway now. The left side is all windows. We can see most of the plant. There must be twenty ships down there. They're humongous."

"Make sure Saphoro gets all of the data for the surveillance and cloaking equipment."

"Roger. We just reached the computer section. I'll contact you when we're done."

****

Neelon poked Maya's arm and said excitedly, "Look at this! Four battle cruisers. They must have come through a portal."

Maya exclaimed, "Oh shit!"

"We don't have much time. What do we do?"

Maya called Celine on the intercom, "Celine, are you there?"

"Go ahead, Maya."

"There are four heavies coming your way."

"That's not in the plans."

"No kidding. We have to lay low until they pass by. Let Will know that he's on his own for a bit."

"Will do. Call when you're clear."

Talia appeared on the DMS and said, "You see them, too, Maya."

"Yeah. Play dead until they pass, then we'll figure out what to do."

"Gotcha'. Talk to you then."

Celine relayed the information to Will, Jack and Kalin.

Will asked, "Everybody hear that? No cover for a while."

Kalin yelled, "We're going downstairs for my crew."

"Good luck. Watch your backs."

Kalin left the room.

Will asked Shanna, "Can you walk?"

"Yeah."

"Don't lie to me. If you can't, I've got to get you out of here."

Shanna grumbled, "I can walk. You worry about finding the main power; I'll cover your back."

Will was unsure of Shanna's ability to keep up with him. Will grabbed the soldier and pulled him to his feet. Will ordered, "You're going with us. Lead the way."

The soldier hobbled out the doorway with Will holding his collar. Shanna struggled to keep up.

Two soldiers fired at them from the end of the hallway.

Will tackled the wounded soldier and fired back. He struck one of them. The other retreated.

Will got up and dragged the soldier onto his feet again. Another soldier fired from behind them.

Shanna fired back and hit him in the face.

Will yelled, "You can't let them get off a shot, Shanna!"

"Sorry. It won't happen again."

When they reached the elevator, Will pressed the button and waited anxiously.

The soldier asked, "Are you going to kill me?"

Will noted a bit of sarcasm in the soldier's voice. "Probably not, but I'm sure I can think of something better if you prefer."

"No. At this rate, I'll be dead before we get there."

Will snapped, "Then you'd better get a move on. I'd hate to see you leave the party early."

The elevator doors opened. Will pulled the soldier inside.

"Come on, Shanna!"

Shanna backed into the elevator and fell to the floor. She crawled to the wall and leaned against it.

Will encouraged her, "Come on, Shanna. I need you."

"I'm fine."

"You said that before. Why don't I believe it?"

The doors opened. Will and his hostage stepped into a foyer. Ahead of them was a thick plated door with a digital lock and a card reader.

Will shook the soldier, "It's show time. Get out your card and open the door."

The soldier reached into his pocket.

Will pressed the barrel of his gun against the soldier's temple.

The soldier asked, "What's that for?"

"In case you get second thoughts."

The soldier obediently took out the card and slid it through the reader. The door opened quietly.

Will pushed him through. He looked back at Shanna. "Do you want to wait here?"

"Yeah, I'll hold the elevator for you."

"I'll be back soon."

Will inquired, "Where is the control room?"

The soldier replied, "Straight ahead. The first door on the left."

Will pushed him along.

The soldier was bleeding profusely from his side and grew weaker.

The door slid shut behind them.

Will ordered, "Give me the card."

The soldier reluctantly handed his keycard to Will.

The soldier said arrogantly, "Tenemon is on his way with four cruisers. You and your rebel friends will be squashed like bugs."

Will answered just as arrogantly, "You really think so. Well, Tenemon and I go back a ways. He hasn't had much luck dealing with me."

"Perhaps your luck has run out."

"I guess we'll find out, won't we?"

Will opened the door to the control room and looked around. There were three panels with numerous controls and switches. Will backed into the hallway.

Across the hall was a thick watertight door. Will ordered the soldier, "Open it. We're going in."

The soldier hesitated and replied, "We can't. It's a high radiation zone."

Will held the gun to the soldier's temple and said, "You've got one chance to open that door and get in there or I'll kill you right here."

"You don't understand. There are two reactors in there. We can't enter that area at power."

"Oh, yes you can."

The soldier reluctantly opened the door. Will pushed him inside and quickly surveyed the huge compartment. The soldier fell to the floor and begged, "Please don't leave me here."

"Sorry, pal. I've got to go."

The soldier crawled back to the door.

Will exited and sealed the door. He felt bad for a moment as he closed the lock on the door but he rationalized, "I guess all's fair in war."

Will entered the control room and looked at the equipment. He had no idea what to do. He examined the controls and decided, "If I put all the switches in 'manual', that should create quite a problem for them."

Will raced back and forth in front of the controls taking every switch out of 'auto' and placing each one in 'manual'. For good measure, he turned all the dials to their maximum position.

Several trouble alarm windows flashed and an alarm sounded from the annunciator panel.

"That should do it."

He yelled into the headset, "Jack. Kalin. How are you guys doing?"

There was no response. Will rushed down the corridor to the exit. He quickly carded through the reader. The door opened and he rushed into the foyer.

Shanna was lying across the elevator door path unconscious. The door bumped her side repeatedly.

Will scooped her up in his arms and begged, "Come on, Shanna. Don't give up. We're almost out of here."

Shanna just stared with a glazed look in her eyes. He carried her into the elevator and waited anxiously for it to reach the top level.

****

Jack, Breel, Arasthmus and Regent fought desperately against ten soldiers barricaded at the end of the hall.

Jack hollered, "How's it coming, Saphoro?"

Laneia held Saphoro's palm-sized transcoder while Saphoro monitored the files on the main terminal's display.

Saphoro looked at the mini-display and answered, "I'm almost finished downloading."

"How much time?"

"Just a little bit longer."

Jack ordered Breel, "Cover me. I'm going to try Mynx's technique."

"You can't! It's too dangerous."

Jack glanced back at Breel and asked, "Got a better idea?"

"No, I don't."

Jack instructed Arasthmus and Regent, "I'm moving up. Keep me covered."

Jack crawled up the hallway toward the soldiers. He kept his pistol pointed forward. When the first soldier stood to fire, Regent picked him off.

Two more soldiers fired at Jack.

Breel and Arasthmus hit both of them.

As Jack got closer, the soldiers became impatient and exposed themselves to fire at him.

Jack hit the first soldier. Breel and Regent hit two more.

Jack rolled across the hall to the other side for a better angle. He taunted the soldiers, "Hey, losers. Come on out and play. I got something for you."

One of the soldiers kicked over his barricade and fired at Jack. He rolled quickly and fired back.

The soldier ducked against the wall, but Breel shot him before he could reach shelter.

Will called on his headset, "Jack. Kalin. What's going on?"

Jack replied, "Not now, Will. I've got my hands full."

Kalin replied, "I have my crew and about four others. We're pinned down by the entrance to the spaceport."

Will hollered, "Celine, can we get them any support."

"Negative. As soon as the *Luna C* and the *Ruined Stone* are clear to fire, I'll let you know."

"Roger."

Will asked, "You hear that, Kalin."

"Sure did. We're holding."

****

Neva set Mynx down inside the *Phantom's* main quarters.

Mynx ordered Neva, "You make sure you get that piece of trash and make sure he suffers."

"I will. You take it easy."

Neva hugged her.

She closed the hatch and left the *Phantom*. She entered the plant and saw dead soldiers in the main and secondary hallways. Neva took the stairs to the upper level. She heard Nester's voice nearby and ducked back into the stairwell. She ascended the steps to the roof.

When she opened the door, she saw Nester's small craft parked nearby.

"This is my lucky day!"

Neva entered the small ship and searched for a hiding place. She opened several cabinets, only to find them full of equipment. She fretted as she looked around the cabin for a place to hide.

Voices outside the ship frightened her. She stooped down low and hid in the corner. She noticed a handle to a floor panel.

Neva whispered to herself, "Oh, please be empty!"

She pulled the handle and raised the panel. Inside was a small man way, with circuit boards and wiring harnesses on four sides. Neva crawled in and closed the panel.

****

Celine called Will from the *Phantom*, "The heavies are getting close. What do you want me to do?"

Will set Shanna down. "If you leave now, can you escape?"

"I think so, but what about you and the others?"

A loud siren made it impossible for him to hear. Will picked Shanna up and carried her into another room.

He called Celine, "Are you there?"

Jack cut in and asked urgently, "Will, what did you do?"

Will replied, "What do you mean?"

Jack answered, "What did you do to set off the sirens. The loudspeakers announced a radiological emergency. Everyone's evacuating."

"I messed up their reactors."

"Well, we're in trouble now!"

Kalin cut in and yelled, "The soldiers are running! We can get to the ship."

Will ordered, "Get out of here as fast as you can, Kalin!"

Kalin replied, "We'll see you on the outside."

Will asked, "Jack, where are you?"

"We're on our way out the door. All of the soldiers are running away."

"Get on the *Phantom* and get out of here!"

"What about you?"

"We'll never make it. Get out of here. Celine, did you hear that?"

"Yes I did. I'll give you a last call when we're ready to leave."

Will replied despondently, "Just go. Shanna's hurt. We'll never make it.

Where's Neva?"

Jack said, "She took Mynx back to the *Phantom*."

"Take care of everyone. I'll miss them all."

Kalin's voice carried across the headset loudly. "Will, get to the roof. We'll try and pick you up."

"Just get out of here. You're gonna' have four cruisers breathing down your back real soon."

"If you get there, we can grab you on the fly. Be there."

Jack urged him, 'There's your ticket buddy. Good luck."

Celine responded, "Everyone's inside. The hatch is closed. Good luck, Will."

"It was fun, Celine. Take care of Bastille."

****

Maya watched nervously as four battle cruisers glided past them. Maya targeted the area behind the pilots' cabin of the closest cruiser.

Neelon asked, "Do we have a chance?"

"If we take out one and Talia takes out one, we have a chance."

"Should we call her?"

"No. We can't risk being spotted."

"How will she know when to fire?"

"I'm sure she's watching us closely."

Neelon complained, "This sucks."

"Just be ready to crank up the engines and get us out of here. This is gonna' be dirty."

Maya focused intently on the closest cruiser as it passed them. She looked ahead to the second one but it was a long shot for her.

"Neelon, raise Talia and tell her to fire and run when I give the signal. Get ready."

Maya's brow became sweaty and her hands and fingers itched. She waited for the precise moment.

"Neelon, now!"

Maya fired three shots and refocused on the second ship. She fired several more shots at it.

She saw traces of cannon fire from the invisible *Ruined Stone*. Two of the cruisers exploded into fiery masses. The third cruiser took multiple hits from Maya's cannon.

Neelon powered up the *Luna C* and in a few moments, they were racing away from Ramses-3.

The *Ruined Stone* was right behind them.

The *Phantom* took off from the damaged dock and darted into space.

Celine saw two of the cruisers explode. She called Talia and Maya.

"Nice shooting, girls!"

Maya answered, "We're on the run! We have a trailer."

Celine replied, "You left me a cripple. I'll finish it off and catch up with you."

Celine fired three torpedoes and destroyed the third cruiser.

Bastille burst into the cabin in time to see the cruiser explode.

"That's my girl."

Celine cried, "Bastille, you're okay!"

"Yes, I am. Who didn't make it?"

"Will, Shanna and Neva. We've got injuries as well."

Celine sniffled and said, "I can't believe Will and Shanna didn't make it."

A tear formed in her left eye.

Bastille comforted her, "I know. There's nothing we can do."

****

Will carried Shanna up the stairs to the roof. He saw two men enter a small craft. He ran and dove through the hatch with Shanna in his arms. They tumbled across the floor.

One of the men jumped on Will and punched him. The other started the ship and took off.

Will fought with the stronger of the two men.

Neva lifted the panel and peeked out. She saw the man raise a metal bar to strike Will. She lunged from the man-way and tackled him. She punched him repeatedly and screamed, "You bastard, Nester! I'll kill you."

The man at the controls selected 'autopilot' and darted after Will.

Will wrestled desperately with the man. They punched and clawed at each other.

Shanna opened her eyes and saw Will fighting. The metal bar was on the floor next to her. She strained to get up. After much effort, she got on her hands and knees.

Will was on his back and the man sat on top of him. The man punched him three straight times. Will's face and mouth were bleeding profusely.

Shanna picked up the bar and lunged at the man. She buried the metal bar in his back and fell on her face. The man shook violently and fell to the floor. The flesh fell away revealing a Weevil.

Shanna was repulsed by the creature.

Will pulled the bar out of the Weevil and handed it to Neva. "Kill the SOB!"

Neva had a sick smile on her face as she pierced Nester's chest with the bar. She put her face close to his and said sadistically, "Sayonara, asshole."

She twisted the bar and moved it back and forth.

Nester shook wildly and convulsed. The flesh fell away from his face and arms. Neva didn't seem to care.

A bright flash filled the cabin and sent the ship in to a wild spin.

Will, Neva and Shanna were tossed around until the ship stabilized.

Neva yelled, "What the hell happened?"

Will replied humbly, "I think that was my fault."

Neva got up and rushed to the controls. She turned on the scanners and directed them behind their ship. The display illuminated and showed a glowing cloud on Ramses-3 where the plant used to be.

Neva asked, "What the hell did you do to cause an explosion like that?"

"I don't know. I just flipped a bunch of switches for their reactors."

Neva exclaimed, "Holy …!

Will helped Shanna to sit up on the floor. He hugged her tightly.

"How are you feeling?"

"Like hell. I feel so weak."

"You picked a good time to get up. Thanks for saving me."

Shanna wiped some of the blood from Will's mouth with her hand.

She quipped, "You look worse than I feel."

****

Maya raised Talia on the DMS and informed her, "There was a major explosion on Ramses-3. It looked nuclear."

Talia asked, "Any word on Will and Shanna?"

"Negative. Neva's missing, too."

Talia said solemnly, "I'm sorry, Maya."

"Me, too."

"We're getting some distance between us and the cruiser."

"Good. Stay in touch."

****

Will asked Neva, "Did everyone else get away?"

"I don't know. It appears that the *Ruined Stone* and *Luna C* got away but there's an Attradean battle cruiser on their tail."

"Try to raise them on the DMS if you can."

Will helped Shanna to her feet. He escorted her to the co-pilot's seat and sat down.

Shanna sat on his lap and nestled her head against his shoulder.

Neva received three beeps from the DMS and informed Will, "We've got an incoming signal."

238

Shanna sat up so Will could see the display.

Tenemon's face appeared on the display. He screamed, "Nester, what the hell happened down there?"

Will slid Shanna off of his lap. He leaned toward the display.

"Tenemon, you dumb son-of-a-bitch."

Tenemon yelled, "You're not Nester! What the hell are you doing on his ship?"

Will chastised Tenemon, "What did I tell you about making this personal? Once again, you stuck your nose where it didn't belong."

****

Maya watched the display in utter shock. Her split screen showed Will and Tenemon. She shouted at Talia through the DMS, "Do you see what I see?"

"I sure do. Don't interrupt. I want to hear this."

Celine called in from the *Phantom*, "They're alive!"

Maya answered, "Let's see where they are."

She activated rear sensors and selected 'search' mode.

****

Tenemon snarled at Will, "You're a dead man. You've destroyed my plant."

Will explained, "As I told you before, I was paid to take care of some dirty business."

"What are you talking about?"

Will explained with a laugh, "You hired someone to steal technology from the Fleet and install it on your ships. That's dirty business."

"Who hired you?"

Will answered arrogantly, "That's confidential information."

Tenemon threatened, "I'm gonna' get you, Saris, if it's the last thing I do."

239

Will taunted him, "Don't make statements you can't back up. It's bad for your credibility."

Tenemon's cruiser turned around to chase after Will's ship.

"I'm coming for you, Saris."

Will yawned and replied, "I don't have time to play, Tenemon. I've got other business to attend to."

Tenemon's face disappeared from the screen.

Neva was concerned. "What are we going to do when he catches us?"

The display monitor beeped three times.

"Here comes your answer."

Neva pressed the 'receive' button. Celine's face appeared on the screen.

"Will, you son-of-a-bitch! You're alive. I see Shanna and Neva, too!"

Neva replied, "Hi, Celine. How's everyone else?"

"We thought you were the only casualties. We did take a few injuries but no deaths."

Will sighed, "What a relief."

"Bastille tells me that we can retrieve you from that little piece of junk you call a ship and bring you onboard the *Phantom*."

"Bastille never ceases to amaze me. When can he do it?"

"Bastille has a lock on you now. Three of you, correct?"

"That's right. Give us a minute and do your thing."

"See you then."

"Thanks Celine."

Will instructed Neva, "Set a course directly for Tenemon's ship and put us in 'autopilot'."

"I'd be glad to!"

Neva set the coordinates and activated the autopilot system. She stood up and spit on the Weevil that was Nester.

Will kidded, "Is this the end result of a lovers' quarrel."

"I never trusted that sneaky bastard."

****

Bastille activated the transporter controls. He ordered Celine, "Keep an eye on the Attradean cruiser. I'm going downstairs to make sure the extraction worked."

Bastille rushed down the steps to the main quarters. He whispered to Jack, "Will, Shanna and Neva should be on the way to the transporter room."

Jack pulled Breel's arm and said, "Come with us."

Jack and Breel followed Bastille to the transporter room.

Will, Shanna and Neva appeared on the platform.

Will did a flying leap into the arms of Jack and Breel.

Jack yelled, "How the hell did the three of you escape?"

Will replied, "By the hair on my chinny-chin-chin."

Breel was confused and asked, "What does that mean?"

Will explained, "My Aunt Penny used to say it when something was really close. I think it's an Earth saying."

Jack and Breel hugged Shanna and Neva.

Jack exclaimed, "It's great to have you all back."

"It's good to be back. I didn't think we were going to make it."

"There are a lot of people that will be glad to see you alive."

XII.   **Phase Two**

Will put his arm around Shanna and helped her to the front of
the cruiser. He stopped at his quarters and lay Shanna down on his
bed. He kissed her forehead.

"I'll bring Arasthmus in to check on you."

"Thanks, Will."

Will and Neva entered the main quarters.

Laneia and Saphoro sat in the chairs along the wall. When they
saw Will, they rushed to him.

Will hugged the girls.

Saphoro exclaimed, "Thank goodness, you're alive!"

"Did you get the data?"

"I sure did. It's downloading into our computer as we speak.
There's just one problem."

"What's that, Saphoro?"

"I got their entire database."

"I'm sure there's a lot of interesting things in it."

"You wouldn't believe what's on there."

Laneia asked, "Where's Shanna? Did she make it?"

"She's in my quarters. She's a little banged up."

Arasthmus stormed out of his berth and yelled, "What's going on out here? It sounds like…"

Arasthmus stared at Will for a few seconds. He stuttered, "What… What in the world …? How did you get here?"

Will teased, "I'm sorry I disappointed you."

Arasthmus hugged Will and explained, "I thought you were done for. How did you get here?"

"Thank Bastille for that."

Celine's voice came across the intercom, "If you turn on monitor six, you'll notice a small ship about to collide with Tenemon's cruiser."

Neva turned the monitor on.

Everyone watched as the small ship collided with Tenemon's cruiser. A small explosion ensued and the cruiser slowed down considerably.

Will jumped up and shouted, "Yes! Neva, you're a genius."

He hugged her and high-fived Breel and Jack.

Neva asked, "Where's Mynx?"

Arasthmus pointed to the third room down the hall.

"Is she alright?"

Arasthmus informed her, "We had to amputate her arm. She'll be okay."

"I'd better go see her. Where's Regent?"

Arasthmus answered, "He's in the second room down. He lost an eye."

Will was saddened. "Can I see him?"

Arasthmus pointed to the room. "I think he'll appreciate a visit from you."

"Can you check on Shanna for me? She's in my quarters."

"Sure."

Will entered the second room down the corridor. He saw Regent lying flat on his back. A gauze pad was taped over his left eye. A tear streamed down from his right eye.

Will called to him softly, "Regent, it's me."

243

Regent opened his right eye slowly. He almost fell out of bed he became so excited.

"Will! It's really you. It's so good to see you."

Will asked, "How are you feeling?"

"Better now."

"I'm sorry about your eye."

"I'm fine, now that you're back."

"I haven't forgotten about Keira. I'll make sure I bring her back to you."

Regent said bravely, "I'm going with you. I've lost an eye, not my ability to fight."

"Then I'll be glad to have you by my side."

"Do you think we still have a chance?"

"Tenemon's ship is crippled. He won't be back to Attrades for a while."

"No way!"

"That's right. We're moving up the timetable."

"Where's Shanna? Is she okay?"

"I think so. Get some rest and I'll see you later."

"Thanks, Will."

"I should be thanking you, Regent."

Will left Regent and entered Mynx's room.

Neva sat on the edge of the bed and held Mynx's only hand.

Will sat next to Neva and put his hand on the covers over Mynx's legs.

"Hi, Mynx. How are you feeling?"

"Miserable. I guess I'm out of a job now."

"Why's that?"

"GSS won't keep me with only one arm."

"Do you really think I would let you go back there? I need people like you and Neva on my crew."

Mynx replied, "That's sweet. I'd love to stay on your crew."

"Did Neva tell you how she took care of Nester?"

"No, but I'm anxious to hear?"

Will asked, "Before we get into that, what are you going to tell GSS?"

"What do you think I should tell them?"

"How soon before they expect you back at GSS?"

"Neva and I can stay out here a long as necessary until the problems are resolved."

"Well, I wouldn't tell them about your injury. Let them keep paying you."

"That works for me."

"Tell them that the base and the factory have been destroyed. I'm awaiting the balance of the payment."

"What happens when they say 'no'?"

"Tell them that it will cost double to catch the remaining destroyer that already left Ramses-3. Also tell them we'll want the money up front."

"Gladly."

Will added, "And of course you and Neva will receive equal shares as before. Advise your contact that there really is a destroyer with the technology out there."

"I'll take care of that immediately."

"Oh, yeah. Welcome aboard, ladies. It's a pleasure to officially have you on my crew."

Neva said gratefully, "Thanks, Will. I really appreciate everything you've done for us."

Will asked Neva playfully, "Wasn't it you that saved my life?"

Neva and Mynx chuckled at him.

Neva said proudly, "We're a hell of a team."

Will responded, "We're the best!"

He patted Mynx's knee and departed the room.

****

Will entered the pilot's cabin. He sat down between Bastille and Celine.

"Well, well. My two favorite pilots."

Celine hugged Will. She said, "I can't believe it! You pulled this off."

"It was a bit sloppy, but we did it."

Bastille asked, "What's next on the agenda?"

"We're going after the destroyer and then hit Attrades."

Celine was stunned, "What? After all this?"

"Now is the perfect time. Tenemon's ship is crippled. We hijack the destroyer now, while he's away."

Bastille asked, "What about the Seers?"

"I'll take care of the Seers. Take us to Eve's for a meeting with Kalin."

"I'm looking forward to this."

Will remarked, "I hope this plan works better than the last one."

Celine suggested, "Why don't you get a shower and some rest. You look like hell."

"Good idea."

Will departed the cabin and returned to his room. He knelt by Shanna and kissed her forehead. She opened her eyes and placed her hand on his cheek.

Will said, "I'm going to shower. I'll be back to check on you."

Shanna smiled at him but said nothing.

Will felt the pain she was enduring in her head. He felt responsible for not protecting her.

He entered the lavatory and turned the hot water on in the shower. He disrobed and stepped into the steaming hot shower.

Steam quickly filled the shower stall. Will leaned against the wall and thought about the Seers on Attrades.

Shanna pushed the shower door open and stepped inside.

Will was surprised to see her on her feet. Shanna placed her arms around him. He pressed her against the wall with his body. They kissed passionately. The two made love in the hot, steaming water.

Later, when they returned to Will's quarters, Shanna climbed into his bed and slept.

Will sat on the edge of the bed and admired Shanna as she slept. He lay down next to her and slept for several hours.

****

Celine placed the Phantom on 'autopilot' and relaxed in her seat. The display monitor beeped three times. She pressed the 'receive' button and watched the monitor.

Maya's smiling face appeared.

Celine sat up and asked, "What's up, girlfriend?"

"How are Will and Shanna doing?"

"They're resting now. I spoke with Will a short while ago. He's insistent on hijacking the destroyer and rescuing the Seers, especially since Tenemon's ship is limping back."

"The timing does seem good."

"I'm nervous about this. Something tells me we should quit while we're ahead, Maya."

Celine's monitor beeped three times. "I'll call you back. I have another signal coming."

"I'll be waiting."

Celine pressed 'receive' again. Kalin's face appeared.

"Hello, Celine. Long time, no see."

"How are you doing, Kalin?"

"Very good, but we have a problem."

"I expected as much. Things were too quiet."

"Eve's was raided by the Attradeans. They took a lot of prisoners."

Celine interjected, "So we'd best not meet there."

"I owe Will for helping me recover my ship and crew. We're ready for a strike against the Attradeans. Just give me the word."

"I have your signal locked in."

Bastille entered the pilots' cabin and greeted Kalin, "Hello, my friend."

"Greetings, Bastille."

"What news have you got for us?"

"Eve's is out. The Attradeans hit it and took prisoners."

"How far are you from us?"

"Not too far. When we left Ramses-3, I headed straight for Eve's."

Bastille asked, "Do you know where Yord is?"

"Sure. That's the barren planet where they used to keep the lepers?"

"Close enough."

"What about it?"

"Meet us there as soon as you can."

Kalin was surprised. "Do you have a secret hideout or something? There isn't anything near there for light years."

"I'm sure Will wants to share the surprise with you. I'll let him tell you."

"Can you give me Talia's signal designator? I'd like to speak with her."

"I can't, but I can have her contact you."

Kalin replied, "That would be great. I'll see you on Yord."

"Until then, my friend."

****

Celine called Maya back, "It's me again."

"What's up, Celine?"

"Kalin called in. Eve's was raided by the Attradeans."

"Good. Our boys don't belong hanging out there anyway."

"He's going to meet us on Yord."

"You didn't tell him about the base, did you?"

"No. We'll leave that up to Will."

"Smart move. So it's back to Yord we go."

"That's the plan. By the way, Kalin wants Talia to contact him. I'll stream his designators to you. You can pass them on."

Maya giggled aloud.

Celine asked, "What's so funny?"

"It's just hard to believe that Talia would fall for someone like Kalin."

"Why? I think it's cool."

"Oh, I think it's great. I just had a different idea of what her type of man would be."

Celine teased, "I won't tell you what we thought your type would be."

May said defensively, "You two talked about my love life."

"Well, your lack of it is more like it."

Maya snapped, "That's cruel."

"Not anymore. Now that you have Jack, you're a sweet loving commander."

May kidded, "You and I will settle this over a drink."

"I'll think about it. See ya' on Yord."

"Bye, Celine."

****

Will heard a tap on his door. He was nestled against Shanna. He hated to get up, but he gently pulled away from her. Still asleep, she sighed and turned over.

Will quickly dressed in clean clothes. He looked around the room and realized he lost his sword on Ramses-3. He felt bad about it.

Will opened the door and stepped into the corridor.

Jack was waiting with a smile on his face.

"How are you feeling?"

Will replied groggily, "Better since I slept."

Jack touched Will's swollen lower lip.

"Ouch!"

Will pulled back and asked sorely, "What did you do that for?"

Jack kidded, "You need to learn how to fight."

"I can fight. I just became so distracted that I forgot everything I could do."

"You can't afford to do that too often."

"I know. I was concerned about Shanna."

"When you lose your focus, people could die. You have to stay at your peak regardless of what happens around you."

Jack put his arm around Will and consoled him, "I know you're a young man. It's going to take time to understand everything that's happening in your life."

"Thanks, Jack. I'm glad someone knows what I'm feeling inside."

"Remember, I was your age once."

Will shook hands with him.

"Thanks again."

"We'll be landing on Yord shortly. Kalin's meeting us here."

Will followed Jack out of the room and down the corridor.

"What for? What happened to Eve's?"

"The Attradeans raided it. It's not safe right now."

"Damn. What a pity?"

Will and Jack entered the main quarters. Will sat down at the large table in the middle of the room.

Jack asked, "Do you want to talk about anything?"

"No. Not right now."

"I have something of yours."

Will looked up with interest and asked, "What?"

Jack reached behind his chair and pulled out Will's sword and scabbard.

"Did you lose this?"

Will gratefully took it from Jack and strapped it on his waist.

"Where did you find it?"

"It was on the floor of the secondary hallway."

Will replied, "It must have come off when I was crawling."

"Keep an eye on your weapons. You don't want to get into the habit of losing them."

"Thanks, Jack. I'll get my act together."

Bastille entered the main quarters from the pilots' cabin and announced, "We just entered the canyon. We'll be docking shortly."

"Thanks, Bastille."

Bastille commented to Will, "You look much better."

"Compared to what?"

"You were pretty beat up."

"Thanks for noticing."

Celine's voice interrupted their conversation. "We're on the ground. You can open the hatch."

Bastille pressed the knob and the hatch opened slowly. The three of them watched the *Luna C* and the *Ruined Stone* ease into their berths.

Shanna entered the main quarters and sat on Will's lap.

Will greeted her, "Hi, honey."

Shanna kissed him on the cheek and said, "Hi."

"We're home."

"I see."

Will asked with concern, "How are you feeling?"

"My head feels like a bell that's been rung too many times. But it's getting better."

"You had me worried."

"It didn't seem too bad at first but then it got worse."

Will and Shanna departed the *Phantom* first. Jack, Arasthmus and Regent followed next. Bastille and Celine exited with Mynx and Neva last.

Maya and Zira joined them on the dock. Maya hugged Will and Shanna. She had a tear in her eye. "I was worried sick about the two of you. I thought you were goners."

Will replied, "So did we."

Talia approached them and cheered, "To the victors go the spoils."

She hugged everyone. When she reached Mynx, she hugged her and said, "I'm so sorry about your arm."

Mynx responded gratefully, "Thanks. I'll get used to it."

Maya teased, "Where's your spoils, Talia?"

Talia answered, "Kalin is on the way in. I gave him directions."

Will informed them, "We'll meet in the hall. There's a lot to discuss."

He led Shanna up the granite stairs to the marble concourse.

Mariel greeted them, "Welcome back."

Will and Shanna approached her with extended arms. Mariel hugged each of them and said, "It's good to see you back. We were worried."

Shanna replied, "It's good to be back."

Mariel asked, "How was your mission?"

Will answered, "Successful, but costly. We suffered some serious casualties."

"Sometimes that makes victory all the more sweeter."

"We're not done yet. That was only the first phase."

Mariel pushed apart Shanna's hair and examined her cut. She was concerned after looking it over.

"Shanna, dear, that's a very bad cut on your head."

"I know. It really hurts."

Mariel asked, "How about you, Will? You seem to have some bumps and bruises."

Will covered his swollen lips and replied, "No big deal. I got beat in a fist fight."

Mariel was surprised.

"A fist fight. Isn't that a bit primitive for you?"

"I was caught up in the action and forgot the other things I could do."

Mariel suggested, "I could help you work on your concentration. We have exercises for that."

Shanna wrapped her arms around Will and countered, "I can help him with his concentration. I have my own ways."

Will blushed.

"Thanks anyway, Mariel. I've learned much from this experience."

Maya, Zira and Jack entered the hall.

Jack informed Will, "Kalin's here. He's on the way down."

"Thanks, Jack."

Will asked Mariel, "Can we bother you and your staff for a meal? I will repay you for your kindness when we return."

"Nonsense. If you can return the Seers and the Eye, that would be payment enough."

"Thank you, Mariel."

When everyone was seated in the hall, Will stood up to address them. He looked around and realized that Kalin brought quite a large group of men with him.

Will announced, "Welcome to our new friends and congratulations on a great victory. That, however, was just a warm up for what's coming. Fortunately for us, the element of surprise is now on our side."

Everyone cheered Will.

He walked from the table to the main floor and continued with his speech, "I'd like to welcome Kalin and his men. We're grateful to have their help in the next stage of our plan."

Four servants entered the hall with ewers of wine and distributed them at each table. Two more entered and distributed wooden mugs.

"I'm sure everyone is wondering how we are going to accomplish this next phase."

Kalin shouted, "Death to Tenemon and his forces!"

Will grinned. "I have something better in mind for Tenemon. Death is too easy."

Will perched himself on top of a chair, facing everyone.

"Kalin, I would like you to provide a distraction for Tenemon's forces at the palace. Whether you sit nearby and make them nervous or land and attack, that's your call. If you choose to loot on the way, that's also your call. I'm fine with that."

Kalin laughed loudly and bellowed, "Just like pirates, eh!"

"Just like pirates, except we're selective about who we prey on for tactical and financial reasons. Speaking of which, give Jack your names and he'll set up a non-alliance account for each of you. There will be some monetary incentives when this is over."

Kalin's men banged their cups on the table in gratitude.

Will resumed his instructions, "The rest of us will lead an assault on the new destroyer which is awaiting Tenemon's arrival for christening. Once we have control of it, I want Bastille and Celine to get it back here as quickly as possible. Saphoro will work with them to remove all of the surveillance and cloaking technology from it. As soon as you've completed that, get it installed on the *Phantom*."

Saphoro asked, "How much time do we have?"

"Not much. I'm counting on you to be quick."

Will sauntered to the next table where Mynx and Neva were seated.

"My negotiators here will give GSS a chance to settle an old account. If they fail to comply, the girls will break GSS's heart with some bad news."

Mynx and Neva nodded cheerfully.

"The rest of us will rescue the Seers. Either Maya or Talia will transport us up from the palace and we'll be gone. At some point, Tenemon will arrive in a crippled cruiser. He probably has reinforcements coming from other parts of the galaxy already. If it gets too hot, I want the ships out of there, immediately. The remainder of us will tough it out. Any questions?"

Kalin asked, "Can you tell me what will happen to Tenemon?"

"Only that I don't want him killed. He's worth more to us alive. Besides, I have big plans for him. I can tell you this. Tenemon will pay us handsomely for something he doesn't have."

Kalin replied, "That will suffice."

Six women entered the room carrying trays of food. They served everyone at the tables.

Will shouted, "Eat well, my friends!"

He returned to the high table and sat next to Shanna.

Shanna said, "Well done, my prince."

"Thank you, my princess."

Mariel commented to Will, "You've become quite an orator. Your people respond to you. That's very good."

"Thanks, Mariel. It's from the heart."

"That is the best way to speak to your people."

Will finished eating and stood up. He announced to everyone, "I'm returning to the *Phantom*. I ask each of the ship commanders to check in when you're ready to leave."

Will and Shanna thanked Mariel for a fine meal and exited the hall. They descended the granite stairs and crossed the dock.

Will paused in front of the *Phantom* and stared at it.

Shanna asked, "What's wrong, Will?"

Will replied, "I guess we really did beat up the paint job on our ship. Laneia and the others did such a nice job, too."

"I'm sure they'll be happy to repaint it when we return."

254

Will led Shanna onboard and into his quarters. He sat her on his bed and placed his arms around her waist. She immediately responded by kissing him.

Will asked, "Why is it that every time I kiss you, we make love?"

"Is that a problem?"

"No, just an observation."

Will laid her gently on her back. He lay next to her and nibbled on her neck. She rolled him onto his back and sat on him. She held his hands in hers and spread them apart. She lay against his chest and kissed him.

After making love, they slept peacefully.

****

Will awoke and dressed himself. He kissed Shanna on the forehead as she slept. After watching her for several moments, he left the berth and entered the main quarters.

Bastille sat at the table, patiently waiting. He quipped, "I was afraid that I might need to send Arasthmus in to revive you."

Will asked, "What's wrong?"

"What's wrong? We're ready to move on Attrades. Kalin has already started his attack from the east side of the palace. We're moving in from the west. The *Luna C* and the *Ruined Stone* are in position and cloaked."

"Wow. I slept through all that?"

"Tenemon's on the way. He's fairly close. His reinforcements still have a ways to come yet. I took the liberty of firing torpedoes at the two cruisers on the palace grounds. Scanners indicate one large ship is inside the docking facility on the hill."

"Excellent."

"I told Maya and Talia to let Tenemon land. You did want him on the ground didn't you?"

"Absolutely. You did well, Bastille."

Shanna entered the main quarters and joined Will. She placed her arm around his waist.

255

Bastille teased, "Hello, Sleeping Beauty."

Shanna rubbed her eyes and asked, "What's the matter?"

Will explained, "I think we overslept a little bit."

"Are we ready to leave, yet?"

"We're a little bit past that."

"Oh. How long before we reach Attrades?"

"Get your stuff on. We're heading down now. Kalin started the battle already."

Shanna was surprised that they had slept for so long.

"I'll be right back. Don't leave without me."

She rushed up the stairs to her quarters.

"I'm impressed, Bastille. You took care of all this without my help?"

"Well, Jack and Celine handled some of it as well."

Mynx ambled into the main quarters. She saw Will and teased, "So, you are alive. I have news for you."

Will teased, "Enlighten me, oh wise one."

"GSS says they aren't paying the balance. It was too high to start with. I informed them that there is one destroyer on the loose with the stolen technology. They're offering five thousand credits to capture it."

Will was insulted. "Five thousand! Are they nuts?"

"It gets better. I told them one million credits and they laughed. I explained that you were sure Tenemon would have no problem paying one million credits to retain possession of his ship."

"Good girl! You did well."

"Unfortunately, they fired me and Neva. I told them we quit, though, I did mention that we'd give them one opportunity to bid on the destroyer when we have it in our possession, but I couldn't guarantee the price. Oh and I did mention that next time, you want the money up front."

"That's outstanding, Mynx. I'm proud of you. Where's Neva?"

"She's cutting up her GSS uniforms. She has a bit of an attitude sometimes."

Will kidded, "Yeah, I saw how she handled Nester. She literally beat him to death."

256

Celine announced, "We're landing. Get your butts in gear, people."

Will asked, "Who's piloting the *Phantom* if we get our hands on this destroyer."

Bastille answered, "Saphoro is. Celine gave her a little course on the *Phantom's* instrumentation."

"Good move. I like it."

Will and Bastille left the pilots' cabin and returned to the main quarters.

Jack handed out RG-23 pulse pistols to everyone.

"Party time, people. Let's make it a good one."

Shanna entered the main quarters and stood by Will's side. She was wearing Tera's leather and knives. She handed Will his sword and scabbard.

She teased, "Did you forget these?"

Will replied foolishly, "Oh, yeah. Thanks, Honey."

Will was embarrassed as he strapped on his sword.

Jack teased, "There you go again, forgetting your weapons."

Bastille asked, "Are we ready?"

Everyone nodded in agreement.

Will yelled, "Open the hatch and kick some ass!"

As soon as the hatch opened, they encountered gunfire. Will and Shanna darted from the ship and hid behind a crate. They fired at six soldiers lined up near the end of the dock.

Shanna hit one and wounded another.

Will fired and hit a third one. The remaining soldiers retreated behind a barricade.

Will got his first look at the destroyer and gazed at it in awe.

He asked Shanna, "Did you ever see anything so big?"

Shanna replied with a little humor, "Well, if you must know…"

Will covered her mouth with his hand and said, "Smart ass."

Regent led the remainder of the group off of the ship. They rushed toward the destroyer.

Will and Shanna covered them from the dock.

After a short exchange of gunfire, Regent and Jack entered the destroyer.

Will and Shanna hurried to catch up.

Bastille and Celine entered the cabin and examined the controls.

Will peered into the pilots' cabin and asked, "Can you fly her?"

Bastille replied, "She's very similar to the *Phantom*. It shouldn't be a problem."

"Good. Give us a few minutes to secure the rest of the ship and we'll be out of the way."

Celine said, "Good luck, Will."

"Thanks, Celine. Good luck to the two of you."

Will turned around and an Attradean soldier pointed his gun at his head. He put his hands up.

Shanna crept from the stairwell into the main quarters and saw the soldier. She took a knife from her armband and threw it.

The knife embedded itself in the back of the soldier's neck, just under the brim of the helmet. The soldier collapsed to the floor.

Will yelled, "Nice throw, Shanna!"

"I owed you from the last battle."

Ten minutes later, Jack descended the stairs to the main quarters. He announced triumphantly, "The ship is secure. Let's get out of here."

Will banged on the door to the pilots' cabin. "The ship is yours. We're leaving."

Bastille proclaimed, "Just like clockwork!"

Will raced to the front of the destroyer. He waved with a thumb up to Celine and Bastille.

The destroyer's engines roared to life and eased the big ship out of the hangar.

Will left the hangar and hurried down the hill with Shanna close behind.

Shanna asked, "What about the others?"

"They'll catch up. We need to secure the area for them."

Will and Shanna reached the palace gates. Two soldiers fired from the top of the wall. They ducked inside the gateway, close to the wall.

Shanna indicated, "Tenemon has the soldiers guarding the palace instead of his regular guards."

"What's that mean?"

"This isn't going to be easy."

Will heard gunfire from the west.

"I hope Kalin drew some of the soldiers out of the palace."

"It's possible."

Will pushed the large wooden gate. It moved a few inches.

He whispered, "I'll push it open and rush in. Here's your chance to show me more of your knife-throwing skills under pressure."

"Come on, Will. After all this, you still doubt me."

Will teased, "Put up or shut up."

Will pushed the heavy gate open far enough so the soldiers above could take notice. He dashed along the inside wall and raced toward the white prison building.

The soldiers fired at him repeatedly.

He skillfully dodged them and dashed to the entrance.

Shanna backed away from the outer wall until she could see their backs. She took two knives from her armbands and fired them at the soldiers. The knives struck the back of their necks and the soldiers fell to the ground inside the palace wall.

Shanna stepped inside the gate and searched the area. She saw Will in the doorway of the prison waiting for her.

Will used his telepathy to communicate. "Follow the wall and hurry your cute little butt over here."

Shanna giggled and darted toward him. She cautiously retrieved her knives from the dead soldiers. When she was close enough to the prison, she dashed across the grounds to the entrance.

Three soldiers rounded the corner and spotted her. Will drew his gun and fired at them. He took them out easily.

Shanna reached the doorway and teased, "It's about time you learned to shoot straight."

"Keep it up, girl."

Will descended the stairs to the second level. Shanna followed him closely.

Will saw two soldiers coming down the hallway.

"You want them, Shanna?"

"Sure. I'll see you downstairs."

Shanna took two knives from her armbands. She checked her leg straps and saw that she had four more.

Will descended the stairs to the third level and searched the area cautiously.

There were no soldiers or guards in sight.

Will continued down the stairs to the bottom level. He quickly crossed the stone floor. When he turned the corner, he saw the four Seers huddled around the Eye. They were chanting incantations in the Yordic language.

Will used his telepathy to communicate with them.

"Seers, I have returned to release you."

The Seers stopped praying and looked across the mist at Will. The elder Seer asked, "Who are you?"

"Will Saris. Give me some time to figure out how the mist is controlled."

One of the Seers called to him, "The controls are in this room over here."

She pointed to a small room along a ledge behind them.

The Seers watched anxiously from their stone island.

Will studied the ledge, which wrapped around to the backside of the chamber. He carefully stepped along the ledge until he was on the opposite side of the chamber from the stairs.

One of the creatures leaped at Will's leg but missed. His heart raced, as he feared he would fall.

Will located the small room with ten blue valves and ten red valves on the wall. Each valve had a number. Will began closing the valves, one at a time. He found that the lower numbered red valves were for the creatures' lair, so he turned those back on.

He closed the higher numbered red valves and stopped the flow of ammonia into the channel at the end near the stairs. When he opened the blue valves, oxygen was pumped into that particular part of the channel, thus forcing the creatures to retreat into their lair.

After a few moments, he drew his sword and stepped down into the channel. Although he still smelled traces of the ammonia, it was bearable.

Shanna appeared at the edge of the chamber floor over the channel. She saw Will and asked, "Is it safe to cross?"

"Yes. I turned off the ammonia."

Will looked up and saw four guards behind Shanna. Before he could say anything, they grabbed her arms and pulled her away from the channel.

One of the guards stepped along the ledge to the small room.

Will thought, "Damn, this isn't good."

He hurried up the steps to the island where the Seers waited anxiously.

The guard turned on the ammonia and the creatures rushed out of their lair. They sensed fresh meat in the area and were rabid with hunger.

The soldier laughed at Will and said, "Looks like you've got no place to go. Tenemon will be happy to see you."

Another guard dragged Jack's body in and dropped him on the ground. Blood streamed from the side of Jack's head.

That guard added, "So much for your buddy."

Will paced the floor, trying to think of a way out.

Shanna cloaked her thoughts and used her telepathy to speak to Will. "Do you think it's a good time to use my alter-shape?"

Will answered telepathically, "If you think you can. I'll keep the guards distracted."

"I'll give it a try."

Shanna pretended to be ill. She dropped to the floor and laid still.

The two guards let her fall to the ground. One guard kept his gun pointed at her.

Will taunted the guards. "If you don't let me out of here, I'll transform into your worst nightmare!"

One of the guards asked curiously, "How would you do that?"

"I'm a shape-shifter. Haven't you ever heard of Firenghians?"

The guards looked at each other, uncertain if Will was serious or not.

One of them replied, "I've heard of them. They don't exist anymore."

"Says who?"

"Tenemon sent the Boromeans to wipe out the last of them many cycles ago."

"Do you believe everything Tenemon says? He's having a lot of difficulties lately with his credibility. In fact, the Boromeans are attacking several of your outposts as we speak."

The guard asked the others, "Have you heard anything about that?"

The second guard replied, "Yeah. The Boromeans think one of our ships attacked their base and destroyed it."

"Wow. That would be enough to set them off."

Will asked, "Have you ever seen a Boromean up close?"

The guards were interested in Will's conversation.

The talkative guard replied, "No. Have you?"

The fourth guard returned from the small room.

Will explained, "My mother was killed by them. She was Queen of the Firenghians. Boromeans are ugly, ruthless and dangerous."

The second guard asked, "What do they look like?"

Will explained, "They have mandibles instead of jaws. They wear dreadlocks with poisonous stingers on the tips. They prefer to kill their prey slowly and tend to eat their victims while they are still alive."

The guard said with a frown, "That's nasty."

The other guard looked down and Shanna was gone.

"Hey! Where did she go?"

Will teased, "Come on, guys. She's a girl. Where's she gonna' go?"

The first guard said to the second guard, "Go find her. Kill her if you have to."

The second guard left. Now there were only three remaining.

262

Will paced back and forth. He noticed that Jack stirred slightly.

Shanna contacted Will telepathically. "I'm in the small room. What can I do?"

Will responded to her, "Turn off nine and ten red. Turn on nine and ten blue."

The first guard asked Will, "Can you really change shape?"

"Come on. I can't tell you for sure. What if I need that to escape?"

"You can't escape. It's hopeless."

Will looked down and saw the creatures retreating from the section of channel to his left.

He answered, "I could leave right now and these creatures wouldn't touch me."

The guards laughed heartily.

The third guard said, "I like him. He's entertaining."

The first guard asked, "Why wouldn't the creatures attack you?"

"Because I have special powers that frighten them."

Will noticed Regent and Arasthmus peering around the corner at them.

"Watch this."

He walked down the steps into the channel.

The guard shouted, "Stay right there!"

Will advised him, "You should come down and tie me up; otherwise I might walk out of here."

Will knew the creatures were watching him, waiting for an opportunity to pounce on him.

The third guard said, "I'll take my chances from up here."

Will laughed at them and walked across the channel toward the steps near the ledge.

The guard hollered, "Get back here or I'll shoot!"

Will laughed at them. "You don't understand. You can't kill me. I'm not mortal."

The guard became irate and said, "Let's find out."

He raised his gun to fire but Arasthmus and Regent fired at the guards first. They fell to the ground dead.

Will returned to the island inside the channel.

He shouted from the platform, "Boy, am I glad to see you guys!"

Regent replied, "Glad to oblige."

Will instructed Shanna, "Turn off red valves four through eight."

Regent called out to the Seers, "Keira, are you there?"

One of the Seers approached the edge of the floor. She asked excitedly, "Regent, is that you?"

"Yes it is, dear. I've come for you."

Will announced, "It's safe to cross the channel. The ammonia is turned off."

Regent crossed the channel first and climbed up the steps. He picked Keira up and carried her back across the channel.

The remaining Seers quickly followed them.

Arasthmus crossed the channel and picked up the Eye. It was heavy for him but he managed to get it back to the other side.

Jack stood up shakily and leaned against the wall. He placed his hand over the wound on the side of his head. He heard footsteps in the stairwell and warned them, "Hide quickly. Someone's coming."

Will waited on the island. He ducked behind the pedestal. The others hurried around the corner out of sight.

Tenemon entered the chamber with ten guards. He stomped across the floor to the edge of the channel.

Will instructed Shanna, "Turn on the ammonia, quickly."

The mist thickened and the creatures roamed the channel freely again.

"Get out of the room and hide. Wait for my instructions."

Shanna obeyed his instructions.

Will stepped out from behind the pedestal.

Tenemon recognized him immediately.

He shouted at Will, "At last, I'll have the satisfaction of cutting you into little pieces, Saris."

Will sat on top of the pedestal and taunted Tenemon, "How many ships have you lost over this little feud? How many prisoners have you lost? How many outposts have been destroyed?"

Tenemon's face turned beet red. He asked angrily, "What do you know about the outposts?"

Will happily related the story about how they attacked the base with an Attradean vessel.

Will paced along the edge of the channel to capture the attention of the guards.

Tenemon screamed, "Where is my destroyer?"

Will explained, "Certain people paid a lot of money for this job. They paid even more to make sure there were no more of the destroyers under construction."

Tenemon ordered one of the guards, "Turn off five and six. I'm going to kill him myself."

Will teased, "Tenemon, I really have to wonder about how you got to be king. It seems that ever since we first met, you've had nothing but misfortune."

Tenemon drew a saber from a sheath under his thick robe. He warned Will, "When I get my hands on you, I'm going to skin you alive."

The guard shouted from the small room, "Five and six are off."

The guard left the room and rejoined the other guards.

Tenemon watched the creatures retreat from that section of channel. He ordered his guards, "I want you in the channel. Make sure he doesn't escape."

Tenemon stormed down the steps and crossed the channel.

Will contacted Shanna, "When the guards enter the channel, turn five and six on. Turn nine and ten off. When I escape, quickly turn nine and ten on."

Tenemon stormed up the steps to the island.

He said coldly, "You have one chance to return everything you took from me."

Will drew his sword and laughed.

He taunted Tenemon some more, "I have to hand it to you, Tenemon, you've made this job entertaining."

Tenemon stalked him with his saber positioned to strike.

Will continued goading him, "Don't you want to know how much your life is worth to my employers?"

Tenemon asked angrily, "Who are your employers?"

Will was about to answer when Tenemon struck at him.

Will blocked the jab and spun away from Tenemon. He backed toward the open section of channel.

Tenemon screamed at his guards, "Get in the channel, now!"

The guards reluctantly filled the oxygenated portion of the channel.

Will noticed Breel and Laneia hiding near the steps. He saw the others quietly exit the chamber and ascend the stairs.

Will ordered Shanna, telepathically, "Open five and six, now!"

Tenemon lunged at Will with the saber pointed straight at him.

Will used his hilt to deflect the saber wide. Will rolled away from Tenemon and stuck Tenemon's right calf with his sword.

Tenemon stumbled to one knee.

The guards began choking.

Suddenly, the creatures pounced on them.

Four of the guards scrambled up the steps but Breel and Laneia were there. They shot the guards in the legs. The wounded guards fell down the steps and were quickly devoured by the creatures.

Will teased, "I really hate to leave you like this, but I'm sure we'll meet again."

Tenemon groaned and lunged at Will. He caught Will by surprise and buried his saber in Will's side.

Will staggered backwards and said shakily, "You finally got one good shot. Sorry but I do have to go."

Will contacted Shanna, "Are nine and ten closed?"

"Yes they are. Are you alright?"

"No."

Will hobbled down the steps and crossed the channel.

"Make sure you open nine and ten when I …"

Shanna shouted to Breel, "Will needs help! Get him out of the channel."

Breel hurried to the ledge and carefully stepped across it.

"Will, over here!"

Will staggered toward Breel.

Breel grabbed him and pulled him from the channel.

Shanna opened valves nine and ten.

Tenemon screamed, "Come back here! You can't escape me."

Tenemon tried to descend the steps and cross the channel but the creatures raced toward him. He quickly backtracked onto the island.

Tenemon screamed, "Damn you, Saris!"

Breel pulled the saber out of Will's side and tucked it under his belt. He put his arm around Will and carried him carefully along the ledge to the other side.

Shanna had just finished dressing after shifting back. She and Laneia took Will from Breel as he cleared the ledge.

Will was breathing heavily and dripped sweat from his brow. His shirt was soaked with blood. A trail of red spots followed him.

Breel hyperventilated for a minute.

Laneia asked, "Are you alright, Breel?"

"Yeah. The smell of ammonia makes me a little nauseous."

The girls laid Will down on the ground.

Shanna examined his wound.

"We've got to get him back to the ship. It looks bad."

Tenemon recognized Shanna. He yelled at her, "I know you, Seer! I'll get you, I swear."

Shanna grew angry and walked to the edge of the channel. She yelled, "One day, if Will doesn't kill you, I will. That's a promise, you piece of garbage."

Tenemon fumed, "Screw you, bitch!"

Shanna replied with a smile, "No, it looks like you're the bitch and I'd say you were screwed. See ya', bitch."

Laneia walked to the edge of the channel and asked sarcastically, "Do you know who I am?"

Tenemon recognized Laneia. He pleaded, "My sweet daughter. Help me across this channel."

"I can't. I'm not your daughter anymore. I was an accident, remember."

Tenemon pleaded, "Come back, Laneia. Please don't leave me like this."

Laneia said defiantly, "You're only alive because of me. Consider this a gift. Next time, you will die."

Laneia joined her friends.

Breel picked Will up and carried him.

Tenemon screamed, "I hope you die, Saris!"

Will replied weakly, "I'll call again. Perhaps we'll do lunch."

Tenemon bellowed, "I hate you, Saris!"

Breel carried Will up the stairs.

Will yelled from the stairwell, "Good luck with your kingdom."

Shanna put a finger over Will's mouth. "That's enough. Save your strength."

When they exited the prison, they found Jack waiting nearby with two guns. His shirt was blood-soaked and he was somewhat delirious.

He managed to crack a smile and said, "Aren't we a pair?"

Will smiled briefly, but lost consciousness.

Jack contacted the *Luna C*, "Maya get us up, fast."

"How many, Jack?"

"All of us."

The gate opened and twenty soldiers rushed into the prison toward them.

Jack muttered, "Oh, boy!"

A brief flash from the transporter returned them to the *Luna C* just in time.

XIII.   Leviathan

The *Phantom* and the *Leviathan* reached Yord together. Saphoro guided the *Phantom* gracefully into Devil's Canyon and into the cavern. The *Leviathan* circled above and waited patiently.

Mariel approached her and asked, "Well?"

Saphoro proclaimed, "We made it! The others are on the way."

"That's great, Saphoro! It's finally over."

"Not yet. Our work is just beginning."

"We'll help you in any way we can."

"I have to start downloading the Attradean database and figure out how to remove the cloaking and surveillance systems from *Leviathan*."

"Sounds like a real challenge. Good luck."

"Thanks, Mariel."

****

Shanna entered the pilot's cabin and asked, "How are we doing, Maya?"

"We'll be hitting the first portal shortly."

"Good."

"I sent the *Ruined Stone* to keep an eye on things for a bit in case Tenemon tries to strike back at us."

"Excellent."

What happened to Will?"

"He, uh, got hurt in a sword fight."

"With whom?"

"Who do you think?"

"Not Tenemon."

"Yes."

"What an ass!"

"He seems to have a flare for the dramatic."

"I've noticed."

Shanna departed the cabin and returned to Will's quarters.

Arasthmus placed a patch over the wound in Will's side.

Will stirred and awoke.

"How is it, Arasthmus?"

"This one's gonna' be tricky. I inserted a clamp to stop the bleeding, but this is a dangerous wound. Don't you dare move."

"I won't."

Arasthmus gave Will an injection.

Will asked, "What's this for?"

"To make sure you don't move."

Will cracked a brief smile and fell asleep.

Shanna kissed Will's forehead. "Get well, my love."

She touched his cheek gently.

****

The *Luna C* approached Yord.

Maya turned on the intercom and announced, "We're home everyone. As soon as the ship is secure, we can exit."

Everyone in the main quarters cheered and hugged each other.

Regent and Keira kissed passionately.

The *Luna C* glided smoothly into the second dock.

Saphoro crossed the dock from the *Phantom* and hurried to greet them.

The hatch slowly opened and she boarded.

Saphoro asked, "Is everyone alright?"

Breel answered, "No. Will's hurt pretty bad."

"What did Arasthmus say?"

"We haven't heard anything in a while."

Shanna entered the main quarters.

"Hey, Shanna. How is Will doing?"

"Not too good. Arasthmus has stopped the bleeding. Now it's up to Will. We don't know how far his healing abilities can go."

"Let me know if anything changes."

"Sure will. I'll see you in a bit."

"Bye."

Shanna left the main quarters and entered the right hall.

Arasthmus stopped her and said, "Will and Jack are going to need some down time."

Jack yelled from one of the berths, "Not now! We've got work to do."

Arasthmus explained, "I'm going to give Jack something to immobilize him. He's a pain in the ass."

Shanna laughed. "That's been said on many an occasion from what I hear."

"We'll have to keep Will in bed. He has an internal injury and it may not heal as fast as a surface injury."

Shanna smiled fiendishly. "Leave that to me."

She returned to Will's berth.

Regent picked up the crystal Eye and escorted the Seers off the ship.

When they appeared on the dock, everyone cheered for them.

Mariel rushed to greet them.

Keira exclaimed, "Mariel! I never thought I'd see you again."

"Neither did I. It's great to have you back."

Mariel and the Seers hugged each other and cried tears of joy.

271

Mariel asked Regent anxiously, "How did it go?"

"Not bad."

Keira stepped aside from Regent, revealing the Eye in his arms. She informed Mariel, "We have recovered the Eye of Icarus."

Regent stood before them with the Eye.

Mariel gazed at the crystal object and proclaimed, "We are born again. Yord will become the centerpiece of galactic civilization that it once was."

Mariel waited patiently for Will and Shanna. She finally asked Regent, "Where are the others?"

Regent explained, "Will was injured. They're still inside."

Mariel proposed, "We can pray in the temple for healing for all who were injured, including you, Regent."

"Thank you, ma'am."

"I must see how Will and Shanna are doing. My servants will have food and drink in the hall for all of you."

Mariel hurried onto the *Luna C.*

****

The huge destroyer, dubbed *The Leviathan*, hardly fit into Devil's Canyon. Bastille sweated as he focused on the monitors which zoomed in on the canyon's steep, rocky sides. He felt a bit relieved when they glided just above the canyon floor.

Rows of lights on either side of the canyon illuminated the path to the hidden gate.

Bastille commented to Celine, "Well, will you look at that – a welcome mat."

Celine asked, "Will we fit through the gate?"

"It's gonna' be tight. We might have to touch up the paint a little once we dock her."

The destroyer vibrated briefly, sending chills down Celine's back.

"What was that, Bastille?"

"Looks like the port side's going to need a little bit of that paint I was talking about."

Bastille carefully maneuvered her through the deep cavern.

The hidden gate slowly opened on *Leviathan's* left side.

Bastille wiped the sweat again from his brow and said, "I'm glad they're learning to use the controls inside the base for the lighting and the gate."

The *Leviathan* squeezed through the entrance and eased into the far berth, just past the *Phantom*.

Celine remarked, "Not bad. Did you ever pilot anything this size before?"

Bastille laughed at her.

"What's wrong? Is it something I said?"

Bastille blurted, "Before the *Phantom*, I never piloted anything in my entire life!"

Celine's eyes widened with surprise.

"Well, how did you ever get this far?"

"My brother owned a transport and I traveled with him. He explained how to navigate and pilot but he never let me try."

Celine was shocked.

"Bastille, all this time… We could have been killed!"

"Relax, Celine. It's just like one of those virtual reality games. I spent a lot of credits visiting the virtual reality clinics."

Celine sat back in her chair and covered her eyes with her hands.

Bastille asked seriously, "Are you alright, Celine?"

"Is there anything else you 'forgot' to tell me, Bastille?"

Bastille rubbed his chin and thought for a few seconds.

"Yeah, I guess there is."

"Well you'd better get it out now before I lose my patience with you."

"I used to fix things in my village. Sometimes I would even make new things for the people. Because it was a small village, there was never much money in it. One day, my brother invited me to work for him. I learned about his ship and how to fix it. The ship didn't break very often so I didn't have a lot to do, but it paid good."

Celine listened stoically and said, "Uh-huh."

"I'm sorry. I wouldn't have done it if I didn't know how to. I just didn't have the experience."

Celine asked impatiently, "What else is there, Bastille?"

Bastille hesitated and reached for Celine's hands. He held them in his and said, "I love you, Celine. I never felt this way about anyone in my life."

Celine giggled at him.

Bastille asked defensively, "What's wrong with that?"

"Hell, I don't think anyone's ever loved me in my entire life. I was always thought of as a certifiable nutcase."

"Well, I don't. I see the real you and I like it."

Celine lowered her head and tears rolled down her cheek.

"I'm sorry for getting mad at you, Bastille. I love you, too."

Celine lifted her head and kissed Bastille.

He blushed but didn't resist.

Bastille glanced out the front viewing shield and saw a host of people waiting at the dock.

"Damn, I guess we'll have to wait."

Celine looked out and saw Saphoro at the front of the *Leviathan*, waving to them.

"I'll have to talk to Saphy about her timing."

Bastille stood up and extended his hand to Celine. She graciously took it and followed him out of the *Leviathan*.

****

Bastille and Celine met Maya at the *Luna C's* hatch. Bastille asked, "Where's Will, Shanna and Jack? I see everyone else."

Maya explained, "Will and Jack are injured. They're inside."

Celine asked, "Will they be alright?"

"Arasthmus thinks so."

Bastille looked at the hatch and said, "Here they come now."

Breel and Arasthmus carried Will on a stretcher.

Jack hobbled behind them.

Mariel and Laneia escorted Shanna.

They looked deeply concerned about Will's condition.

Jack spoke groggily from the injection Arasthmus gave him. He suggested to Bastille and Celine, "Why don't you two get with Saphoro. We're going ahead with Will's plan, with or without him. Let me know if you need any help."

Bastille replied, "Jack, you're in no shape to ..."

"Don't worry about me. I'm fine. Timing is everything right now."

Celine asked sadly, "Keep us posted on Will's progress."

"I will."

Bastille and Celine left the *Luna C.*

Neva stood nearby alone along side of *Leviathan.*

Jack noticed and joined her.

Neva forced a smile and said, "Now what?"

"Where's Mynx?"

"She's lying down. Arasthmus gave her something for the pain."

"How is she taking it?"

"Not well. She knows that she's done as a GSS agent. She's worked for them all her life."

"Well, you and Mynx are our chief negotiators. Tell her we need her on our side."

Neva asked, "Where do we start?"

"Get a hold of GSS and tell them we have the destroyer. Work your magic from there."

"I'll do that."

"Neva, you and Mynx did real good. You're a big part of our success. The two of you always have a place with us. If Will was here, he'd tell you that himself."

"Thanks, Jack. That means a lot."

Neva returned to the *Phantom* leaving Jack alone on the dock.

Maya joined him and kidded, "You're supposed to be off your feet."

Jack gazed into Maya's eyes and said, "I love you Maya."

Maya was surprised. "I ... I love you, too."

Jack became dizzy and almost fell.

Maya caught him.

"Guess what, Jack? You are going to lie down, whether you like it or not."

"I'm fine."

"If you want to keep this relationship, Jack, don't ever lie to me."

"Alright, I feel …"

Jack passed out in Maya's arms.

Maya called for the servants to help her take Jack inside the *Phantom*.

****

Maya arrived at the hall later in the day.

Mariel was giving everyone an update on Will's condition. She stood at the head table and explained, "Will's going to be alright. It's going to take a little time, but he's going to recover."

Everyone in the hall cheered.

Mariel stepped down and left the hall.

Neva entered the hall and approached the table where Regent sat with the Seers.

Neva introduced herself to Regent and the Seers.

Regent asked, "What can we help you with?"

Neva requested, "Can you and the Seers return the Eye to its pedestal now?"

"Sure, but why the urgency?"

"I want to know what Tenemon is doing. We'll need the Seers to find out for us."

"Well, of course we can. Is there something particular that you're concerned about?"

"We're starting the negotiations with GSS, the Fleet and Tenemon for the destroyer. I want to make sure none of them is in a position to ambush us."

Regent asked, "What do you think, girls?"

Mira, the oldest of the Seers answered, "We'll be happy to start on it. The only catch is that we'll need Shanna with us."

Neva said, "I'll talk to her. I don't think she'll have a problem with it."

Regent replied, "We'll get on it, right away."

"Thanks, everyone. I appreciate your help."

Neva left the table and approached one of the servants. "Excuse me. Can you tell me where Will Saris' room is?"

The young lady answered, "It's on the second floor. I'll take you to it."

"Thank you very much."

Neva followed the servant woman to the second floor. She was amazed at how big this underground complex was. They traveled up marble steps to a balcony high above them.

Neva wavered a bit as she looked down.

The servant asked, "Are you alright?"

She became red with embarrassment.

"Yeah. I'm a little bit afraid of high places."

"That's hard to believe. You and your friends don't appear to be afraid of anything."

"I don't know if we're that stupid or that brave."

"I think you are all very brave."

"Thank you."

They crossed the balcony and entered a carpeted hallway.

She pointed and said, "He's in the room at the end of the hall."

"Thanks again."

The servant nodded and left her.

Neva walked down the hall to the door and knocked lightly.

Mariel opened the door and motioned for her to come in.

Neva entered and felt immediate remorse when she saw Will and Shanna both on the bed. There were tubes connected to both their arms.

Arasthmus stood nearby, monitoring the tubes.

Mariel whispered, "Talk quietly. Arasthmus is counting the amount of blood that Shanna is giving to Will."

Shanna said meekly, "Hi, Neva."

"Hello, Shanna. What's all this?"

Arasthmus clamped the tubing and breathed a sigh of relief.

"I think it's going to work."

Arasthmus removed the tubes from Will and Shanna's arms.

"Hello, Neva. This is called a transfusion. Will lost too much blood so we're replenishing it with some of Shanna's."

Neva was amazed. "You can do that?"

"In the old days, this is how people replaced lost blood. Today, on our advanced worlds, we have machines to manufacture blood and pump it into the patient."

"I've heard stories about this transfusion business but it seemed so primitive."

"It is but it works. The key is not to take too much from the donor or you could lose both individuals."

Neva asked, "How do you feel, Shanna?"

"A little tired."

"It's good that you are all here. Mariel, I'd like to use the Seers to monitor the area during the negotiations for the destroyer. I'm concerned that if they were able to monitor our escape, they could trace us back to Yord."

"That's a reasonable request."

"The only catch is that we'll need Shanna to help the Seers."

Mariel replied, "Shanna must rest. I will take the fifth spot."

"Thank you, Mariel. Regent is taking the Eye to the temple as we speak. The Seers are with him."

"I will join them."

Mariel bent down and kissed Shanna's head.

"You are a brave young girl. Look after your man."

"Thank you Mariel. I will."

Mariel left the room.

Arasthmus remarked, "Will's taking a beating so far. He's got to slow down.

Neva asked, "What's your prognosis on Will?"

"I think he'll be okay in a cycle or so."

"I hope so. This plan is his baby. I don't want to ruin it."

Shanna replied, "This baby belongs to all of us. All of our freedom is at stake."

"I'm afraid we'll let you down."

Shanna praised her, "You and Mynx are too smart for that. We all believe in you."

"Really."

"Of course. Do the best you can. That's all the rest of us are doing."

"That means a lot, Shanna."

"Just think, Neva, with this technology and these ships, we can sneak around the galaxies without being seen. Tenemon is going to lose his mind when his, I mean our ships keep popping up and creating problems."

"I'm sure he will. What scares me is that he is a mad man. I'm sure the rest of his life will be committed to getting even with Will."

Arasthmus explained, "That's where we come in. We have to keep him safe and help him make smart decisions."

Shanna added, "Will believes in all of us, just like we believe in him."

Neva approached the bed and took Will's hand in hers. She whispered, "Get well, soon, friend." She withdrew from the bed.

"I've got to negotiate our deal. Take care of him."

Shanna replied, "I will. Thanks, Neva."

Neva thanked them both and left the room.

Shanna prayed over Will.

****

Mariel entered the temple. She saw the four Seers and Regent erecting the Eye onto its pedestal.

She said proudly, "This could be one of the greatest moments in the history of civilized worlds."

Regent asked, "Why is that?"

Mariel explained, "With the recovery of the Eye, we can stop the invading forces of Tenemon and restore peace. We can form a new alliance dedicated to peace and prosperity and still have the weapons to deter our enemies. That's where we failed before."

Regent suggested, "If Will is able to disrupt Tenemon's alliance as he says he can, we might be able to end this thing without a fight."

Mariel warned, "Will and Shanna are very bright, but they are young. Mistakes will be made. All of us are responsible to help them mature wisely and lead us in the right direction. This is a big responsibility for two young people like them."

"I will offer to act as Council and Advisor to Will and Shanna. But they'll require your help as well. You know the history of your people and the mistakes that were made along the way. Together we can build a new society."

Mariel complimented Regent, "Your wisdom is exemplary. Will is lucky to have a friend like you."

"Thank you, Mariel."

Keira approached them. "Mariel, Regent and I have a request."

Mariel looked both amused and curious at the same time. "What is it, Keira?"

Regent and I knew each other before Tenemon disrupted our world. We love each other."

Mariel replied, "That's admirable."

Regent announced to her, "We would like to be married, quietly."

"That could be arranged. Why is it that you prefer to keep such a joyous occasion from your friends?"

"We don't want to take away from the importance of other events happening around us. In addition, it's been a long time since Keira and I were together. We want to spend some time rebuilding our relationship."

"Very well. As soon as negotiations are over, we will perform the ceremony. In the mean time, our presence is required to monitor the Eye."

"Thank you, Mariel."

"It looks like I'll have to train two new Seers."

Keira replied, "I'm sorry, Mariel."

"Don't be. It is a joyous reunion for you and Regent. Exceptions will be made."

"Thank you again."

****

Neva entered Mynx's cabin.

Mynx lay in bed on her side facing the wall.

Neva sat on the edge of the bed and placed her arm on Mynx' shoulder.

"Are you okay?"

Mynx said tearfully, "No. What am I gonna' do without my arm? I can't believe GSS fired us."

Neva became irritated and said, "Screw them, Mynx. They've been using us for years. As serious as this mission was, we got absolutely zero help from them."

"But who knew that Nestor was a Weevil?"

Neva replied, "Suppose all of GSS is Weevil? Then what?"

"Well, what do we do then, Neva? We've got no place to go."

"What do mean we have no place to go? Look around you."

Mynx whined, "These people don't want us around."

Neva replied emphatically, "I beg to differ. We've been invited to stay here with Will and his friends."

"Will only said that because he had a little action under the sheets with me. He feels guilty."

"I hate to disappoint you but Shanna extended the invitation. Will is still unconscious."

Mynx asked, "Why would Shanna do that?"

"They're good people. We're making a lot of money with them as well. If you don't like it here, you can walk away and go wherever you want."

"What about you?"

"It depends on you. If we pull this off on GSS, the Fleet and Tenemon, we're all going to be very wealthy. We won't have to worry about working the rest of our lives."

"They hardly know us, Neva. How can we call them friends?"

Neva reminded her, "How long have these people been together? They know us about as well as they know each other."

281

"Do you really believe that?"

"Of course. Didn't you listen to their stories? The only person Will knew from before was Maya."

'So you think they would accept us as part of them?"

"Yes I do."

"I hope so, Neva. I really would like to be part of all this."

"It's going to be tough on you, getting used to doing things with only one arm. I'll do my best to help you, but you have to make the commitment to overcome your disability."

"I'll try."

"Regent lost his eye in battle. It sucks but it happens. Right now, your savvy as a negotiator is critical. I can't do this without you."

Mynx sat up and studied her image in the mirror. "I can do this, Neva."

"Well come on, girl. Let's get it done."

The two girls entered the comm/nav area of the *Phantom* and sat down in front of a large communication panel.

Mynx grinned at Neva as she activated the computer. After several keystrokes, the screen illuminated and a man's face appeared.

"Well, well, well. Mynx and Neva. I thought you forgot about us."

Neva inquired, "I was wondering, Dru, how is it that a Weevil like Nestor was able to infiltrate the organization and climb the corporate ladder as far as he did without arousing any suspicion?"

"Neva, you've known me a long time. If I had the answer to that I'd either be dead or out there with you."

"We have the destroyer. Make your bid."

"You know I can't do that. I have to talk to our superiors. "

Mynx explained, "It's simple, Dru. GSS wants it or they don't. This is a one call opportunity."

Dru asked, "Why are you playing hardball with me? I'm on your side."

Mynx explained, "A ship of this caliber in the hands of the Weevil could change the whole war. The Weevil would hold all the cards and the Attradeans would be their lackeys."

"What are you saying, Mynx?"

"I'm not saying anything. Make an offer."

"Five hundred thousand credits."

Neva sneered, "Not even close."

"I can't go higher without the proper authority."

Mynx threatened, "Then our business is concluded. You're out of the bidding."

Dru called out desperately, "Wait! Seven hundred thousand credits."

A light beeped on the panel above the monitor.

Neva whispered, "They're tracing our signal."

Mynx laughed at Dru.

"I guess you lose. Better luck next time."

Mynx terminated the connection. She looked down at the keyboard and frowned.

Neva asked, "What's wrong?"

Mynx looked up again and said sadly, "You were right. GSS is controlled by the Weevil."

"How could you tell?"

"Dru was always a protocol person. He would never get involved in the bidding except to relay information. I was testing him."

"You think he was killed?"

Mynx replied curtly, "Absolutely."

"So, we're finished with GSS."

"No, I think they're finished with us."

Neva vowed, "There will be another day and another place. We'll get them, I promise."

Mynx nodded in agreement. She pressed several keys and watched another face appear.

A bearded man asked, "Who are you? This is a military channel."

Neva answered, "If Tenemon isn't too busy, can you put him on?"

"No. You'll speak to me."

"We have his destroyer. If he wants it back, he can bid for it. GSS has already made an offer. We're giving him an opportunity to make a bid."

"We aren't bidding on anything. We want that destroyer back."

"Then you are out of the running. Goodbye."

"No, wait! Here is King Tenemon."

Tenemon appeared on the screen. His once green face was beet red and veins bulged in his forehead.

"Who are you?"

Mynx greeted him, "Good evening, King. You seem to have lost your color."

Neva chuckled and added, "As well as a few of your ships."

"I will hunt all of you down and kill you."

"Look, King, we're very busy. If you want to hunt us down, it's a big corporation and it's your business how you waste your time. Do you want to bid on the destroyer or not?"

"What did GSS offer?"

"We can't divulge that?"

Neva teased, "You and GSS know each other, huh?"

"That's none of your business!"

Mynx warned, "Look, King, make a bid or we're done talking."

"All right! One million credits and I want that ship fast."

Mynx explained, "We have one more call to make. You'll be notified of our decision shortly."

"What does Saris have to do with this?

"I'm sorry but there's no one here by that name. We'll be in touch. Thank you for your time."

Mynx disconnected the signal and the screen went blank.

Mynx and Neva laughed hysterically. They high-fived each other and stomped their feet.

Mynx said, "This is getting to be fun."

Neva chimed, "These guys are so gullible."

"Come on. We've got to see if Maya's back."

"What for?"

"We might want to make an offer to the Fleet as well."

"Hell, the more, the merrier."

Mynx and Neva shut down the communications system and left the ship.

****

Jack hobbled up the short ramp to the *Leviathan*. He entered the hatchway and looked around.

"Hello. Anybody here?"

Jack heard Celine's voice, "Up here."

He looked up at the missing ceiling panels and wondered what they were up to.

"Where are you, Celine?"

"Right above you."

Jack strained to see through the fiber optic cables and steel piping. Finally he located Celine.

"What in the world are you doing?"

"I'm reading a book. What does it look like I'm doing?"

Jack replied sarcastically, "I don't know. I can't tell from here."

"We're removing power cables from the surveillance systems."

"Where are Bastille and Saphoro?"

"They're installing the cabinets on the *Phantom*."

"No kidding."

"We'll be done here soon."

"Who else is up there with you?"

"Breel and Laneia."

"Good work."

Celine answered cynically, "You don't know how much that means to me, Jack."

"Why do you dislike me so much, Celine? Have I ever done anything to you?"

"Yes. You made Maya miserable for years and I had to pay the price."

"How is that my fault?"

"You should have straightened her out a long time ago. She needed someone to take the burden off of her."

"I thought I tried that. She broke off our friendship for quite a while, if I remember correctly."

"Just so you know, her crew paid the price."

"Do you want her back? I could stop seeing her."

"Heavens no! It took this long to get her in tune with the living, don't jeopardize it now."

"Well, you'd better start treating me better or else."

"I'm telling her you said that."

"I wouldn't if I were you. She's very stubborn. She'd purposely dump me and become her old self again, just to prove a point."

"Damn you, Jack Fleming."

"I love you too, Celine."

Jack departed the *Leviathan* and walked slowly to the *Phantom*.

The *Luna C* glided into the cavern and landed nearby.

Jack waited for Maya to exit the ship.

The hatch opened and Neelon stepped out.

"Hi, Neelon. Everything okay?"

"I think so. Maya's inside speaking with the Fleet Commander on the comm/nav system."

"Thanks. I'd better get in there and see what's up."

Jack boarded the *Luna C* and entered the pilots' cabin.

Maya held up a finger for him to be silent.

The monitor in front of her had a woman's face with long dark hair. She wore a highly decorated Fleet uniform.

"Well, Commander, you'll find that your reward money has been transferred into the designated account. I can't believe you were able to rally enough forces to execute such a plan."

"To tell you the truth, Imperial General Furey, I was as surprised as you. Renegades aren't the most trustworthy people but things just fell into place."

"We're launching an investigation into GSS and we'll weed out those Weevil. I should have known they had something to do with this. Congratulations on a job well done."

"Thank you, ma'am."

The screen went blank.

Jack laughed at Maya.

"What's so funny, Jack Fleming?"

"I only caught the end but it sounded like one heck of a story you fed her."

"Well I couldn't tell her the truth, could I?"

"I know. I'm teasing."

"The Fleet has put up another two hundred thousand credits for the attack we coordinated with renegades on King Tenemon's Palace. There is a lot of fighting between the Attradeans and their allies, but the Boromeans are sitting back and waiting for an opportunity to take over Tenemon's alliance. The Fleet is counting on the *Luna C* and the *Ruined Stone* to keep a handle on things out here."

Jack knelt down next to Maya's seat. He placed his arms around her and hugged her.

"I'm so happy to have you back in my life, Maya."

"You say that now, but what about later."

"Why would you say that? Did you talk to Celine?"

"I was just checking in on her by comm-link. She left me hanging while she moved some cables."

"So you heard our conversation?"

"Of course I did."

"I was only teasing her."

"Well, I didn't think it was very nice. Now I'm holding you responsible to make sure I don't go back to being my miserable self."

"How do I do that?"

Maya unbuckled her seat belt and stood up.

"Jack Fleming. I'm surprised at you."

Maya took his hand and led him back to her cabin.

Jack asked, "Are you sure there's time for this? We have a lot to do."

"Yes we do and it starts here with me."

Jack said merrily, "I'm really gonna' enjoy working around you, Maya."

Maya smiled seductively.

They entered her cabin and Maya closed the door.

****

Shanna fell asleep with her head resting on Will's chest.

Will began to talk incoherently in his sleep.

Shanna opened her eyes and felt a strange sensation in her head. She saw a Boromean ship gliding toward the *Ruined Stone*. Shanna then saw a Boromean ship fire three shots at the *Ruined Stone*. Immediately, the ship erupted into a fireball. A moment later, there was nothing left.

Shanna knew that the Seers were using the Eye. She raced out of Will's room and hurried down the stairs.

Neva and Mynx approached from the other direction.

Shanna yelled, "Where's Maya?"

Mynx answered, "We're looking for them, too. I thought they'd be in Will's room."

Neva asked, "What's wrong?"

"The *Ruined Stone* is in trouble! We have to warn them."

Mynx replied, "Come with us. If they aren't at the docks, we'll search for them."

"Thank you so much."

Shanna was in tears.

The three women raced down the stairs to the docks.

Neva volunteered, "I'll search the *Leviathan*."

Mynx said, "We'll take the *Luna C*."

Mynx and Shanna searched the main deck and saw no one.

Shanna pleaded, "Can't you do something, Mynx? They're going to die."

"Go get Neva. I'll try to raise them on the comm/nav system."

Shanna bolted from the *Luna C*.

Mynx sat down at the comm/nav panel and studied the controls. She turned on the power and began operating the system. She traced the *Ruined Stone* to a position halfway between Attrades and Yord. Next she tried to contact them but a block signal appeared.

"Damn. They're in blackout mode."

Shanna and Neva returned to the *Luna C*.

Shanna asked Mynx, "Did you contact them?"

"No. I can't get through."

Shanna asked, "How could that be?"

"They're hiding. Something must be going on out there."

Neva inquired, "Can you pilot this type of ship?"

"I can do it but I'll need help. Someone has to work one side of the controls for me."

Neva replied, "No problem. I'll help you."

Mynx instructed Shanna, "Close the hatch and press the 'seal' knob to the left."

Shanna obeyed.

Neva suggested, "We should let someone know where we're going."

"There isn't time. Besides I need you up here."

Shanna returned. "It's sealed."

"Good. Let's get out there and find the *Ruined Stone*."

Mynx powered up the *Luna C* and glided toward the entrance. She halted the ship near the gate sensors and waited anxiously for the gate to open.

Shanna watched nervously as the ship eased through the canyon and gained altitude.

She asked, "How long before we get there?"

Mynx replied, "About a quarter of a cycle. We should be able to make good time if the Fleet hasn't closed the portals."

289

Neva suggested, "Why don't you monitor the comm/nav station, Shanna. If anyone tries to raise us, let me know."

Shanna left the cabin and went to the comm/nav station.

****

Bastille, Celine, Breel, Laneia and Saphoro exited the *Leviathan*.

Bastille looked around and saw that the *Luna C* was gone.

"That's strange. Where did they go?"

Celine replied, "Shanna was looking for Maya in a hurry. I wonder what for."

Mariel rushed down the stairs toward them.

"The *Ruined Stone* and the *Luna C* are in trouble!"

Bastille placed his arms on Mariel's shoulders and said, "Relax, Mariel. Tell us what's going on."

"We were using the Eye to watch for trouble. We saw the *Ruined Stone* attacked and destroyed by a strange ship. When the *Luna C* appeared, an armada of ships ambushed them. They were also destroyed."

Bastille asked, "Where is everyone?"

Mariel replied, "I sent Keira to find Regent. He should be here shortly. I haven't seen anyone else."

"Damn. This is bad."

Celine warned, "If there's an ambush waiting out there, two, even three ships won't be enough."

Bastille looked at Saphoro.

She grew nervous and said defensively, "Wait a minute! I never piloted a ship into combat."

Bastille explained, "The cloaking device is operational. One of us will go with you to program the torpedoes. They'll never know you're there."

Saphoro asked, "What are you going to do?"

"We're going to make an appearance with the *Leviathan*. If the ships aren't Attradean, they'll think that Tenemon is playing both sides. That will make things even hotter for him."

"Why are we worried about that now?"

"Because, when the battle is over, that's when we'll see about delivering the destroyer to him, assuming his bid is the highest."

Saphoro asked, "Why do you think his will be the highest?"

"Because he has the most to lose."

Regent raced down the steps toward them.

"I heard what's happening. What are we doing?"

Bastille decided, "Celine, you go with Saphoro. Regent, you go, too."

Celine was very concerned and asked, "Who's going with you?"

"I'll take Breel and Laneia with me."

"Bastille, I have a bad feeling about this. Be careful."

"I will."

Bastille kissed her and hurried to the *Leviathan*.

Breel and Laneia followed him.

****

Will opened his eyes and sat up. He saw the images of his ships being destroyed. He felt the bandages around his stomach and climbed out of bed. He hobbled out of the room.

"Hello! Shanna! Mariel!"

Will felt pain in his side and placed his hand over the wounded area.

Two servants appeared from the balcony.

Will asked urgently, "Where are my friends?"

The first servant girl answered, "Everyone was headed to the docking area."

"Help me get down there. It's really important."

The girls each took an arm and helped Will down the stairs.

When they reached the dock, Will saw the *Phantom* pulling out. He noticed that the *Leviathan* was powered up, too.

Mariel was shocked to see him there. "Will, get back to your room."

"I've got to help them."

"You're going to hurt yourself. You aren't ready."

"Mariel, I've got to help them."

"You'll all be killed!"

"Then so be it."

Will turned his attention to the two servants and said, "Come on, girls. I've got to get their attention."

They helped him to the front of the *Leviathan*. He waved frantically at the pilots' cabin.

Laneia sat in the co-pilot's seat and Breel knelt in the middle. Bastille explained how the torpedoes are programmed from the panel near Laneia's arm.

Laneia looked up and noticed Will in front of their ship.

"Look! It's Will."

Bastille blurted out, "What in bloody hell is he doing?"

Breel offered, "I'll go get him."

"Hurry up!"

Breel ran down to the hatchway in the main quarters. He released the 'seal' lever and opened the hatch.

Will's bandages were showing blotches of blood already.

Breel was afraid for him. He picked him up and carried him into the ship.

"Will, what are you doing? You're bleeding!"

Will coughed and his voice started to weaken.

"Breel, they're in trouble."

"We know. We're going to rescue them."

Breel laid Will in the nearest cabin and returned to the hatch. He immediately closed it and returned to the pilots' cabin.

"All secure. Let's go."

Laneia asked, "Where is he, Breel?"

"I put him in one of the cabins downstairs."

Bastille was annoyed with the distractions. He asked angrily, "Laneia, do you remember how to program the torpedoes?"

"I think so."

"That's not good enough. If you forget, our friends are going to die."

Bastille reviewed the operation of the torpedo control panel as he piloted the *Leviathan* into space.

****

Talia looked out at the stars. She thought about Kalin and the fun she had the night before.

Zira sat beside her and noticed her far away look. "What are you thinking, Talia?"

"Oh, lots of stuff. Have you checked the tracking screens for intruders?"

"Not yet, but I'll do it soon. Besides, no one knows we're out here."

"I'm surprised we haven't seen any activity on Attrades, yet. I expected to see all kinds of ships coming and going."

"Maybe Tenemon is still stuck where Will left him."

"Could be. That's okay. I'm up for a boring night. Tomorrow we'll go back to Yord and the *Luna C* will take our place for a cycle or two."

Zira complained, "I can't believe Will is actually going to marry that witch."

"She's not a witch, Zira. She's a Seer."

"Whatever. It's still wrong."

"Zira, Honey, you'll never get a man with an attitude like that. Maybe that's why Will chose Shanna over you."

"I think she put a spell on him. She probably hates all of us."

"Come on, now. You're being bitter."

An annunciator alarm sounded on the panel to Talia's left.

"What the hell! Someone's got a lock on us."

Talia quickly powered the ship and lost its cloaking ability.

"Get those tracking screens up, fast!"

The *Ruined Stone* shook violently.

Zira pressed three switches and entered a series of numbers.

"Here it comes now, Talia."

The tracking screen showed a Boromean ship approaching from the rear.

Zira screamed, "It's right behind us, Talia!"

"We're getting out of here."

"What about torpedoes?"

"No time to turn and fight with them right behind us."

Another explosion rocked the *Ruined Stone*.

Talia yelled, "Damn! We lost an engine."

Zira cried, "What can we do?"

"Keep watching that screen. We'll see if we can get a firing position on the ship."

"I'll activate the torpedo panel."

"When was the last time you checked the long range sensors, Zira?"

"Um, I don't remember."

"Damn, girl. Check them now. We might be heading into an ambush."

****

Bastille turned on the DMS and called, "*Phantom*, do you read me?"

Saphoro answered, "Go ahead, Bastille."

"Do you remember how we extracted Will, Shanna and Neva from Nestor's craft?"

"Yes, I do."

"If things get bad for either the *Ruined Stone* or the *Luna C*, we're extracting them. I want to make sure we don't try to extract from the same ship at the same time, or we'll kill them."

"I understand."

Bastille asked Laneia, "What do you see on the long range sensors?"

"There are lots of ships out there? I can't tell who is who."

"I'm going to autopilot. I'll check it from the comm/nav station."

Bastille set the 'autopilot' and instructed Laneia, "Call me if anything changes up here."

Laneia nervously watched the control panels.

Bastille took a seat at the comm/nav station and powered the system up. He immediately brought up the long-range sensors. He saw eleven Boromean ships forming a gauntlet. A twelfth was slowly stalking the *Ruined Stone*, forcing her into the gauntlet.

"Holy hell! They'll be slaughtered!"

****

Maya and Jack left her cabin and walked down the hallway.

Maya asked curiously, "Jack, does the ship feel like it's moving to you?"

"I think so."

"I'd better see what's going on."

Maya hurried to the pilots' cabin. She was surprised to see Mynx and Neva at the controls.

Maya asked, "What's going on?"

The girls were startled by Maya's appearance.

Neva scolded her, "Can't you knock! You scared the living hell out of me."

"Sorry. Now, what's going on?"

"We have big problems. We looked for you and Jack but couldn't find you."

"Slow down, Neva. Tell me what's happening."

Bastille's voice came across the DMS. "Come in, *Luna C.* Do you read me?"

Shanna appeared behind Maya. "Maya, what are you doing here?"

Neva interrupted, "Hold on. It's Bastille."

Neva turned on the DMS monitor and Bastille's face appeared.

Bastille was very upset. He yelled, "You're heading into a trap. The *Ruined Stone* has been set up."

Maya panicked and hollered, "What's he talking about?"

Mynx said sullenly, "This is bad."

Neva asked, "What do you recommend Bastille?"

"The Boromeans have set up a gauntlet. If you try to help the *Ruined Stone*, you'll be slaughtered."

Maya pleaded frantically, "A trap! We've got to do something, Bastille. We can't let them die."

"We're on the way. We should catch you in about a tock."

Jack entered the pilots' cabin and asked urgently, "Maya, show me how to use the cannons."

Maya was still stunned. She watched Mynx and Neva working the controls to her ship and wondered how this happened.

Jack chastised her, "Come on, Maya. Now's not the time to lose your nerve."

He took Maya by the hand and led her out of the cabin.

Bastille's voice crackled again on the DMS. "Hey, Mynx. Did you take bids yet on the *Leviathan?*"

"Yeah, why?"

"Who's the winner?"

"Looks like the king."

"Good. Call him and tell him to transfer the money. When we finish here, we'll drop the destroyer off with a few surprises on board."

"I'll take care of it right away. By the way, Maya and Jack are on board."

"Tell Maya that we have a surprise on board as well. Will showed up on our doorstep, just before we left."

"What? He's crazy!"

"No kidding. Be careful."

"Thanks for the heads up."

****

Bastille studied the tracking screen and pondered.

Will appeared in the doorway and sat down next to him.

Bastille took one look at the bloody bandages and yelled, "What the hell is wrong with you? You'll bleed to death!"

"Shut up, Bastille. Let me see the screen."

Bastille slid back, giving Will room to see.

Bastille asked, "What do you think?"

"What if the *Leviathan* waits back here away from the gauntlet? The *Phantom* can enter the gauntlet in cloak mode with guns blazing."

Bastille pondered and replied, "How about we have the *Phantom* race through the gauntlet, don't fire, but transport Talia and Zira on board their ship. Once they are safe, we can light up the Boromeans. They'll be watching the *Luna C* and never expect us."

"Who's in the *Phantom*?"

"Saphoro."

"She's new at this."

"I know."

"Won't that make the *Phantom* a target?"

"No. She can cloak while in flight. I took care of that problem with the instrumentation from the *Leviathan*."

"That's even better, Bastille."

"The *Phantom* is already in position."

"We'll lock onto the *Luna C* in case they get into trouble. We'll need to extract them fast."

"I'll contact the other ships now."

"Notify the *Ruined Stone* to target the ship at the end of the gauntlet. Have them program their fire for twenty tocks."

"Why twenty?"

Because, at that time, they're either joining the fight or they'll be extracted from it. The end ship in the gauntlet is the command ship. Take that one out and shoot up a few of the others, I can guarantee you the rest of the fighters will run."

Will wobbled a little and grabbed onto the table.

Bastille ordered him, "Get back to the cabin and lay down. You're bleeding and I can't help you right now."

Will nodded in agreement. He got up slowly and carefully descended the stairs. When he reached the bottom, he staggered past the cabin to the rear of the deck. He grabbed onto the ladder, which led to the upper turret and climbed. He strapped himself into the seat and watched the stars go by.

****

Bastille returned to the pilots' cabin.

Laneia asked anxiously, "What did you find out?"

"I talked with Will and we have a plan. The other ships have been notified as well."

"Does it have a good chance of succeeding?"

"I think so. We'll probably lose the *Ruined Stone*, but at least Talia and Zira will be alive."

Bastille looked at the tracking screen in front of Laneia. An unknown ship was approaching the gauntlet.

"Now who in the world could that be?"

Bastille turned on the DMS and finally contacted the *Ruined Stone*.

"Talia, it's Bastille."

Talia sobbed as she answered, "What is it, Bastille?"

"Do you see the ship approaching from your aft?"

Talia checked her tracking screen. She sniffled and replied, "Yes, I do. It looks like a freighter."

"Any idea who it is?"

"No. No, wait! It's Kalin!"

Bastille spoke sternly, "Talia, Tell him to get out of there. He'll ruin the plan. Whatever it takes, get him away from there."

"I'll try."

"Good girl."

Bastille toggled a switch and entered a three digit number. He spoke into the speaker. "Come in, *Phantom*. Are you there?"

Saphoro answered, "Go ahead, Bastille. I'm listening."

"Kalin's freighter is approaching the *Ruined Stone*. If Talia can't turn him around in time, he's toast. If that happens, you are to go in cloaked. Do not fire or you'll give away your position. Attach the tractor beam to the *Ruined Stone* and yank her out of there. There should be enough chaos between the freighter's arrival and our gunfire to confuse the daylights out of the Boromeans."

Saphoro asked, "We can't cloak and run, can we?"

"Now you can. I took care of that problem."

298

"I understand. You won't forget about us, will you, Bastille?"

"No way! We're all going home."

Laneia alerted Bastille, "The *Luna C* is coming into view."

"Good. Breel I want you to monitor the comm/nav panel. Just listen for anything strange that I should know about. I'll monitor the DMS up here."

Breel obediently left the cabin."

****

Talia contacted Kalin's freighter.

Kalin answered, "Talia, we'll be there shortly."

"No, Kalin. It's a trap. Get out of here."

"Get ready to run when we arrive."

"Kalin, we can't. We lost our number two engine. We can't outrun anybody."

"Well, they're going to pay for messing with my girl."

"Kalin, listen to me. My friends have a plan. They're on the way. If you interfere, you'll jeopardize any chance we have of escaping."

"I can't sit back and watch you die, Talia."

Kalin's freighter approached the gauntlet. Seven Boromean fighters left formation and targeted the freighter.

****

Bastille directed the *Leviathan's* extractor beam to the freighter. He programmed it for twelve people and pressed the start sequence.

****

Talia watched on the screen as the Boromean fighters swarmed around the freighter.

Talia pounded her fist on the control panel and cried, "Why didn't you listen, Kalin? Why?"

The freighter disappeared from the screen.

****

Bastille contacted the *Luna C* by DMS.

Bastille hollered, "Go in, Saphoro! I repeat, go in and pick them up."

Bastille ordered Laneia, "Program torpedoes one through six like I showed you."

Maya appeared on the DMS. "Bastille, we're going in, too."

"No, Maya. Cover the *Phantom*. They're going to pull the *Ruined Stone* out. If it looks bad, coordinate an extract with Saphoro."

"I understand. Maya, out."

Bastille warned Laneia, "Here we go. It's show time."

Bastille guided the *Leviathan* into what remained of the gauntlet. The Boromeans had no idea that neither the *Phantom* nor the *Leviathan* was coming.

Bastille instructed Laneia, "On my mark. Three. Two. One. Fire!"

Laneia attempted to launch the first six torpedoes. Nothing happened.

Bastille asked, "What's wrong?"

Laneia panicked, "The panel went blank. It lost its power."

"No, no, no! Not now."

"We must have done something to the wires when we removed the cloaking system."

"This is not good."

****

Will raised his head and looked out from the turret. He saw the Boromean ships coming toward them. He instinctively activated his turret and prepared to fire his cannon. At first, he felt dizzy, but as he leaned into the cannon's sights, he thought about his dad.

"Once upon a time, dad fought the Boromeans from a turret like this. Dad I wish you were here."

Will tightened his grip on the cannon's controls and began to fire.

Will's memories fueled his rage. He exclaimed, "This is for my mother, you rotten bastards."

The first series of shots sailed wide right, but the second series struck two of the fighters.

****

Bastille asked Laneia, "Did you see that explosion on the right?"

"Yes, I did."

"What was it?"

"Two Boromean fighters just exploded."

Bastille pondered aloud, "Now what's going on?"

Laneia looked toward the rear of the ship from the viewing plate and saw cannon fire from atop the *Leviathan*.

"Bastille, someone's firing the cannon on the top turret."

Bastille cracked a smile and said, "That's got to be Will."

Bastille took a big turn and swooped through again. He saw two more of the fighters explode into fiery masses.

Bastille spotted the *Ruined Stone*.

She was towing at a fairly high rate of speed. Three fighters closed in on the *Ruined Stone* and three others were pursuing the *Luna C*.

The *Luna C* couldn't help the *Ruined Stone* while being pursued.

"Damn. It doesn't leave us much choice, Laneia."

Bastille veered toward the *Ruined Stone*.

Bastille called Will on the intercom and warned, "Will, watch your fire. The *Ruined Stone* is being towed by the *Phantom's* tractor beam. Remember, the *Phantom's* cloaked."

Will replied, "No problem."

301

Bastille watched anxiously as cannon fire darted from the top of their ship at the fighters. Two of the fighters exploded. The third one was pounding away at the *Ruined Stone* with gunfire. Finally, the third fighter was hit and exploded.

Bastille headed for the *Luna C* as fast as the ship would allow him.

A destroyer isn't designed for a dogfight with small fighters.

The *Luna C* was bobbing back and forth, avoiding much of the gunfire.

The *Leviathan* couldn't quite catch up to it.

Will steadied the cannon and aimed carefully at the nearest fighter to the *Luna C*.

He waited patiently for several seconds and fired a short burst. The fighter exploded, causing the other two to divert around the wreckage.

Bastille's voice crackled from the intercom, "That was a hell of a shot, Will."

"I'm not done yet. Get us as close as possible."

"Sorry, pal. This is all we got."

"Contact the *Luna C*. Tell them to turn around and head toward us."

Bastille replied, "Right away."

Will focused on the sights and lined up on the second fighter as it circled behind the *Luna C*.

Will fired a stream of cannon fire but was too far ahead of the fighter. Fortunately, it was enough to divert the fighter away from the *Luna C*.

Will saw the *Luna C* go into a turn and head back toward them. He targeted one of the two remaining fighters and calculated his shot. Finally he pulled the trigger. His cannon fire struck the side of the fighter and damaged it.

There was a small explosion on the wing, but the fighter turned and fled the battle. The remaining fighter fled with it.

Will leaned back in the seat, took a deep breath and passed out.

Bastille cheered from the pilots' cabin and yelled into the intercom, "We did it, Will! We did it."

Bastille noticed the silence. He turned the *Leviathan* on a course for Attrades and set the 'autopilot'.

"Laneia, I'll be right back. Keep an eye on things."

Bastille hurriedly left the cabin.

A few moments later, Breel appeared.

"Laneia, where's Bastille?"

"He went to check on Will. What's wrong?"

"The Attradean frequency is programmed into this surveillance system. I can hear the Boromean leader screaming at Tenemon."

"About what?"

"About the Attradean destroyer attacking his armada. They want to know why he is helping us."

"That's good, isn't it?"

Breel replied happily, "I think it's great."

Laneia informed Breel, "Bastille went to get Will. He didn't look too good when he left. His bandages were stained with blood."

"Where did he go?"

"He was firing the cannon upstairs."

"Oh, dear. I'd better go help him."

Breel rushed out of the cabin.

****

Ten men stood confused in the lower bay. They were bloody and bruised.

Bastille entered the bay and recognized Kalin.

Kalin asked anxiously, "Is Talia okay?"

Bastille replied, "I don't know yet. The *Ruined Stone* is in tow."

Breel advised the men, "Sit down and rest. We'll get you back as soon as possible."

Kalin asked, "What happened to my freighter?"

Breel explained, "If we had waited a little longer, you'd have gone up in flames with it."

Kalin replied sadly, "Thank you for saving us."

Breel said, "Save it for later. There are a whole lot of people to thank for this rescue."

Bastille climbed the ladder to the turret. He saw small blotches of blood on the floor under Will's seat.

"Will, are you all right?"

Will's head was slumped over.

Bastille squeezed into the turret far enough to unbuckle Will's straps.

Breel arrived and called to Bastille, "If you can lower him down the ladder, I can take him from there."

"Get ready, he's coming down."

Bastille awkwardly twisted Will's body over the small hatch opening and lowered him halfway down the ladder.

Breel took Will's limp body and laid him down on the floor. He immediately checked his pulse and heart rate.

"Bastille, he's in bad shape. We've got to get help for him."

Bastille climbed down the ladder. "We're going to transport him to the *Luna C* and get him home. Stay with him for now."

Kalin watched in disbelief. "Holy Mother of God! Is he alive?"

Breel answered, "So far."

Bastille hurried back to the pilots' cabin.

Laneia asked, "Is Will alright?"

"No. Not at all."

Bastille turned on the DMS and programmed three codes. He ordered emphatically, "Listen up, everyone. Here's what's happening. We're transporting Will to the *Luna C*. He's in bad shape and has got to go back to Yord ASAP. Has anybody heard from Talia?"

Maya answered, "Their communications are out."

"Get someone on board and assess their situation. If there's core damage, jettison it. We don't want radiation leaking all over Yord. I need the *Phantom* for the delivery of the destroyer. What is the status of the *Luna C*?"

Maya replied, "Not good. We've got core damage and we're at twenty percent power. We'll never make it back."

"Jettison your core. The *Phantom* will have to tow you back."

304

Celine asked, "You're coming back with us, right?"

"No. I'm going ahead with the drop-off."

Celine cried, "You can't. Tenemon's soldiers will kill you."

"Relax, Celine. I know what I'm doing."

"You'd better, you big oaf."

"Alright, everybody, do your thing. I'm going off the air until after the drop. Mynx and Neva, it's your show, now."

Mynx replied, "Be careful, Bastille."

"Bastille, out."

Bastille programmed the transporter and locked in the coordinates for the *Luna C.* He spoke into the intercom, "Breel, place Will on the transport platform. Let me know when he's clear."

Breel lifted Will up and carried him to the platform. When he set Will down, he nearly cried. Will's bandages were completely soaked in blood. Breel hugged him and said, "Hang in there, friend. We won't let you down."

Breel went to the intercom and announced, "He's ready, Bastille. Get him out of here."

Breel watched sadly as Will's body disappeared in a flash."

* * * * * * * * * *

On board the *Luna C*, Shanna and Jack waited anxiously for Will to arrive on the transporter platform.

The space above the platform hummed smoothly and a shadow began to appear. In a few seconds, Will laid before them, his face ashen and his midsection blood-stained.

Shanna rushed to him and cried, "Look at him! He's dying."

They lifted Will up and carried him into one of the cabins.

Jack ordered Maya, "Tell Saphoro to get us tagged and back to Yord as soon as possible."

Jack and Shanna sat next to Will.

Shanna held Will's hand tightly. She tried to communicate with him through their telepathy but all she saw was darkness.

Jack asked, "Is there anything we can do?"

Shanna sobbed, "Not that I know of. We need Arasthmus."

"You can do that mind thing with Will, can't you?"

Shanna was confused, "What mind thing?"

"You know, when you can talk to each other without anyone knowing."

"Yeah. I tried that. It didn't work."

"Keep trying. If you can reach him, maybe you can convince him to fight or maybe convince him to heal."

"What if it doesn't work?"

"It had better. Shanna, I don't think he's going to make it back to Yord and there's nothing we can do for him here. You're his last hope."

Shanna covered her mouth with her hands and muttered tearfully, "He can't die."

She wrapped her arms around his chest and hugged him. She cried, "Don't you leave me, Will! Don't you leave me."

Jack had tears in his eyes. He left the room and entered another vacant cabin. For the first time in a long time, he prayed.

Maya entered the room and when she saw him, her heart broke.

"Jack, I'm sorry to interrupt you."

Jack reached out to her and hugged her. "Will doesn't look good. I don't think he'll make it."

"Please, don't say that. I need your help."

"What for?"

"I'm going on board the *Ruined Stone*. Can you help me?"

"Yeah."

"Are you sure?"

"Yeah. Let's go."

Jack wiped tears form his eyes and followed Maya.

They stepped onto the transport platform. Maya pressed five buttons on a panel above her head.

There was a brief flash and they were on board the *Ruined Stone*.

Everything was dark, except for sparks shooting from several panels.

Maya went straight to the pilots' cabin. Jack searched the main deck. The ship was a mess.

Maya entered the cabin.

The rear circuit panel had fallen on Zira. She was bleeding badly. The floor sopped with blood as Maya stepped between the seats.

Talia's head rested against the left viewing plate. She had a deep laceration over her head. Blood streamed down her face onto her lap.

Maya checked her pulse. She was barely alive.

Maya cradled her and cried, "Talia. I'm here, Talia."

Jack entered the cabin and felt pity for them.

Talia opened her eyes and whispered faintly, "You came for us, Maya."

Maya answered, "We all did."

"Thank ..."

Talia lost consciousness.

Maya cried uncontrollably.

Jack pulled her away and hugged her. "Come on, Maya. We've got to get them out of here. Don't lose your nerve."

"I can't do this! Look at them."

"Yes you can. You're still a commander. Act like it."

Maya fought to regain her composure. "I'm trying, Jack."

"I know you are. What do we do about the *Ruined Stone*?"

"We'll set the self-destruct sequence on it."

Maya reached over Talia's body and pressed three switches. The monitor illuminated dimly. Maya entered a long series of codes into the system and watched impatiently.

A voice came over the intercom from the computer, "The self-destruct sequence has been initiated. You have seventy five tocks to evacuate the ship."

Maya replied, "That should be long enough."

Maya lifted Talia away from the controls and pulled her into the main quarters.

Jack pushed the rear circuit panel off of Zira. He set the switch on the DMS. Mynx' face appeared. "How are they, Jack?"

"Not good at all. We're coming back with them. The ship is set for self-destruct. Notify Saphoro to terminate the tractor beam on the *Ruined Stone*."

"Will do."

Jack replied, "See you soon."

****

The DMS beeped three times. Mynx anxiously turned on the DMS and saw Tenemon's face. She smiled gleefully and asked, "What took you so long?"

Tenemon snarled, "Where's my ship?"

"We took it for a test ride just to make sure everything was working properly. The Boromeans think so."

"What do the Boromeans have to do with this?"

"Well. It seems they were preparing to mount a surprise attack on you. We felt bad about all the misfortune you've had to endure as a result of our employers and your enemies; therefore we decided to help you out. We took care of the Boromean armada for you."

Tenemon was enraged, "They were there to keep an eye on you!"

"I don't think so, King. They had an ambush set up and I really think they had ideas of confiscating the *Leviathan*."

"Where is it now?"

"Where are the credits?"

"Alright. Half a million now, half when I get the ship."

"Sorry, no deal. However, what we'll do for you is this. Send three quarters now, and when the *Leviathan* is in sight, you send the remainder. Otherwise she cloaks and disappears."

"How soon will it be delivered?"

"Sooner than you think. There are three associates on board. Once the ship is docked, we'll extract them and be out of your hair."

"I'll be waiting."

"Don't be late on the payments, King."

Neva keyed into the non-alliance account and watched anxiously. The main account balance leaped by three quarters of a million credits.

Neva replied happily, "First payment received."

Mynx answered, "Good. I don't trust him."

"That's funny. I don't think he trusts us either."

"I wonder why."

Maya interrupted, "We're back."

Neva said, "We're sorry about the *Ruined Stone*. We got out here as quickly as possible."

"I know."

Mynx pressed three switches and pulled a lever. She replied, "The core is ejected. We only have backup power from here on out."

Neva asked, "How is Will?"

"Not good. The *Phantom* is taking us in as quickly as she can without risking an accident. It's going to be rough going through the canyon and docking will be tricky."

Mynx remarked, "So long as we get our feet back on the ground."

"Thank you for taking the initiative to come out here and help the *Ruined Stone*. I'm sorry that I wasn't there when you needed me."

Neva explained, "We didn't know what else to do."

"It means a lot to me. Let's go home and pray that Bastille is alright."

XIV.   A New Beginning

Will awakened in a strange room. He looked around and saw beautiful drapes hanging on the walls. He could see daylight through three different windows.

Shanna contacted him telepathically, "So, you're finally awake."

"Where are you?"

"I'll be there shortly."

Will waited anxiously. He tried to get up, but he was very weak. His side was wrapped tightly.

Shanna burst through the silver door. She hopped on the bed like a little kid. Will saw the innocence of a young girl in Shanna but he knew better.

She leaned over and kissed him.

"How do you feel, Will?"

"I guess I'm alright."

"We've got so many surprises for you."

"I don't need surprises, just you."

Will placed his hand on Shanna's cheek. "If you hadn't gotten through to me, I wouldn't have survived. I kept hearing your voice."

"You did!"

"Yes. You said something about starting a family."

"That's right. You couldn't leave when we have so much ahead of us.

He asked, "How long has it been since we got back?"

Shanna said, "It's been about two klogs. I was afraid you'd never get up."

"How long is two klogs in Earth time?"

"I keep forgetting you don't know this system of time. It's about three weeks."

"That long?"

"Arasthmus did a lot of work on you. He had to take blood from my body the first time, Maya's body this time, and then he put it into yours. I think he called it a transfusion."

"Can I ask you something? It's something that I really want to know."

"Sure."

"Did you transform into your alter-shape on Attrades?"

Shanna smiled slyly and said, "Maybe."

"What's this 'maybe' stuff?"

"Maybe, if you're good, I'll tell you about it."

"But I'm curious. What did you become?"

"I'll get Maya and you can talk to her about female transformations."

Will complained, "Don't bring that up to Maya, please."

He took Shanna's hand and said, "I guess you saved me again."

"We have a wedding coming up. I want you in one piece. What good is a husband who can't satisfy his wife?"

"Will asked defiantly, "Who says I can't satisfy you?"

Shanna teased, "Well, I'm waiting."

Will replied, "That's not fair. I'm hurt."

"Well, I guess you owe me."

"How is Jack?"

"He's coming. We lost the *Ruined Stone*."

"Talia and Zira?"

"Maya took them back to Fleet for medical attention. They were in bad shape beyond Arasthmus capabilities."

"Damn. Where's Regent and Keira?"

"It seems that they had a lot of catching up to do. They're away for a little while but they'll be at our wedding."

"That son-of-a-gun."

"Kalin's freighter was destroyed by the Boromeans. We extracted them before the explosion."

"Wow! Have we heard from Tenemon?"

"You don't worry about him for a while."

"Why not?"

"I'm sure he's got his hands full."

"So what do we do now?"

Shanna leaned over and kissed him slowly.

Will muttered, "Here we go again."

Shanna asked seductively, "Is that a problem?"

Will chuckled and kissed her passionately.

****

Later in the day, Will opened his eyes and was surprised to see Mynx, Mariel, Jack, Maya, Regent, and Keira in front of his bed.

Shanna was under the covers with him.

Will blushed. He asked, "How long have you been here?"

Jack teased, "Long enough."

Shanna opened her eyes in surprise. She said innocently, "Oh, hello, everyone."

Mariel chastised her, "Will is supposed to be resting. What do you think you're doing?"

She giggled, "I'm helping him with his concentration."

Everyone laughed at her response.

Jack kidded, "I hope it helps. Will needs it."

"Thanks, pal."

Mynx informed Will, "Bastille took care of the *Leviathan*."

Will was elated, "Great. So now we can make the offer."

Mynx answered, "Easy, Will. It's taken care of. GSS offered seven hundred thousand credits. Tenemon offered a million credits, just like you said he would."

"So I guess Tenemon gets his ship back."

Neva corrected him, "You mean 'Tenemon had his ship back'. It seems that after he got it, he found that it was just an ordinary ship. He got on the DMS to bitch about it and, while we were talking, someone happened to take the destroyer right from under his nose. Since the Boromeans are blaming Tenemon for the destruction of their armada, he didn't have time to chase after it."

Will laughed. "Tell me Bastille handled all that."

"Yes he did. They're docking as we speak."

"I feel left out."

"Just today, GSS called back. They raised their offer to one million credits if we can get the destroyer back and give it to them."

Will was giddy over GSS' change of heart. He asked, "So, then what?"

Mynx replied, "I told them three million and we want half up front, plus expenses."

Will said proudly, "That's our senior negotiator. Mynx, you're the best."

Jack added, "The best part is that GSS is considering Mynx offer. They need time to get the money together, though."

Will remarked, "We have all the time in the universe."

Mariel interrupted the meeting and said, "Everyone must say goodbye to Will for a little while. He has much to learn before the wedding and the coronation."

Will was befuddled and asked, "Did you say 'coronation'?"

Mariel replied, "Yes I did. It's only proper for a king and queen to be inducted regally."

Will complained, "This sounds like a lot of work."

Everyone laughed and bade him goodbye.

Will yelled, "Don't go anywhere without me!"

He asked Shanna, "They won't go anywhere without us, will they?"

Shanna rubbed her nose against his and said, "Who cares?"

Will muttered, "Oh, boy. Here we go again."

Mariel pulled Shanna away and said, "That's enough, young lady, until after the wedding. You have a lot to do as well."

Shanna pleaded, "Just give us a little time together, Mariel."

"No. That's enough."

Will remarked, "You're wearing me out, Shanna."

"But, Will, we're just getting started."

"Oh, boy."

ABOUT THE AUTHOR

Michael, a life-long Philadelphia area resident, began his writing career in 1999 while performing a tour of duty in Kuwait. He was a weapons crew chief for 22 years before retiring from the Pa. Air National Guard, performing several tours in the Middle East. During the nineties, he worked as a nuclear field engineer designing system upgrades for the power industry. He's received Associates degrees for Electronics Technology, General Education, Liberal Arts, Aircraft Systems from various schools and a Bachelors degree for Technical & Industrial Administration from Widener University.

Michael is an active sports enthusiast who enjoys music, traveling and writing when not working as a nuclear controls technician in a local power plant. He enjoys participating in science fiction conventions around the country and is anxious to promote his new works particularly overseas. His goal is to see his novels become movies on the big screen.

CPSIA information can be obtained at www.ICGtesting.com
Printed in the USA
BVOW04s1446090415

395392BV00005B/15/P